Foreword

The following work of fiction is inspired by true events. With limited exception, every character is based loosely off a real historical figure. The vast majority of locations are true to London in 1888. Every occult society featured within truly existed, and the magic featured throughout this book is heavily based off real grimoires that inspired the rise of occultism throughout the Victorian Age.

Though the details of the murders perpetrated by *Jack the Ripper* are both gruesome and difficult to believe in equal measure, I have taken very few liberties in describing the heinous nature of the crimes he committed.

Shadow

of the

Golden

Dawn

By D. R. Hill

To my fiancée,

Thank you for sharing my greatest passion. Your love and support inspires me in all my work.

I

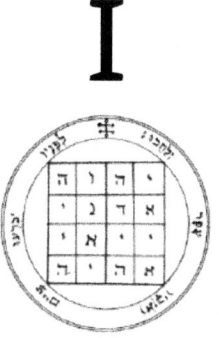

Buck's Row, Whitechapel
5:52 a.m. August 31st, 1888

PC John Neil pocketed his watch. He stood anxiously beneath the amber glow of the antiquated gaslight illuminating the shadowy confines of Buck's Row. Further onlookers were starting to amass in the dim alleyway. Workmen emerged from their cottages, pausing on their way to the docks, factories, and slaughterhouses to gawk at the supine body of a woman surrounded by policeman.

"Come on folks," urged PC Thain, "move along."

Several of the workers murmured amongst themselves, and with their morbid curiosity sated, turned back up Buck's Row to make their way around the police blockade.

"We should have had her on the back of that ambulance and out of here an hour ago!" muttered the disgruntled Sergeant Kirby as he trudged over beside Neil. "We're going to have a situation on our hands soon enough."

Neil looked onwards in dread as more men and women emerged from the rows of cottages to garner a peek at the prostitute lying dead outside the gates of Brown's Stableyard. "I fear you are right, sir," confirmed the Irish constable, wishing to God that it had been some other copper out on the plod to first lay eyes on her.

Had the killer struck half an hour earlier, Kirby might instead have been the one to stumble upon the mutilated corpse, or perhaps even Thain, who had patrolled down the impoverished street not long beforehand. Instead, Neil had seemed destined to be the first officer on the scene.

Almost three hours earlier, Neil had discovered the woman lying in the street. At first, he had merely taken her for a drunkard, passed out after a night spent in one of the many local public houses; such a sight was commonplace in Whitechapel these days. But as Neil leant closer, examining her with the orange light of his bullseye lantern, he descried the blood soaked into her hair and clothes. Peeling back the crimson stained collar of her ulster, the copper unveiled her pallid neck. It had been slashed!

Neil recoiled in alarm. The distant clopping of hard-soled boots echoed down Buck's Row. Steeling his resolve, he turned his lantern towards the approaching heavy footfalls: the characteristic stomping of another copper on the beat. The footsteps were echoing from down Brady Street; help was near at hand.

Dimming his lantern several times in quick succession, Neil signalled the other policeman as he approached the turning to Buck's Row. For a brief moment, the heavy footsteps ceased. Seconds later, the stomping quickly resumed, faster now as the approaching bobby hastened towards Neil. From out of the shadows, PC John Thain, a fellow officer from Bethnal's J division emerged.

Thain silently greeted Neil with a look of intrigue before his eyes sank ominously over the body bathed in Neil's lamplight.

"Not another one," breathed Thain with dread.

"Her throat's been cut," explained Neil, guiding the centre of the bullseye over the blood specked across her chin and neck. "I just found her lying here."

"Dear God," sighed Thain, "what a hell-forsaken place this is!"

Moments later, another set of boots clattered across the cobbles, this time emerging from the opposite end of the backstreet. Fingers curled anxiously around his billy club, Neil issued a sigh of relief as Jonas Mizen from Whitechapel's H division emerged from the gloom.

The H Division man seemed to know already that something was awry. Silence choked the alley so thickly that not one of the three policemen dared utter a word. Stepping aside, Neil and Thain revealed the sprawled-out body slumped at the foot of the stable gates. Mizen shut his eyes and pinched the bridge of his nose; he had already known.

Mizen had been alerted to the murder whilst walking his own patrol down Hanbury street; two men had come upon the body prior to Neil on their way to work. Uncertain in the darkly lit alley as to whether the woman was in fact dead or merely inebriated, they had decided between them to inform the first copper they saw on route of their discovery; that first copper being Mizen.

With three constables now on the scene, Thain was sent to fetch Dr Rees Llewellyn from his surgery on Osborn Street about a half mile away. It was in Thain's absence that Neil had first spotted *it*. It was lying in shadow across the gates to the stableyard, completely obscured by the darkness bathing the narrow street. As Neil paced nervously back and forth awaiting Thain's return, the beam of his lantern had swung across the gates, briefly illuminating the image.

Catching glimpse of the shape out of the corner of his eye, Neil retrained his bullseye lantern on the entranceway, for the first time illuminating the bizarre graffito in full. Cocking his head in befuddlement, Neil edged closer, raising his lantern to further study the dark markings painted across the gates.

Various interconnecting lines formed a triangle subdivided into four smaller ones, all ringed inside two concentric circles. Throughout the strange graffito, dozens of unusual characters were scrawled; at first Neil had assumed them to be letters from the Hebrew alphabet, yet as he moved closer, he began to doubt that theory. The symbols were too foreign to be Hebrew; they looked more like Egyptian hieroglyphs, or stranger still.

"What the...!?" breathed Mizen in equal bewilderment as his attention too now fell on the mysterious markings painted beside the corpse.

Neil stepped passed the dead prostitute and observed the dark paint shimmering beneath the glow of his oil lamp. He dabbed his fingers gently against the wood, confirming his suspicion: the graffito was still wet. He rubbed the congealing substance between his fingertips and his heart sank. Shining his lantern down at his hand, Neil examined the crimson fluid clotting between his fingers with dread. He staggered back, gasping in terror, nearly tripping over the corpse, raising his beam of lamplight back across the graffito, then, to the victim sprawled out at his feet.

"What is it!?" demanded Mizen, seeing that Neil was seconds away from hysteria.

Lost for words, he merely raised his hand to show the cop from H division his bloody fingers.

"Shit," breathed Mizen, glancing to the freshly painted graffito.

"Blood...!?" stammered Neil. "It's painted in her blood!"

That was the moment everything had changed.

A shiver rand down Mizen's spine as he realised the gravity of the situation. The two men stood staring at one another in panicked disbelief. Finally, regathering his senses, Mizen took off towards Whitechapel High Street, sprinting for the nearest police box, leaving Neil alone with the cadaver. His heavy boots pounded across the cobbles. Lungs panting, heart racing, he swung right onto Brady Street. The dim glow of antiquated gaslighting yielded ahead to the bright dazzle of newly installed electrical arc lamps. Humming loudly as they flickered down the stretch of Whitechapel Road, the cold white glare of the modern streetlights far outshone the defunct gas lanterns that still burned throughout much of the East End.

Mizen bore right once more, charging past commuters emerging from the entrance of Whitechapel station, and skidded to a halt in front of the blue police box. Yanking open the door, the constable stepped inside the small booth and lifted the receiver to his ear. Steadying his breathing, Mizen waited as the telephone rang out in H division headquarters on Leman Street. Within seconds, Mizen was through to the Whitechapel police station a mile away, warning his superiors of the situation.

Back on Buck's Row, the first onlookers had arrived to ogle at the bloodied corpse lying cold in the street. Composing himself, Neil adjusted his helmet and directed the beam of his lantern on the three dishevelled men, ensuring that the lamp's glare obscured their view of the body, and more importantly, the graffito.

Going on the offensive, PC Neil demanded their names, addresses, and occupations. They worked at the knacker's yard on Winthrop street, only a few hundred yards away, and one of them was even a resident on Buck's Row. They had every business being there, but the constable pressed harder, hoping that if they feared they might be suspects, they'd not loiter long. Neil asked for their whereabouts for the last hour; if they knew the victim? The trio grew anxious as Neil grilled them, their demeanour quickly shifting from inquisitive to furtive.

Hurried footsteps from the west end of Buck's row signalled the return of PC Thain with Dr Llewellyn in tow. With the arrival of a second bobby, the three men needed little dissuasion from loitering at the crime scene. The knackers making their retreat into the night, Dr Llewellyn planted his bag down on the cobbles. Stepping aside, Neil slowly cast his bullseye lantern back across the gateway, steadily unveiling the corpse from beneath a pall of shadow.

A length of eerie silence smothered the alley, before, after a long moment of hesitation, Dr Llewellyn drew a handkerchief from his pocket, dabbed his brow, and approached the body. Kneeling in the entranceway to the stableyard, he quickly studied the woman, tentatively peeling back the collar of her blood-soaked ulster. Glancing uneasily to the pair of policeman stood over him, he issued a singular grave nod. Dead.

With the official pronouncement given, the doctor turned his attention back to the victim to begin a preliminary assessment. He began to mutter under his breath, scribbling notations on a pad as he examined the prostitute's injuries in greater detail. Cause of death: two deep lacerations to the throat, one all the way down to the vertebrae. Her spine was all that had prevented complete decapitation.

Suddenly, Mizen trundled out of the darkness. He was panting, face as white as a ghost. Shakingly, he repeated the instructions given to him direct from Leman street: they were not to move the body. Under no circumstances was the crime scene to be tampered with. Against both their better judgement and standard procedure, their orders were to set up a cordon, securing the perimeter until reinforcements arrived.

Normal protocol saw bodies shipped away to the nearest mortuary as soon as possible, crime scenes scrubbed down before they started to draw crowds. The otherwise inevitable arrival of sightseers and rabble-rousers more often than not sparked trouble. Whitechapel consisted mostly of deprived slums filled with unemployed drunkards frustrated at their lot in the world. Work was scarce and booze was cheap, and many lived in filth, squalor, and destitution. What fuelled the anger of the populace moreover was that, a mere mile away, past Aldgate, the City of London had entered into a golden age, thriving under the riches that industry, trade, and technology had brought to the wealthiest city in the world. The disparity between Whitechapel and the City of London stoked a rage that frequently turned to rioting, and the Met often bore the brunt of the violence. Keeping this body out on the street was just asking for trouble!

Only a few minutes earlier, Neil had hoped that the prostitute's corpse was not far from the back of a police ambulance. Once she was en route to the morgue, the matter would be handed over to the Criminal Investigation Department of the Metropolitan Police. Neil's stake in the investigation would be more or less done with, aside from a few statements he would have to give. But now, he knew this night was far from over. He regretted more than ever discovering the body, but more so, the discovery of the strange markings painted across the stable gates.

In the half hour that followed, various officers from both H and J division arrived on the scene, helping Neil, Mizen, and Thain to cordon off the majority of Buck's Row. The residents of the street and the surrounding neighbourhood began to issue forth to investigate the commotion. Murmurs whispered through the crowd of murder, several speculating as to whom the victim might be, whilst others more brazenly demanded answers from the police officers guarding the perimeter.

Detective Inspector Edmund Reid of H Division was soon to appear, bringing with him a photographer armed with a small-format camera to take record of the scene. The police ambulance was pulled in, but the body was not loaded inside; instead, the draught horse was uncoupled, the cart wheeled across the alley to obscure the stableyard gates from the public.

Several camera flashes illuminated the crime scene. Onlookers amassed at the barricades gasped in horror as the bloody corpse was unveiled time and time again in the glare of the magnesium flash lamp, the body near wholly visible beneath the ambulance's undercarriage. But Neil and the other officers present knew all too well that the intention had never been to obscure the corpse. The ambulance's positioning was to hide something else entirely: the graffito painted above it. And just as well; several reporters from The Star had not long ago arrived and were already firing questions at the officers along the perimeter.

Neil fumbled in his tunic and drew out his pocket watch. Five fifty-two; his beat should have been coming to an end soon.

"We should have had her on the back of that ambulance and out of here an hour ago!" grumbled Sergeant Kirby as he took up position alongside Neil. "We're going to have a situation on our hands soon enough."

"I fear you are right, sir," agreed Neil.

Kirby reached into his pocket and produced a pair of freshly rolled cigarettes. "Do you smoke, Constable?"

"Tonight, sir, I do," nodded Neil.

"Good man," nodded his superior, handing the Irishman one of the cigarettes before placing the second between his lips. The sergeant struck a match, lighting both their rollups, and took an extended drag.

Neil stifled a cough as he drew a puff of smoke into his lungs and exhaled wheezily.

"Rumour is, Special Unit are on their way down here now," explained Kirby.

"Special Unit?" questioned Neil.

"Malleus," affirmed Kirby. "Hammer."

"Hammer are on their way *here*!?" breathed Neil. "Then that means...!?" he continued looking back towards the graffito obscured by the ambulance.

"That's what the boys are saying," nodded Kirby.

"Oh shit!" cursed Neil, looking down at the crusted blood beneath his fingernails. He wiped his hand on his trousers again, fearful of what any contact with the blood could mean for him.

"Calm yourself, Constable," growled Sergeant Kirby.

"But sir... I touched it!"

"And you're fine, ain't you?"

Neil remained quiet.

"If you're concerned, I am sure the boys from Special Division can take a look at you when they arrive."

Neil bowed his head. "No sir, I don't think that's necessary."

"Good," nodded Kirby as smoke issued from his nostrils beneath the orange glow of the gaslight.

With the photographer beginning to pack away his equipment, Detective Inspector Edmund Reid stooped to study the body of the streetwalker. His eyes slowly rose to the arcane graphic painted in the victim's blood. Curious, he thought, that a pattern such as this should cause more upheaval within the force than the nearly decapitated body sprawled out beneath it. Were not the graphic painted in blood, the officers to arrive on the scene might have merely dismissed it as nothing more than graffiti; unusual graffiti yes, but nothing too extraordinary. Yet the medium in which it was painted changed the very nature of the discovery, from one of vandalism to something infinitely more sinister.

Inspector Reid stepped closer, observing the symmetrical shape in which the unusual hieroglyphs were ordered; in a macabre manner, the image was pleasing to look at. It could be considered art in its own right. Reid had always held a fascination for the arcane and inexplicable, and staring at the glyph inscribed in blood before him, he felt an insatiable curiosity to understand its purpose.

"Reid!" warned a gruff familiar voice from out of the shadows. "Step away from that."

Reid cautiously backed away, ensuring to

leave little imprint on the surrounding crime scene. "Apologies Chief Inspector," mumbled the detective, removing his hat respectfully.

From out of the gloom emerged a tall greying man in a dark suit and coat with wiry mutton chops sprouting from his cheeks. At his side stood a handsome, suited Indian man, six inches shorter than his superior, but equally finely dressed.

"Just be careful," warned Frederick Abberline.

"Of course, sir," apologised Reid again.

"Edmund, might I introduce my new partner: Detective Sergeant Kalpesh Khatri. Khatri, this is Inspector Edmund Reid of H division."

"A pleasure, sir," smiled Inspector Reid, replacing his hat atop his pate and extending a hand to the Indian.

"The pleasure is mine," insisted Kalpesh with a well-spoken British accent, devoid save the subtlest hint of his true ethnicity.

"Gentlemen," huffed Abberline, "now is hardly the time for pleasantries!"

"Quite so," agreed Reid, turning back to gaze at the strange arcane sigil emblazoned in the victim's blood.

Abberline stepped closer, studying the glyph for himself, rubbing his whiskered chin. "Sweet lord," breathed the aging detective. "This city is going to hell!"

"Not literally, I trust?" questioned Reid

fearfully.

"Regrettably, I cannot give you any such assurance, Reid," replied Abberline as he continued to study the unworldly graffito. "Khatri," spoke out the greying man after a time, "this is more your area of expertise. See what you make of this gibberish."

"Of course, sir," nodded Kalpesh as he carefully stepped around the supine woman sprawled on the cobbles. He moved closer, scooping up a bullseye lantern and directing its beam across the sigil. "It's a pentacle," he announced.

"That much is surely apparent," mocked Abberline, expecting a more in-depth analysis from his newly appointed partner than mere statement of the obvious. "Anything else you care to ascertain, Sergeant Khatri?"

"It is familiar enough," remarked the Indian. "I believe I have come across it before." Kalpesh reached inside his coat and withdrew a black leather journal from his inner breast pocket. He quickly leafed through pages and pages of his scribbled shorthand and annotated sketches before finally arriving at the pentacle in question. "Here," he indicated, tapping the page. "It's as I feared. It's from the Key of Solomon; it's the third Seal of Mars."

"Now that's more like it," remarked Abberline. "What does it do?" questioned the detective as he placed his hands on his hips.

Kalpesh was already skimming his scrawled notes. His heart sank with dread. He raised his gaze to Abberline. "It is for the invocation of war—it incites wrath... discord... chaos!" he uttered.

Frederick Abberline absorbed the news silently. A grave expression elongated his greying face.

"Discord? Chaos?" questioned Reid nervously, glancing past the cover of the carriage obscuring the crime scene to the rabble growing steadily more restless beyond the police cordon.

"The lad didn't stutter, did he Reid?" muttered Abberline.

"Forgive me, Chief Inspector, but I am not so well versed in esoteric matters as the men at Special Division; might I ask, what is it that we are to expect? What, if any, ramifications are to come from the painting of this so called, *Seal of Mars*?"

Abberline exhaled and tightened his jaw before turning to face the detective from H Division with a sombre glare. "At this stage, Reid, your guess is as good as mine."

Edmund Reid swallowed hard, his eyes falling to the corpse at his feet. "Perhaps then it would be appropriate to remove the body from the scene; lest upheaval is stoked within the residents of Buck's Row by this... *pentacle*."

"Not yet," refused Abberline, his greater concerns far from the potential riot kindling mere yards away.

"If it pleases the inspector, I have

ensured that the scene has been meticulously recorded," explained Reid. "The victim has been photographed from an array of angles, with great effort made to capture the positioning of her body and the details of her surroundings. Likewise, photographic record has been taken of this... *graffito*. Moreover, a local surgeon has already carried out a preliminary inspection of the deceased."

"I said not yet, Reid!" growled Abberline, cutting off the detective before he could make another insistence on removing the body from the street.

Reid fell silent, lowering his head.

"Is there anything else, Sergeant?" asked Abberline as Kalpesh continued to study the sigil painted on the gates.

"The symbols," began Kalpesh immediately.

"What of them?"

"Most of the characters utilised in any of the forty-four pentacles depicted in the Lesser Key of Solomon are from the Hebrew alphabet," explained Kalpesh.

"And that most definitely is not Hebrew," stated Abberline. "Any idea what it is?"

"I cannot say for certain," replied Kalpesh, "but if I were to hazard a guess, I would say they are letters from the Enochian alphabet."

"Enochian?" questioned Abberline.

"Similar to celestial," explained Kalpesh. "The supposed language of angels."

"Is that so?" mused Chief Inspector Abberline. "Any theory as to why it is in Enochian?"

"None," Kalpesh shook his head. "But if the killer knows Enochian..."

"Then we aren't dealing with just any second-rate sorcerer," stated Abberline.

"Precisely."

"Good work," grumbled Abberline, clearly impressed with the man newly assigned to him.

"Thank you, sir," replied the Indian as he resumed turning the pages in his black leather journal.

"Reid?" Abberline turned back to the head of H division.

"Sir?"

"What did this doctor of yours have to say about the body?"

Reid knelt aside the murdered woman and indicated to the lacerations across her throat. "Cause of death was through blood loss as a result of severing of the carotid artery from these two cuts; The second of the two is deep—down to the spine."

"I would have thought that obvious enough," replied Abberline. "But I cannot see any splattering about the scene."

"The doctor suggested she might have been strangled beforehand to subdue her; doing so would likely have caused a reduction in blood pressure."

"Therefore, no arterial spray," surmised Kalpesh as he shut his journal and knelt alongside Reid.

"Yes," confirmed the plain clothes detective.

"Anything else the surgeon made mention of?" asked Abberline.

"No," replied Reid. "He has been awaiting the arrival of the body at the mortuary for some time though now, where he means to perform a proper autopsy."

"Do we have a name yet?" questioned Abberline.

"Not yet," replied Reid. "But we have gone door to door. It would seem the deceased is not a resident of Buck's Row. More likely, she is a regular of one of the nearby dosshouses."

"Do you smell that?" questioned Kalpesh as he leant closer to the body. The smell of excrement seemed obvious now as he stooped over the woman. He noticed a crease in her ulster clotted with blood about her abdomen.

"Smell what?" mused Abberline. "Whitechapel?"

Kalpesh cautiously drew back the prostitute's skirt and two petticoats before stepping away in horror. The three men stood over the woman looking down in disgust at the brutal mutilations across her lower abdomen.

"It would seem this surgeon of yours, Reid, failed to notice something of interest;" uttered Abberline gravely. "This poor woman has been disembowelled!"

II

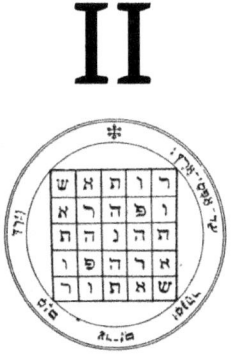

**Whitechapel Infirmary, Old Montague Street
7:33 a.m. August 31st, 1888**

"The victim has been identified as Mary Ann Nichols," explained Abberline as he entered the morgue. "But it would seem she went as Polly to those who knew her around here."

"Any family of note?" questioned Kalpesh as the bare Edison bulb hummed overhead, its warm light falling upon the naked body of the mutilated prostitute.

"She has been estranged from her husband,

William Nichols, for some time it would seem," replied Abberline. "He's on his way up from Southwark to make a formal identification. The pair had five children, of which the youngest four still live with their father."

"The oldest?"

"We haven't verified it, but we have reason to believe he lives with his grandfather, south of the river."

Kalpesh nodded as he studied the horrific wounds that had been inflicted upon the body.

"First impressions from the questions we've asked are that she was reasonably well-liked by those that knew her," continued Abberline as he moved aside his partner to observe the victim laid bare. "No enemies of note."

"Anyone she owed money?"

"None we've turned up," answered the detective. "Seems she spent all she had on booze. Her doss money included."

"What do you mean?" questioned the Indian.

"She was lodging in a doss house on Thrawl Street," returned the detective. "But she was turned away last night—didn't have the four pence she needed for the night. Last person to see her alive: another streetwalker by the name of Emily Holland—claims that Polly here reckoned she'd already earnt her doss money three times over, but had squandered it on each occasion."

"So she was looking for another customer?"

surmised Kalpesh.

"So it would seem."

"Then it would be safe to assume that whoever killed her might well have posed as a customer."

"Chances are, she'd never seen the man before," nodded Abberline.

"It makes sense," sighed the Indian. "She served as the sacrifice for a ritual. Her identity was unimportant to the killer. He merely slaughtered her for her blood—her lifeforce—to fuel some form of black magic."

"What did the coroner have to say?" asked Abberline, indicating to Mary Ann Nichol's lifeless body.

"Well," began Kalpesh, "despite appearances, she is actually in her forties. She's missing a number of teeth, though they weren't lost particularly recently."

"What else?" pressed Abberline, eager to cut to the details relevant to the murder.

"There's bruising around her neck and face on both sides."

"So our man was right about something: she *was* strangled."

"It would appear so, yes," confirmed Kalpesh.

"What about the weapon?"

"A long knife of moderate sharpness, I am told; one used with *'great violence.'* The same blade was used to inflict the wounds to the throat and abdomen," explained Kalpesh. "Oh, and supposedly the killer could be left-handed, given the bruising and the direction of the cuts."

"Something to keep in mind," muttered Abberline, "but we can't base our manhunt on it; I've known coroners proved wrong about these things in the past."

"Noted."

"And what of your opinion?" questioned Abberline, turning his scrutinising gaze now on his newly appointed partner. "What do you make of those wounds? What is the nature of the killing?"

Kalpesh met his superior's eyes, observing the same expression that he had received in Buck's Row. This was a test. Abberline demanded to be impressed by the next few sentences Kalpesh was to deliver; anything less than an insightful observation from the Indian detective would be a failing.

"The blade used was more than likely an athame," stated Kalpesh. "It matches the description and dimensions given by the coroner, and given the ritual nature of this murder, it fits."

"An athame?" questioned Abberline, his stare falling momentarily to the jagged wounds stretching across Polly Nichols' lower abdomen.

"It's a ritual blade used by occultists, representative of fire, one of the four classical elements." explained Kalpesh. "One of four components often used in ritual magic; the other three being a wand, typically representing air, a chalice is symbolic of water—earth, interestingly enough is often represented by a pentacle."

"The Pentacle of Mars at the scene of the crime?"

Kalpesh nodded.

"What was the killer trying to do?" pressed Abberline. "Why paint that sigil in this poor woman's blood?"

"I can only begin to speculate," muttered Kalpesh as he slowly fingered through his journal, hoping to find some answer scrawled across the pages. "The pentacle is only one piece of the ritual. Polly Nichol's body is another, but there must be more—there are too many variables we don't know to determine the exact purpose of this ritual."

"But what are you thinking?" questioned Abberline, wanting more concrete answers.

Kalpesh closed his journal, sliding it neatly back inside the breast of his coat before turning his full attention once more to the body supine on the cold table before him. "These mutilations would not have taken long to perform," declared the detective, thinking aloud. "But there is a level of intricacy to the Third Seal of Mars, especially given that the text within it is in Enochian, rather than Hebrew."

"This woman wasn't exactly found in a back alley," remarked Abberline. "She was lying almost directly underneath the window of one of the cottages. Our killer couldn't have had long to act. It was out in the open; he could have been discovered at any moment."

"Exactly," nodded Kalpesh. "The man that painted the Third Seal of Mars on those gates wasn't merely copying the sigil from a page; doing so would have taken too long."

"I agree," remarked Abberline, "but what are you getting at, Khatri?"

"Whoever painted the pentacle either had it memorised completely, or they not only know Enochian, but are fluent in it."

"You are saying that we are dealing with someone high up in the occult?"

"I'd say they would have to be," insisted Kalpesh. "This isn't the sort of magic any low-ranking occultist could feasibly get their hands on. Grimoires containing these secrets... the only copies left in existence are hidden deep in the vaults of the most secretive esoteric orders; they do not find themselves into the hands of common practitioners. Save for our own reference copy in the archives, Malleus has systematically destroyed every book of the Key of Solomon it has ever seized. Enochian is a dead language amongst all but the most secretive and underground occult fraternities."

"Then why is it that we just found it written in blood on the streets of Whitechapel!?" demanded Abberline in frustration.

"That is what makes it all the stranger," mused Kalpesh. "Any high-ranking occultists—

anyone privy to such closely guarded arcane secrets—you'd have thought they would not have performed such a macabre ritual so brazenly and so publicly on the streets. The Freemasons, The Brotherhood of Luxor, The Theosophical Society —they all have secret headquarters, places hidden deep within the city unbeknownst to us, where they'd be able to perform a ritual such as this in secret. And yet, this ritual took place out on the open streets; in the dead of night, granted, but along a street patrolled every half an hour by the men of J Division."

"You think it is a message?" mused Abberline.

"Maybe," shrugged Kalpesh. "But if so, it is not a particularly clear one to send."

"Then what?"

"It is perhaps too early to say."

"Then take a guess," insisted Abberline. "Gut instinct?"

Kalpesh ruminated in silence for a long moment.

"Khatri!" urged Abberline impatiently.

"I think this is just the beginning of something," supposed the Indian. "We've not seen the full extent of this crime; just a small part of a much larger picture. This could merely be the first stage in an extensive ritual."

"You're saying this murder might just be the first of many?"

"I fear so," responded the junior detective

solemnly.

"Shit," cursed Abberline through gritted teeth.

"Whatever the case," continued Kalpesh, "the implications of what happened last night are hard to stomach. Our killer is a dangerous warlock; perhaps one of the most dangerous Malleus has encountered this century."

"Then we had better catch the bastard," replied Abberline sternly, "before he strikes again!"

III

Tower of London, City of London
9:11 a.m. September 1st, 1888

Black smoke billowed upwards in rising clouds from the murky Thames as hundreds of barges chugged through the noisome water. The clattering of pistons roared over the clanging of bells as dense traffic clogged the greasy waterway serving as the main artery for London. Hooves clopped, axels creaked, and wheels rattled as dozens of carriages and stagecoaches navigated the street, parting every so often to give way to an electrified tram car screeching down the rails embedded in the road. Pedestrians wove between them, mingling with the traffic, stepping off and onto trolleys and ferries, but mostly keeping to the pavement as they chattered and shouted to one another in the bustling throngs. Meanwhile, high in the sky, a dozen massive airships hung suspended on invisible strings, silently drifting against the backdrop of clouds, looming over the capital of the British Empire, serving as a constant reminder of the relentless progress of industry.

Kalpesh strolled down the waterfront, gazing out from the embankment at the chaos of the bustling city before him. He meandered through the crowds of tourists gathering outside the gates of the Tower of London to gaze upon the medieval castle. Emerging from out of the gathering, the Indian detective found himself confronted by a line of Yeoman Warders standing guard outside the barbican. Kalpesh greeted them with a smile, flashing the nearest beefeater his badge and identification papers. The yeoman studied the Malleus badge, briefly raising his gaze to the man presenting it, before nodding silently with a look of contempt, stepping aside to wave him through.

Kalpesh cleared the security line and marched through the gatehouse beneath the raised portcullis, heading out onto the bridge spanning the fetid river water that flooded the moat. As he made his way towards the second barbican, Byward Tower, he glanced upwards to the rows of antiair turrets and mounted machineguns that lined the battlements, all manned by the redcoats patrolling atop the ramparts. From outward appearances, the military garrison stationed within the Tower appeared to be protecting the fortress against invading forces. But in truth, as many Maxim Machine guns pointed inwards as out; in reality, the defences and personnel served more to protect the city outside from those who were contained within.

As Kalpesh approached the far end of the bridge, two more yeomen armed with bayonetted rifles stood at a secondary security checkpoint. The Indian halted before the guards, presenting once more his badge and papers before offering up his service pistol and kukri. Whilst his relevant identifications were scrutinised more thoroughly this time, the second of the beefeaters patted him down. A hand fumbled inside his breast pocket and drew out his journal. The guard flicked rapidly through the pages before his eyes glazed over and he returned the black leather-bound notebook to its owner.

With both yeoman content, the first returned Kalpesh his badge and papers and shouted, "Raise the gate!"

The buzz of an electric motor powering up preceded the clattering of the second portcullis and the steel grating was lifted from the gateway of Byward Tower. Kalpesh stepped into the shadowed archway, hastily crossing into the Tower's outer ward.

Malleus headquarters had been located within the Tower of London since the order's inception in the mid-16th century. Created to enforce Henry VIII's Witchcraft Act of 1542, Malleus, named for the infamous witch hunter's treatise Malleus Maleficarum, or Hammer of the Witches, originally operated out of the White Tower itself. But, with the rise in modern occultism that had spread across the globe in the last century, the organisation had needed to expand. In 1845, the new Malleus headquarters, frequently referred to as Anvil, was constructed in the southeast corner of the inner ward.

Imprisoned within the heavily guarded dungeons situated deep below ground, Anvil held some of the most dangerous persons in the world: occultists awaiting trial, and those already sentenced destined for the gallows on Tower Green. Anvil's prisoners were held tightly under lock and key, with trials expedited and the death penalty serving as the final sentence of all found guilty of practises that breeched the laws against sorcery.

Many successful prison breaks had been made from the Tower of London throughout the course of history, but since the construction of Anvil, not a single convicted occultist had ever again set foot outside its walls, save for the short walk they all made to Tower Green. It was said the prison was utterly inescapable. Any who stepped into the dungeons beneath Anvil was destined to meet their end at the gallows. It was into those very dungeons that Kalpesh was now headed.

Passing beneath the raised portcullis of the Bloody Tower, Kalpesh stepped into the inner ward and made his way east towards Anvil. Glancing briefly in the direction of the White Tower at the heart of the complex, the Indian detective finally made for the neo-medieval castellated limestone building that dominated the southeast corner of the courtyard. More riflemen stood to attention either side of the steel reinforced doors of Malleus headquarters, maintaining their statuesque composure as they guarded the entrance. Cutting between them, Kalpesh stepped through into the opulent entrance hall.

Daylight streamed through venetian stained glass, casting a mosaic of colours across the encaustic tiles in the form of the Malleus heraldry: a flaming cruciform sword. A grand crystal chandelier humming with Edison bulbs hung from the vaulted ceiling, whilst carved walnut panelling lined the lower walls, rising upwards into the ornately sculpted limestone arches that converged overhead.

Several statues stood about the atrium, most notably Henry VIII himself. On the right side of the Tudor king's effigy stood a statue of Heinrich Kramer, the German-born inquisitor who authored Malleus Maleficarum, whilst on the left of the king was Jacob Sprenger, a Dominican Friar also credited to the authorship of the treatise. Controversially, Sprenger's contribution to the Hammer of the Witches was frequently brought into question by historians, many claiming his name had been added long after both Sprenger's death, and the book's first publication. Yet to this day, his effigy stood in the atrium of Anvil, regardless of whether the man in question would have approved of its placement.

"Kalpesh," a voice called out the moment the young detective entered the building.

"Melville," returned Kalpesh affably, turning to see his old friend Melville Macnaghten approach.

"I believe that is *Assistant Chief Constable*, to you, Detective" winked the officer, jestingly.

"It's official then?" questioned Kalpesh in surprise. "Warren has resigned?"

"Indeed," replied Melville, his moustache bristling as a smile curled beneath it. "That bastard has finally folded under the pressure. The Home Secretary seems to have taken his resignation rather well; in fact, as I hear it, he sounded positively thrilled!"

"Then I suppose Monro is best pleased also?"

"I'll say," smirked Melville again. "He's finally where he should be; none of us quite understood how it was that Warren beat him to Commissioner in the first place. Now James answers directly to the Home Secretary, as it should have been from the start."

"Good," nodded Kalpesh with admiration. "He deserves it. You both do."

"Maybe now that we don't have that overbearing liberal breathing down on us constantly, we can actually get some real policing done."

"We still managed before," replied Kalpesh.

"Hardly," returned Melville. "It's a wonder we ever succeeded last year against the Jubilee Plot."

"But we did," insisted Kalpesh.

"*You* did," corrected Melville. "Heavens knows what would have happened had you not acted."

"I just did what anyone would in my position," insisted Kalpesh.

"No," refused Melville, "you performed above and beyond the call of duty. And because you did so, Malleus thwarted the greatest act of treason against this country since the Gunpowder plot!"

"Thank you, sir," returned the Indian detective, bowing his head in gratitude.

"Oh, don't turn all formal on me, Khatri," returned the Assistant Chief Constable. "You proved I was right in bringing you into Malleus— not to me of course; I never doubted you would excel here—but to all the bigots and naysayers who were against an Indian ever being made detective within Special Division. You have done us proud."

Kalpesh beamed back at his mentor.

"How's your new partner, Abberline?" questioned Melville, changing the subject.

"Somewhat prickly," responded Kalpesh. "But I believe I have gone some way to earning his respect."

"He may be new to Malleus," explained Melville, "but he has been a detective for the better part of fifteen years, and he was a uniformed officer for another decade before that. The arcane might be outside his field of expertise, but the man lives and breathes detective work. He turned down a promotion in Whitehall to transfer here."

"Any idea why?"

"He never gave a clear answer. But I suspect it had something to do with the Jubilee Plot; until last year, I believe much of the Met underestimated the threat of the occult. I imagine Abberline believes he can do more good here at Special Branch than in the regular CID."

"That's admirable."

"Quite so," agreed Melville. "He's a good man, Frederick Abberline is; as you put it yourself: a little prickly at times, but a distinguished policeman. I suspect you can see why it is I had the two of you partnered?"

"My guess would be that you believed we would complement each other's shortcomings?" returned Kalpesh with a raised eyebrow. "He is not well versed on esotericism, but has a lifetime of experience in criminology, whilst I on the other hand *do* have a broad academic knowledge of magic, and yet am lacking in police experience."

"Nothing escapes you, does it, Khatri?"

"A rather calculated decision from you, it would seem, Melville."

"Would you expect anything less from the newly appointed Assistant Chief Constable?"

"I supposed not," smiled the Indian.

Melville offered another broad grin, the whiskers of his moustache ruffling as he did so, before his amiable demeanour quickly dissolved into a stern professionalism. "Come on," beckoned the man. "Monro is waiting for us."

"Monro is here?" questioned Kalpesh in surprise.

"He came straight down from the Home Office the moment word reached him."

Kalpesh stood silent and dumbfounded.

"Henry Steel Olcott, cofounder of the Theosophical Society, chief orchestrator of the Jubilee Plot, asks as his last request to speak privately face to face with you by name, and you didn't think that the head of Malleus would head down river to oversee it?"

"When you put it that way..." conceded Kalpesh.

"We need to find out everything we can from that zealot; how he came to learn of your identity first and foremost!"

IV

Anvil, Tower of London, City of London
9:38 a.m. September 1st, 1888

"Are you ready, son?" asked Commissioner James Monro, thin wisps of smoke diffusing from his nostrils as he took another puff from his pipe.

Kalpesh swallowed, his heart throbbing in his chest. "Yes, sir," he replied anxiously.

"Be careful," warned Monro, "he'll try and get inside your head."

Kalpesh nodded.

"He'll be fine," insisted Melville. "We'll be watching everything. If you decide you've had enough at any point, just let us know and we'll pull you straight out."

Kalpesh nodded silently once more.

"Are you sure you want to do this?" pressed Commissioner Monro apprehensively.

"Yes."

"Alright," nodded Melville before looking to the two guards stationed at the cell door. "Let him in."

"Yes sir," agreed one of the jailers, pulling a lever with two hands. "Cell door opening!" he shouted, before pushing a large red button mounted on the wall.

An electronic bell clattered loudly down the dungeon corridor and a warning bulb flashed crimson above the massive steel door. All fell suddenly quiet before the motors surged to life and the round vault door began to slowly rotate as it was geared away from across the entrance of the high-security cell. Soon, the aperture to the cell was entirely agape and the motor whir died, replaced in its stead by the deafening whine of arcs of electricity bolting outwards from two giant Tesla coils erected within the room.

Monro nodded to one of the jailers and the guard pulled the circuit breaker, killing power to the coils. The flashes of lightning faded along with the droning tumult. Tentatively, Kalpesh stepped forth into the cell of one of the most dangerous warlocks in the world. The motors for the cell door hummed again as the huge mass of steel revolved back over the doorway, sealing the Indian detective inside.

A large Faraday cage was erected in the heart of the room, centred in which sat Olcott silently meditating in the lotus position. This was the first time Kalpesh had looked upon the man since he had apprehended him in June the previous year; he appeared more haggard and withered than the Indian detective could ever have imagined, aged by the year of torture and interrogation he had been subject to since his arrest. His unruly beard had doubled in length, but the wiry hair upon his scalp had thinned and was now balding in patches. He was gaunt from malnourishment, his eyes sunken into the wrinkled sockets of his blemished face; the meagre meals he had been supplied with were unfit to sustain a man for any prolonged duration. Were his execution not imminent, Kalpesh suspected the man would soon perish from starvation alone.

Kalpesh stepped closer, his hard-soled shoes reverberating across the concrete floor as he approached. Henry Steel Olcott remained silent and motionless, only the subtle rise and fall of his chest indicating that his feeble body had not yet failed. Heavy shackles and manacles bound his wrists and ankles, chaining him to the floor in the centre of the room.

Kalpesh examined the powered-down Tesla coils positioned either side of the cage; so long as the sorcerer remained inside the protective

Faraday shield without touching the mesh walls, he was safe from the high-voltage surges of lightning continually forking outwards from the large resonant transformers. The electrified coils were normally kept in constant operation, only powering down in instances where others needed to safely enter the cell; beyond mealtimes, the only situations where this was the case tended to be for the lengthy sessions of interrogation that Olcott was often subjected to. Yet, in the entire time that the occultist had been imprisoned within Anvil, he had not once been overcome by Malleus interrogators. Olcott had a seemingly unbreakable resolve that allowed him to endure torture in a way that had not been previously documented by Malleus, even dating back to the middle ages when techniques of eliciting confessions were far more barbaric than the methods employed today. As such, Olcott had gained something of a fearsome reputation among the jailers. Many dreaded being stationed outside his cell, whilst others profited, taking the shifts of fellow guards in exchange for money or favours.

The Faraday cage also served another purpose beyond containing Olcott and protecting him from the electric arcs fired from the Tesla coils; in the same way it formed an impenetrable barrier to electromagnetic radiation, it formed a blockade to the Aether, interfering with any and all kinds of spellcasting, negating the powers of any occultist contained within by preventing them from drawing on the powers of the cosmos that flowed outside the cage.

Kalpesh moved closer, observing that Olcott's eyes remained shut as the man stayed fixed in meditation; he did not appear to be aware that anyone had even entered the cell. The Indian peered over his shoulder to look upon his dim reflection in the glass wall behind him; on the other side of the half-silvered mirror, Kalpesh knew Melville and Moro would be watching, recording the entire encounter on film and phonograph for the Malleus record archives. He looked back to Olcott and took an abrupt step backwards as a set of blue eyes shot open to behold him.

The chains binding the occultist jangled as he mechanically rose to his feet. He shuffled forwards stiffly, until, restricted by the full reach of his restraints, he came to a stop several inches short of the steel mesh of the Faraday cage. Throughout his automaton-esque shuffle, Olcott never averted his gaze from Kalpesh. An eerie silence descended as the two men continued to stare fixedly on one another.

Kalpesh was the first to speak. "You asked for me?"

Olcott stayed disquietingly silent.

"You requested me by name, I am told."

Still, Olcott's cracked lips remained sealed as he studied the young Indian, his head subtly cocking as his stare penetrated him.

"How is that?" pressed the detective. "How did you come to learn my identity?"

A long moment of quiet passed.

"Why am I here?" questioned Kalpesh in annoyance.

Silence.

"It looks as if we are done here," finalised Kalpesh, not in the mood for mind games. He turned to make for the door.

"Do you know who you are?" the rasping voice of Olcott spoke after him.

Kalpesh halted, slowly revolving back to face the prisoner. "*I* know who I am," he replied. "The question is: how do *you*?"

Olcott cleared his throat before his chest rose and fell in a deep inhalation. "The universe speaks to me."

"The universe speaks to you?" questioned Kalpesh sceptically. "Not in here it doesn't. You are in a Faraday cage; it blocks every form of scrying and divination we know about. What's more, this entire room is lead lined, and if that isn't enough, this cell is so far underground that neither the cage nor the lead should even matter."

Olcott remained cold and motionless, his blue eyes locked unwaveringly upon the man before him.

"Would you care to revise your answer?" pressed Kalpesh.

"Your inventions..." he began in his broad American accent, "this cage, this room—you are right, they smother the anthem of creation, but the chorus is not drowned out completely. Even from within this prison that you have erected, still the universe whispers, and every so often, I am able to hear what it says."

"And what is it saying, exactly?" asked Kalpesh sceptically.

"It speaks to me of destiny," he replied. "It speaks to me of you."

"Of me?"

"Indeed."

Kalpesh momentarily glanced at his reflection once more in the one-way glass. "You know nothing about me," he refuted.

"On the contrary, my boy," Olcott declared matter-of-factly, "I may be the only person who truly does."

"Would you care to elaborate, or do you wish to merely keep up this exchange of cryptic statements?"

"The mark you carry…" began the American.

Kalpesh balled his left hand into a fist.

"Do you know what it means?"

"Yes," replied the detective abruptly.

"But you don't know why you bear it?"

This time Kalpesh remained silent.

"I first saw it when you apprehended me last year," explained Olcott, "but it is only through introspection that I have come to understand its true meaning."

"What are you talking about?"

"At the time I had merely assumed it to be nothing more than what it appeared to be: a tattoo; one perhaps serving as a reminder of your homeland—of your heritage. But through meditation, a memory I had long forgotten presented itself to me that provided the truth."

"And what truth is that?"

"Your identity."

"You are talking in circles," replied Kalpesh patiently.

"You've had that mark as long as you can remember, have you not?"

Kalpesh felt his knotted fist clench involuntarily tighter.

"Who would tattoo a child, you ask?"

"And I suppose you have some answer to that?"

"A mother who knows she is to be parted from her son, but hopes in time to find him again —in a different land, with a different name."

"What are you suggesting?" pressed Kalpesh, taking a step closer to Olcott.

Olcott smiled. "It really is you, isn't it?"

"Answer me," demanded Kalpesh coldly.

"You've been asking yourself these questions your whole life, and now you find answers for the first time, in a man imminently destined for the gallows—the greatest irony of all being that you yourself are the one that condemned him to that very fate."

Kalpesh turned away and began to walk

towards the door.

"The subcontinent has a rich cultural history of tattoos," spoke Olcott after him. "Caste markings, identification, ritual purification, esoteric empowerment; all of these apply to that mark on your hand."

Kalpesh halted.

"I trust you have heard of Rani Lakshmibai?"

Kalpesh revolved. "Rani of Jhansi? The warrior queen of the Indian Rebellions?"

Olcott smiled crookedly. "A powerful sorceress who fought for the independence of her people—your people. Since her death, she has risen as a martyr—a symbol of resistance to British rule in India."

"I am familiar with the story," returned Kalpesh. "I was a company man. I served in the Bengal army—the same Bengal army that quashed the rebellion."

"But you did not grow up on the subcontinent," asserted Olcott.

"No," replied Kalpesh. "I was raised in an orphanage in Whitechapel."

"You were smuggled out of India when you were just a babe, secreted away to the birthplace of your father."

"What are you trying to suggest?"

"I knew your father. I met him during my travels in India. It is through his account that I learnt all of what I tell you now: it is that mark on your palm that identifies you as his; it is that mark on your hand that identifies you as Indian royalty —the son of Rani Lakshmibai."

"Rani Lakshmibai had no son," refuted Kalpesh. "The entire reason for her revolt was that the Company did not recognise her adopted son as her husband's legitimate heir. Her biological son died in infancy."

"Your half-brother," nodded Olcott. "You were conceived during the rebellion; your father, a Civil Service Officer and rebel sympathiser, came to meet Rani Lakshmibai during the siege of Jhansi, and you were born days before the fall of Gwalior—days before your mother fell in battle."

"This is ridiculous," proclaimed Kalpesh.

"You were given that mark and smuggled out of Gwalior by your father's contacts—shipped back to England, in the hope that in the wake of the rebellion, your mother might travel here and find you. But Rani Lakshmibai fell in the aftermath of the battle, and somewhere along the journey home, you were lost to your father. He scoured this city for you high and low, but like so many children in London before you, you had been lost. Assuming the worst, he returned to Jhansi, without his son."

"You are lying," replied Kalpesh. "How could you know all of this?"

Olcott shook his head. "It is all true."

"Then who is he?" questioned Kalpesh. "What is the name of this British father of mine?"

"He has been dead some time."

"Then give me a name," shrugged the detective.

Olcott silently refused.

"You are trying my patience!"

The American continued to stare back at the Indian detective.

"You have offered no proof for any of these claims. Why is it I should believe a word of what you say?"

"Because you know it in your heart to be true."

Kalpesh sighed exasperatedly.

"It has happened, hasn't it?" asked Olcott, his eyes narrowing.

"What has happened?"

"The Ripper... he has finally struck! The Beast has awoken. I can sense the disturbance in the Aether his work has caused."

"What are you talking about?" pressed Kalpesh, his eyes narrowing.

"Last night?"

Kalpesh scrutinised Olcott suspiciously as his mind briefly flickered to images of Buck's Row.

Olcott nodded in confirmation. "The ritual has begun. It is only a matter of time."

"If you know something, I suggest you stop playing these games and come out with it."

"The horrific murder that occurred in that dark alley last night was merely the first step in a series of cataclysmic events that will tear at the very fabric of reality. He must be stopped."

"What do you know?" demanded Kalpesh in frustration.

"Only that he cannot be allowed to succeed, and that you are to play a role far greater than I can foresee in what is to come!"

"Then help me. Prove to me that you are not merely guessing. Give me something concrete that I can use! What do you know?"

Olcott stood silently, his ghostly face giving nothing away. Suddenly a faint buzzing sounded and his body crumpled. The theosophist collapsed to the ground and convulsed as an electrical current conducted through his manacles from a generator concealed beneath the floor.

"Answer him!" the voice of Monro crackled over the loudspeaker in the corner of the room.

The hum fell quiet and Olcott's body slumped against the concrete. The old man whimpered as he rasped for air.

Kalpesh closed his eyes, turning away from the man in pity. "What do you know about what happened last night?"

Olcott continued to pant wheezily as he lay on the floor of the cage. "Only that no one deserves to die the way she did… ripped."

"What do you mean?"

"She will be the first of many," spat Olcott.

"Did you have something to do with it?" pressed Kalpesh. "Do you know the man responsible?"

The theosophist refused to answer.

The generator powered up again and Olcott yelped as more electricity surged through his body, earthing via his shackles. The buzz cut out and he began gasping again.

"Answer the questions, Olcott!" came now the voice of Melville.

"They won't stop," warned Kalpesh. "You need to cooperate. What do you know?"

"You must seek her out," murmured Olcott, strings of saliva stretching between his numb lips and the cold floor.

"Seek who out?" questioned Kalpesh, crouching nearer to the American.

Olcott paused in his response. His head lurched back as he was electrocuted again.

Kalpesh averted his gaze.

The clicking of the generator fell silent.

Olcott moaned as he caught his breath.

The generator whirred up again, this time followed by Olcott's screams.

"Tell us what we want to know!" demanded Monro.

The current cut out and Olcott vomited across the floor of his cell. He shuddered and groaned. The hissing of the generator surged again and Olcott screamed harrowingly. Kalpesh could smell burning flesh as blisters began to form beneath the irons clapped around Olcott's ankles and wrists. Kalpesh signalled to the mirror before him, gesturing for Monro and Melville to stop the torture, but electricity continued to zap through

Olcott's manacles and the theosophist screams howled unabatingly throughout the cell.

"Blavatsky!" roared Olcott through gritted teeth as the shocking current shut off. "Blavatsky," he whimpered.

"Blavatsky?" questioned Kalpesh.

Olcott nodded as a trickle of blood issued from the corner of his mouth, mixing with the bile and sputum pooled around his head. "Find Blavatsky," he wheezed.

"Blavatsky is in Belgium," replied Kalpesh.

"No," spat Olcott, his head rolling back. "London."

"Helena Blavatsky is here!? In London?" pressed Kalpesh.

Olcott hesitated in his answer and his body began to spasm again.

"Stop it!" demanded Kalpesh, rising to his feet and confronting his reflection. "He's had enough!"

The generator cut out and Olcott slumped limp on the floor.

"Tell us where Blavatsky is, Olcott!" came the artificial voice of Melville through the loudspeaker.

Olcott's eyelids flitted open and his blue gaze fell upon Kalpesh.

"Where is she?" urged the detective.

Olcott lay motionless.

"You have to help me out here!"

The theosophist's chest quivered with

irregular breathing as he lay silently looking up at Kalpesh. Suddenly, his muscles tightened and convulsed again.

"Stop!" cried Kalpesh, storming back over to the one-way mirror until he was face to face with himself.

"Tell us where we can find Blavatsky!" demanded Melville over the speaker.

Olcott let out a bloodcurdling scream.

"He can't take any more!" warned Kalpesh. "You'll kill him!"

The whirring of the generator continued for several more seconds before finally it cut out.

"I think he's had enough," crackled the voice of Monro.

Kalpesh walked over to Olcott as he lay helplessly sprawled inside his cage. His lips were trembling as his tongue stumbled in an attempt to form words.

"We need a doctor in here!" declared Kalpesh loudly.

"Find her," murmured Olcott, his eyes fixed on Kalpesh. "Only... you..." he whispered almost inaudibly. "Save us."

Foam began issuing from Olcott's mouth and his eyes rolled back in their sockets. The occultist began to convulse again, but this time there was no accompanying sound of the electrocuting generator.

"Get a doctor in here now!" bellowed Kalpesh as he rushed to the gate of the cage. He shook the mesh door on its hinges, but without a key to the padlock, there was no way inside.

The electric motor of the steel door roared into action and the reinforced bulwark rolled away from the entrance. The two jailers rushed in, one forcing Kalpesh aside as the other fumbled through a ring of jangling keys. The padlock clicked open as the Malleus resident doctor swiftly rushed into the cell, followed by Monro and Melville. The cage door swung open and the doctor darted inside, but before he had made it to Olcott, the theosophist's convulsions had ceased and his head slumped back.

The doctor pressed two fingers beneath the man's bearded jawline, concentrating as he felt for a pulse. After a lengthy still moment, the physician looked up at Monro and Melville and offered a solemn shake of his head. He checked his pocket watch.

"Time of death: nine fifty-nine."

V

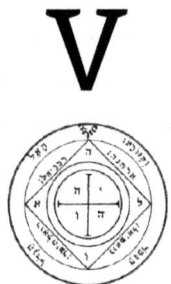

Anvil, Tower of London, City of London
10:15 a.m. September 1st, 1888

Kalpesh took a swig of gin as he sat in front of the desk of Commissioner Monro. Placing the glass back on the desk, he reclined in his chair and continued to examine the faded markings tattooed in the centre of his left palm, tracing his thumb over the blurred lines of ink. His glass chinked as Monro topped it up from the decanter, subsequently replenishing his own, then Melville's. The Commissioner replaced the decanter back on top of his spirits cabinet before sitting on the corner of his desk in front of Kalpesh.

"Let me take a look, son," insisted Monro, gesturing for Kalpesh's hand as he took a puff from his pipe.

Tobacco smoke wafted his way as Kalpesh extended his arm and presented the tattoo to Monro.

"And you say you've had this as long as you can remember?"

"Yes sir," confirmed Kalpesh.

"Any idea what it is?"

"It is the Devanagari symbol for Om."

"Devanagari?" questioned Monro.

"It's an Indian script; one used in Hindi, Nepali—Sanskrit... It's incredibly widespread on the subcontinent."

"And the symbol, 'Om?' What is the significance of it?"

"It is hard to say, sir," responded Kalpesh.

"How so?"

"It has a plethora of meanings and connotations," explained the Indian.

"Give me some examples."

Kalpesh shrugged. "Eternal truth, self-knowledge, power, awakening? It is widely used in prayers and mantras in Hinduism and Buddhism. It is a syllable, one used in worship and meditation. Depending on where you travel throughout Asia, it has differing significance."

"And the circle that surrounds it?"

questioned the Commissioner.

"I'm not so sure," replied Kalpesh. "It might be representative of a sun, but that is at best a guess based on the research I've done."

"You've spent a lot of time researching it?" questioned Monro, releasing Kalpesh's hand.

"Sir, I grew up in an orphanage with no knowledge of where I was from or who my parents were. This mark is the only link I had to my past. With all due respect, I have spent an exhaustive amount of time researching what it could mean."

"And do you think it has any esoteric significance?"

"I suppose it's not impossible," admitted Kalpesh. "But I suspect it is more likely of cultural or religious symbolism."

"What do you make of what Olcott claimed?" asked Melville, speaking up for the first time. "Is there any truth to it? Could you be the child of Rani of Jhansi?"

"I suppose anything is possible," conceded Kalpesh. "I am of the correct age."

"Olcott provided no evidence," uttered Monro dismissively, sucking on his pipe. "I suspect he was merely attempting to manipulate you. To what purpose, who can say now? But there were too many holes in his tale for us to take it seriously; for one: he provided no explanation as to how he knew you as Kalpesh Khatri! His story doesn't explain how he came to learn your name. Most likely, at some point he either coerced a jailer into giving it to him, or he simply overheard it in conversation between the men guarding him."

Kalpesh and Melville nodded in agreement.

"And just as likely he acquired knowledge of last night's killing in Whitechapel through the same means."

"Olcott was a Buddhist modernist," explained Kalpesh. "He would have instantly recognised the symbol of Om if he had indeed seen it on my hand back in June of last year. To him, it would have held a significance—certainly one he could construct a story around; all he would have needed to get me in the room would have been my name."

"We need to look at the rotas—see who was stationed outside the cell, identify anyone who might have had contact with Olcott," began Monro. "If the guards have been talking about investigations in front of the prisoners, we need to put a stop to it. Melville, can you see to this?"

"Yes sir," agreed the assistant chief constable.

"Best keep it on the sly," suggested Monro. "We need the jailers to be frank with us; if they believe that they will be reprimanded, then they will likely prove uncooperative."

"Understood."

"What do the two of you make of this whole affair?" posed Monro.

"Isn't it obvious?" questioned Melville. "He was set for the gallows at the end of next week. He was seeking some way to stay his execution, or at least delay it. He gave us what information he had in the hope that we would assume he knew more than he was letting on. Depending on how the investigation went, he could have bought himself months!"

"A likely theory," agreed Monro.

"There's another possibility that we perhaps haven't considered, sir," spoke up Kalpesh.

"Go ahead, Khatri."

"What if Olcott was truthful with us? What if the Faraday cage and the lead lining of the cell aren't quite as effective at magical suppression as we had assumed them to be, and somehow Olcott had indeed managed to divine some of the information he gave us today?"

"Unlikely," put in Melville. "The countermeasures have been designed and approved by some of the world's leading scientific minds."

"But such minds have been proved wrong in the past," conceded Monro. "Very well Khatri, I take your point. It cannot hurt for us to make certain. I'll speak to the Home Secretary—see if we can get Alexander Graham Bell in here to look over the cell, maybe make a call to our friend Tesla across the Atlantic and see if he has any opinions."

"Agreed," chimed in Melville. "It always pays to check that our security is up to scratch."

"Very good, sir," approved Kalpesh.

"What of his suggestion that Madame

Blavatsky is currently residing in London?" questioned Melville.

"It is something that we cannot rule out," asserted Monro.

"If what you suggest is true, Commissioner," began Kalpesh, "that Olcott somehow learnt the details of last night's murder from overhearing the prison guards, or something of the like, then it could perhaps have benefitted him immensely to offer up something to us that we did not already know as a means of gaining our trust."

"You are suggesting that Blavatsky may well be in London?" asked Monro.

"If she is, then Olcott might have believed giving her up to us might have earnt him favour," supposed Melville.

"A sound suggestion," nodded Monro. "But do you believe that Olcott would have betrayed Blavatsky in this way? He practically revered her?"

"If he believed it might save him, why not?" shrugged Melville.

"They have been travelling the world together for over a decade," added Kalpesh. "It could be reasonable to assume that she arrived here in England the same time Olcott did. She may even have played a role in the Jubilee Plot."

"All reasonable assumptions to make," nodded Monro. "I'll get on the telephone to Brussels and see if they can give us any intelligence on Blavatsky's movements. In the meantime, Khatri, I know you are on the Whitechapel murder case with Abberline, but I am assigning you to this also; I want you to do some digging and see if you can find anything that might indicate Madame Blavatsky is indeed here in London."

"Yes sir," nodded Kalpesh.

"Is that all, sir?" asked Melville.

"You are dismissed," affirmed the commissioner.

Melville necked the remainder of his gin, planting the crystal glass atop a filing cabinet before pulling his jacket and hat off the stand and making for the door. Kalpesh likewise rose, leaving a portion of his drink unfinished, yet as he moved to leave Monro's office, the commissioner interrupted his exit.

"Khatri, if you could stay behind..." he requested. "I'd like a private word."

Kalpesh momentarily looked to Melville who was already out of the door. His old friend offered him a shrugging smile before placing his hat atop his pate and making for the stairs.

"Yes, of course, sir," complied the young detective.

"Shut the door," instructed the commissioner as he rose from the desk and moved to gaze out of the window across the inner ward to the White Tower.

The Indian complied, closing the door behind him and once more taking his seat.

A long silence endured before finally the commissioner was the first to speak. "It was a messy affair today, but you handled yourself well."

"Thank you, sir," replied Kalpesh distantly as he stared at the light refracting through the gin glass sat on the desk before him.

"I know it was your first time as interrogator. It's not easy, especially when you're faced with a man like Olcott."

"I fear there is more we might have learnt from him."

"I fear the same," affirmed Monro.

Kalpesh took a sip of gin.

"I know it shook you," continued Monro. "It doesn't often end the way it did today, but Olcott was in poor health. We merely hastened the fate of the hangman's noose."

Kalpesh swirled the viscous gin about silently, watching as the spirit coated the edges of the crystal before sinking smoothly back into the bottom of the glass.

"Speak freely, Khatri. I want to know your thoughts on what happened."

Kalpesh paused, looking up at the commissioner as he stepped away from the window and seated himself in the chair behind his desk. "We went too far, sir."

"That much is clear," agreed Monro. "Melville was somewhat overzealous with the electrocution switch, but it was not his intention to kill Olcott."

"I understand that, sir. But I believe there was no call for it in the first place."

"Is that so?" remarked Monro with amusement. "As I recall, we only got Blavatsky's name after we pushed him hard enough."

"I believe he would have given us her name regardless," argued Kalpesh. "He has never folded under torture in the past; why should today have been any different? I believe his intention from the moment I first entered that cell was for him to tell us about her—there may have even been more he intended to reveal."

"An interesting take away," pondered Monro.

"Olcott was difficult; he was attempting to control the direction of the conversation. But I don't think torture was called for. With all due respect, sir, I believe we murdered him today."

"Olcott was days away from execution," replied Monro. "You are right in saying that we pushed him beyond what we should have done, but we most certainly did not murder him. What happened this morning was an accident and nothing more; torture is an important part of Malleus—it has been used since the order's inception. Heinrich Kramer laid down the framework himself for how to elicit confessions and extract information."

"I'm fully aware of that sir," nodded Kalpesh.

"And yet you disagree with it as an interrogation technique?"

Kalpesh bit his tongue.

"Please, give me your thoughts on the matter, Detective," insisted Monro.

"Yes, sir," nodded Kalpesh. "I don't object to torture on a fundamental level, but I believe Malleus should be less eager to dole it out. And, I fear that the confessions and information that are coerced from it are not always as reliable as they are taken to be."

"Let me explain something to you, Detective," began Monro condescendingly. "We are at war. Nobody in parliament wants to admit it, but our very way of life is under attack! The occult is growing day by day; practitioners of the dark arts grow bolder each year in their experimentation, and maleficium is on the rise. You of all people understand that. When other's dismissed threats made against the crown as mere scaremongering, (many high-ranking officers in this very order included,) you saw merit in the dangers and acted without instruction from those above you. You avoided the assassination of Her Majesty the Queen and many of her subjects, all because you understood the claims being made were not merely hollow threats.

"The heathens we face in this war have advantages that we cannot hope to match; they can see events before they happen, divine critical information by satanic means; they can travel distances in the blink of an eye, vanish from plain sight, and summon untold abominations into this world. These are powers that God never intended to fall into the hands of mortal men. These are the tools and weapons of angels and demons. And yet it falls to us to protect this great country from those who would seek to unravel all that we hold dear.

"In this fight we have few weapons at our disposal. The miracles of scientific progress that we have made in recent decades may yet stem the tide of the occult uprising, but currently it is not enough. Those we face can telepathically read minds and see through the vibrations of the Aether. These are feats we cannot perform. Instead, we must rely on the medieval techniques we have employed for centuries that have been tried and tested again and again. Now, that does not mean we should take pleasure in the act of torture; I find it as distasteful as you do, Khatri —of that I can assure you. But I understand it's necessity. It is an invaluable tool that must responsibly be used in every instance where it can aid us, to ensure that we stay one step ahead of those that seek to do us harm!

"Now, what happened to Olcott today was unfortunate. But at some point throughout your career, it *will* happen again! I don't ask you to enjoy this grisly practice, nor do I even ask that you pretend to; but what I must insist upon, is that you find the stomach for it; because I can assure you Detective, it is paramount to the work we do here."

Kalpesh lowered his head.

"Do I make myself clear, Khatri?"

"Yes sir," mumbled Kalpesh.

"Very good, Detective. You are dismissed."

VI

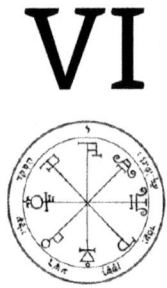

Kings Cross St Pancras Underground Station, Finsbury
7:21 p.m. September 2nd, 1888

Tracks screeched and whined with ear-splitting intensity as the electrified locomotive ground to a halt in the dimly lit underground passage. Kalpesh rose from the wooden bench and negotiated his way between the various passengers packed inside the confines of the cramped carriage. Reaching the door, he stepped out onto the platform, straightening his tie in the muggy heat of the subterranean station. The detective made for the stairwell, ascending rapidly in several brisk strides as he sought to escape the suffocating air of the underground railway system. Ascending a short flight of steps, the Indian joined the mass exodus from the platform before stepping onto the rising escalator. Climbing quickly past the tourists leisurely stood on the moving staircase, Kalpesh emerged out onto the tumultuous streets at ground level, before cutting west along Euston road.

Pausing in front of the redbrick gothic-revival frontage of the Midland Grand Hotel, he drew his pocket watch from his waistcoat, comparing the timepiece to the clock of the soot-stained building. Pulling out the crown, he made a slight adjustment, synchronising his watch to the clockface atop the two hundred-and-seventy-foot-high tower. Seven twenty-one. Pocketing the chronograph, the Indian took note of the newspaper stand a few yards away from him. Strolling past, he skimmed the headlines.

ANOTHER AWFUL MURDER IN WHITECHAPEL

WOMAN FOUND BRUTALLY HACKED TO DEATH IN THE STREET

BARBAROUS AND MYSTERIOUS MURDER

HORRIBLE MUTILATION

Kalpesh supressed an internal sigh and continued on his way. Spotting a gap in the traffic, the detective dropped off the curb and passed behind a tram, pausing briefly to allow a stagecoach to roll in front of him before he hurried the rest of the way, stepping back onto the pavement on the far side of Euston Road. Swerving between pedestrians, he quickly walked the final quarter mile of his journey down the busy thoroughfare as the heat of the summer day began to fade into evening warmth. Passing the white pillars and red doors of St Pancras New Church, the Indian detective rounded the corner onto Upper Woburn Place.

The buzzing traffic and crowds faded as Kalpesh drew away from Euston Road, until after a hundred or so yards, he came to a set of terraced commercial buildings, the nearest of which drew his attention. The ground floor was boarded up, whilst the decrepit sign above the entrance of the disused printing house was flaking paint.

Reaching inside the inner pocket of his coat, Kalpesh once more drew out the crumpled pamphlet he had obtained the evening before. He studied the creased cover.

LUCIFER

THEOSOPHICAL MONTHLY

The cover art depicted a negative image of Lucifer, the 'morning star.' The celestial being took the form of a naked child raising above his head a flaming torch as he levitated low in the night sky. The title was an obvious attempt at controversy from the magazine's listed editor 'HPB,' three initials famously known within the occult as none other than Helena Petrovna Blavatsky. Though Lucifer was widely regarded throughout the Christian Church as an angel synonymous with Satan, this was a mere misconception; in truth, Lucifer was the 'bringer of light' symbolised by the planet Venus. It was the celestial movement of Venus that stemmed the original misconception, often appearing brightly at dawn before sinking below the horizon as the sun ascends. As such, throughout various mythologies, the morning star represented a fall from grace: an angel descending from heaven to the underworld. Through various translations of the Bible, this fable came to be associated with Satan's own fall from grace, and as such, the Light-Bringer and the Devil became regarded as one and the same. By entitling her magazine 'Lucifer,' Blavatsky was making a joke at the expense of the Church, and simultaneously alerting readers to the ignorance of organised religion. Beneath the title read the publication's tagline, *'To bring to light the hidden things of darkness.'*

The magazine had been circulating in the back alleys of the East End for the better part of a year, and Kalpesh's copy hadn't been too difficult to acquire given the contacts he had made in Whitechapel's underbelly throughout his short stint at Special Branch. The magazine was not strictly speaking prohibited, as it did not distribute illegal occult materials; it contained neither the teachings of witchcraft nor any means by which to uncover them. Instead, it merely served as a medium through which Blavatsky spread her world views and controversial ideas regarding creationism and philosophy. However, given the author, and its association with the criminal organisation of the Theosophical Society, the magazine had been deemed as occultist propaganda, and as such, any copies being distributed through vendors were ordered to be seized and destroyed. Circulation of Lucifer had been monitored for some time by Malleus, but given various legal technicalities and a lack of resources, many of the leads had not been followed up, and the London print house responsible for its publication had not been located. Malleus had however narrowed down it's likely whereabouts to an area measuring just over a square mile in the vicinity of Camden.

Kalpesh had spent much of the previous day eliminating the registered presses within the area one by one, but after having discovered no evidence that Lucifer was in print at any of them, he had been forced to change tactics. Scouring through various archives in the Public Record Office, he compiled a list of print houses that had closed within the last few years. This list was far smaller than those in operation, and as such, it had quickly delivered him to where he stood now.

Folding the pamphlet, he pocketed it once again and pressed himself up against the nearest boarded-up window. He peered through the gaps in the planks to peek inside at a vacant ground floor sparsely furnished with a few broken chairs and an overturned desk. Thin streams of light cut through the barricaded windows and motes of dust danced about in the slanting rays. The main reception counter was covered in a dustsheet and wallpaper peeled from the plaster inside the abandoned building, but there was no sign of any printing press, operational nor dilapidated. Kalpesh took a step back defeatedly and crossed out another address from his journal. All out of options, he sighed in annoyance and began to slowly trudge back in the direction of Euston Road. He swiftly passed another newspaper stand on the corner of the terraced row and hesitated for a moment. This time he ignored the headlines reporting on Friday night's events on Buck's Row and studied the young boy selling the broadsheets.

"Care for a copy, mister?" questioned the newspaper hawker holding up the Daily Star. "Only a ha'penny!"

Kalpesh drew his wallet and produced a threepence, showing it to the newsboy. "Are you here every day?"

"Most days, sir," nodded the lad. "What's it to you?"

"That building there," continued the detective, indicating to the derelict printing house, "ever see anyone go in or out of it?"

The newsboy shook his head.

"Okay," nodded Kalpesh, flicking him the coin. "Here you go." He pocketed his wallet and turned to walk off before the boy spoke again.

"This about the noises, sir?"

"Noises?" queried Kalpesh. "You've heard noises from in there?"

He nodded again.

"What sort of noises?"

"Drumming, whirring… you know the like."

"Machinery?"

"Yeah," agreed the boy.

"Is it loud?"

He nodded again.

"When do you hear it?"

"More so recently, sir. Mostly in the middle of the day."

"And is it continuous? Does it go on a long time?"

"Hours, sir," confirmed the hawker.

"Thank you," smiled Kalpesh, producing another penny and giving it to the boy before tussling the child's hair and returning back to the frontage of the press. Peering briefly down Woburn Walk, Kalpesh made his way along the façade of the terraced row of commercial buildings until he came to the wrought iron railing that fenced off the gap between the street and the lower ground floor of the old press. Stepping through a gateway, the detective descended a flight of stone steps into the recess. Several narrow windows on this lower level faced outwards into the sunken walkway. Old broadsheets were pasted over the glass from the inside to prevent any would-be-intruders or squatters from peering in. Whoever had covered the glass had done so thoroughly. A number of windowpanes were cracked with a few shattered altogether, yet in these places the windows had been boarded from the inside; as such, Kalpesh was unable to find any gaps in the veil of newspaper pages through which to glimpse into the ever more suspicious looking building.

Reaching the end of the sunken path, the detective came to an unassuming door, its black paint cracked and flaking away from the wood. The detective looked up over his shoulder to the street above to ensure that he was not being observed; lacking any form of warrant to search the premises, he knew he technically should not attempt to force entry without the owner's permission. However, Malleus detectives were afforded greater privileges than conventional officers, and given that this building had fallen into receivership when the printers had declared bankruptcy, Kalpesh deemed it was within his authority to attempt to search the premises; even still, it would be better to not be seen breaking and entering by random passers-by.

Satisfied that he was not being watched, Kalpesh tried the brass handle. It rotated stiffly, but the door did not budge. Locked. Kneeling on the cobbles, Kalpesh withdrew a leather case from one of his coat pockets, opening the folder to reveal a set of lockpicks. Taking a moment to briefly study the mortise lever lock in front of him, he selected a pick and torsion wrench and inserted both into the keyhole. Rotating the tensioning tool, Kalpesh applied pressure to the cam inside the lock until it maxed out and gently began to nudge the first of the levers inside the mechanism with the pick.

Pressing his ear close to the door, he listened against the din of the street above until he both heard and felt a gentle click as the bolt step slid marginally into the gate of the first lever, binding it in place. Withdrawing the pick slightly, the detective moved onto the second lever in the series, gently lifting it inside the lock until it too clicked into position. Working his way through the series, Kalpesh nudged each into place until the final gate opened, the bolt step slid through, and the tension on the wrench lifted. Rotating the picks a full turn, the detective felt the bolt retract from the doorframe and retreat inside the lock.

Stowing his picks back in the case, Kalpesh

rose to his feet and pocketed the folder. Once more checking the coast was clear, he revolved the brass handle again and slowly eased open the door. The hinges creaked as the detective sergeant stepped through the threshold into the dim room. He closed the door behind him and allowed for his eyes to quickly adjust. Dusky light filtered through the newspaper pages plastered across the windows, illuminating the basement and the rows of machines concealed inside. Kalpesh shook his head in disbelief as he looked at the series of rotary printing presses before him.

Making his way across the edge of the room, he clasped hold of a circuit breaker lever, lifting the stiff switch until it flipped upward into position. Bulbs buzzed and flickered one by one across the ceiling, better revealing the printers before the machines themselves began to hum, the rotors whirring with increasing volume as they powered up. Moving over to the nearest machine, Kalpesh grabbed a stack of blank paper from a box beside it and fed it into the press. Moving over to the far side of the machine, he watched as the first sheet emerged. Snatching it up, the detective flipped over the leaf in his hand and read the title page that had been freshly printed upon it.

THE SECRET DOCTRINE
VOL. I

HELENA PETROVNA BLAVATSKY

The press continued to spit out copies of the same page as Kalpesh folded over the warm paper and slid it inside his coat. He walked between the rows of printers until he had crossed the room completely. There he spied several small wooden crates stacked against the far wall. Most of the containers were empty, yet a couple had been sealed and addressed. Drawing his kukri from the scabbard concealed at the rear of his belt, Kalpesh wedged the blade beneath one of the lids and carefully prised open the nearest crate to him. The nails eased slowly out of the wood, and once the Indian detective had worked free one side, he used his hands to pull the lid completely off.

Inside were packaged a score of bound books, their leather spines were facing upwards, embossed with gold lettering spelling out once more, *'The Secret Doctrine Vol. I.'* Kalpesh drew a copy from the centre of the box and flexed open the stiff binding to the very same title page that had moments earlier emerged from the press. Turning the page, Kalpesh unveiled the seal of the Theosophical Society: an ouroboros, a snake eating its own tail, encircling a star of David inside of which was the ankh, the Egyptian key of life. Between the head and the tip of the snake's tail sat a swastika, and above that, the Devanagari symbol of Om, whilst surrounding the lower portions of the seal read the words, '*There Is No Religion Higher Than Truth.*"

He turned the page again, his eyes skimming briefly over the foreword, picking out words and phrases that sent alarm bells ringing through his mind. He steadily flicked through the rest of the book in rapid succession; sigils, pentacles, and seals littered the pages; he caught glimpse of Sanskrit mantras, Norse runes, Icelandic staves, the Kabbalistic tree of life, Egyptian hieroglyphs, and pages upon pages of text translated into English, French, Italian, Russian, Arabic, and Hindi. Reaching the end of the tome, Kalpesh began leafing through the pages once more in dread as he studied the content in greater detail. Inside were contained ritual instructions, detailed incantations for curses and malefic enchantments, techniques for scrying and astral projection, all interlaced with Blavatsky's own commentary and exposition bearing an overtone of indoctrinating ideologies and dangerous philosophies that painted the Empire as an oppressive totalitarian state dedicated to crushing freedom of thought. The Secret Doctrine was not a code of belief, but a weapon with its sights aimed directly at the establishment; it was a handbook of maleficium intended to be used against Malleus and the Crown.

"Shit," breathed Kalpesh as he closed the book, dropping it atop the crate.

His mind raced as it continued to process the images he had just seen. He tried to comprehend the consequences of this dark grimoire being distributed to even a few of the secret occult societies. This book had to be Blavatsky's magnum opus, an entire lifetime's knowledge of witchcraft and sorcery distilled into a single encyclopaedia of the arcane; what made it all the worse, was that it was entitled, 'Volume I.' As he began to come to grips with the impact this book could have, his eyes focussed on the lid of the crate he had prised free.

The detective shook himself out of the stupor that had seized him and realised he was staring at an address penned onto a card stapled to the wood. It was a location in London: Lansdowne Road in Notting Hill. He checked the other crate aside the one he had opened; the address was the same.

Kalpesh's ears pricked up as a door on the far side of the room flung open. A gunshot sounded over the roar of the printers. Lead clanged against steel as the bullet ricocheted off the rotary press nearest to the sergeant. The bullet whistled as it deflected inches away from Kalpesh's ear. He threw himself to the ground and the gun sounded again, the second shot crunching into the brickwork behind where he had been stood less than a second earlier.

Hitting the concrete floor, Kalpesh rolled over, his hand reaching for his holster. Drawing his Mauser C96, the detective scrambled back to his feet, taking cover behind the thundering printer as another shot pinged deafeningly off the machine's exterior.

"Police! Drop your weapon!" screamed Kalpesh over the din of the press.

No response came. Kalpesh peaked out of cover and caught a glimpse of a young, spectacled, dark-haired man prowling behind the printers on the far side of the room. On spotting Kalpesh emerge, he fired off another shot from a revolver. Kalpesh ducked back down just in time for the bullet to streak over his head and shatter more of the bricks in the wall behind him.

Kalpesh's thumb flicked the safety on his Mauser. He shimmied to the side, moving around to the opposite edge of the whirring presses, nosing out from behind cover. Another gunshot sounded as he was spied by his adversary, the bullet shattering against one of the printer's cylinders. Kalpesh returned fire. He squeezed the trigger of his Mauser twice and it coughed loudly. The muzzle flashed and a pair of .30 Mauser Automatic rounds ejected from the barrel in rapid succession. The first shot smashed through a windowpane papered with broadsheet. The second met flesh, ripping through the shoulder pad of his assailant's jacket, slicing the skin beneath as it clipped him. The gunman let out a cry and dropped behind a machine.

Kalpesh rose and began to advance on the shooter's position, his own pistol raised in front of him as he kept the sights trained on the man's location.

"Drop the gun now!" boomed Kalpesh authoritatively. "I'm with Hammer!"

The shooter's hand popped over the top of the press and shot blindly. The revolver fired wildly once more, the slug sailing clear over Kalpesh's head. Sparks and glass showered down as a hanging bulb overhead exploded from the gunshot. The detective flinched, stooping as he protected his eyes. The Webley revolver clicked several times more, the hammer now striking the firing pin against spent cartridges. The shooter emitted a panicked whimper as he broke the gun to reload. Empty cartridges jingled as they spilled over the floor.

Composing himself, Kalpesh rushed between the machines, charging towards his foe as the gunman fumbled with a full-moon clip. Kalpesh slid to the ground upon hearing the characteristic crack of the revolver barrel snapping shut over the droning printers. Another hail of shots popped as several bullets plugged wildly into the floor, ceiling, and walls in Kalpesh's general vicinity.

Footsteps scrambled across concrete as the shooter rushed for the door through which he had emerged. Blood dripped in pools behind him as he fled. Kalpesh stepped out from the protection of the next printer and took aim. The gunman blindly squeezed at his trigger repeatedly as he routed in fear. One shot narrowly missed Kalpesh, smashing another pane of glass, whilst the final bullet plugged into the wall on the opposite side of the room to the detective. Once again, the hammer ticked uselessly as the empty chambers turned over.

"Freeze!" commanded Kalpesh one last time, hoping the criminal in his sights might finally surrender.

The gunman continued to scramble away, heedless of the policeman's warning, racing towards the door. The Mauser C96 drummed once in Kalpesh's grip. His shot met the mark, slamming into the fleeing gunman. The impact of the bullet knocked the man off balance, sending him tumbling headfirst. He screamed through the fall, but as he slammed into the side of a whirring printer, his cry was snuffed out.

With his gun still raised, Kalpesh rushed towards the man's location. He was laying facedown and motionless on the floor. As the detective neared, he understood why. The top of the man's skull had been cracked clean off at the crown where his head had struck one of the machine's spinning flywheels. Blood was pooling rapidly around the body, spreading out in an incarnadine puddle across the floor of the printers. Kalpesh grimaced at the grisly end the shooter had met. He took a step back and felt something crunch beneath his heel. Peering under his shoe he looked at the shattered blood-flecked lenses of the man's round spectacles. Making certain the coast was clear, he made his way back over to the circuit breaker and killed the power.

VII

Upper Woburn Place, Bloomsbury
7:52 p.m. September 2nd, 1888

Crossing the gloomily lit press as the roaring printers whirred down, finally dying away to silence, Kalpesh avoided the body of the shooter in the expanding pool of blood and made for the door through which the gunman had first appeared. It hung slightly ajar, artificial light spilling out from the room beyond. Keeping his pistol raised, Kalpesh gently swung open the door and peered into the underground passage ahead of him. Bare bricks lined the narrow, subterranean corridor with bulbs hanging from bare wires running at intervals from the low ceiling. The floor of the passage was compacted soil, extending a dozen yards ahead to a turn in the way.

The Indian detective stepped inside and crept along its length, poking his head around the corner with his gun raised in front of him. The tunnel continued beyond the turning for a half-dozen more yards, before ending in a ladder that rose to a trapdoor above. Standing at the foot of the ladder, Kalpesh could make out faint natural light from the room above. He stood quietly, listening for any sounds overhead before cautiously ascending the ladder.

Presently, he emerged through the trap door into what appeared to be a painter's studio, or rather, the supply room for one. Art supplies littered the shelves with opened tins of paint, countless brushes, and jars of murky water covering numerous work surfaces. Several canvases in various stages of completion were sat on easels and stacked against the walls of the workroom. Kalpesh heaved himself up into the room, scanning for anyone who might be lurking out of sight behind the shelves.

Proceeding through an open doorway, the detective emerged behind a counter in a gallery. Dozens of paintings hung on display throughout the shop. The frontage of the gallery was caged by latticed security grilles drawn across the windows. Kalpesh cautiously cross the shop floor and peered through the steel shutters out onto Woburn Walk. He checked the grille to see that it was padlocked shut, but even still, he gave it a reassuring shake, ensuring it was secure. Satisfied no one could gain entry to the shop, nor, more importantly, the passageway, without a key, Kalpesh returned to the back room, sliding down the ladder to return to the printing press.

Giving the body of the shooter a wide berth as he re-entered the basement, Kalpesh made for the door back out to the street. Two bullet holes through the newspaper-pasted glass issued straight beams of half-light from the dusk-lit streets outside; as Kalpesh observed motes of dusk quivering within the faint rays, he saw them each dim in turn as a shadow glided across the windows. The Malleus detective snatched his semi-automatic pistol rapidly from out of his holster, and ducking beneath the height of the windowsill, he took aim for the door, his pulse hastening as he watched the brass handle slowly rotate.

A darkly dressed figure crept through the entrance and Kalpesh cocked the hammer of his Mauser to announce himself. "Not another step!" he warned, rising to his feet as he kept the gun trained on the man.

"Lower your weapon!" gulped the man as he pointed a billy club the detective's way, altogether failing to conceal the terror prevalent in his voice.

The detective's mind fell at ease as he

realised the man stood before him was a bobby. "Relax," he assured the fellow policeman as he made a gesture of holstering his weapon. "Detective Sergeant Khatri, Special Branch," he dug out his badge and presented it to the copper.

The patrol officer sighed audibly as his demeanour calmed. "Thank heavens, sir," he chuckled. "You had me worried there."

"I trust you are responding to the shots fired?"

"Yes indeed sir. Yes indeed!" he replied. "I trust you have the situation under control?"

"I took down the gunman," confirmed Kalpesh, leading the patrolman a few steps further into the room to allow the officer a view of the cadaver.

The constable took a step back in horror; even in the dim light, Kalpesh could see the colour drain from his face.

"I believe the area is secure," continued the Indian detective. "But I need to call in the cavalry..."

The bobby nodded weakly as he covered his mouth with a handkerchief and braved a closer look at the young man lying in his own blood. "What happened to his head!?"

"I think he clipped one of the spinning flywheels."

The bobby grimaced, retreating as he did so.

"Listen," instructed Kalpesh sternly in an attempt to regain the man's attention. "I need to go make a telephone call. Whilst I'm gone, you lock down this room. Use your whistle; see if there are any other officers nearby that can stand watch with you outside. Don't let anyone in. And see if you can send a man to guard the door to the gallery around the corner on Woburn Walk."

The constable continued to gawk haplessly at the man with his head staved in.

"Do you hear me?" pressed Kalpesh forcefully in frustration.

The constable swallowed, averting his eyes from the scene to look at Kalpesh. He nodded with anxious obedience.

"Good," said Kalpesh. "Where is the nearest Police Box?"

"Um…" stammered the bobby through muddied thoughts. "Euston Road."

"Alright," replied the detective. "Come on," he gestured, leading the man back out onto the street. "I won't be gone long," he assured as he rapidly clambered up the steps back to street level.

Darting off down the centre of the way, Kalpesh made for the junction of Euston road as the sharp burst of a policeman's whistle cut through the evening air. The arc lamps that illuminated central London began to flicker alight atop the rows of lampposts as Kalpesh jogged across the street back towards King's Cross. After a couple of moments, he arrived at the blue police box erected on the pavement and stepped inside. He dialled through to Anvil and waited for the call to be connected. Barely a few seconds had passed before the receiver at Malleus headquarters was lifted off the hook and Kalpesh was speaking directly to the Special Branch operator.

With Malleus informed of all that had transpired and the severity of the situation, Kalpesh hung up the receiver and exited the police box, swiftly returning in the direction of the secret printers on Upper Woburn Place. By the time Kalpesh had returned, the first police carriage dispatched from Finsbury's G Division was arriving on the scene. The siren cut out as the driver applied the brakes and reined in the draught horses. As the carriage skidded to a halt, a dozen policemen armed with magazine-fed Lee-Enfield rifles and Greener Police Shotguns issued from the carriage.

"Detective Sergeant Khatri of Special Branch," called out Kalpesh, producing his badge and identification as he approached the armed officers.

"Superintendent Charles Hunt," replied the most senior officer amongst them as he stepped forwards to meet Kalpesh. "You are the detective who called this in?"

"Yes, sir," replied Kalpesh courteously, though the truth of the matter was that under these circumstances, he outranked the superintendent.

"What's the situation?"

"You there?" called out Kalpesh to the constable who had first appeared on the scene some time ago. "Is anyone watching the entrance to the gallery around the corner?" he pressed, noting the other patrol officer standing beside him.

The constable shook his head nervously.

"For God's sake!" muttered Kalpesh in frustration under his breath. "Right," he continued, addressing the superintendent once more, "I need two men stationed at the entrance to the gallery around the corner on Woburn Walk, and I want a cordon set up here; no one is allowed in or out until the rest of Malleus arrives!"

"Done," replied Hunt, issuing a series of gestures to his men. "What else?"

"I haven't conducted a proper search of the gallery yet; I don't know if there is anyone upstairs. I need a team to accompany me inside to ensure the premises are secure."

When Kalpesh finished speaking, another blearing siren howled from down the street as a second Police carriage skidded to a halt beside the first, carrying reinforcements from Holborn's E Division.

"Huntley," said the Superintendent. "Coordinate a perimeter with the boys from Bow Street."

"Yes sir," agreed the policeman nearest to him.

"Moore, Beard," Hunt continued, looking to the two remaining men at his side. "You are with the detective and I."

Both nodded, readying their rifles.

"Remember lads, this is a crime scene," reiterated Hunt. "Do not touch anything unless absolutely necessary, or the boys at Anvil will have you hanged at Tower Green by Friday! Isn't that so, Sergeant Khatri?"

"Quite right," agreed Kalpesh, unholstering his pistol.

"We follow your lead," insisted Hunt.

Kalpesh nodded, moving to descend the stone steps. They entered the printing press once more to find that the dying light from outside was now failing altogether to filter through the papered windows; the lower ground floor was now shrouded completely in darkness.

"Moore," whispered Hunt. "Go fetch some lanterns from the carriage."

"No need," insisted Kalpesh, producing from within his jacket a brass cylinder. As he rotated the switch on the side, a tungsten-filament bulb powered by a series of dry batteries flashed on, casting a beam of directed light from its end.

"Huh!" remarked Superintendent Hunt as he marvelled at the electric torch. "I take it that is standard issue for Special Branch?"

"Yes," confirmed Kalpesh, sweeping it across the shadows to reveal the rows of rotary presses.

"Sir, any chance we can get some of those for G Division?" asked Moore.

"Why don't you write to Scotland Yard

and put in a requisition order?" mocked the Superintendent.

"Come along," insisted Kalpesh. "And stay clear of the body," he added, shining the light over the young man he had shot not half an hour earlier.

The three men from Finsbury remained silent after seeing the man's head cracked open and followed Kalpesh into the tunnel. The bulbs hanging from the ceiling of the passage were still lit up, and as such, Kalpesh clicked his torch off as he entered. Together, they ascended the ladder to the artist's storeroom, carefully sweeping the area to ensure that no one was lurking out of sight in any corner recesses. They fanned out into the shop to see several men stood guard on the far side of the security grille with officers beginning to establish a cordon down Woburn Walk.

Sweeping across the shop floor, they converged on the stairwell and filed up it one by one with Kalpesh taking point. Arriving on the first-floor landing, Superintendent Hunt overtook the detective to check the next flight of steps were clear whilst Beard took up the rear. Kalpesh and Moore moved either side of the single doorway on the floor ahead, and cautiously, Moore rotated the knob, allowing Kalpesh to enter first.

Streetlighting spilled through a set of partially drawn curtains, illuminating the apartment enough for Kalpesh to find the light switch beside the door. As several bulbs lit up about the room, the detective studied the flat in precursory detail. A fireplace with a single wing-backed chair opposite it sat central to the long room. Several bookcases were positioned either side of the door through which they had emerged, and as Kalpesh's gaze flitted between the titles, he noted a large quantity of classical literature and poetry. Down the far end of the room a small kitchenette area surrounded a gas stove and basin, whilst set against the bay of the first-floor window, Kalpesh sighted an open writing desk.

Silently signalling Moore not to touch anything, he stepped further into the flat and approached the desk. Pages of unfiled letters and scribblings littered the surface, and amongst them were what appeared to be numerous poems. Gently lifting a sheet from atop the scattered pile, the detective read a single stanza poem scrawled upon it.

> NOR dread nor hope attend
> A dying animal;
> A man awaits his end
> Dreading and hoping all;
> Many times he died,
> Many times rose again.
> A great man in his pride
> Confronting murderous men
> Casts derision upon
> Supersession of breath;

He knows death to the bone
Man has created death.

Scanning the various works and letters, he saw a single name continually appear signed across the work and at the bottom of several correspondence: William Butler Yeats.

Kalpesh sighed heavily as he returned the page to the desk and made for the far end of the room where two doors hung slightly ajar. Peaking inside the first, Kalpesh discovered a fully plumbed lavatory, whilst stepping through the second he came upon Yeats' bedroom. The bed was unmade and various discarded items of clothing were littered about the floor. Atop the nightstand was a copy of the Secret Doctrine. Inspecting the volume of Blavatsky's grimoire, Kalpesh saw that Yeats had folded over the corners of numerous pages to bookmark them, whilst the margins were scribbled with notes in the young poet's hand. Beneath the book atop the nightstand were further pages of notes in what appeared to be some form of cypher. Kalpesh replaced the book atop the bedside table and returned back out into the corridor with Moore.

Together, the three men of G Division accompanied the Malleus detective up the next flight of steps to the top floor of the building. Moonlight spilled down through large skylights into what was clearly the artist's main studio.

Dozens of canvases sat upon easels whilst more paints and brushes cluttered the various worksurfaces. Nobody was in sight. The coast was clear.

"Building is secure," declared Hunt with an unnecessarily hushed voice.

Kalpesh nodded. "Let's get out of here. Malleus will want to tear this place a part the moment they arrive, which I imagine will be soon."

VIII

**Upper Woburn Place, Bloomsbury
8:26 p.m. September 2nd, 1888**

When Kalpesh emerged back out onto Upper Woburn Place, Malleus was arriving in full force. By the looks of it, a perimeter had been established all the way back to Euston Road. Crowds of onlookers were beginning to gather at the cordons.

"Khatri!" the gruff voice of Abberline called out to him.

"Sir?" Kalpesh greeted his partner as he saw him cut through a gathering of Holborn constables.

"I hear you took down a gunman?"

"Yes," nodded the Indian as he holstered his Mauser.

"You didn't think to bring me along with you?"

"I didn't want to bother you with this, sir," Kalpesh explained. "I thought it was a fool's errand coming here."

"Didn't want to bother me?" Abberline's eyes narrowed. "Khatri, this is big. Why were you even out here?"

"I was chasing down a lead on the Lucifer case," replied the Indian. "Monro assigned me to see if I could find any evidence that Blavatsky was in the city."

"Sergeant Khatri," began Abberline sternly, "I may be new to Special Branch, but I am not new to police work; now, I don't know how things were done in the Company, but in the Met, we watch each other's backs! I may be your boss, but I am also your partner. Now, had *I* been on the hunt for one of the most dangerous witches in all of the civilised world, I am pretty sure I'd've wanted you along for the journey, not least to while away the hours spent chasing down bootless errands, but perhaps more importantly in case I stumbled upon a bedlamite with a revolver! So, if in future, should you choose to go looking for anyone on Malleus's most wanted list, I trust you will think twice about leaving me to twiddle my thumbs filing paperwork back in Anvil!?"

"Yes sir," replied Kalpesh, unsure whether he was mistaking the scolding for genuine concern from his partner or if that were mere wishful thinking.

"That's a good lad," replied Abberline with a raised eyebrow. "Now," he continued patting the Indian detective firmly on the arm, "look alive, the boss is coming this way."

"Sergeant Khatri!" cried out Melville upon sighting him.

"Sir," Kalpesh and Abberline said in unison.

"DCI Abberline," Melville nodded in greeting before turning to Kalpesh. "Good work Kalpesh," he applauded. "Is the site secure?"

Kalpesh nodded. "I just finished a sweep with the men from G Division."

"Excellent. Do we have an ID on the gunman?"

"I believe his name was William Butler Yeats, sir."

Melville nodded, leaning to peer down Woburn Walk to where Malleus officers were prising open the security grille of the gallery. "The shop and apartment are being rented to a John Butler Yeats, an Irish national who moved to London last year with his family, but they appear to be living out Ealing way in Bedford Park."

"A son then?" suggested Abberline. "One serving as caretaker for his father's gallery?"

"It seems likely," agreed Kalpesh. "Does John

Butler Yeats have any ties to the occult?"

"Not according to our records," replied Melville. "Even still, we are taking him into custody as a precaution; we've got men on route to him now."

"Very good, sir," put in Kalpesh.

"What's next, boss?" asked Abberline.

"We turn this place over," answered Melville, "see what we find."

"Sir," Kalpesh drew from his inner breast pocket a card he had ripped from the lid of one of the crates containing the Secret Doctrine and handed it to Melville.

"What's this?" questioned the assistant chief constable.

"Just maybe the location of the Blavatsky Lodge," supposed the Indian.

"Huh!" smiled a bemused Melville as he studied it. "If it is, you might have just earnt yourself a promotion, Kalpesh."

"Good work, Khatri," added an impressed Abberline as he placed his hands on his hips.

"We'll get straight on it once we are done here," insisted Melville.

"Sir," pressed Kalpesh, "I think we may need to act even sooner."

"Go ahead, Khatri?" returned Melville, allowing Kalpesh to elaborate.

"People are already gathering," explained Kalpesh. "We have made a scene here. If that address is indeed the location of a Theosophical

Society lodge, and if they catch word that we have discovered their printers, they might well realise we know their whereabouts."

"Point taken," nodded Melville as he glanced about at the civilians gathering at the police checkpoints to catch a glimpse at what was going on. "There's a good chance they might have a look out watching us now. They could learn of what has happened before the night is up."

"Then send us, boss," spoke up Abberline. "Khatri and I'll head over to the place immediately. We'll see if it's the hideout for the Russian bitch, sir."

"Very well," agreed Melville. "But you aren't going alone."

"Boss?" questioned Abberline.

"If this address is indeed the Blavatsky Lodge, then we cannot hesitate on a chance to make an arrest. I'll send you in with a squad of armed officers. Don't bother staking out the premises ahead of time; this is a straight up raid, pure and simple. Go in fast and take anyone you find inside into custody. We'll deal with the fallout afterwards."

"Is that permitted, sir?" questioned Abberline apprehensively.

"Malleus isn't standard CID, Inspector; we are called Special Branch for a reason. We don't have to deal with all the red tape if we have reasonable grounds on which to act."

"Then a raid it is," agreed Abberline, rolling

his shoulders in anticipation.

"I'll head over to the location once we are set up here," insisted Melville. "Hopefully by the time I arrive, that *'bitch'* will be in cuffs!"

"Right you are, boss."

"You ready for this, Kalpesh?" questioned Melville, momentarily abandoning the position of his senior officer to resume the role of friend and mentor.

Kalpesh nodded, eager but nervous.

"If this goes off as I hope it does, then there shall be special commendations for you both."

"If we can finally bring Blavatsky in, that will be all the reward I need," insisted the Indian sergeant.

"Come on," beckoned Melville, "let us get you boys kitted out."

Melville led the two of them over to an armoured police carriage and silently signalled a nearby Malleus armed officer to unlock the luggage trunk fixed to the rear.

"You boys are going to be the first to use this," explained Melville as the officer before them rotated the key in the padlock and lifted the lid.

"What in God's name!?" questioned Abberline in disbelief.

"Courtesy of our friend Nikola at the Edison Tesla Electric Company," explained Melville.

Kalpesh stared down into the crate to see what could only be described as a weaponised miniature Tesla Coil. Two prongs extended from the outer coil to direct the electrical arcs in what would hopefully be a controlled manner, whilst the gun itself appeared to link via cables to a pack of batteries and capacitors welded together, complete with a set of shoulder straps.

"I'm told it is called the *'Teleforce,'* but the men in the armoury have already nicknamed it the *'Peace Ray,'*" smirked Melville as he watched the two detectives gape at the futuristic weapon that appeared to be something straight out of a Jules Verne novel.

"They should have called it the Leyden Rifle," responded Kalpesh.

"Peace Ray?" questioned Abberline. "Is that an attempt at a joke?"

"I am assured that it is non-lethal," explained Melville, "at least for the most part."

"Right," responded Abberline, hard pressed to believe it.

"Obviously, attempt to take Blavatsky and any other suspected occultists in alive," reiterated Melville. "This here weapon is intended to help you do just that. But you are authorised to use lethal force if required. Don't let Blavatsky get away; stop her and anyone else by any means necessary."

"Understood," nodded Kalpesh.

"There's more," assured Melville, shutting the lid of the trunk and leading them to the next Malleus carriage. "These here are also new," explained the assistant chief constable as he opened the carriage door and pulled out a crate, planting it on the pavement. "Starting next week, these are going to be issued to a select number of Special Branch officers. They are the result of a year's collaboration between the Bell Telephone Company and Edison and Tesla."

"Surely these aren't the Mark II wireless telephones?" questioned Kalpesh.

"Take a look and see," replied Melville, handing him a crowbar.

Kalpesh carefully prised off the lid of the crate.

"Given where you gentlemen are heading, I think it only fair you get them early."

The lid came loose and Kalpesh found himself indeed looking at the second generation of the famous Hertzian wave communicators that had been invented little over a year ago. Yet this was more than a simple iteration on a proven design, instead it was an entire reinvention that had far reaching implications. The Mark I design was a large device, portable only in the sense that it could be installed inside a carriage and thereby transported from location to location, allowing Malleus officers to rapidly contact Anvil without needing to journey to the nearest police box. This second incarnation of the technology was a massive leap towards the full realisation of wireless telecommunication, or perhaps rather, it *was* the full realisation of it.

Kalpesh lifted one of the wireless telephones from out of the crate and examined it in bewilderment. A single casing, by appearance designed to affix to a belt, housed the power supply and the Hertzian wave transmitter and receiver. Out of the case extended a braided wire that attached to a secondary unit that looked as if it affixed to a shoulder strap. The secondary unit of the wireless telephony device consisted of both the earpiece receiver and microphone, whilst extending upwards was a wire aerial intended to convert broadcasted waves into electric power and likewise the reverse.

"We are calling it the Airwave," explained Melville. "It's going to change police work beyond recognition!"

"It's going to change *the world* beyond recognition!" insisted Kalpesh as he handed one to Abberline to inspect.

"Just like telepathy, huh?" remarked the inspector.

"Indeed," agreed Melville. "After all of these centuries, the odds are finally starting to even out in Malleus's favour."

"Then let's take the fight to them," insisted Kalpesh.

"That's what I want to hear," smiled Melville. "There are combat uniforms and cuirasses inside the chest atop of here," he said banging his fist on the side of the Malleus carriage. "Suit up. I'll get you a squad together. Be ready to move out in ten."

IX

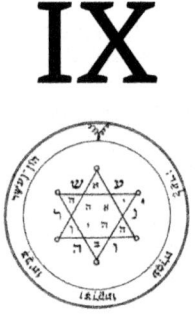

Lansdowne Crescent, Notting Hill
9:31 p.m. September 2nd, 1888

The carriage jostled and rocked as it rode across the cobbled streets of Notting Hill. Drawing back the curtain from the window, Kalpesh peeked out at the wealthy borough; parks and gardens stretched in the spaces between the terraced townhouses of the Ladbroke Estate, whilst horse chestnut trees rowed the paths, their leaves soughing gently beneath the flickering arc lamps lining the broad boulevard. This side of London was a far cry from the cramped slums of the East

End.

The six men inside the carriage sat in tense silence as they locked eyes with one another, knowing that they were mere moments away from their destination. Abberline and Kalpesh sat opposite each other in the centre of the two benches. On the right sat Sergeant Patrick McIntyre and Sergeant Mansfield Smith-Cumming, an ex-naval officer who had joined Malleus shortly before Kalpesh. On the left sat Sergeant Basil Thomas and the very young Detective Constable Robert Nathan.

Together, they were outfitted with four teleforce guns, equipped to Kalpesh, Abberline, McIntyre, and Cumming, whilst Thomas and Nathan had been given an ample supply of wooden baton slugs for their pair of modified Greener Police Shotguns. Along with these non-lethal weapons, the squad had been supplied with a trunk loaded full of riot control equipment. If the situation escalated, they were each armed with their Mauser C96 service pistols.

"That should do it," grumbled Abberline as he banged his fist against the side of the carriage interior behind his head, signalling the plain-clothed driver to halt.

As the black carriage shuddered to a stop, the door clicked open and out stepped the six Malleus officers into the night. Kalpesh adjusted the metal cuirass encasing his torso and tightened the straps to his teleforce pack. Together, they moved around to the rear of the carriage as Abberline unlocked the storage trunk and began dispensing their additional equipment. Kalpesh was handed an Airwave by Sergeant Cumming. He clipped it to his belt before threading the wire through the straps of his breastplate; finally fixing the speaker and microphone to his shoulder, he straightened the foot-long aerial, allowing it to protrude upright above his head.

"Here," said Sergeant Thomas, handing the Indian a helmet and gasmask.

Kalpesh placed the helm over his head, allowing the respirator and goggles to hang freely to the side as he flicked the switch on his Airwave. The speaker popped and let out a high-pitched whine, before, fiddling with the small nob on his belt, Kalpesh tuned the device to the correct frequency.

As one by one the other Malleus officers followed suit, Kalpesh leant his head closer to the mouthpiece and spoke into it, "This is Detective Sergeant Khatri. Does anyone read me?"

To his amazement, his crackling voice emitted from several of the nearby devices with a fraction of a second delay. As all fell quiet, a few delighted chuckles emitted from the men around him in wonder at the technological marvel. Then, suddenly, all of the Hertzian wave devices fizzled again.

"Sergeant Khatri, this is Assistant Chief Constable Melville. We read you loud and clear!"

This time a few audible gasps of astonishment sounded amongst the Malleus officers before Melville spoke again.

"What is your situation? Have you arrived at the address?"

"Negative, sir," replied Kalpesh, holding down the transmit button on the mouthpiece. "We have stopped a few hundred yards away outside a church on Lansdowne Crescent. We are preparing to proceed the rest of the way on foot."

"Copy that, Sergeant," replied the sizzle of Melville's voice over the airwave. "We are just finishing up here in Bloomsbury. I should be en route to your location shortly. Hopefully I'll be there in person to shake all your hands once you've taken Blavatsky into custody."

"Let's not get ahead of ourselves, sir," warned Cumming as he first tested the Airwave for himself. "We don't yet have any confirmation that this is actually the Blavatsky Lodge."

"I've got a good feeling about it," assured Thomas eagerly to those next to him.

"Don't worry, boss," insisted Abberline down the airwave. "We'll bring her in alive!"

"Good man," crackled Melville. "We'll keep silent over the Airwave from here on out to ensure we don't give you away as you close in."

"Very good, sir," replied Abberline.

"And gentlemen..." Melville paused for dramatic effect. "Good luck!"

The airwave fell silent and Kalpesh drew the

map of Notting Hill from out of the carriage to study it one final time.

"Khatri, you take point," instructed Abberline. "You have the most combat experience, and none of us would be here if it weren't for you."

"Thank you, sir," replied Kalpesh. "I think we should attempt to enter the property through the garden at the rear. The trees should prevent us being seen by anyone as we approach." He took a moment to trace the proposed movement across the paper with his finger.

"Sounds good to me," approved Abberline.

"Then that's what we'll do," confirmed Kalpesh, folding the map away and stowing it in a pouch on his belt. "Everyone ready?"

A series of silent nods followed.

"Move out," he instructed, pressing the stock of his teleforce tightly into his shoulder as he set off. Making past St John's Church, they cut south towards the wrought-iron-fenced gardens that sat to the east side of Lansdowne Road. Stepping through the gates to the park, they rushed along the gravel path beneath the shadows of the trees, before coming to a halt on a lawn that looked out to the line of houses.

"Take a knee," instructed Kalpesh as they stooped and huddled together to survey the property in question. Spreading the map on the grass, Kalpesh clicked on the electric torch fitted to his cuirass and let the light spill across the page. "That's the one," he confirmed, pointing to the smaller of two semidetached houses ahead as he stowed the map once more.

Pulling a miniature set of binoculars from a case on his belt, he surveyed the building. The lights were on in numerous windows, visible through cracks in the drawn curtains.

"Someone is definitely home," confirmed Abberline, peering through a set of his own binoculars.

"Considering how many rooms are lit up, there could be a good few of them in there," added Cumming.

"Let's do this quick and cleanly," insisted Kalpesh. "Thomas, Nathan, the two of you take the bay window on the right. Smash out the glass and get a gas grenade in there."

The two young detectives nodded.

"Cumming, McIntyre, you two move around to the side of the house, see if you can do the same from the front."

"Understood," agreed Cumming.

"Sir," continued Kalpesh, looking to Abberline, "you and I are heading in through the back door."

"Sounds good, my boy!"

Kalpesh issued him a smile before clipping the gas mask across the front of his face. His breathing rasped as the diaphragm flexed in and out. "Let's do this," he mumbled through the respirator as the others fitted their own masks.

They quickly cut the rest of the way

across the public garden, pausing on the far side with their backs against a feather-board fence. Gently easing the latch on the gate, they let themselves quietly into the back yard. Rushing across the lawn, Kalpesh and Abberline took up position either side of the rear entranceway. Abberline readied a teargas grenade, drawing the pin and issuing the Indian a nod from behind his respirator. Kalpesh peered over his shoulder to see Thomas and Nathan pressed against the wall bordering the rear bay window. He waited as Cumming and McIntyre vanished around the flank of the property, and a few seconds later, a quiet fizz emitted from the radio.

"In position."

"On my mark," breathed Kalpesh, holding down the button to talk. He inhaled deeply, steadying his racing pulse. "Now!"

Glass shattered. Kalpesh drove his full weight into a kick, his heel connecting powerfully with the lock on the door. The bolt ripped through the wood of the frame and the door flung violently open. Abberline lobbed the teargas grenade into the corridor ahead. A detonation thundered from inside. The grenade began to hiss as noxious gas spooled across the floor.

Raising his teleforce, Kalpesh darted inside. He heard cries. Muffled shouting. There was a second deafening explosion, and then, screams. Suddenly, heat and smoke started spilling out from under the door on the right up ahead.

"Kalpesh!" the voice of Melville crackled in alarm over the Airwave. "Abort! Abort!"

"What is it?" demanded the Indian as he fumbled to turn down the speaker volume.

"It's a trap!" warned Melville. "They know you are coming!"

"Shit!" cursed Abberline, rushing towards the doorway from under which black smoke was now billowing.

"Sir, wait!" warned Kalpesh as the inspector brushed past him. He watched as the rug under his feet creased, revealing etchings scratched into the floor. "Look out!"

Kalpesh drove his shoulder into Abberline, knocking him off balance, but the inspector's boots clipped across the arcane glyph regardless. As the carpet bundled, a portion of a pentacle was unveiled. Abberline suddenly lifted from the floor of the corridor, his body hurtling upwards as his weight inverted. The plaster above crumbled as the Malleus detective slammed hard into the ceiling. Bouncing off the wooden laths, the inspector rolled against the wall and came crashing back down in a rain of plaster. His limp body thudded into the crumpled rug and he fell motionless.

A fierce roar sounded from up ahead, and from around the bottom of the stairwell, two men rushed outwards at Kalpesh. A pistol sounded and a bullet plugged into the wallpaper inches from the Indian detective's head. The second occultist charged him, brandishing an athame like a dagger as he stormed through the fog of teargas.

Instinct seized hold of Kalpesh, overriding the shock; he felt his finger curl hard around the trigger of his teleforce. The corridor blazed white and a shrieking thrum tore at the air. A web of continuous lightning crackled between the gun's forks, and a bolt of electrified energy arced outwards. The ray of electricity collided with the oncoming occultist, and in the blink of an eye, he was driven off his feet, into the floor, his body crumpling in convulsion under the strain of a thousand volts surging through him.

At the far end of the corridor, the pistol snapped loudly again. Kalpesh felt his helmet violently jolt as the second shot glanced off the rim. He squeezed at the trigger again. Another streak of lightning lanced out of the miniature Tesla coil, licking across the wall, scorching the wallpaper black as it traced down the length of the hallway.

The occultist leapt back into cover to avoid the arc of plasma, but even his rapid reactions failed to save him, the jagged whip of energy swerving clean around the corner, striking him square on behind the wall. The villain slumped against the stairwell, his unconscious body sliding to the floor. Kalpesh stood mesmerised by the two incapacitated men, taking a second to examine the remarkable weapon in his hands.

Yet the moment of admiration was short

lived; realization soon set in, his eyes falling back to Abberline, the inspector lying motionless at his feet.

"Abberline!" he breathed in horror, skirting the unveiled pentacle as he rushed to his partner's aid. His fingers fumbled for the man's neck; he felt a pulse. Kalpesh leant his head near to the unconscious detective's lips; he was breathing faintly.

Grappling the shoulder straps of Abberline's teleforce, he heaved the lump of a man upwards and dragged him steadily back down the corridor, out the door, laying him flat on the lawn of the backyard.

Smoke was billowing out of the side of the house, flames licking through the shattered windowpanes. The room into which Nathan and Thomas had entered had been consumed in a raging inferno. Gunshots began to clatter faintly over the roaring flames. Kalpesh made out the distinctive whine of a peace ray firing in retaliation.

"Cumming, McIntyre!?" Kalpesh called into the Airwave as he trudged back into the corridor now flooded with teargas. "What's your situation?"

No response came, the device remaining silent as the Indian detective stepped past the pentacle trap that had thrown Abberline into the ceiling. He made for the door to the fiery backroom. He clasped the doorknob, but immediately retracted his hand; even through gloves, the brass handle was scalding hot to the touch. He stepped back and delivered another kick. The singed frame splintered and the door pivoted open. A wall of blazing heat slammed suddenly into Kalpesh. He could hear harrowing screams gurgling from inside.

"Thomas! Nathan!" he screamed, daring to poke his head into the room swallowed in a blistering conflagration. He descried two bodies consumed in the firestorm, one utterly motionless, the other crawling towards the door, flesh cooking, meat slopping from his bones. Within seconds, he succumbed, slumping dead beside the first, the two carcasses bubbling as the conflagration engulfed them entirely. As Kalpesh withdrew from the threshold, an afterimage welded itself momentarily to his retinas; it had been glowing through the charred floorboards: a second pentacle, more than likely a deadly trap that had set the room ablaze when the two young detectives had entered it.

Suddenly, a whirlwind of frigid air swelled out of the heat and swept throughout the room, quenching the flames in a matter of seconds. Poking his head back inside, Kalpesh saw smoke still rising from the smouldering floorboards; but seemingly all of the fire had been dispelled. He was merely guessing, but Kalpesh suspected the flames had been vanquished by a second layer of enchantment scripted into the fading pentacle; no doubt designed to prevent the entire building from being consumed in the inferno. Kalpesh winced as he looked at the immolated remains of the two young detectives smouldering amidst the cinders.

"Khatri!" the faint voice of Cumming whistled over the Airwave through a static of distortion.

"Cumming!?" gasped the Indian, readying his weapon as he continued down the corridor.

"Khatri, we are pinned down!" the fizzling voice cried as gunshots continued to pop in a room up ahead. "McIntyre's been hit!"

"Hold on!" urged Kalpesh as he continued to tread lightly, scanning the walls, floor, and ceiling through the mist of teargas for any other arcane traps that might have been laid for them. He heard retching and coughing sputter from the stairs ahead. He poked his gun around the turn and saw a woman curled up in a fit of tears, her chest writhing in agony as she sucked in lungfuls of the surrounding toxic fog. Knowing she was unlikely to pose any threat, Kalpesh ignored her and pushed on towards the front room.

"Cumming, I'm seconds away," he whispered, pressing himself close to the wall as he shimmied around the fringes of a magic seal drawn into the ceiling above.

"I can't see a thing!" buzzed Cumming. "It's so dark!"

Twisting the doorknob to the front room, Kalpesh lurched inside, gun raised. As he stepped through the threshold, he was suddenly blinded. Gunshots echoed around him, firing wildly as a preternatural black smoke swirled throughout the room so densely, that any and all light was shrouded by the sinister gloom. It was an invocation: a magical screen of smoke that clotted the air, obscuring anything caught within its radius. The summoner of the cloud had to be nearby, within line of sight of the arcane haze, therefore, all most certainly within the room itself.

Kalpesh swivelled his head about the smothering black fog; it was dense, but not impenetrable. He snatched a flashbang hanging from his belt and drew the pin; releasing the lever, he rolled the grenade across the floorboards. He covered his ears, but counterintuitively, peeled wide his eyes. A thunderous snap cut through the air, setting Kalpesh's ears ringing even beneath the protection of his palms, but the explosion was also accompanied by a flash. The instantaneous sheet of light was only faint, but it was bright enough to cleave through the spell. A split-second glimpse of the room revealed itself to Kalpesh as a grey oil painting of silhouettes and shadows. In the corner, a table was overturned with two ghostly figures hunched behind it. On the far side, near the blurred outline of a fireplace, had appeared three more spectres; one stood with his hands raised overhead in a somatic gesticulation, whilst the other two were aiming weapons vaguely in

Kalpesh's direction.

Darkness collapsing back in around him again, Kalpesh used the remembered image to orientate himself. Swivelling his body, he dropped to his knees. He heard cries of distress as everyone else in the room was deafened by the stun grenade. Wood splintered around the Indian detective as gunshots fired wildly in his direction, shredding the floorboards, and whizzing through the air mere inches from his head.

Taking aim from recollection alone, Kalpesh fired the teleforce. An electrical hum zapped through the darkness, a faint ribbon of lightning dimly tracing into the fog. He fired again, altering his aim for the second target. Suddenly, the room flooded with light as the smothering blackness immediately dissipated. The invocator dropped unconscious with a thud, and the final occultist loomed into full view. His eyes flicked from his collapsed accomplice to see Kalpesh aiming directly at him. He swung his gun, but before the villain could set his sights on the detective, Kalpesh clicked the trigger a final time and a torrent of electricity conducted through the air, rippling across the man's body, jolting him off his feet. The occultist slammed into the mantlepiece and thumped into the empty hearth.

"Shit!" breathed Cumming, rearing his head from behind the flipped dining table. "Good aim, man!"

"Thank you," breathed Kalpesh, unclipping

his gasmask as he climbed to his feet.

"Who did you say you served with?"

"The First Royal Bengal Fusiliers," replied Kalpesh distractedly.

McIntyre groaned loudly from behind the table. Kalpesh rushed over to inspect the man with the aid of Cumming. A bullet hole was punched into the shoulder of his cuirass just below his collar bone. Blood was soaking through the uniform beneath his breastplate. Kalpesh knelt beside him and reached behind the man's shoulder. The cuirass seemed intact across his back.

"The bullet is probably still inside him," deduced Kalpesh.

"You alright, Patrick?" questioned Cumming.

McIntyre nodded faintly as sweat beaded on his brow.

"Help me get his breastplate off!" insisted Kalpesh as he fumbled at the clasps under McIntyre's arms.

McIntyre grimaced as they jostled him about, before finally, they lifted the armour over his head and leant him back against the table.

"There's no exit wound," confirmed Kalpesh.

"I'm good," groaned McIntyre, gritting his teeth into a smile.

"You are going to be fine, old boy!" insisted Cumming as he pressed a handkerchief firmly over the wound. "What happened to the others?" he turned to Kalpesh.

"Thomas and Nathan are dead," lamented Kalpesh.

"Abberline?"

"Unconscious," he explained, "but otherwise, I think he's okay."

"We really botched this!" grumbled Cumming.

"They knew we were coming," Kalpesh growled in frustration.

"Khatri..." crackled the Airwave. "Kalpesh... come in!?"

"This is Khatri?"

"Kalpesh!" fizzled Melville's voice in relief. "Jesus Christ! Thank heavens you are alright!"

"Melville, we've got officers down," warned the Indian sergeant.

"Copy that," replied Macnaghten solemnly after a long pause. "What's the situation?"

"Nathan and Thomas are dead. Abberline and McIntyre are both down but stable."

"Understood," crackled Melville. "We've got back up heading your way along with a medical team. Standby; they should be with you in half an hour."

"Pat, can you stand?" asked Cumming.

McIntyre nodded.

"We need to get him out of here!" insisted Cumming.

Kalpesh stayed quiet as he heard footsteps

moving about upstairs.

"Help me get him to his feet," added the Sergeant.

Kalpesh knelt back down beside the injured policeman and carefully lifted him from under the armpits. McIntyre grimaced as they heaved him up off the floor. Together they hoisted his arms above their shoulders, each taking a portion of his weight so that he could stumble out of the room. Donning their gasmasks, they pushed down the corridor towards the tiled foyer by the front door. More footsteps thumped on the floor above, this time accompanied by the indiscernible murmuring of voices.

"I'll get the door," whispered Kalpesh, letting Cumming take McIntyre's full weight as he turned the key in the lock. The door opened out to the street. "Get him clear," instructed the Indian detective.

"You aren't coming with us!?"

Kalpesh shook his head, turning to the sounds coming from upstairs.

"Are you mad!?" hissed Cumming.

"We can't let them escape," refused Kalpesh.

"They aren't going anywhere! Now come on, let's get out of this hell hole!"

"No," refused Kalpesh. "They'll get away. They'll be working on a teleportation circle—if they haven't completed one already. By the time backup arrives, Blavatsky will be gone!"

"Damn it," cursed Cumming, knowing the

Indian detective was right.

"I've got to finish this now."

"No!" urged Cumming. "There'll be another time. If you go up there now, they'll slaughter you!"

"They won't expect me," assured Kalpesh. "It has to be now. Malleus won't get another chance to bring Blavatsky in alive. Not after this."

"You are a brave man," uttered Cumming gravely as he locked eyes with Kalpesh. "A bloody foolish one—but brave all the same."

Kalpesh nodded solemnly.

"Here," breathed Cumming, drawing a Mauser from his holster and offering it to the Indian sergeant.

Kalpesh took the pistol, tucking it inside his belt alongside his own.

"Make that bitch pay!"

"I will," he assured, gripping his teleforce and turning to walk slowly back inside.

X

The Blavatsky Lodge, Notting Hill
9:49 p.m. September 2nd, 1888

Stepping over the weeping occultist on the stairs, Kalpesh crept upwards to the first-floor landing. His breathing rattled inside his mask as the thinning teargas swirled about in the air. Emerging from out of the toxic cloud, the sergeant progressed to the upstairs corridor. A doorknob rattled ahead, and out of a room strode a wiry-haired man in a set of long robes. He stopped dead in his tracks the moment he saw Kalpesh appear from out of the stairwell. The theosophist froze, his eyes widening as he looked on at the armoured, masked Malleus agent aiming a miniaturised tesla coil his way. His hand lurched suddenly as he reached beneath his robes for the gun concealed at his waist, but before he could draw, Kalpesh clicked the trigger of his teleforce.

Lightning sizzled in a melodic arc, connecting instantly with the occultist, grounding through his body as it electrocuted him into submission. He dropped, smacking the floorboards face-first, yet in the blink of an eye, another man in robes took his place, leaping out of the same room, brandishing a revolver of his own. But before the villain could take aim, Kalpesh discharged another bolt of plasma. Streaking across the wall in a searing flail of energy, the tendril of light finally lashed the occultist, his body contorting in a twinge of uncontrolled muscle spasms. The gun fired off in his grip; the bullet smashing a mirror hanging on the wall sending shards of glass flying.

Kalpesh heard a door thump open on his flank, but the goggles of his mask narrowed his field of view like a set of blinders. He swivelled his head in search, yet before he could lock eyes on the foe storming his way, he was barged off his feet, driven hard into a closed door on the opposite side of the hallway. The latch buckled under impact and the door gave out, sending Kalpesh and his tackler tumbling through the threshold and into a room lit by dozens of flickering candles. The tip of a knife scraped against the steel plate of Kalpesh's cuirass as he and his assailant grappled on the floor. Kalpesh drove a boot into the man atop of him, sending him reeling backwards.

Finally locking eyes on his foe through the narrow field of his gasmask, he took aim from the floor with his teleforce at the occultist scrambling back to his feet. The trigger clicked, but to Kalpesh's dismay, not so much as a spark projected from the prongs of the electricity gun. Regaining his footing, the occultist lunged for him athame-first, sinking his blade towards the floor where the Malleus sergeant lay.

Swinging wildly with the weight of the dead weapon in his hands, Kalpesh clouted the man across the forearm, deflecting the inbound ritual blade. The occultist reeled sideways, parried away by the blow. Kalpesh threw the teleforce aside, rolling over, fingers nimbly darting for the haft of his kukri. Unsheathing his Gurkha blade from the scabbard on his belt, Kalpesh leapt back to his feet, narrowly jinking clear of another wild swing from the theosophist's athame. His foe lunging for him once again, Kalpesh moved to intercept, grappling the swinging wrist of his assailant and driving his own blade deep between the man's ribs in a singular swift motion.

He drove forwards, pinning the occultist against the wall beside the door. The athame tumbled from his grip. A gunshot clapped suddenly beside Kalpesh's ear as another theosophist darted inside the room. Plaster ruptured outwards from the wall; the shot missing by a good foot. The gunman took aim for the Malleus agent again. With his blade still sunk into the side of the first theosophist, Kalpesh twisted, heaving the weight of the dying man locked in his embrace around him. He tucked himself in tightly behind the body just as the next succession of shots were fired his way. The bullets plugged into his human shield. Gunfire dying away, Kalpesh shoved the limp theosophist in the direction of the shooter, ripping his blade free in the same movement.

The gunman stumbled back as the dead warlock smacked into him. He staggered, fighting to stay upright as he shoved the body aside. A fraction of a second later, Kalpesh speared into him, tackling him powerfully to the ground. Gunshots cracked and bullets flew wide as Kalpesh batted the shooter's aim upwards towards the ceiling. Wrestling frenziedly on the floor, the two men knocked over a dozen flickering candles, immediately setting fire to a sheet strewn across a bookcase. Rolling over in the growing embers, the gunman drove the butt of his pistol down at Kalpesh. The weight of the gun struck the detective in the face, shattering an eyepiece in his mask. Kalpesh's head lurched backwards from the force of the pistol-whip, his helmet smashing against a skirting board.

The gunman pressed down atop of him,

pinning Kalpesh to the floor, straining against the Indian's grip as he fought to direct the barrel of his pistol towards the Malleus agent. The Indian swivelled his neck just in time for a shot to narrowly miss his head, the bullet punching through the floorboards in the corner of the room.

Releasing his grasp from Kalpesh's elbow, the gunman grappled the revolver in two hands, using the strength of both arms to try and turn the pistol towards the detective's head; but in doing so, he forfeited restraint of Kalpesh's blade. The Malleus officer clove his Kukri upwards, carving the edge deep into the warlock's chest. The gun went off. Skirting board exploded in a rain of splinters, the shot sailing wide. A gush of blood spouted into the air, spraying from the gunman's severed carotid artery, painting a wide splatter across the wallpaper. The occultist slumped heavily atop Kalpesh, the arterial spray steadily weakening with each pulse as the blood began to pool thickly across the floorboards.

Heaving the dead weight off himself, Kalpesh cast the cadaver aside. He clambered up from the floor, retreating from the heat of the growing fire ignited by the toppled candles. Goggles cracked and smeared with blood, respirator near enough suffocating him, Kalpesh ripped the mask and helmet free of his head, gasping for air as he discarded them. Sheathing his Kukri, he turned to see his teleforce in the centre of the floor; the cable that attached the gun to the powerpack across his back had been severed, most likely cut by his assailant's knife. Slipping out of the shoulder straps, he dropped the heavy pack of capacitors and cells to the floor and reached for the pair of C96 Mausers holstered at his side. Staggering exhaustedly across the room, he braced himself against the doorframe and poked his head out to peer up the corridor.

The architrave exploded inches from his brow, sending a shower of splinters into Kalpesh's face before more gunfire clapped from up the hall. Tucking his head back into cover, he squinted, allowing several beads of sweat and tears to clear the debris from his eyes. Pistols continuing to cough deafeningly outside, the Indian detective exhaled, preparing himself as he readied for a lull in the fusillade. The instant the firing stopped, he sprung, throwing himself shoulder-first out through the doorway. Hitting the carpet, he combat-rolled across the hall, tucking in his limbs before snapping back upright into a crouching stance. Years of military training took over, and before his mind had time to process what was happening, he found himself peering down a set of sights trained on the gunman at the far end of the corridor.

He opened fire. The hammer of his Mauser struck thrice. The muzzle flared and a triplet of bullets spat down the corridor. Two missed, but the final slug flew true. A fine mist of blood puffed into the air as the shot punched through the man's cheekbone. His head snapped backwards and he collapsed.

Rising from his knees, Kalpesh trudged warily down the hall, readying for any other occultist that might suddenly pounce out of the warren of open doorways. He kept his gun raised, sights trained ahead as he steadied the pistol on the wrist of his other arm, his second Mauser clutched in his left hand, ready for the moment his first magazine clicked empty. Panting heavily, he anxiously advanced towards the rear of the property, stepping over the motionless bodies he had left in his wake. How many more members of the Blavatsky Lodge could be awaiting him?

He reached the end of the landing and found the next staircase; it doubled back the way he'd come, rising towards the top floor. Everything had fallen eerily silent. Whoever was left had to be preparing something up ahead. He ascended the flight, step by step, the wooden staircase creaking under his boots as he climbed. He cocked his Mauser anxiously. His laboured panting slowed to calm, controlled inhalations as his pulse steadied.

A naked bulb hanging above the landing ahead began to flicker and buzz. Kalpesh paused, watching as the lightbulb dimmed and quivered; it could be a faulty connexion, but he suspected something more sinister was awry. More likely, the Aether was being distorted by something or someone in proximity to the light. He held his breath. A faint susurration of incantation was audible ahead. He was edging closer to a trap; but there was no way around, and he was steadily drawing short of time. If Blavatsky awaited him at the end of this gauntlet, and if she were (as Kalpesh suspected) plotting to escape by means of a teleportation circle, the ritual would be nearing completion, had it not already been finalised. He had moments left, if not seconds. The only way forward was through.

Kalpesh pulled the trigger. His pistol snapped and the bulb atop the stairway exploded in a shower of sparks. He heard a female voice yelp in surprise as he powered up the stairs, sprinting for the corridor above. A ring of candles lit the hallway atop the landing, and knelt before a glyph marked in wax and chalk upon the floorboards, was a witch. She panicked as Kalpesh rushed out of the stairwell, storming down the corridor her way. She frantically sliced an athame against her palm and smear blood across the wax pentacle to activate it.

Kalpesh charged, hurling himself from his feet as he dove clean across the sigil. The floor and walls of the corridor tremored and shook as the Indian detective flew through the air. A clamour of splitting wood and rupturing brick and mortar imploded around him. He struck the floor on the far side of the pentacle and piled shoulder-first into the theosophist priestess. Together, they slid across the floorboards, tumbling over and over one another as a rug folded and bundled beneath them, finally slowing them to a halt.

Kalpesh rolled over on top of the woman, pinning her beneath his weight. She screamed and thrust with her athame, but the detective snatched hold of her forearm before she could land the blow, delivering a blunt strike with the butt of his Mauser to her forehead. Instantly rendered unconscious, her eyes rolled back and the witch fell silent.

The detective glanced back over his shoulder to the imploded ruin that had mere seconds earlier been a hallway. Jagged lengths of floorboards had constricted, piercing upwards into rows upon rows of downward spearing ceiling laths. The walls on either side of the corridor had likewise choked inward, great boulders of aggregated brick and plaster smashing together on either flank, the hallway sealing shut in a giant fanged maw of rubble and debris.

The way back was now shut off. Had Kalpesh been any slower to react, he would either have been barricaded on the other side, unable to reach the far end of the house, or worse, swallowed up in the crushing jaws of the implosion.

Climbing to his feet, he retrieved Cumming's pistol from the floor beside him and moved towards the final door at the end of the corridor. With his gun raised, he drove the sole of his boot hard into the wood. The door clattered open and Kalpesh rushed inside. He swung his pistol from left to right and back again, sweeping his sights across the unlit bedroom.

Several bookcases filled with illicit material leant against the far wall; in between them stood a writing desk. Next to the bed was a nightstand covered with various medicine bottles, a bedpan tucked beneath it. In the corner, an empty wheelchair sat facing Kalpesh. Otherwise, the room was vacant, devoid of Blavatsky or anyone else. The window was open, a gentle evening breeze blowing the drapes inward. Kalpesh rushed towards the opening and poked his head outside. He gazed out across the backyard and glimpsed movement down below in the shadows.

"Stop!" Kalpesh cried, aiming his gun at a figure shuffling around beneath him.

"Khatri!?" came the befuddled voice of Abberline.

"Abberline!?" Kalpesh shouted in relief.

"My head is killing me!" moaned the inspector as he stepped into the light cast by the open backdoor.

"You took quite a hit," replied Kalpesh.

"What's happened?" pressed the detective. "Have you found her?"

"No," sighed Kalpesh in frustration. "She's not here!"

"Blast!"

"I've taken out everyone else," explained the Indian.

Abberline shot the detective a bewildered look. "Good man!" His eyes fell to the incinerated remains of the back room and the cremated bodies visible within. "I take it Thomas and Nathan didn't make it?"

Kalpesh shook his head.

"What about the other two? Cumming? McIntyre?"

"They're out front," returned Kalpesh. "McIntyre has been shot, but it's not life-threatening. Cumming is out with him waiting for backup to arrive."

Abberline nodded. "Stay there, I'll make my way up to you."

"You can't," explained the detective. "The corridor's been smashed apart by a spell!"

Abberline nodded again, exhaling deeply as he examined the building. "Alright," he mumbled finally, clearly undeterred. "Hold on," he insisted, unstrapping his teleforce and laying it on the grass before momentarily disappearing from the Indian's field of view as he moved closer to the house.

Kalpesh leant further out over the sill as Abberline began to emit several exasperated grunts. The Indian detective's eyes adjusted to the dim light of the moon to see that his partner was scaling a waterspout fixed to the wall that rose to a hopper situated just above his head. It took the man only a few seconds before he had climbed the drain all the way up to Kalpesh. Abberline extended his fingers, fumbling for the window ledge. Curling his grip around the sill, he shifted his weight across until he was dangling entirely from the window. Then, with Kalpesh's help, he heaved himself up, wriggling through the frame, clambering into the bedroom beyond.

Straightening himself, the inspector puffed as he caught his breath. Studying his immediate surroundings, he then peered out of the bedroom into the corridor, spying both the unconscious witch and the crumpled remains of the hallway beyond.

"Christ, Khatri!" exclaimed the man. "How many of them did you take down?"

"She makes twelve," replied the detective.

Abberline raised his eyebrows in disbelief. "Remind me never to get on your bad side, detective!" Abberline turned away and began to examine the contents of the room, starting first with the writing desk.

Kalpesh stepped back out into the corridor to glance at the unconscious witch. As he examined the iris of jagged laths and floorboards sealing off the way back, a sudden realization struck him. He raised his gaze, tracing his eyes along the ceiling until he spotted what he was searching for: an attic hatch.

"She was definitely staying here!" called the voice of Abberline from within the room as he leafed through several letters with the initials 'HPB' scribbled at the top.

"Sir!" hushed Kalpesh, beckoning his partner.

Abberline's eyes narrowed, sensing the urge for silence as he dropped the pages and made his way out of the bedroom with his gun drawn. Kalpesh pointed silently upwards to the loft hatch. Abberline nodded, clicking the safety off his pistol. Kalpesh drew his kukri, raising it above his head to reach the full height of the ceiling, pressing the point against the trapdoor. It immediately swung open, and suddenly, a ladder on a rail slid down to thud against the floorboards at their feet. There was a sudden kerfuffle from up top before the commotion fell silent enough for the two detectives to hear more murmured incantation.

Abberline gestured to the ladder and Kalpesh nodded apprehensively. Drawing his Mauser, he quietly placed a foot on the bottom rung and silently ascended. He kept his pistol above his head, aiming at the opening, ready to fire if anyone or anything appeared from above. Nearing the top, he prepared to climb through the hatch gun-first, knowing full well that anyone in the loft would likely be waiting for him. He could still hear murmuring: a deep but distinctively female voice. Kalpesh swallowed. Unable to delay any longer, he sprung his head and gun through the hatch.

He swung the pistol in a wide arc, ready to shoot anything that fell in his sights, yet before he could complete the sweep of his gun, an iron poker arced from out of the shadows, clattering against the pistol in his hand. The Mauser flew clean from his grip, bending Kalpesh's fingers back painfully. A set of hands grabbed hold of his collar and heaved him upwards. He lost his footing on the ladder as he was dragged across the floor of the dimly lit loft. A gunshot sounded from Abberline below as the inspector fired at the shadow moving overhead, but the bullet drove uselessly into the rafters.

Kalpesh fought against the man throttling him, but the wind exploded from his lungs as a second blow from the poker struck him across the abdomen, denting the plating of his cuirass. Kalpesh clawed at the hands constricting around his trachea as the villain straddled his chest, pinning him to the floor. Clawing wildly with an arm, he managed to grab a handful of hair.

Footsteps sounded on the ladder rungs as Abberline attempted to scramble up to Kalpesh's aid, but a powerful boot from the man wielding the poker stomped the inspector's face. Dazed from the blow, Abberline lost his grip, slipping down the rungs to land hard on his back on the floor below. Before the inspector could rise back to his feet, the ladder retracted, and Kalpesh heard the distinctive sound of the loft hatch slamming shut.

Kalpesh ripped out a clump of hair from the scalp of the occultist atop of him. With a sudden effort, he flipped the weight of his adversary off his chest. The grip around his throat loosened, but as he rolled on top of his assailant, the toe of a boot drove into his hip. A fiery spasm of pain surged up his nerve from the joint. He toppled over, narrowly avoiding another swing from the iron poker aimed for his head. A blade unsheathed from beneath a cloak as the first man attempted to seize hold of Kalpesh again. Struggling against flailing limbs, Kalpesh felt his fingers snag around Cumming's pistol holstered at his side. A knee slammed down onto his hand as it locked around the broom handle of the Mauser inside the holster. The edge of an athame pressed against his throat. He fought with his free arm, forcing away the ritual knife as it slowly cut into his neck.

Suddenly, the room was lit ablaze with azure flames, as on the far side of the attic, the veil of the Aether tore open. The blue fire condensed into a circle of smoke and a puncture in the cosmos twisted together two different spatial locations. A blurred image of a far-flung destination congealed and began to take focus.

The Mauser exploded in Kalpesh's hand as he pulled the trigger with the gun still inside his holster. The man atop of him screamed as a chunk of kneecap was blown clean off. The weight lifted from the gun, and suddenly, his arm was free. The occultist wielding the poker swung for him again, the iron rod cleaving down at the supine detective. Kalpesh fired once more, his gun still holstered, but this time angled up away from the floor. The muzzle flashed and his assailant screamed. Bullet struck bone, the occultist's shin snapping as the slug drove clean through his leg. He toppled over mid-swing, slamming hard into the floorboards beside Kalpesh. Flailing on the ground, he lunged in one last vengeful strike at the Indian, yet before he could land the blow, Kalpesh finally pulled his pistol clean out of the shredded holster, pressing the barrel firmly into the occultist's breastbone.

The Mauser emitted a doublet of smothered coughs, eviscerating the man's heart inside his chest. An enraged and agonised scream erupted from the other knee-less occultist beside Kalpesh. He stabbed for the Indian with his athame. Rolling over the corpse of the man he'd just killed, Kalpesh narrowly avoided impalement, the ritual knife sinking into the cadaver instead. Taking aim from the ground yet again, the pistol in Kalpesh's grip clapped twice more, the two bullets obliterating the remaining theosophist's throat as they met their mark.

Kalpesh heaved himself to his feet. Up ahead, he caught full sight of the portal. Through it he saw the watery shadows of a darkened warehouse as sapphire mist whirled clockwise around the aperture. Upon the floor of the attic before it, was marked the elaborate pentacle of a teleportation circle surrounded by rings upon rings of runes and Hebrew characters. Rising clumsily to her knees in the centre of the intricate glyph was Blavatsky herself. The obese woman turned to behold Kalpesh with her bulging eyes before she stumbled forwards with her walking stick towards the portal.

The loft hatch swung open again. "Stop her, Khatri!" barked Abberline as his head reared through the trap door.

Kalpesh's feet were already in motion. He raised his gun, pulling the trigger as he took aim for her legs, his intent: to cripple her before she could reach the portal. But the Mauser clicked uselessly in his hand. He cursed, realising the slide was kicked fully back. Fumbling for a charger clip, he started to run. He reached into his ammo pouch and snatched a fresh charge from the belt. He clicked it nimbly into the receiver slot and forced the cartridges down into the magazine before pulling out the stripper.

Helena Blavatsky vanished, the liquid surface of the gateway rippling as she passed through. The moment the portal swallowed its summoner, it began to collapse. The blue smoke billowing around the periphery evaporated, and the phantasmal veil of energy started to distort and contract. Kalpesh accelerated from a run to a sprint, before hurling himself with all his might at the narrowing passage. He felt his stomach flip inside his abdomen. His ears popped, his sinuses stung, and his eyes bulged as the air around him compressed and crumpled his body. He screamed as he felt himself being ripped apart. Then everything went black.

XI

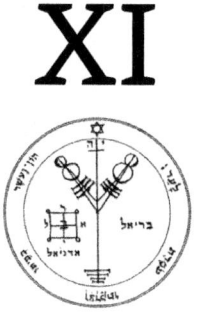

**Unknown Location
10:01 p.m. September 2nd, 1888**

"Khatri!?" crackled the Airwave speaker affixed to Kalpesh's shoulder. "Khatri!?" Abberline's voice fizzled again through a susurrus of static.

Kalpesh opened his eyes and groaned. Every muscle in his body felt sprained. His head was spinning dizzyingly. He was facedown, pressed onto a concrete floor. He grumbled, struggling to lift his heavy torso from the ground. The spinning slowed, the groggy haze gradually lifting from his mind.

"Khatri!?" buzzed the Airwave again. "Khatri, can you read me?"

Picking himself up off the floor, Kalpesh glanced shakily around at his surroundings. His blurred eyesight steadily adjusted to the faint moonlight spilling down through the gaps in the roof above. He was inside a derelict warehouse of sorts. Broken glass and rusted lengths of steel littered the floor; piles of rubble strewn about from where the ceiling had collapsed in places.

"Kalpesh!" stuttered the speaker. "If you can hear me, pick up!"

Kalpesh lifted a leaden arm and pressed the button on the communicator. "I'm here, sir."

"Sweet Mary!" exclaimed the inspector. "You are hard to put down, son!"

"I'm not so sure," Kalpesh wheezed. "I've had my bell rung pretty hard!"

"You alright?"

"Maybe," he winced. Rolling his shoulder, he felt the searing pain of several torn muscles.

"Just stay on your feet," instructed Abberline. "Tell me, where are you?"

"I don't know," coughed Kalpesh as he glanced groggily around himself. "Some kind of warehouse. It's abandoned."

"Well, you can't be too far," insisted the inspector. "You must still be somewhere in London, or else I doubt we'd be talking to one another over these contraptions!"

"Yeah," chuckled Kalpesh, before gasping from the pain it induced. "You are probably right."

"What about Blavatsky?" questioned Abberline. "Can you see her anywhere?"

"No," he swallowed, glancing about once more.

"Well, she can't be far," insisted the inspector. "You went through that portal straight after her. There can't have been more than a few seconds in it!"

"Right," agreed Kalpesh.

"Look around. She must be there."

Kalpesh scanned his surroundings, searching for any sign of the nearly lame witch.

"And Khatri..."

"Yeah?"

"Be careful," Abberline warned. "She is on Malleus' most wanted list for a reason!"

Kalpesh nodded and forced forward the slide on his C96 Mauser. He knelt, looking at the dust across the warehouse floor. Even in the dim light, he could make out the scrapes of shuffling footsteps punctuated by the marks of a cane. He elevated his gaze, tracing the path Blavatsky had taken to a steel support pillar a dozen yards ahead. Raising his gun, he trained his sights on the column.

"Step out!" he shouted. "I know you are there! This is it. Nowhere left to hide."

Only the echo of his own voice responded.

"Surrender!" he warned, edging closer as he

began to circle around the column to get a line of sight on Blavatsky. "Don't make me shoot you!"

Suddenly, a deep cackle sounded from up ahead. Kalpesh glanced down as movement in the periphery of his vision drew his attention. The dust under his feet was swirling preternaturally, and in a matter of seconds, a series of lines began to trace out through the dirt, quickly taking shape into a glyph. Kalpesh darted into motion, desperate to get clear of the rapidly forming seal, but before he could make it to safety, the pentacle had fully formed and the arcane trap triggered.

Blackness enveloped Kalpesh, blinding him completely. Demonic whispers roared through the strangulating smoke as torrents of hot air buffeted him from all sides. He fired his gun, aiming only through best guess as to where he thought Blavatsky was hiding. Lead clanged against steel as the bullets ricocheted uselessly off the support pillar, his spent cartridges pinging as they clattered to the concrete floor.

Suddenly, Kalpesh's stomach lurched and the ground fell sharply away from him. He dropped violently upwards, flying into the air, momentarily clearing the cloud of darkness. Almost immediately, gravity reverted and he was spun head-over-heels. He tumbled in a sickening whirlwind of dizzying distortion, plunging headfirst back down into the vortex of black mist.

His body smacked into the ground. His cuirass crumpled inwards. A rib cracked inside

Kalpesh's chest. He screamed. The force exerted on him doubled down, driving him harder and harder into the floor. Air squeezed out of his lungs, the weight growing second by second. He was restrained beyond all hope, entirely paralyzed by the malefic forces crushing him into the concrete.

Darkness washed away as the black mist evaporated. A sniggering cackled sounded as a cane began to tap against the concrete floor. Out from behind the steel support pillar appeared the bloated high priestess of the Theosophical Society, Helena Petrovna Blavatsky herself.

"You little pig!" she spat in her thick Russian accent, shuffling over towards Kalpesh as he lay helpless on the ground. "You thought you could stop me?" she laughed. "You know nothing. You are slave. You serve your oppressive masters with no understanding of true powers of cosmos!"

Kalpesh's vision began to tunnel; unable to breathe, he was quickly losing consciousness.

"I pity you. Your eyes are shut. You are blind to the forces of nature. You think that which you do not understand is unnatural; you seek to destroy that which has existed for thousands of years, simply because it cannot fit within your narrow and pathetic worldview!"

Kalpesh's eyes rolled over to the pistol lying on the ground at his side. It was well within his reach, but unable to move, he had no hope of obtaining it.

"You persecute those of us brave enough to

search for what lies beyond veil of Aether. Those who can see into dimensions beyond our own existence are burnt alive for their gifts!"

Kalpesh felt the blood draining from his head. She was killing him, slowly but surely. He did not know how much longer his body could survive the immense weight crushing down on him, but he knew he was mere seconds away from blacking out.

"You call us monsters... but it is you who are real creatures of evil!"

A prickling sensation began to spread across Kalpesh's hand. At first, he thought it a mere tingling from the failing blood circulation in his extremities, but the odd sensation began to grow, expanding from the centre of his left palm, flowing quickly down into his fingertips before ascending to his elbow.

"Change is coming," insisted Blavatsky as she finally reached Kalpesh and leant over him, beholding him with a set of swollen, beady eyes. "The world stands on a precipice, it needs only select few to push it over the brink!"

Kalpesh flexed his fingers, something that seconds ago had been impossible. He balled his hand into a fist. He was still restrained, but for whatever reason, the overwhelming force acting across the rest of his body was letting up on his left forearm.

"A new world is just beyond the horizon. But you will never see it!"

"No," wheezed Kalpesh, his lips pinned against his teeth.

Blavatsky's eyes narrowed in confusion. She leant closer as Kalpesh began to whisper what she assumed were his last words.

"Neither... will... you!" he rasped, his fingertips groping at cold steel.

Blavatsky's face contorted in an expression of horror as the Malleus officer's arm lifted impossibly from the floor.

Kalpesh pulled the trigger. The Mauser C96 shook with recoil as a single bullet clapped out of the muzzle. The shot punched through Blavatsky's shoulder. She lurched backwards, her feet and walking stick flailing out from under her. As she struck the ground, Kalpesh felt the tonnes of force driving down on him dissipate. Air flooded back into his lungs and his chest burned hot in agony.

Peeling his body up from the concrete, Kalpesh threw himself on top of Blavatsky as she moaned, clutching her bloodied shoulder. She struggled feebly as the detective flipped her prone and straddled her back. Cursing loudly in Russian, she began to frantically mutter another hex. But striking her hard across the pate with the butt of his pistol, Kalpesh successfully managed to silence the crone before she could finish her invocation.

Holstering his gun, he reached for the set of iron manacles on his waist and forced the old woman's thick arms behind her back. Snapping the cuffs tightly around her engorged wrists, he began to speak.

"Helena Blavatsky, I hereby place you under arrest in accordance with the 1542 Witchcraft Act for the crimes of distribution of prohibited esoteric materials, maleficium, practicing of black magic, and for conspiracy against the Crown."

She began to curse again, but the detective shoved a gag inside her mouth and restrained it in place with a bit which he tightened around the back of her head. Clambering off the obese sorceress, Kalpesh collapsed, gasping to catch his breath. When he was ready to speak again, he reached for the transmitter on his shoulder to find that the Airwave was no longer attached to its strap.

He sat up and looked around. The shoulder component of his communicator lay only a few feet away. He picked it up to inspect the damage. The casing had been cracked and dented when he had slammed into the ground, the braided wire ripped out.

Prising open the casing, the detective contacted the frayed ends of the cable dangling from his waist against the terminals inside the receiver. The Airwave suddenly crackled and whined with static. Turning the dial on his waist, Kalpesh tuned the device until suddenly the voice of Assistant Chief Constable Melville fizzled over the communicator.

"—Kalpesh? If you can hear us, come in! Repeat! Sergeant Kalpesh, do you read us? Are you okay?"

"Melville," breathed Kalpesh.

"Kalpesh!? I don't believe it! Where are you? Are you hurt?"

"I don't know exactly where I am," replied the Indian. "I'm in a warehouse somewhere. Judging by the smell, I'd say somewhere down by the docks."

"Don't worry. We'll get men out to you—"

"Melville..." he interrupted.

"What is it?"

"I got her!" he smiled. "I've got Blavatsky in custody!"

XII

Anvil, Tower of London, City of London
9:00 a.m. September 5th, 1888

"Forgive the mess," apologised Monro as he shut the door to his office behind Kalpesh, gesturing for the Indian detective to take a seat amidst the boxes of paperwork stacked across the desk and floor. "I'm in the process of moving over to the Home Office, but with everything that has happened in the last week, I haven't given the process the attention it needs." He smiled, taking a moment to look Kalpesh up and down. "How are you feeling?"

"Still a bit sore, sir," replied Kalpesh as he rolled his shoulder and felt a dull twinge in his ribs, "but the laudanum does the job of relieving the pain."

"You took quite a battering," replied the commissioner, "but I figure it's safe to say you gave as good as you got." Monro grinned. "Can I offer you a drink? Gin perhaps?"

"Thank you, sir, but I fear my senses are already somewhat blunted by the laudanum," refused Kalpesh.

"Of course," nodded Monro before heading over to the spirits cabinet in the corner of his office to pour himself a glass from the decanter. Once he had finished, the commissioner removed his jacket, draping it over the back of his chair, and perched on the corner of his desk to face Kalpesh. "You've done yourself proud, Khatri," he remarked finally.

"Thank you, sir." He smiled politely back at Monro.

"They'll be telling stories about you in Malleus long after I'm out of here," the commissioner insisted. "Five other officers incapacitated, and you managed to fight your way through over a dozen of those bastards to apprehend none other than Blavatsky herself!"

Kalpesh stayed silent, unsure how to respond.

"All I can say to you, Khatri, is that you are a damn fine officer!"

"That means a lot to me sir, hearing you say that."

"There were a lot of men on this force who were against us hiring an Indian to a detective position, and I must admit, I was among them. Not that I think any less of you or your people; I was an Indian civil servant for the better part of thirty years; I served as district judge in Bombay, as you well know. I was merely concerned with how others would react to your appointment, particularly the uniformed officers of Malleus unable to make detective.

"But, Macnaghten persuaded me, as he often does. He downright insisted upon your appointment. He told me, *'To hell with what everyone else says!'* He was right of course; now I find it hard to believe that I was once reluctant to see you made a plainclothes officer. And here we are—for the *second* time in two years, I am sat congratulating you on bringing to justice one of the greatest threats to the crown!"

"I was just doing my job, sir."

"Bollocks!" replied Monro sternly. "Cumming was just doing his job. The moment things turned sour, he got McIntyre out of there and waited for backup to arrive. Abberline was just doing his job, going back into that house to help his partner. But you Khatri—don't you pretend for a moment that any other officer would have done what you did. I doubt there are many officers that even *could* do what you did!

"Saying that you went above and beyond the line of duty is underselling it! You saved Abberline's life and pulled him out of that house. Then, seeing that Basil and Thomas had been obliterated, you had the balls to head back inside to help Cumming and McIntyre. You got the two of them out of there, but that still wasn't enough! You fought your way through that hellhole, taking out sorcerer after sorcerer until you reached Blavatsky! Do you even know how many of those bastards you took down?"

Kalpesh knew the answer but chose to stay quiet.

"Fourteen!" continued Monro. "Five dead, nine subdued nonlethally and now in custody, and that doesn't even include Blavatsky herself."

Silence.

"*You* did that. You did that *alone*!"

Kalpesh looked back at the commissioner, unsure what Monro expected him to say.

"One man... against fourteen!? Don't you see how extraordinary that was?"

"There was a lot of luck involved, sir," offered Kalpesh finally.

"I don't doubt it," returned Monro matter-of-factly. "But there must also have been a hell of a lot of skill involved! If I didn't have access to your Company service records, I'd have half a mind to investigate you for maleficium!"

"I can assure you, sir, that is not necessary."

"You don't need to tell me, Khatri. I know

you are as clean as they come," he assured. "We need more men in Malleus like you. You are a shining example. I cannot sing your praises high enough. That is why, effective immediately, I am promoting you to Detective Inspector."

"Thank you, sir!" beamed Kalpesh subduing his elation.

"Not only that, but I am recommending you for special commendation. Provided no one objects, you'll be awarded the Queen's Police Medal for your service to the force."

"I don't know what to say, sir..."

"Then don't say anything—Inspector. Just keep up the good work."

"I will, sir," he promised.

"Very good," nodded Monro.

"Is there anything else, sir?"

Monro chuckled softly. "No, I think that is quite enough for now. Are you near enough ready to return to work?"

"The time off wasn't my choice to begin with," reminded Kalpesh.

"No, but it came recommended," explained Monro.

"I am ready to come back, sir."

"I am sure you are eager to," agreed Monro. "But I am going to insist you take the rest of the week to recover. Things have gone quiet these last few days since the news broke that we took down the Blavatsky Lodge. It would seem the rest of the occult has gone to ground; they fear we are closing in on them."

"Very well, sir," replied Kalpesh disappointedly.

"Don't worry, Khatri. If we need you, we'll call you in."

Kalpesh nodded.

"You're dismissed," smiled Monro.

Kalpesh rose and exited the commissioner's office. He descended the stairs to the lobby, making for the exit back out to the Tower of London's inner ward, when a familiar voice called out to him from across the atrium.

"Khatri!"

Kalpesh spun to see Abberline striding towards him across the tiles.

"How are you?" he asked, looking at the fading bruising across the side of his face and the two stitches in his neck.

"On the mend," insisted Kalpesh.

"You are a tough son of a bitch, I'll give you that!"

"What about you?" asked the Indian. "How's the head?"

"Oh," stammered Abberline, his hand reaching to his crown, feeling where his pate had struck the ceiling in the Blavatsky Lodge. "Just a concussion; nothing too serious."

"Good," smiled Kalpesh.

"How have you been?"

Kalpesh sighed wearily. "I just want to be back. I'm going stir crazy at home; but Monro has insisted I stay off until the end of the week."

"I know the feeling," insisted Abberline.

"Well..." continued Kalpesh, "I'll see you in a couple of days. Take care of yourself, sir." He turned, making for the door again when Abberline spoke after him once more.

"Thank you... for pulling me out of there when you did!"

"Don't mention it," beamed the Indian detective.

"Listen," continued Abberline, "my wife... Emma... she's asked me to invite you to dinner at ours."

Kalpesh hesitated, taken back by the request.

"I understand if you'd rather not," continued Abberline quickly. "It's just, Emma wanted to thank—"

"Okay," smiled Kalpesh. "That sounds nice."

"You'll come?" remarked Abberline somewhat surprised.

"Yes."

Abberline nodded. "Um... does Friday work for you? At seven?"

"Yes," smiled Kalpesh. "I'll see you then."

XIII

Commercial Road, Whitechapel
6:55 p.m. September 7th, 1888

    Kalpesh clicked shut his pocket watch, sliding it back into his waistcoat. He looked up at the unassuming terrace house facing out onto Commercial Road bathed in dusky light. He anxiously ascended the steps. Removing his hat, he took a deep breath and quickly rapped his knuckles against the door, immediately taking a step backwards. He heard movement from inside and took a second to frantically straighten his tie as the latch clicked and the door swung open. Before him stood Abberline. The inspector was dressed far more casually than Kalpesh had ever seen him; his cuffs were rolled up to his elbows and his collar hung loose and open. His thinning hair lacked its usual slickness, whilst his wiry moustache and side whiskers appeared more bristling than ever.

"Kalpesh," the man greeted him warmly, using the Indian's given name for what might have been the first time ever.

"Sir," Kalpesh nodded respectfully.

"Please…" muttered Abberline, "Fred will do just fine for tonight."

"Fred," agreed the young detective apprehensively as he continued to loiter on the porch. "I'm not too early, am I?" he apologized, gesturing to the chief inspector's state of dress.

Abberline shot him a curious look, stepping back through the threshold to grant himself a look at the grandfather clock in the hallway beyond. "I think you're a couple minutes early, but you haven't caught us off guard…?" replied a befuddled Abberline.

"Fred?" called a female voice from inside. "Is that him?"

"Yes, my dear," replied Abberline, as from out of a doorway at the far end of the corridor emerged a slight woman in her early forties.

"Well—why is he still out on the doorstep!?" she demanded with an affable smile drawn between two plump cheeks. "You must be

Kalpesh," she said, running her hand up her husband's arm as she took her place beside him.

"A pleasure to meet you, Emma," returned Kalpesh, bowing his head.

"Please," she insisted, ushering her husband out of the doorway, "come inside."

Kalpesh obliged, taking a moment to wipe his feet on the doormat before stepping out off the street into the carpeted hallway. He paused, revolving to take in the wallpaper lining the corridor depicting a dozen species of birds perched on blossoming branches. He turned full circle to see Emma elbow Abberline gently, prompting him to speak.

"Erm... can I take your hat and coat?"

"Err... yes," Kalpesh nodded, equally as awkward, handing Abberline his hat as Emma aided him in removing his coat.

With both items hung on the hat stand, Emma gestured towards one of the front rooms. "Fred, why don't you sort the two of you some drinks whilst I finish up in the kitchen?"

"Yes dear," obeyed Abberline as he leant in for a kiss.

Kalpesh watched as the inspector's wife disappeared back into the rear of the property, vanishing behind the kitchen door.

"Come on, Khatri," beckoned Abberline, indicating he accompany him through the nearest door.

Kalpesh followed, stepping into the living

room behind Abberline. The golden light of the late summer evening was spilling through the sash windows across a Persian rug.

"Have a seat," instructed the chief inspector, gesturing to the settee and armchairs arranged around a coffee table in the centre of the room.

Kalpesh perched tentatively on the edge of a wingback and habitually checked his pocket watch. Seven o'clock dead.

"What's your poison?" questioned Abberline as he made his way over to a small cabinet tucked in the corner. "You're a gin man, if I remember correctly?"

"A gin would be lovely," replied Kalpesh, gently probing his ribs with his fingers. He had taken his last draught of laudanum in the morning and the effects had long since worn off.

"Gin it is then," smirked Abberline, producing two crystal glasses and filling them amply from a bottle of Beefeater. "Here," he said, offering Kalpesh one of the glasses before placing the bottle down on the coffee table and taking a seat on the settee opposite the Indian.

Abberline lounged back across the sofa and took a swig from his glass. Kalpesh took a more tentative sip, and the two men found themselves sat facing one another in awkward silence. A clock ticked above the mantlepiece, and the distant sounds of Emma moving things about in the kitchen made their way faintly through to the living room. A tram rattled down the road outside.

A few moments later, the muffled conversation of a pair of pedestrians walking the pavement of Commercial Road could be heard as they passed the window.

"So…" began Abberline after an uncomfortable length of time, "what have you been doing whilst you've been off?"

"Um, reading mostly," replied Kalpesh as he took another sip from his glass.

Abberline nodded. "Anything interesting…?"

"Just mostly work-related research," explained Kalpesh. "I refamiliarised myself with Tesla's theorem on the Aether and how electromagnetism and magic interfere with one another."

"Oh?" nodded Abberline disinterestedly, leaning forwards to swirl the gin in his glass.

Another lengthy silence fell.

"I also recently finished Jules Verne's Robur the Conqueror," added Kalpesh.

"Right," smiled Abberline sheepishly.

"Do you read much… Fred?"

"Err… no, not much these days," he replied. "Edmund Reid is an avid reader," he said after a short time.

"Inspector Reid of H Division?"

"Yes," returned the grizzled detective. "A good man, Edmund Reid; one I felt happy to leave in charge of H Division in my stead."

"Are you local to Whitechapel?" questioned

Kalpesh.

"Hmm," smirked Abberline. "No, I'm from Dorset originally—moved to London twenty-five years ago."

"What brought you here?"

"All manner of things," explained the detective. "I was a clockmaker... or at least apprenticed to one. But money was tight; my mother had a hard time bringing me and my siblings up by her lonesome. But the real reason is, I was drawn to the police... to detective work. I grew up reading Penny Dreadfuls and got the bright idea that I might solve a few crimes myself!"

"Then you were once *too* an avid reader?"

Abberline chuckled. "I suppose I was."

"Do you ever regret it?" questioned Kalpesh. "Leaving your home to come here and become a detective?"

"Never," replied the man definitively.

"What about you?" questioned Abberline. "What made you leave India? Why'd you leave the Company?"

"I grew up here, believe it or not," replied Kalpesh.

"Here in Whitechapel?"

Kalpesh nodded. "In an orphanage just north of here."

"You never knew your parents?"

"No."

"And so, when you were old enough, you signed up for Company service?"

"I wanted to see the world—or rather India."

"Understandable," remarked Abberline. "How did you end up back here, and a detective in Malleus for that matter?"

"I suppose I made friends with the right people," explained Kalpesh. "I was stationed in Bengal several years back. One day I was out on patrol when I came upon a British man being attacked by Indian land rioters; I intervened and defended him. I suppose I might have saved his life. That man was Melville Macnaghten."

"Something of a fateful encounter, some might say."

"Quite so," agreed Kalpesh. "Melville and I became good friends in the years that followed, as did he and James Monro who was District Judge of the Bombay Presidency at the time. When Monro resigned from civil service in India, he returned to England and became the Met's first Assistant Commissioner. A couple years later, Melville arrived back in London after years of managing his father's tea plantation on the subcontinent, and Monro offered him the position of Assistant Chief Constable in the Met."

"But Warren didn't exactly like Macnaghten as I hear it?" remarked Abberline.

"That's one way to put it," remarked Kalpesh sardonically. "The Commissioner didn't much like Monro either. A lot of people are glad he's finally been pushed out."

"Namely Monro and Macnaghten," observed Abberline.

"I suppose," agreed Kalpesh, "but it's not hard to see why."

Abberline shrugged, bowing out of passing comment on either man.

"After Melville's appointment to Assistant Chief Constable was vetoed by Warren, Monro resigned as Assistant Commissioner and transferred to become director of Special Branch, taking Melville with him."

"And where do you come into all of this?" questioned Abberline. "Why'd you leave the East India Company?"

"They were gearing up for another war with Burma. I'd had enough after Afghanistan; I'd lost too many friends and did not want to go through it all again. I came back to London and sought out Melville. He got me into the Met as a uniformed officer; I studied hard and passed the tests needed to become a Special Branch detective, and—with a great deal of pull from Melville, I was able to transfer to Malleus at the start of last year."

"Right in time to foil the Jubilee plot as I hear it...?" returned Abberline.

"Well, that's another story altogether," shrugged Kalpesh with a smirk.

"You are full of surprises, Khatri, I'll give you that," grinned Abberline. "What's your secret?"

"You first," riposted Kalpesh.

"What do you mean?"

"The way I hear it, you've left an impression wherever you've worked. There's not a man on the force, in Malleus, CID, or any other department that has worked with you that doesn't sing your praises!"

Abberline leant back and chuckled, taking another long swig of his gin before plonking the glass down on the coffee table. "The secret, my boy, is good old-fashioned hard graft!" Abberline refilled his glass and topped up his guest's. "But I'm willing to guess that you've figured that out for yourself!?"

Kalpesh nodded.

"Your turn," insisted Abberline, redirecting the question back to his partner.

"I've immersed myself in the arcane," he explained. "I figured that the best way to catch a sorcerer was to think like one; in order to be able to do just that, you need to understand witchcraft. So far, that philosophy has served me well."

The door to the living room creaked open and in popped Abberline's wife Emma. "Supper is ready," she beamed cheerily.

"Come on Khatri," insisted Abberline as he rose to his feet, following his wife as she led the two of them to the dining room on the opposite side of the corridor.

The evening light was beginning to wane. Emma flicked the light switch as they entered the dining room and several bulbs within wall mounted sconces hummed softly to light. Kalpesh took a seat aside Abberline who placed himself at the head of the short dining table as his wife vanished back towards the kitchen. The two men sat in silence and waited for Emma, who soon re-emerged carrying a steaming pie dish which she placed in the centre of the table, before disappearing once again to return seconds later with several plates of vegetables.

"Fred wasn't sure if you were Muslim or Hindu, so I played it safe and went for lamb in the pie," explained Emma as she took a seat at the opposite end of the table to Abberline.

"I suppose I'm a Hindu," explained Kalpesh, "though I wouldn't exactly describe myself as a practicing one. But thank you regardless."

"Oh," replied Emma, not quite sure how to react. "Well, would you like to say grace with us?"

Kalpesh quickly looked to Abberline who offered him a subtle shake of his head that relieved him of any sense of obligation. "I wouldn't know what to say, Emma," he offered diplomatically.

"It's nothing too special, just a few words to tell God that we are thankful," she smiled.

"Emma..." interrupted Abberline from across the table.

She nodded and bowed her head, holding her hands together in her lap.

Abberline likewise lowered his head, cupping his hands atop the table, but unlike his wife, he neglected to shut his eyes as he allowed

Emma to speak the words.

"For what we are about to receive, may the lord make us truly thankful, Amen."

Before Emma had fully opened her eyes, Abberline had risen from his seat and began plating up the pie for his wife and guest.

"So tell me, Kalpesh, are you married?" asked Emma.

"Oh… err… no, not me," replied the Indian as Abberline set down the lamb pie in front of him with ample servings of roasted potatoes and garden peas.

"No?" she questioned in surprise. "I thought most Indians had arranged marriages?"

"Emma!" cut in Abberline for a second time.

"I'm just asking, Fred," she returned sharply. "I'm not trying to be impolite, Kalpesh, I am just ignorant to these things."

"No, it's no problem at all," insisted Kalpesh as he was passed the gravy boat by Abberline. "Arranged marriages are typically organised by one's family—whereas I grew up in an orphanage, you see."

"Oh, I'm so sorry, I didn't realise!"

"No, it is quite alright, really," insisted Kalpesh.

"Even still," continued Emma, "you are a very handsome young man—and a successful one at that; Fred told me that you've been promoted to Inspector! How is it you have not wooed a lady of your own choosing?"

"I err…" stammered Kalpesh uncomfortably. "I… I suppose I haven't really had time—what with work."

"Emma, can't you see you are making the poor lad squirm?

"I'm just trying to get to know our guest," she insisted. "Perhaps *we* could find you someone! Are you looking for an Indian girl, or would you prefer an Englishwoman?"

"Emma!" repeated an irked Abberline.

"I'm sorry," apologised Emma. "It's just… I feel like I am indebted to you… after you pulled my Fred out of that building. You saved his life, and I would just like some way to repay you."

"Please, Emma," began Kalpesh, "this dinner is more than enough!"

"I'm sure Kalpesh does not need our help in finding a wife, my dear."

"Okay," she agreed defeatedly.

Silence fell as they began to eat.

"This is delicious," said Kalpesh after finishing his first mouthful.

"Mm!" nodded Abberline in agreement with his mouth still full. "You have outdone yourself again, my love."

"It's my grandmother's recipe," she explained, masking her pride.

Another silence descended before Kalpesh next spoke. "You have a lovely home."

"Thank you," beamed Emma. "We've been here quite a few years now—since Fred was head of

H Division. Where is it you live?"

"Oh… it's not quite like this," he explained. "I just rent a small apartment."

"Whereabouts?" she pressed.

"Opposite the Jewish graveyard on Brady Street."

"Brady Street?"

"North Street, my dear," explained Abberline.

"Oh, yes," she nodded, realising now where Kalpesh meant. "I'm not sure why they felt the need to rename it."

"Isn't that just around the corner from where we were the other night?" questioned Abberline.

"I thought you were in Notting Hill the other night?"

"Before that, my dear," explained Abberline, "back where there was the…"

"Yes," confirmed Kalpesh. "Right around the corner."

"Where there was the what, Fred?"

"The murder, my dear," mumbled Abberline.

"Oh," replied Emma, clearly regretting having asked.

"Let's not talk about work," insisted Abberline as he shovelled another forkful of pie into his mouth.

"That's a good idea," agreed Emma. "So, Kalpesh," she continued, "if you have no wife, nor a family, you must have friends?"

"Well…" began Kalpesh taking a moment to think whether the neighbours in his building he occasionally shared idle chitchat with could be considered his friends. "I had a few friends back in the Company…" he began.

"He's an old chum of Macnaghten," put in Abberline. "The new Assistant Chief Constable at Hammer…" he elaborated for the sake of his wife.

"Oh, that's nice," remarked Emma. "Do you two spend much time together outside of work?"

"Erm… sometimes," lied Kalpesh with a weak smile. "Less so now."

"Well, Fred spends a good deal of time in the pub these days," teased his wife. "I am sure he'd be happy to take you along with him every now and then."

Abberline looked from his wife to Kalpesh as he continued to silently chew a mouthful of food.

"Isn't that right, Fred?" Emma pressed.

"Yes dear," smiled Abberline when he had finally swallowed.

"I wouldn't want to intrude," insisted Kalpesh.

"No, please!" insisted Abberline's wife. "He'd be glad for the company—wouldn't you Fred?"

"Yes dear," repeated the inspector.

A long silence elapsed as the three of them continued with their meal.

"How does tomorrow night sound?"

questioned Abberline.

"Tomorrow night?" repeated Kalpesh.

"The Ten Bells?" added Abberline with a wry smile.

"The Ten Bells?" parroted the Indian detective dumbfoundedly.

"Do you know it?"

Kalpesh suddenly clocked that Abberline was referring to a pub. "Near Spitalfields Market?"

"That's the one."

Kalpesh hesitated.

"Well then?" pressed Abberline. "Do you fancy a pint or not?"

"Err... yes!" stammered Kalpesh.

"Good. I'll meet you there after I'm done at Anvil."

"Great," remarked Kalpesh as he saw Emma smiling to herself as she cleaned her plate. "Tomorrow night," he repeated to himself.

The three of them continued to make small talk as they finished up with dinner, after which, Emma cleared the table and began washing up in the kitchen. As pots, pans, plates, and cutlery clattered and sloshed in a basin behind the kitchen door, Kalpesh and Abberline retired once more to the front room. Abberline poured them both another liberal serving of gin without bothering to ask Kalpesh if he actually wanted one, and the two took up their previous positions across the coffee table from one another, albeit in a more relaxed manner than prior to dinner. Finally, conversation began to fluidly ebb between the two men as they briefly discussed work, then politics, before easing into a wider range of more trivial topics. Emma rejoined them some time later, placing herself beside her husband, until the hour of eleven drew near and Kalpesh began to feel he had outstayed his welcome.

"We'll have to have you around again soon," insisted Emma as she lifted the young detective's coat for him to slip his arms into the sleeves. "Isn't that right, Fred?"

"Yes, dear," agreed Abberline passively again as he had done so many times already that evening before returning Kalpesh his hat.

"Thank you both for having me," beamed Kalpesh sincerely. "I really enjoyed myself."

"Our pleasure," smiled Emma as she opened the door for him.

"I'll see you tomorrow," said Abberline as Kalpesh exited out onto the doorstep.

"Tomorrow," agreed Kalpesh as a cool breeze ruffled his collar.

"Good night, Kalpesh," grinned Emma, bidding him farewell.

"Good night," the Indian detective offered in return before descending the steps to the pavement.

The door clicked shut behind him and Kalpesh set off down the path; his head spinning gently from the gin, he began the short walk back to Brady Street in the quiet lamplit alleys of

Whitechapel.

XIV

Brady Street, Whitechapel
6:32 a.m. September 8th, 1888

The floorboards beneath Kalpesh's bed shuddered as a fist pounded forcefully against the door. He sat upright, snapped out of sleep by the banging. His head was tingling hazily, the beginnings of a headache setting in. He rubbed his eyes and reached for the pewter mug set atop his bedside table and gulped down several mouthfuls of stale water. Light was streaming through the cracks in the shutters, casting a pale glow around the dingy, cramped bedroom. His hand deposited the mug back atop the nightstand and his fingers slid over the rough wood until they curled around his pocket watch. Habitually winding it, Kalpesh flicked it open and observed the hour: just gone six-thirty. Another quintet of thuds thumped against the door.

Groaning as he pulled himself out from beneath his tattered blanket, Kalpesh heaved on a set of trousers and threw a shirt over his torso, half buttoning it as he made his way barefoot towards the knocking. A third round of bangs shook the door as the Indian fumbled at the bolt and chain before finally he opened the door to the top floor landing.

"Khatri," Abberline greeted him. His dress, and the fact that he had reverted to using Kalpesh's surname, inferred that this was not a social visit.

"Fred?" Kalpesh murmured in confusion as he rubbed his eyes again.

Abberline looked about the dusty corridor at the cracked and damp-stained plaster, then to the peeling paint of Kalpesh's door frame; peering past his partner, he turned his attention inside the claustrophobic confines of the detective's neglected apartment.

"How can I help you?" asked the Indian, leaning further across the entranceway in a poor attempt to screen the apartment from Abberline's view.

"Get dressed," instructed his superior.

"There's been another one."

Kalpesh nodded. Stepping out of the doorway, he gestured for the Chief Inspector to enter. "Make yourself at home," he insisted. "I'll be two minutes."

Abberline moved inside, shutting the door behind him as Kalpesh made for his bedroom. Removing his shirt, he cast it on the floor and poured water from a ewer into a basin set on a dresser in the corner of the tiny room. He cupped his hands and wet his face before wringing a flannel in the cool water and using it to scrub the sweat and grime of the previous day from his face and torso.

"You are a slob, Khatri!" called out Abberline's voice from the kitchen as the detective no doubt eyed the unwashed pans and crockery with scrutiny.

Kalpesh ignored him as he wet his toothbrush in his mug and dabbed it inside his pot of toothpaste. As he scrubbed his teeth, the taste of gin was slowly replaced with cherry. He spat and rinsed his mouth. He looked to his razor set beside the basin and ran his palm over the day-old stubble sprouting from his chin; shaving could wait.

Oiling his hair, the detective fished out a fresh shirt from the wardrobe stood crookedly in the corner. He wrapped a tie around his neck, folded down the collar, lifted his elasticated braces over his shoulders, threw on his waistcoat, pocketed his watch, slipped on a pair of aging socks, laced his shoes, and emerged from the bedroom only a couple moments later. Abberline had made his way into the dingy room that passed for a lounge. A single wooden chair was nestled in the corner, a sheet of folded paper shoved under one of the legs to prevent it rocking, whilst the remaining floorspace of the small room was piled with stacks of books in various states of disorganisation.

Abberline stood turning over a copy of Mary Shelley's *Frankenstein; or, The Modern Prometheus* in his hand as he looked around at the unsorted collection of books that formed Kalpesh's library. "Have you read all of these?" he questioned.

"Most of them," nodded Kalpesh as he retrieved his jacket and hat hung from a hook mounted on the wall. "You can borrow that if you'd like," he added, indicating to the copy of Frankenstein in his partner's hand.

"Um... thanks," replied Abberline, looking more closely now at the book he had picked up before politely tucking it into his coat's side pocket.

"I'm ready," announced Kalpesh.

Abberline nodded, taking another long moment to study the squalid conditions in which Kalpesh lived. "We need to find you a nicer apartment, Khatri," insisted the detective.

"I can't really afford much better," replied Kalpesh.

"You have just been promoted, haven't

you?"

Kalpesh nodded.

"I know a detective sergeant isn't on much these days, but I'd have thought it would do you better than this!"

"I imagine it could," agreed Kalpesh.

Abberline's eyes narrowed. "Then what the bloody hell are you spending all your wages on Khatri!?" he demanded.

Kalpesh's body language betrayed him as his eyes flitted momentarily to Abberline's surroundings.

Abberline once more glanced about at the various waist-high stacks of literature ranging from prose to poetry, novels to non-fiction, newspaper clippings, serials, textbooks, and scientific papers all intermingled in disordered heaps. "Good god, Khatri... I think you've got a problem!"

"It's not that bad," insisted Kalpesh.

"Judging from the rest of this place, I'd say it probably is!" scalded Abberline. "There's more to life than reading!"

"I know that," agreed Kalpesh. "Most of it is research for cases."

Abberline exhaled loudly. "Alright," he said more sympathetically. "But no more books until we get you moved into a nicer place!"

Kalpesh nodded in reluctant agreement.

"Maybe somewhere that doesn't overlook a graveyard," he added as he peered out through the soot coated windowpanes to the Jewish cemetery hidden through a row of tactically planted trees.

Abberline checked his own pocket watch, reminding himself that they were in a hurry. "Come on," he urged, "there's a carriage waiting outside."

"Where are we heading?" questioned Kalpesh as he opened the door and stepped out onto the landing with Abberline.

"Hanbury Street."

"We are taking a carriage to Hanbury Street?" questioned Kalpesh as he twisted his key in the lock before testing the handle to double check his apartment was secure. "It's only a fifteen-minute walk from here?"

"And it is only a five-minute carriage ride," returned Abberline as they descended several flights of unnervingly steep stairs. "We are against time."

"Why so?" questioned Kalpesh.

"I think you'll understand why the moment we arrive."

"Okay," returned the Indian in submission as they reached the ground floor, exiting through the front door onto Brady Street where a black Hackney Carriage was awaiting them.

Abberline opened the cab door for Kalpesh to climb inside. "Twenty-nine Hanbury Street. And be quick about it!" he instructed the driver, before clambering in and seating himself opposite his partner.

The carriage jostled into motion, heading south down the road, veering right onto Buck's Row after little more than a hundred yards. Kalpesh peered out of the window as they passed the gates to the stableyard were only a week ago the body of Polly Nichols had been discovered. They soon left the first murder scene behind, turning right onto Baker's Row before cutting northwest directly onto Hanbury Street.

"Looks like we might be having that pint early," remarked Abberline as they neared their destination.

"What makes you say that?"

"The Ten Bells is just around the corner from the scene of the crime."

"That's convenient," chuckled Kalpesh as the cab began to decelerate.

Kalpesh's ears pricked up over the rattling of the carriage wheels across the cobbles to the sound of unrest. Cries and shouts of a not-too-distant throng became audible as the carriage pulled up, and as Kalpesh and Abberline stepped out onto the street, they sighted the mob forming before a line of uniformed policemen cordoning off the entrance to a terraced house.

Abberline paid the driver and the horses nickered as it moved off, turning south down Brick Lane to avoid the unruly mob hurling abuse at the police before them.

"Step aside!" instructed Abberline forcefully as he and Kalpesh began to fight their way through the thickening hoard.

Kalpesh took note as several members of the crowd seemingly recognized Abberline and did as commanded, parting to allow the reputable detective through until they reached the line of uniformed officer struggling to restrain some of the more agitated Whitechapel citizens at the front of the crowd. Inspector Abberline pushed his way through the angry frontline of the rabble, dragging Kalpesh with him by the sleeve of his coat.

"Stay back—!" began a uniformed constable before immediately recognizing the man emerging from the crowd as the ex-local Chief Detective for H Division. "Inspector, sir!" the man greeted him almost standing to attention.

"PC Mizen," Abberline returned to him.

"The crowds grow restless, sir," explained the constable. "They fear the man that has done this! They say we are failing them. People fear to walk the streets!"

"Keep them out of here, Jonas," instructed Abberline cogently.

"We're trying, sir," insisted Mizen.

Whilst the two men spoke, Kalpesh's gaze fell beyond the periphery of the crowd gathering outside number twenty-nine, to the door of the adjacent house; a queue seemed to be taking shape, extending from the entranceway out into the street. At the front of the line a couple of shady characters served as doormen, and, as the young detective watched coin exchange hands, he realised a price of admission was being paid. One by one, the queue of onlookers paid their entrance fee and slipped inside, no doubt thereafter climbing the stairs to the rooms with overlooking views of the rear yard of number twenty-nine.

"I presume the body is out in the open?" asked Kalpesh, turning to the constable. "Out the rear?"

"Err... yes," returned Mizen.

Abberline shot Kalpesh a quizzical look, intrigued as to what had led him to such an insight.

Kalpesh met his partner's gaze before silently indicating in the direction of the queue extending out into the street from the doorway of number thirty-one. Abberline swiftly arrived at the same conclusion about the transactions being made before he spun around and glanced above the heads of the throng to the door of number twenty-seven to see that a second queue was beginning to take shape, the owners of the similarly overlooking rooms having taken inspiration from their entrepreneurial neighbours two doors over.

Abberline cursed under his breath. "What is this!?" he demanded of Mizen. "A bloody circus?"

"I... err...!?" stammered the lowly constable as he too realised what was taking place in the adjacent properties.

"White!" the disgruntled Chief Inspector

called out to the uniformed sergeant stood in the doorway ahead.

Hearing his name called, the officer trudged over to Mizen, Abberline, and Kalpesh. "Sir!?" he greeted Abberline upon recognizing the old head of H Division CID.

"Do you mind explaining to me, Sergeant, why it is that you boys are letting next door charge spectators for a better view of the murder scene?"

"Sir? I wasn't aware…" he trailed off as he took note of the ever-lengthening lines to the adjacent properties.

"I suggest you send some of your boys to deal with the situation," growled Abberline. "And best get it done before the superintendent catches wind of this!"

The colour drained from White's face. "Yes, sir," he agreed submissively, "right away! Mizen, Collins, Lamb!" he barked, grabbing the attention of his three nearest constables. "Disperse those bloody queues. And see no one else tries to sell a view of the back!"

"Come on," insisted Abberline as he turned to his partner. "Let's get back there and get a look for ourselves."

Together, Abberline and Kalpesh approached the entranceway to number twenty-nine and stepped through into the dim hallway of the shared property. Several more constables were keeping guard inside, each recognising Abberline before they asked for any form of identification.

Passing the narrow staircase that led to the upper floors of the terraced house, the two Malleus detectives made straight for the open backdoor and emerged out to the rear yard of the building.

Various detectives were gathered throughout the yard, Inspector Edmund Reid being amongst them; he and several others were stooped over a body sprawled up against the featheredge fence that bordered next door, only a couple yards from the backdoor.

"Chief Inspector Abberline, Detective Sergeant Khatri!" Edmund Reid greeted them nervously the moment they emerged from the building. "Thank heavens you have come."

"Reid," Abberline greeted his H Division successor. "And it is Detective Inspector Khatri now," he added gesturing to Kalpesh. "The lad has gone and got himself promoted!"

"My compliments, Detective Inspector," Reid nodded the Indian's way.

"Thank you," replied Kalpesh politely, yet his attention was almost entirely on the cadaver now.

"What have we got?" questioned Abberline, all too eager to skip the pleasantries.

"Where to begin?" mused Reid as he stepped aside to display the body of the woman to the two Special Branch detectives, and more importantly, reveal the blood smeared across the boards of the fence.

"It's definitely our man," muttered

Abberline as he and Kalpesh gawked at another pentacle painted over the wood.

"She's been identified as Annie Chapman," declared Reid. "Forty-seven, and for the past summer at least, a resident of Crossingham's Lodging House just over on Dorset Street."

"She a whore?" asked Abberline somewhat indelicately, eager to hasten through the trivial details.

"Yes..." replied Reid taken back by the bluntness of the question. "Much like Mary Ann Nichols, she appears to have been a *lady of the night,* though it would seem it was a trade she had only taken to recently."

"Oh?" questioned Abberline, raising an eyebrow.

"She was separated from her husband, but

up until a year and a half ago, she was receiving payments from the man."

"What changed?"

"It appears he drunk himself into an early grave," returned Reid sombrely.

"And so, with her regular payments up, she took to the streets to earn her keep?"

"Apparently so," confirmed Reid.

"Even still, it would seem our man is out targeting streetwalkers."

Reid, Kalpesh, and the other present detectives all nodded silently in concurrence.

"What of the injuries? Are they like before? Is the cause of death the same?"

"Similar, indeed," confirmed Reid, gesturing for the man next to him to take the lead.

"Dr Bagster Phillips," Abberline greeted the H Division's Police Surgeon. "What do you have to say?"

"There are two parallel cuts on the left side of the throat, separated by roughly half an inch, that stretch right around the neck," began the overweight surgeon as he gestured to the lacerations with his pen as he examined a set of records he had scrawled in a notebook. "These are most likely the cause of death, though it would appear the victim may well have been subdued by strangulation, evident by the swelling to the face and the bruising around the collar."

"Do we have a time of death?" asked Abberline.

"My estimates are at between four a.m. and four-thirty."

"We have some conflicting information, however," explained Reid. "We've already had a couple of witnesses come forward who claim to have seen the victim after such time, one believing to have seen her as late as half-five, only twenty minutes before the body was found."

"How did you arrive at that estimate?" scrutinised Kalpesh, turning back to Bagster Phillips.

"A simple calculation based on body temperature," explained the police surgeon.

"I trust you took a rectal reading?" questioned Kalpesh.

"That was hardly necessary," returned the doctor dismissively.

"Then how is it you've narrowed down such a timeframe?"

"What are you insinuating?" demanded Bagster Phillips.

"Determining time of death from body temperature is hardly an exact science!" scalded Kalpesh. "And this woman has been eviscerated! With the amount of blood she has lost, and the way she has been carved open—you can hardly expect the temperature of her skin to give you an accurate estimate as to her time of death!?"

"Well...I..." stammered the surgeon, clearly having been unprepared for such a scathing assault of his conclusion. "I suppose it is possible...

given the blood loss, that the time of death might have been later than my initial estimate…" he backpedalled.

"Is there then good reason to assume that our witnesses' accounts of seeing the victim past the hour of five should be believed?" questioned Reid.

"It is feasible," agreed Bagster Phillips reluctantly.

Abberline and Reid looked to one another before both nodding in unison at Kalpesh.

"Very good, Doctor," derided Abberline. "It is good to have everyone in agreement."

"And what of the mutilations?" questioned Kalpesh, as he looked to the bloody mess that had once been the poor woman's waist.

"The abdomen has been entirely laid open," he explained, raising a handkerchief to his nose as he stooped closer to the splayed abdominal cavity from which wafted the smell of excrement. "The intestines have been severed from their mesenteric attachments and laid across the shoulder."

Kalpesh grimaced as the doctor indicated to the entrails drooped across the body.

"Disembowelled," concluded Abberline, "just like before."

"Only, in this case, the mutilations go much further," explained Reid. "Please, George, continue."

Dr Bagster Phillips rose from his squat,

lowering the handkerchief from his mouth and nose. "The uterus, along with all of its appendages, the posterior two thirds of the bladder, and the majority of the vagina have all been removed."

"Removed!?" questioned Abberline, swivelling his head around the small yard. "Well, where the bloody hell are they!?"

"We haven't yet found them," replied Reid gravely.

"You mean our man took them with him when he left?"

"No," refuted Kalpesh, his attention now affixed intently on the pentacle smeared across the fence in the victim's blood. "They weren't taken from here," he explained. "They were used as an offering."

"An offering?" repeated Abberline and Reid in unison as they eyed the arcane markings painted across the featheredge boards before lowering their gaze to the hollowed-out pelvis of the body laid before them.

"You mean to say they were consumed?" questioned Reid in despair.

"In a sense, yes," returned Kalpesh, fishing his journal from his breast pocket, "by the ritual performed here." He leafed through the black leather notebook, swiftly landing on the page he wanted. He looked at the painted lines of blood forming an outer and inner circle, between which was scribed a verse in Enochian. He read aloud the translation from his notes. "He shall give His

Angels charge over thee, to keep thee in all thy ways. They shall bear thee up in their hands."

"What is that?" asked Abberline.

"Psalms ninety-one: eleven," answered Reid. "But what does it mean?"

Kalpesh studied the remainder of the pentacle. At the heart of the seal sat more Enochian characters, surrounded by two more circles encased within a square, surrounded by further angelic letterings.

"Another seal from the Key of Solomon?" questioned Abberline.

"Yes," confirmed Kalpesh. "The Fifth Pentacle of the Sun."

"What does it do?" questioned Abberline nervously.

"It invokes spirits that can transport a person from one place to another in an instant," replied Kalpesh, studying his notes.

"What do you mean exactly?"

Kalpesh shut his journal and glanced about the yard. It was enclosed on all sides. To the east and west, the yard was fenced, each six-foot-high stretch of boarding leading only to an adjacent backyard. The rear of the plot was bordered by the next row of terraced houses. The only way in and out, save clambering over multiple fences, was through the single hallway of number twenty-nine's downstairs.

"There are no witnesses that claim to see a man leaving the scene?" pressed Kalpesh, turning to Reid.

"None that have come forward," replied the Inspector.

"If the murder happened later than five, then it must have occurred in broad daylight," announced Kalpesh.

"And that door is the only way in and out of this yard," concluded Abberline, following Kalpesh's line of reasoning. "But no one saw a man come and go?"

"Sir," began Kalpesh soberly, "I may be wrong, but I believe our killer might have just gained the ability to teleport."

"Well, shit!" swore Abberline.

XV

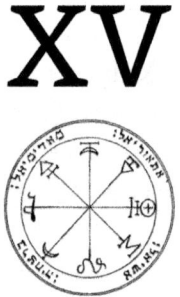

29 Hanbury Street, Spitalfields
7:11 a.m. September 8th, 1888

Flash powder ignited in a blinding glare, flooding the backyard and momentarily bathing the body of Annie Chapman in a white light. Repositioning his camera and readying a second flash, the police photographer continued to record every detail of the murder scene on film. The ruckus of the mob was growing louder by the minute; several detectives in the yard eyed one another nervously as they feared the line of uniformed officers holding the horde at bay might soon be overrun and that number twenty-nine could be stormed by rioters.

"Well, it would seem the first ritual this bastard performed has taken effect," cursed Abberline as he paced the plot, waiting for the photographer to finish up so that they could remove the body and begin cleaning down the crime scene. "Wrath... chaos... discord..." he mused, speaking aloud for both the benefit of himself and his partner.

"Whitechapel's fear of this killer is understandable, and they have long harboured a distrust and resentment for the police," put in Kalpesh, "But you are right; this response... this level of dissonance is excessive. The ritual killing of Polly Nichols has stoked upheaval within the people living here."

"And now you reckon our man can teleport —move from one place to another in an instant?" despaired the chief inspector.

"The ritual for the Fifth Pentacle of the Sun is supposed to grant such powers," confirmed Kalpesh sombrely.

"Sweet Jesus," breathed Abberline in frustration. "As if we weren't having enough trouble hunting down this sadistic bedlamite! Now you are telling me that he can merely appear anywhere at any time and disappear before anyone catches sight of him?"

"Such a power hasn't been documented in any great detail," explained Kalpesh, "...that is to say, at least not in any literature I have studied on the Key of Solomon. The sacrificial cost of attaining such abilities is high, as is perhaps evident from the missing pieces of Chapman's anatomy, and the brutality of her killing," continued the Indian as he turned through his pages of notes, looking for any key insight. "As such, this combined with the esoteric expertise required to perform the ritual in the first place —there are few recordings of any adepts ever attaining such dark powers."

"Speak frankly, Khatri! What are you telling me? That we know the square root of fuck all about this spell!?"

"Not in relation to the exact details or nature of the ability, no," conceded Kalpesh. "But it would be safe to assume the killer can move across locations without having to travel the distance in between."

"So, he could be anywhere by now? On the other side of the Atlantic, India, Australia?"

"I doubt it," replied Kalpesh. "As with all magic, there are limitations, and I would imagine the limiting factors for this ability are in distance and frequency of use. It is more likely that someone granted the ability the Fifth Pentacle of the Sun endows would probably be able to travel a few dozen yards in a single bound, maybe as far as a few furlongs... But as I understand it, anything more than a mile would require a separate ritual in its own right. There is good reason why the preparations for teleportation circles are so intricate and lengthy. They require hours to create from scratch, and the summoned portal only remains stable for a few seconds before it collapses; after which, preparations have to be begun anew for another portal to open."

"So, this man would be able to teleport as and when he desires..." began Abberline, "but only short distances?"

"I am postulating," admitted the detective. "But, yes; in essence, that is what I am suggesting."

Abberline moved back over towards the body as the photographer began to pack away his camera and equipment. He gazed down at the disembowelled corpse the killer had gruesomely exenterated, his eyes slowly rising to the bloody seal. "What is the purpose of all of this, Khatri?" demanded the chief inspector. "What is his plan?"

"It is part of a wider ritual," declared Kalpesh. "Of that I am almost certain."

"To achieve what?"

"I fear it is still too early to say."

"Come on Khatri! You have to do better than that!"

"Sir, I can only begin to speculate..."

"Then speculate!" snapped Abberline. "This animal has struck twice in little more than a week! If you are right—if this is part of something bigger, then we can be sure that come next weekend we'll have another murder on our hands!"

"Sir, you are asking me to take a shot in the

dark—"

"That's what detective work is half the time, Khatri. This killer has left us nothing with which to find out who he is or what he is after; if we want to catch him then we'll need to get inside his head! So, think! What does your gut say? Tell me Khatri, what is he after? What is this all about?"

Kalpesh closed his notebook and slid it back inside his breast pocket. He took up position alongside his partner and likewise studied the body and sigil another time. He stayed quiet, pondering deeply, searching the recesses of his mind for any insight that might aid them in preventing another horrific ritual execution in the streets of Whitechapel.

"It's about power," he announced finally.

"Power?"

"He is building towards something... preparing!"

"Preparing for what?" questioned Abberline.

"Look at the extent of the mutilations; there is an escalation here over the last killing. Polly Nichols was disembowelled—but see the extent to which Chapman's intestines have been drawn from her abdomen. Furthermore, there was no removal of any organs with the last murder. The desecration has intensified; and in doing so he has imbued himself with new power. These first two steps in the greater ritual not only serve as part of the rite, but act as preparation for the next steps.

Poly Nichol's murder set the scene: a borough of the city consumed with unrest, on the brink of upheaval. Now, our killer prepares, taking a first step to empower himself for the latter stages of the ritual. He is readying for what is to come—for what he must face!"

"What must he face?"

Kalpesh wracked his brain for any hint as to what the ultimate goal of the rite could be, until suddenly he understood; he had been staring at it all along! The Enochian symbols were the key. These rituals were the marrying of the Key of Solomon into Enochian magic. Realisation suddenly hit Kalpesh.

"My word..." he breathed.

"What is it?" demanded Abberline.

"I know what he plans to do."

"What!?"

"He intends to summon Choronzon!"

"Choronzon?"

"The Dweller in the Abyss," uttered the Indian gravely.

"Why is it, Khatri, that I do not like the sound of that?" grumbled Abberline, placing his hands on his hips.

"Perhaps because, it is as terrible as it sounds," replied the inspector.

"Start from the top," insisted Abberline. "What do I need to know?"

"The Enochian is the key," began Kalpesh, gesturing to the Fifth Pentacle of the Sun before them. "Enochian magic, and along with it, the Enochian script, were first chronicled by the infamous occultists, John Dee and Edward Kelley back in the sixteenth century. Enochian magic is a type of ceremonial magic—elaborate rituals, intricate pentacles, complicated ceremonies and the like. These sorts of rituals are far more intricate than cantrips and elemental manipulations; they are beyond the realms of typical warlocks or witches and are usually only performed by adepts within occult societies. Enochian magic is performed utilising the Enochian script and is focussed towards evocation and control over spiritual entities."

"Angels?" surmised Abberline.

"Not necessarily," returned Kalpesh. "The Enochian Magic system along with its script were supposedly divined by Kelley through scrying, whilst Dee took record of his partner's visions. The reason for the naming of the system is that, supposedly the angelic entity that communicated the esoteric knowledge to Kelley was none other than Enoch himself."

"Remember, Khatri, I'm not as well-read as you! Who the bloody hell is Enoch?"

Kalpesh sighed, realising he'd need to explain more than he'd anticipated to his partner. "Enoch was the great grandfather of Noah."

"As in—Noah's ark Noah?"

"Yes," confirmed Kalpesh. "Enoch was a favoured prophet, one who supposedly ascended to heaven and there was appointed as chief of the Archangels, tasked with guarding over all celestial treasures. Some sources say he is synonymous with Metatron, the scribe of God."

"Fascinating stuff, Khatri," muttered Abberline sardonically, "but can we skip the Sunday school lesson and cut to the point?"

"Enoch is the author of an extensive apocalyptic religious text excluded from both Christian and Jewish cannon known as the Book of Enoch."

"Never heard of it," remarked the chief inspector.

"That's not unsurprising," replied Kalpesh. "It fell into obscurity after the formation of the Church, despite it being referenced repeatedly in both the New Testament and the Hebrew Bible. However, little more than a century ago, several copies of the manuscript were rediscovered in Ethiopia and brought back to Europe. The text is broken in to five major sections, the first being the Book of Watchers; it chronicles the events leading up to the great flood."

Abberline began to eye Kalpesh again, urging him to hurry to the information that related to the case.

"To sum it up, the book tells of the Fall of the Watchers, the group of angels that rebelled against God and descended to Earth to mate with human women, in the process fathering the Nephilim."

"Nephilim?" questioned Abberline.

"Giants," elaborated Kalpesh.

"Giants?"

"With all due respect, sir, have you ever read the Bible?"

"Well..." stammered Abberline, "not cover to cover..."

"I'll give you the footnotes then. What you need to know, is that, as with the majority of texts throughout Christianity, Judaism, and every other religion for that matter, there are multiple interpretations. Some infer that the Watchers are the fallen angels that were cast out of heaven for their rebellion and imprisoned in hell, where they were twisted and transformed into what we perceive to be demons; others believe that their offspring, the Nephilim, survived in spiritual form when the great flood purged them from the Earth, and that their souls are what became demons. What I am getting at here, sir, is—"

"I understand," interrupted Abberline, raising a hand to cut his partner off from elaborating further. "What you are saying is... these spirits being summoned and invoked by our man, could just as well be demons as angels, and that this Enochian, it is not as divine as one might first assume."

"Precisely," nodded Kalpesh. "The Book of Enoch claims that the fallen angels, before the time of the great deluge, taught mankind various pieces of forbidden knowledge: language, writing systems, weapon crafting, martial arts, and perhaps most importantly—"

"Sorcery?" deduced Abberline.

Kalpesh nodded.

"Then what, or who, is Choronzon?"

"John Dee and Edward Kelley's writings predate the rediscovery of the book of Enoch by about two hundred years, therefore it is logical to perceive that the arcane knowledge they recorded did indeed come through scrying —through communication with some unknown entity, angelic or otherwise.

"Supposedly, the angels banished from heaven were imprisoned in the Abyss: a place that sits beyond the planes of existence. Some claim it is hell itself, others claim that it is the void that exists beyond the material realm, and others believe it is the substance that makes up the Aether. Truthfully, I doubt anyone knows quite what it is. Yet, many believe the fallen watchers, or demons if you'd prefer, are imprisoned there against their will, and if ever they were to escape, they would seek their revenge against heaven and unleash their wrath upon the universe.

"Enochian magic dictates, that there are four 'Watchtowers,' or 'Gates,' that serve as the barriers between the physical world and the Abyss. Each stands in one of the four corners of existence, North, East, South, and West, and each is representative of one of the Elements, Earth, Air, Wind, and Fire, with the fifth element, the Aether, serving as a medium that connects them to each other.

"These gates cannot be opened from the inside, however, from our world, the outside, they can be. Supposedly, the Enochian Keys conveyed to Kelley and Dee can open the four gates that bar the Dweller of the Abyss, Choronzon, inside, preventing his legions of demons from entering the physical world and bringing untold destruction upon humanity."

"You are saying opening the four gates to the Abyss will bring about the apocalypse?" questioned Abberline.

"That is exactly what I am saying," returned Kalpesh coldly.

"And you think this killer is attempting to do just that?"

"I fear so."

"This just keeps getting worse and worse," growled Abberline, forcefully rubbing his face.

"There's more," warned Kalpesh.

"Go on then," groaned Abberline.

"Some claim that opening the Abyss—summoning Choronzon, is the path for an Adept to reach enlightenment."

"Enlightenment?"

"Nirvana, Moksha, Self-realisation..." continued Kalpesh. "They are all terms for basically the same concept: the act of attaining one's ultimate potential—a transcendence to ultimate power."

"You think our man is doing all of this..."

Abberline gestured with a sweep of his hand across the crime scene and in the direction of the tumult from the street, "in the pursuit of power?"

Kalpesh nodded. "I do."

"Then God save us all," breathed Abberline.

XVI

Dorset Street, Spitalfields
9:00 p.m. September 9th, 1888

    The bell of Christ Church Spitalfields tolled for the ninth time as Kalpesh and Abberline rounded the corner onto the worst street in London. The narrow confines of the rookery were lit by a single row of dim gaslights flickering alongside the terraces of soot-coated houses; each lamppost had at least one prostitute leant against it, more often two, whilst the older and uglier of the streetwalkers shunned from the light, remaining hid beneath darkened doorways. Further in the shadows, pimps watched their workforces soliciting on the street, whilst concealed entirely in the darkness, hidden within the deepest recesses of the slum, pickpockets and cutthroats watched any who dared enter the treacherous alley.

The two Malleus detectives drew aside their coats as they strode purposefully into the rookery, displaying their pistols holstered on their belts with their badges on show beside them. The police seldom set foot into Dorset Street, and the times they dared to were within the hours of daylight. The moment Kalpesh and Abberline broached the threshold of the alley, all eyes were upon them. Their prominently displayed pistols served as a threat against any who might try something, yet the real warning came from the badges on show. Two regular officers or detectives foolish enough to get themselves garrotted during a stroll down Dorset Street after dark would more than likely go unanswered; there would certainly be an investigation; feathers would be ruffled, perhaps there might even be an arrest or two; but in all likelihood, there would be no justice done. With the almost negligible chance of any witnesses daring to come forwards and testify, no one would be convicted, the person or persons responsible would walk free, and the whole fiasco would merely serve as another warning to the men of H Division that they held no real jurisdiction in the worst street in London.

For Kalpesh and Abberline however, the situation was different. It was still dangerous nonetheless for two Malleus inspectors to dare set foot inside the lawless slums, yet Hammer had a fearsome reputation of its own, and one that was always upheld. Even the most fearmongering gangsters in Whitechapel were terrified of Special Branch. Malleus's reputation for torture and extraction of confessions had been well earnt in the centuries since its inception, and cases of assault against the men of Hammer were dealt with as vehemently as the crime of witchcraft itself. This assurance, that any attempt made against them would be answered for, and the fact that every cutthroat and marauder that had clocked their entry into the slum knew just that, endowed the two inspectors with the strength to at least feign the authoritative confidence they needed to march unabated into Dorset Street.

"What are we doing here, Fred?" whispered Kalpesh under his breath, trying his utmost to maintain a commanding aura to ward off any would-be-attackers watching from the shadows.

"Trust me," returned his partner in hushed tones. "Just keep quiet and do what I say."

Kalpesh reluctantly sealed his lips as they continued to walk through the narrow gaslit rookery, past the rows of prostitutes lining the street, their heads each turning as they passed them by, staring in confusion at the two witch hunters trespassing in their haunt. After a few dozen yards, they reached the entrance of Crossingham's Lodging House, the doss house where, up until last night, Annie Chapman had resided. On the doorstep outside, an elderly man sat with a gin bottle in hand, his tattered flat cap casting a long shadow over his face.

"Gentlemen," grumbled the nightwatchman as Kalpesh paused in front of the decrepit boarding house.

"Brummy," Abberline greeted him by his nickname.

"You are wasting your time here, Inspector," he croaked standoffishly. "The boys from Leman Street were here all afternoon. I told 'em everything I know."

"You've been a good help, John," agreed Abberline. "We're not here for you—or Tim," he insisted.

"We're not?" Kalpesh questioned his partner in a low murmur.

"Good evening, Brummy," Abberline bid him farewell with a forced smile, tipping the man his hat as he gulped down a swig of gin. Placing a hand firmly on his partner's shoulder, he dragged Kalpesh away from the front of the doss house. "You trying to cause trouble Khatri!?" hissed Abberline seconds later.

"I assumed that was where we were heading!" returned the Indian.

"No assumptions! Just follow me, and keep your mouth shut," muttered Abberline in annoyance.

Now all the more confused as to where they were going, Kalpesh obeyed his partner and followed in silence as they continued to tread deeper into the slums. Halting two thirds of the way down the street, Abberline took a moment to look back over his shoulder, glancing warily about to ensure that they were not being followed. Satisfied that those watching were doing so out of curiosity rather than through criminal intent, Abberline bore a right into the claustrophobic confines of the even narrower alley of Little Paternoster Row.

Not a single streetlamp existed down the dark tunnel that formed the suffocating back alley; the only sources of illumination came firstly from the dim glow of Dorset Street's gaslighting that diffused only around the entranceway to the oppressive side street, and secondly, the moon overhead, tonight it being but a faint waxing sliver. Kalpesh reached into his coat as he pursued his partner into the darkest depths of London's East End and produced his torch. The tungsten filament flickered to light and cast a faint beam down the way that immediately glinted off numerous sets of hovering silver eyes from figures concealed in the array of doorways. Various whores slunk deeper into the alcoves of the alley, shying from the light, several shielding faces disfigured by syphilitic lesions with their hands.

"Turn that out, wog!" growled a thug

lurking in an archway smoking a pipe.

Instinctively, Kalpesh swung the beam cast from the incandescent bulb over the burly figure to reveal a face masked with tattoos leering back at him. The Indian inspector felt a thump against his arm as Abberline struck him.

"Do as he says!" snarled the DCI.

Kalpesh obediently click the torch off and waited in the pressing darkness for his eyes to finally adjust.

"I swear Khatri, if you get us murdered, I'm going to kill you!"

"Sorry," whispered Kalpesh, barely daring to utter a single word.

"Just..." continued Abberline frustratedly, "don't do anything. Just trust me!"

Kalpesh nodded, unsure whether his partner could actually make out the gesture. The two of them crept on across the grimy cobbles, trudging a dozen yards further into the constricted alley until they found themselves outside an unassuming doorway. Pausing before the door, Kalpesh watched as Abberline unclipped the Malleus badge prominently displayed on his belt and pocketed it, before drawing his coat to conceal his Mauser. Though it was near pitch black, Kalpesh could feel his partner's stare penetrating through the darkness, demanding that he do the same. After a long moment, Kalpesh likewise unclipped his badge, dropping it inside his pocket, and moved his coat to conceal his prominently holstered pistol.

Presently, Abberline issued a rhythmic knock on the door before the two men waited for a long moment in silence. Several bolts and chains retracted inside and the door opened a crack, allowing candlelight to spill out into the night. A set of dark eyes appeared through the aperture as an attractive raven-haired woman studied them.

"Vittoria," nodded Abberline in greeting, tipping her his hat.

An expression of recognition registered in the woman's eyes before it was replaced by one of scrutiny. "Who is *he*?" she asked Abberline with a subtle Italian accent.

"A friend," returned the detective.

"Why is he looking at me like that?" she demanded.

"I don't know," returned Abberline. "Why *is* he?" he directed at Kalpesh in annoyance.

"Like what?" whispered Kalpesh.

"I don't like it," insisted the Italian woman through the crack in the doorway.

"Stop it, Khatri!" grumbled Abberline.

"Stop what?" uttered Kalpesh in confusion.

"Is he a sleuth?" questioned the woman.

"Does it matter?" shrugged Abberline.

Her eyes looked Kalpesh up and down once more before the door swiftly closed. The sound of a chain being unhooked rattled and the door opened again, this time wide enough for the two detectives to slip inside. The door shut behind

Kalpesh and a series of bolts were locked back into place by the inhabitant of the tiny apartment. The single-roomed flat had been subdivided by a bead curtain that obscured one corner of the bedsit. In the portion in which the two inspectors found themselves along with their host, was crammed a bed, table, a kitchenette, and a small hearth. The smell of incense hung thickly in the air.

"Put your money on the table," insisted the woman, having secured the door, turning now to reveal herself in full. She was attractive and young, perhaps not yet even in her twenties, with an exotic air about her. Various beaded necklaces hung across her bosom whilst almost every finger bore at least one ring; a pair of heavy brass earrings dangled from beneath her wavy hair, and her lips and eyes were heavily accentuated with makeup.

Kalpesh stood awkwardly by the doorway, unsure what Abberline had led him into. His heart sank further as he watched his partner remove his hat and drop a pair of shillings into a bowl centred on the table. The woman moved about the bedsit, extinguishing numerous candles before letting out her ponytail as she strode, hips swinging, across the room, parting the beads seductively and vanishing from sight behind the curtain into the dimly lit corner.

Kalpesh watched in horror as Abberline doffed his coat and holster, hanging both over the back of a chair before he too made his way over towards the beaded curtain. He paused before passing through, looking back to Kalpesh, who as of yet had not dared enter more than a few feet from the door.

"You coming?" he asked, looking at Kalpesh expectantly.

"Fred... what is happening?"

"Just trust me," insisted Abberline once more. "And don't do anything stupid," he added, before vanishing through the strings of hanging beads.

Anxiously, Kalpesh stepped further inside. He approached the table and began removing his own coat before he caught sight of a magazine face down on the table. Peering back over his shoulder to ensure he was not being watched by their host, the Indian lifted the pamphlet, turning it over to inspect the cover. A depiction of the morning star, Lucifer, was emblazoned across the page.

Placing the magazine back down, Kalpesh hesitantly revolved. He slowly moved towards the strings of beads, behind which Abberline and the woman Vittoria were concealed. He crept closer, feeling his finger's curl around the broom handle grip of his Mauser C96. He reached for the beads, slowly parting the curtain, and peered through the screen.

A half dozen candles flickered atop a tablecloth encircling a smooth, reflective orb balanced on top a plinth. It was an orbuculum, a shewstone, a crystal ball, an artefact of divination used in scrying. Sat across from one another on either side of the table, with the orbuculum between them, were Vittoria and Abberline.

"Sit down, Khatri!" demanded Abberline, his eyes flitting to Kalpesh's hand primed to draw the pistol from his holster.

Kalpesh looked further about the screened corner of the room. A bookcase leant against the wall, and within it, Kalpesh made out several forbidden texts and grimoires. Atop the table sat a wooden bowl filled with knucklebones, and neatly stacked in front of the sorceress was a deck of cards that Kalpesh instantly knew would be a tarot deck.

"Get him out of here!" snapped Vittoria as Kalpesh's grip tightened around his pistol.

Kalpesh drew the Mauser and took aim at the occultist.

"Khatri!" growled Abberline. "What did I say about doing something stupid!?"

"Fred!" returned Kalpesh in distress. "She's a medium! A spiritualist!"

"Don't you think I bloody well know that!?" snarled the chief inspector. "I'm sat in front of a fucking crystal ball!"

"Why aren't we arresting her!?"

"Put your bloody gun away!"

"She's Vittoria Cremers! Isn't she?"

"Yes," hissed Abberline, his face rapidly reddening with rage. "Now holster your weapon!"

"She's a member of the Theosophical Society! That's grounds for her to receive the death

211

penalty…"

"Khatri!" barked Abberline more forcefully than ever as he stood abruptly, the chair screeching out from under him. "Sit down!"

Silence fell throughout the room as Kalpesh looked back and forth between Abberline and Cremers in confusion; both were leering at him.

"I knew it was a mistake bringing you here," Abberline said coldly.

"Fred…" stammered Kalpesh, "I don't understand… why are we here?"

"Just trust me!" he repeated a final time.

Slowly, Kalpesh lowered his gun.

"Get out!" snapped Cremers, rising from her chair. "Both of you! We are done here."

"No," replied Abberline sternly. "We are not."

"I won't scry for you. Not after this!"

"You will," insisted Abberline. "My partner might be a fool, but he is no idiot. He is right about one thing; the witchcraft you offer as a paid service here—your affiliations with Blavatsky—if we took you into Anvil, chances are you'd be hanged by October, my dear!"

"Are you threatening me?"

"No," replied Abberline. "I am merely reminding you that it is because of our deal that you have been allowed to stay living here, instead of inside a cell in Anvil. Now, if you were to fail to uphold your end of the bargain… let's just say you might find your living situation change rather rapidly."

Cremers scowled at Abberline. "You are blackmailing me!"

"That may be so," agreed the inspector coolly, "but I am not the one running an illegal mediumship out of Dorset Street. I needn't remind you, as my partner has already so bluntly pointed it out, that it is my job to apprehend persons such as you. It is only because you have made yourself so indispensable to myself and the men of H Division that we have turned a blind eye as to what goes on here."

"Fine," spat Cremers, "arrest me! It can't be any worse than living in this hellhole!"

"Oh, but my dear," smiled Abberline knowingly, "I assure you it truly can!"

Cremers bit her tongue. "He has to wait outside," she insisted, scowling at Kalpesh.

"He stays right here."

Kalpesh watched the muscles along her jaw contort as she clenched her teeth in anger. "Fine," she agreed. "But you take his gun!"

Abberline nodded. "A reasonable request." Without hesitation, he reached up from his chair and snatched the Mauser from out of Kalpesh's hand, tucking it inside his waistband. "Take a seat, Khatri," insisted the inspector once more, gesturing to the chair beside him.

Apprehensively, Kalpesh eased himself down into the seat across the table from the occultist.

"What do you want to know?" asked Cremers coldly.

"I want you to read for him," instructed Abberline, gesturing to his partner sat beside him.

"For *him*?" she repeated confusedly.

"That's what I said," returned Abberline.

"Is there anything in particular you want to know?" she asked, looking between the two men blankly.

Abberline raised a hand. "Just... indulge me."

Cremers nodded. "Okay." She began shuffling the deck of cards.

XVII

Little Paternoster Row, Spitalfields
9:18 p.m. September 9th, 1888

The pack of oversized cards crackled as Vittoria Cremers shuffled the split deck dextrously back into one. She tapped each edge of the deck on the table in turn until she had neatly aligned every card back into a perfect stack. Pressing the deck firmly down atop the tablecloth, she paused, her eyes rising to gaze at Kalpesh. Yet the look she gave the Indian was more than a cursory glance; her vision pierced him, scrutinising every detail of his being, peering through the shielded exterior of his material self, searching deeper, meticulously analysing the spiritual essence that comprised his soul.

Kalpesh shuddered, momentarily gaining a sense that he had in some way been violated. Cremers detected the writhing discomfit she had installed in him. Her lips curved discretely with mocking satisfaction as she enjoyed a brief moment of perceived vengeance that served to settle the score against the insult Kalpesh had dealt her.

"Just deal the cards," grumbled Abberline impatiently, picking up on the silent exchange ongoing between the two of them.

Cremers' wry smirk morphed into a full-blown mocking grin, and as commanded, she drew the first card from atop the tarot deck, flipping it as she pressed it face up on the tablecloth in front of Kalpesh. The trump card bore the number eleven in roman numerals across the top. The image depicted upon the face was of a king seated on a throne; in his right hand he upheld a sword, whilst in his left he held aloft a set of scales.

"Justice," announced Cremers, her eyes now fixed unwaveringly on the young inspector seated in front of her. The candles seemed to dim about the room and the very air started to congeal. "It is justice for which you fight; justice is the ideal which you hold above all other things in this world. But whilst justice can sometimes be dealt as simply as the swing of the sword, it can just as often be a balancing act. You alone must find the tipping point of the scales. It is not something that others can teach you; lean too heavily in one direction and you risk toppling the ideal for which you strive. Be wary in your fight for justice, it could just as easily be your undoing as your salvation."

Kalpesh looked down at the card, raising his gaze to meet Cremers'. All animosity had vanished from her eyes, replaced now with sincerity and professionalism. A long pause elapsed before she overturned the next card from the top of the deck, curling down the face: number thirteen, a skeleton wreathed in black ropes astride a hellish stallion galloping headlong across a road paved in corpses.

"Death," declared Cremers, the candles fading further as a preternatural darkness pressed harder into the corners of the room. "It is the harbinger of death you hunt; already bodies mount in his wake, those you have found are only those which he bids you discover. Death is the fourth horseman, the herald of the apocalypse, and it is nothing less than the rapture which he has begun to impel upon this world."

Unnatural stillness smothered them as Cremers peeled back the next card in the series. She placed it alongside the other two, revealing the number sixteen, a black tower rising from a pit of flames with dark clouds issuing rain and lightning swirling about the spire at its pinnacle.

"The Tower," the spiritualist continued. "The towers are what Death seeks: passage from one realm to the next. Two of the four Watchtowers have already been torn down. The gate has begun to open. You must act fast to prevent the locks from crumbling, for once the gates have buckled, you know what is to be unleashed..."

Cremers emphatically dealt the next card, revealing the fifteenth of the tarot deck. A monstrous humanoid form stood atop an altar with an inverted pentagram branded across its chest; its legs were the feathered scaly talons of a harpy, bat-like wings extended from its shoulders, and ram horns curled outwards from the being's forehead. Bound in chains, knelt before the altar were the depictions of a man and a woman, stripped of their clothes, their bodies contorted and hunched over in agony at the demonic figure's feet.

"The Devil," breathed Cremers, her own voice faltering as the candles seemed to fail completely at holding the darkness at bay. "If freed from his prison, the world's fate is sealed. Even Death himself does not truly understand what he seeks to unleash, but the fourth horseman is promised to deliver the apocalypse, and with it, tribulation."

Kalpesh and Abberline exchanged looks, and for the first time since the two men had been partnered, Kalpesh saw a look of unrest concealed behind Abberline's stoic expression.

"Your role in the events to come has yet to

be decided," continued Cremers. "Your choices in the days that follow can lead you down one of two paths."

Kalpesh watched as she drew two cards at once, placing them both before him: numbers zero and one.

"Will you be the Magician, or the Fool?"

Kalpesh narrowed his stare on the fortune teller before him, pressing her to elaborate.

"The Fool," she continued, pushing forward a card depicting a wayward traveller adorned in ragged clothing, leaning wearily on a staff, "for all his virtues, for all his ideals, he is destined to wander aimlessly, for the *'Fool's Path'* leads to nowhere. It is the Fool that clings too heavily to that which he holds true, fearing that if he dares release the tenets that support him, that the strength of his own legs and of his will are not enough to allow him to stand. The Fool knows not the balance of the scales, clinging to the sword for all matters of Justice, unwilling to compromise for fear that the scales might swing too far in the wrong direction. The Fool will succumb to Death. The Fool shall find himself bent beneath the feet of the Devil."

Slowly Cremers pushed forward the second of the two cards, a figure raising a wand to the heavens, connecting the four elements, Fire, Air, Earth, and Water, each depicted in the corners of the card. "The Magician is the final card. Known also as the Magus, or the Juggler. The

Magician is the reverse side of the coin to the Fool. Similar in many ways, yet different in one: through wisdom, through experience, through fortuitous circumstance, the Magician has learnt the balancing point of the scales; Justice has two sides, both of which require equal weighting in order to establish equilibrium. The Magician understands that a sword can be used both for justice and injustice; it is both a weapon of war and a symbol of protection. Though the Magician's fate is far from certain, he has learnt to navigate the same path which the Fool is destined to wander aimlessly. He is vulnerable, yet not confined by the fates that imprison the Fool to submission; unlike the Fool, the Magician can stand in defiance against the Devil and may find the means to conquer Death itself.

"Before you lie these two paths; they are intertwined with one another, often intersecting, and there are few signs to determine which is which; but make no mistake, though both lead in the same direction, their destinations differ greatly. It is not clear which path you are on now. Be wary of every step you take, for each decision, each turn in the road, could very easily be your undoing."

Silence descended and the pressing darkness seamed to ease. As Kalpesh awakened from the trance that had grasped him throughout the tarot reading, he became steadily aware that more time than he had perceived had elapsed. The candles surrounding the orbuculum had melted down to stubs, whilst many illuminating the room beyond the beaded curtain had burnt out completely.

Kalpesh met eyes with Vittoria. She shied away from his gaze, retreating into her chair, raising her long, painted nails apprehensively to her lips as she replayed the messages she had divined through the cards over again in her head. The inspector studied her, trying to determine how much of what she had divulged had she known beforehand, and how much had been communicated to her through the Aether by whatever entity she contacted during scrying. Judging by the agitation that had descended upon her, Kalpesh deduced that she had learnt much of what she had said for the first time during the reading.

He looked next to his partner in the seat beside him; Abberline stared back aloofly.

"I think you should leave," stammered Cremers, leaning over to scoop up the dealt cards, rapidly inserting them back into the deck.

"Not yet," insisted Abberline. "We still have more questions."

"No," refused Cremers. "I can't..."

"I needn't remind you again of our arrangement."

"No, please," insisted the medium, rising anxiously to her feet.

"There's something else—something you

aren't telling us—isn't there?"

"Abberline please! I can't—not this time!"

"Vittoria, you have to," insisted Abberline. "You've seen for yourself what is at stake here! We have to stop this monster. We need your help!"

Cremers grimaced. She was on the verge of tears. "Who is he!?" she demanded, casting a finger viciously at Kalpesh. "Who is he *really*?"

Abberline glanced inquisitively at Kalpesh to see that the young inspector was as taken off guard by the question as he was. "He's my partner," returned Abberline definitively. "He's a Special Branch inspector hunting down what might be the greatest threat to the Empire that has ever arisen!"

"He has a connexion to all of this..." she returned. "More so than you. His fate is tied to the man you seek!"

Abberline shot Kalpesh another curious glance before he refocussed once more on the medium. "What is it you see, Vittoria?"

"I can't..." she pleaded.

"You can," assured Abberline compassionately.

Cremers closed her eyes and balled her fists, her body went taught upright. Kalpesh watched as she visibly struggled to calm herself. A long deep exhalation soothed both herself and the two detectives.

"Okay," she whispered, apprehensively retaking her seat. Wiping a tear from the corner of her eye, she took another moment to compose herself before her attention fell upon the crystal ball perched in front of her. Once more, Kalpesh observed her far-seeing gaze of clairvoyance, only this time, instead of peering into him, the medium was staring into the distorted lens of the orbuculum. Her hands rose from her lap, hovering over the table, her slender fingers gracefully swirling around the periphery of the shewstone, yet never touching the crystal's surface. A sudden vacant expression befell Cremers' face and Kalpesh could see that visions were beginning to flicker through the third eye of her mind.

"Vittoria..." Abberline spoke gently. "What do you see?"

"I see..." she began, her lips moving naturally, yet the voice that emitted from them seemed faint and distant, tinged with reverberations as if echoing from out of a deep chasm. "I see the city," she finished finally. "I see a storm... I see a mist... thick, poisonous... it is smog, but magical in origin... demonic in nature."

"What else?" pressed Abberline.

"The city is overrun!" she declared. "I cannot see them... but I know they are there. I can see the shadows they cast, but not their true forms. They are evil creatures... they have slipped through the cracks in the gate..."

"Keep going," insisted the chief inspector.

"No...!" stammered Cremers.

"What is it?"

"I can't see... everything is dark!"

"Vittoria!?" Abberline's voice faltered with concern.

"No!" she pleaded. "No! I can see him!"

"Who!?" demanded Abberline, rising from his chair to lean over the table. "Who do you see?"

"I can see him..." she trembled. "I think he can see me too!"

"Who, Vittoria, damn it!? Who!?"

Her hands suddenly retracted and her neck snapped back. Her head slumped against the rest of her chair as her whole body wilted. Kalpesh watched her eyes roll shut as Abberline darted around the table, catching the medium before she toppled out of her seat altogether. For a brief moment, Kalpesh feared she was dead, but a weak gasp of exhaustion assured him she was still alive. Slowly, her eyes flitted back open as she steadied herself shakily. Abberline eased her back upright, giving her space as she came around. She looked to both of the men before her, her eyes wrought with fear.

"Vittoria," spoke Abberline gently, "what did you see?"

Sweat clung to her brow and her bosom quivered as she struggled to articulate the words. "The Dweller in the Abyss..." she stammered. "I saw... Choronzon."

Abberline rose to his feet, emitting a heavy sigh before glancing over to Kalpesh. "Looks like you were right, Khatri."

Kalpesh sunk back into his own seat as

Abberline took a moment to comfort Cremers.

"You did good," the inspector assured the medium.

Cremers leant forward, cradling her head in her hands as she began to sob.

"We'll be on our way," assured Abberline as he rubbed the woman's back comfortingly before moving away. The chief inspector drew back the beaded curtain, pausing for his partner to follow his lead.

Kalpesh began to rise, when suddenly Cremers lurched across the table, snatching hold of his wrist. She twisted his arm sharply, causing a twinge of pain to surge up from his elbow. His hand reactively fell open, but as he looked back in irritation at the medium, he realised she was transfixed on the symbol tattooed onto his palm. Cremer's reddened and bloodshot eyes slowly levitated to lock with Kalpesh's gaze. Instinctively, the detective ripped free his arm and clenched his hand into a fist to obscure the symbol, studying the witch opposite him in confusion. Tears were pooling in her raw eyes, but she gawked at him now, not with resentment, but rather with a look of desperation.

"You have to stop him!" she wept. "Please!"

Kalpesh nodded before shaking his head with doubt. "I don't know how!"

Without averting her eyes from his own, Cremers reached for the tarot deck and drew one final card. She stretched across the table again and took Kalpesh's wrist, gently this time. He felt her press the card into his palm.

He looked down to see a woman adorned in blue and silver robes seated on a throne with an open tome spread across her lap. Atop the card was the roman numeral 'II.'

"She will lead you to him," whispered Cremers.

Abberline leant over Kalpesh, studying the card in his hand. "The High Priestess?"

Kalpesh rose to look back at the distraught spiritualist issuing him a knowing look.

"Who is she, Vittoria?" questioned Abberline.

But Kalpesh knew perfectly well who she meant. "Blavatsky."

XVIII

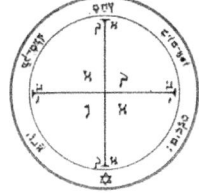

Little Paternoster Row, Spitalfields
10:27 p.m. September 9th, 1888

    Kalpesh and Abberline silently exited Vittoria Cremer's bedsit back into the oppressive, though distinctly non-preternatural, darkness of Little Paternoster Row. From the shadows, Kalpesh could feel the stares of dozens of eyes concealed inside the nooks and crannies of the choking back alley. Yet as the two men hastily marched back onto Dorset Street, turning left back the way they had come towards the exit of the lawless rookery, the young inspector's mind was far from the threat the resenting gazes bore; instead, his thoughts focussed on a looping replay of the events that had just unfolded.

The look of terror that lurked behind the bleary eyes of Cremers had unsettled him deeply; she was a woman who, by choice, conversed and conspired with the beings that whispered from behind the veil; she was used to the riddles and omens conveyed to her by spirits of questionable morality and intent, choosing not to regards such whispers with any sense of scepticism, but instead embracing them as clairvoyance. Her profession was one of looking into the darkness, seeing things and hearing thoughts that mortals were never intended to perceive. Such a practise required a hardened resolve; those who lacked such resolve more often than not succumbed to manipulative malevolent entities, often becoming the victims of demonic possession. Cremers had tonight peered into the dark, looking beyond the veil as she had done countless times before; but for the very first time, she had blinked when doing so. What she had seen had unmade her, breaking her down into a weeping mess.

The bell of Spitalfields Christ Church tolled the half hour as they exited the imposing darkness of Dorset Street back onto the wide, arc-lamp-lit thoroughfare of Commercial Street. Seeking refuge from the night beneath the cold aura of a buzzing streetlight, Kalpesh steadied himself against the lamppost. Routinely, he reached inside his waistcoat pocket, clicking open his watch; he did a double take, checking the hour hand against the church clock tower to ensure his watch was not running fast. Sure enough, it was ten-thirty; it had felt like a mere ten minutes they had spent with Cremers, whereas in fact it had been more than an hour.

"Kalpesh?" pressed Abberline, appearing in front of the Indian.

Kalpesh's eyes narrowed on his partner.

"Everything alright?"

"What the hell was that about!?" demanded the Indian.

"Your guess is as good as mine," returned his partner.

"I'm not talking about Cremers' reading!" he snapped. "What I want to know is, why did we just let her go? Why aren't we taking her into custody? She's on Malleus's wanted list! She's a known clairvoyant, operating out of Whitechapel right under our noses—only, it would seem, that's not the case at all! Not only has her whereabouts been known about for some time by yourself and the men of H Division, but you have also been using her as an informant—an arcane consultant, for lord knows how many cases, behind Malleus's back!"

Abberline's expression hardened.

"Fred..." Kalpesh continued, his anger now fading into concern, "this is corruption! Its obstruction of justice! If Macnaghten or Monro find out about this... you'd lose your job... you could end up imprisoned!"

"You'd tell them?" asked Abberline coldly.

"I..." stammered Kalpesh, not sure what might come out of his mouth if he continued to speak.

"Get off your bloody high horse, Khatri," snarled Abberline. "I thought you were smarter than this! I thought you could think for yourself! That's why I requested you as my partner. But I was wrong! You are just like every other bloody zealot in Hammer: indoctrinated by the fanatical writings of Heinrich-fucking-Kramer!"

"What are you talking about!?"

"Just think for yourself for once, Khatri! Not what some book has taught you to believe— not what Malleus wants you to think! Just look at things with your own bleeding eyes and make an educated observation that is your own for once!"

"I do think for myself!" riposted Kalpesh.

"It doesn't bloody well look that way to me!" growled the veteran detective. "You've got book smarts. You're sharp as a surgeon's scalpel! But it's all wasted—because *you* aren't the one holding the knife. You let others do that for you! Monro... Macnaghten... anything they say you do without question."

"That's not true!"

"Isn't it? If they told you to arrest me tomorrow, would you?"

Kalpesh stayed silent.

"You are just their pawn."

"No. I'm not!"

"Why do you think we just did what we did? So that I could solve the case with Cremers' information, and what—earn myself a promotion? Take a shortcut through the real detective work so that I could catch a killer just to make a name for myself?"

"Of course not," returned Kalpesh.

"Then why would I bloody well take us to see Cremers?"

"Because we need a lead..." replied Kalpesh. "Because you want to catch this man, not for yourself, but to stop him—to help save others."

"And did we get that lead or not?"

Kalpesh looked down to see he was still clutching the tarot card Cremers had pressed into his hand right before they had left: the High Priestess. "Yes," replied the inspector.

"And do you think we'd have gotten that lead if we'd tried torturing it out of Cremers inside some cell beneath Anvil?"

Kalpesh hesitated. "Probably not."

"Exactly!" snarled the enraged chief inspector. "You may not like what just happened, Khatri—hell, I'm not bloody proud of it either! But we got what we came for, and if letting Cremers walk free is the price we pay for catching the monster roaming these streets at night, then I will sleep easy with my decisions."

"I don't know..." faltered Kalpesh. "It doesn't seem right."

"I'll tell you what doesn't seem right, Khatri: there is a world of difference between Cremers and that lunatic slashing streetwalkers in dark alleys throughout Whitechapel—between reading someone's fortune, and trying to open the gates of hell to summon the fucking devil! But do you know who doesn't see it that way? Hammer!

"Heinrich-bloody-Kramer saw all types of magic as evil, all indistinguishable, all equally wicked, all deserving of execution! And because some nut-job inquisitor hundreds of years ago wrote a book on it and convinced the tyrannical king of England at the time, our queen now— God save her— believes the same! So does our government, and so does the Met. But I'll tell you what: *I* don't believe it!

"There's a massive fucking difference between a man stealing a loaf of bread because he's hungry, and a sick bastard who murders whores for his own sexual gratification; just about everyone in this world agrees with that! All crimes are not equal! Yet when it comes to magic, apparently, they are! The law should distinguish between those using magic trying to find deeper meaning in this world and those who use it to harm others! Clairvoyance and Malfeasance are not equal crimes, regardless of which twat in charge in Scotland Yard, or Hammer, or Westminster, or Buckingham-bloody-

Palace says otherwise! We treat soothsayers and necromancers alike—as heretical terrorists, without ever taking into account what their intentions were! We have branded all forms of magic as dangerous and uncompromisingly evil, but how can that be, when magic itself has just steered us back in the direction of hunting down a man I can only describe as the embodiment of evil itself?

"You may disagree with everything I've said, Khatri. You might well dob me in to Hammer in the morning—but nothing you can do or say will make me regret coming here tonight. Cremers has helped me bring dozens of men to justice, and I know for certain that she has done far more good than she has done harm with that bloody deck of cards and her crystal ball!"

"She only helped us because you threatened her!" insisted Kalpesh, still grasping at straws to prevent his beliefs from collapsing.

"Oh please!" returned Abberline sardonically. "Of course she was reluctant to help us! We're men working for the organisation dedicated to purging all practitioners of magic from existence! She's fucking terrified of us—even me, because she reckons that the moment she stops being useful, or the moment I have no bigger fish to fry, that she'll be next. She fears that if I'm not kept happy, that it is only a matter of time before her head is on the chopping block!"

"I..." stammered Kalpesh. "I just..."

"You just what!?" demanded Abberline.

"I don't know," he conceded.

Abberline's aggressive composure steadily melted and the inspector cracked a smile. "Well, that's a first," he chuckled. "I thought you knew everything, Khatri!"

Kalpesh smiled weakly in return. "I understand what you are saying."

"But you don't agree with it?"

"No," insisted Kalpesh. "No, I think that's just it... I do agree with you."

Abberline nodded silently in acceptance.

"Just..." continued the Indian. "Just next time, let me know what I am walking into ahead of time."

"Fair enough," agreed his partner.

Kalpesh sighed audibly, his mind returning to the riddles Cremers had recited to him as he looked at the High Priestess card clutched between his finger and thumb.

"Come on," beckoned Abberline.

"Where are we going?" questioned Kalpesh.

"The Ten Bells," returned Abberline wryly.

"Okay," smiled the Indian. The two men began to walk northward in the direction of the pub. After a few steps, Kalpesh could no longer resist asking something that had been burning in his mind behind the more pressing issues; in Abberline's lecture, something the aging inspector had said stood out to Kalpesh. "You said you requested to be partnered with me...?"

Abberline sighed heavily. "You caught that then?" conceded the grizzled detective.

"Is it true?" smirked Kalpesh.

"If you want to find out, Khatri, the first round is on you!"

XIX

Anvil, Tower of London, City of London
8:06 a.m. September 10th, 1888

Kalpesh peered through the half-silvered glass from the darkened observation room into the cell beyond. Inside, a pair of giant Tesla coils surged with lightning, the tumultuous arcs of electricity buzzing and crackling as they conducted through the air, sparking across the exterior of the Faraday cage. Inside the cage, Blavatsky sat bound in a straitjacket, an iron collar clamped around her neck from which extended several heavy chains affixed to the concrete floor, restraining her from moving little more than a few inches in any direction. The theosophist sat motionless on the hard-wooden chair, her eyes fixed on a stained patch of concrete on the floor of the cell. Kalpesh and Abberline observed her silently for several minutes, throughout which time she barely so much as blinked.

"Barbaric, isn't it?" muttered Abberline under his breath so that the guard stood at the door couldn't hear.

Kalpesh looked to his partner, somewhat caught off guard by the comment.

"Not even Blavatsky deserves to live like this," added the chief inspector.

"She won't for much longer," returned Kalpesh sombrely.

"I suppose that is true enough," agreed Abberline. "Still, it doesn't make this right. No one should be imprisoned like this."

"It's the only safe means of holding her," returned Kalpesh.

Abberline exchanged a sceptical look with his partner. "You reckon she'd be able to escape if she was allowed to stand up or lie down?"

"There'd be greater opportunity..." replied the Indian uncertainly.

"She's dangerous," agreed Abberline. "She can kill a man with a few muttered phrases. But she's inside a Faraday cage with a shock collar round her neck, under constant observation from armed guards—chaining her upright into her seat... it's overkill, don't you think?"

Kalpesh hesitated. "Perhaps you'd feel differently if it was your job to guard her."

Abberline let out a long sigh before smiling weakly. "Maybe," he conceded. "For the most part, we do good work here at Anvil," insisted the inspector. "Despite some of my reservations, I've always believed that Hammer kept people safe; that's why I transferred here from CID. But I've always felt some of the techniques used here are a little too..."

"Heavy handed?" put in Kalpesh.

"Medieval," returned Abberline. "This country has changed so much in the last hundred years... you'd have thought Hammer might have changed with it."

A long period of silence elapsed as the two men continued to watch the imprisoned adept on the far side of the glass.

"Come on, Khatri," beckoned Abberline. "She's not going to question herself."

"You want me to come in with you?"

Abberline looked back at his partner and issued him a smile. "Well, I can't have all the fun myself. Besides, Cremers seemed to think there was something special about you—maybe Blavatsky will think the same?"

"She came close to killing me last time we were face to face," replied Kalpesh.

"And so you shot her, did you not?"

"Exactly," returned Kalpesh. "I can't

imagine she'll be happy to see me!"

"Good," smirked Abberline.

"You want her angry?"

"As I said last night, Khatri, you are sharp as hell, but sometimes you are awfully slow!"

"You want to put her off balance? See if she'll let something slip?"

"Now you are starting to think like an inspector!" praised Abberline. "Now come on, let's get in there."

"Alright," agreed Kalpesh.

"Good man." Abberline patted his partner firmly on the shoulder before turning to the guard at the door. "You there!"

"Yes sir?" questioned the guardsman.

"Get in here and man that button. If we give the signal, you light that bitch up!"

"Err, yes sir," agreed the prison officer.

"But *only* when I give the signal!" warned the chief inspector. "If you jump the gun, so help me Lord, I'll chain *you* into that contraption and set you to fry! Understand?"

The officer nodded, swallowing nervously.

"Come on, Khatri," repeated Abberline, leading him out of the observation room to the reinforced cell door and nodding to the second guard stationed at the controls. "Let's get this over and done with."

"Cell door opening!" shouted the guard, depressing the crimson wall-mounted button.

The warning bulb flashed overhead as the

electromagnetic clapper rattled piercingly against the alarm bell. Slowly, the reinforced steel door slid aside and the drone of the Tesla coils whirred down. Inside the cell, Blavatsky slowly raised her head to watch the two detectives enter. Her bulging eyes squinted with disdain as she recognised Kalpesh.

"Madame Blavatsky," Abberline bowed mockingly as the steel door closed, sealing the two detectives inside with the witch.

Blavatsky muttered several slurs in Russian and spat at the floor of her cage.

"I am Chief Inspector Abberline," smirked the detective. "As I understand it, you have already met my partner, Inspector Khatri." Abberline gestured to Kalpesh who was still lingering close to the door, his arms crossed defensively.

Blavatsky locked eyes with Kalpesh as she studied him silently with disdain. "Are you here to gloat?" she snarled in her thick accent. "You come here to laugh at an old woman? You come to torture me? See if you can make me squeal like pig? It is you who are the pigs!"

"Hopefully it will not come to that," insisted Abberline. "I'm optimistic that you'll cooperate. My partner here though..." he turned around, sliding his hands into the pockets of his waistcoat, and began to stroll commandingly around the exterior of the Faraday cage. "See, you did a number on him the other night—he's still a little sore. Now, I know he put you down pretty hard, and you might well think that makes you about even, only, I don't think Inspector Khatri here quite sees it that way. Isn't that right, Inspector?"

"That's right, sir," nodded Kalpesh, playing the part.

"Now, I know that Inspector Khatri is just itching to deal you some pain," continued Abberline, "only, the thing is, he's not supposed to —that is, provided you are cooperative."

Blavatsky continued to stare menacingly at Kalpesh in silence.

"Were you, however, not to cooperate... well then, it would not be within my power to prevent my disgruntled friend here from—how was it you put it? *'Making you squeal like a pig?'*"

One of Blavatsky's swollen eyes twitched as she bit her tongue in anger.

"Now, I am of two minds as to whether or not to bet on him succeeding; I can see that you are a tough old bird, and as I've heard it, our boys down here haven't had much luck in making you sing since we brought you in." Abberline stopped pacing the cell, planting himself directly in front of Blavatsky. "But, the same was said for your old chum, Henry Steel Olcott, until they let Inspector Khatri in a cell with him; the way I hear things, he became pretty talkative as soon as that happened —that is of course, until his heart gave out!"

Blavatsky's eyes widened until they appeared ready to pop from their sockets as she focussed on Abberline.

"You didn't know?" questioned the Chief Inspector, knowing full well that the information had been kept from her. He tutted loudly. "Well, I am sorry for your loss; I know the two of you got on swimmingly." He continued to pace again, and Blavatsky's focus fell back onto Kalpesh. "It was a nasty business," resumed Abberline, aware of the disquiet he was stirring within the theosophist. "Inspector Khatri pushed him a bit too far. Olcott couldn't quite stand up to the torture. Isn't that right, Detective?"

Kalpesh shrugged as nonchalantly as he could manage.

"We got some good information out of him first though," smiled Abberline. "Hell, as I understand it, he led us right to you!"

Kalpesh could feel Blavatsky's eyes burning a hole in his chest.

"We didn't even realise you were in the country—Hammer had intel that said you were in Belgium. But as soon as Inspector Khatri started putting the screws to Olcott, we quickly cleared that up."

Blavatsky started to breathe uncontrollably, her face reddening, her teeth clenching tightly behind gurning lips as rage boiled visibly within her.

"Olcott said you were in London—told us how to track you down, and sure enough," he turned gesturing to her with both hands, "we found you." Abberline stepped closer, approaching the rungs of the Faraday cage with a taunting smirk. "You mustn't blame him of course—he tried his hardest not to give you up. Only, Inspector Khatri... well, he's just too damned good at his job!"

Blavatsky exploded into a torrent of explicit curses in Russian, then in broken English, before she began murmuring in esoteric tongues.

Abberline reacted swiftly, stepping back from the cage as the theosophist started her incantation, and pointed at the reflective glass walling on the far side of the room. "Do it!" he ordered.

Instantly, Blavatsky's chanting was silenced, replaced by a stifled grunt of pain as electricity fired through the chains, stiffening her muscles into spasm. After several seconds, the guard manning the button in the observation room eased off, and Blavatsky slumped in her chair, gasping to catch her breath.

"Now, now," growled Abberline, "we'll have none of that."

Slowly, Blavatsky raised her head and glowered at both of the men in her cell.

"I'll take your silence as a sign of your cooperation," grumbled the chief inspector, stepping back from the cage to start pacing the room again.

"Why are you here?" hissed Blavatsky.

"We have it on good authority that you have information about a man we are after," revealed

Abberline.

Slowly, the witch began to cackle with malice. "You want me to give someone up?" mocked Blavatsky. "My kind... we seek truth. We are not content in the ignorance you and your country strive for. Like the Church seeking to persecute men of science during the first age of enlightenment, now you stand in the way of the second age of illumination, hoping to purge those who see beyond the veil; but you will not succeed! You want to destroy that which you do not understand, because you are afraid! I am loyal to my cause. I seek to bring enlightenment to those who wish to find true understanding of the cosmos! I will not betray any of my fellow adepts— they are my allies, and *you* are my enemy!"

"Is that so?" growled Abberline in annoyance, his eyes flitting to Kalpesh, unsure how to proceed.

"The Theosophical Society was founded by yourself and Olcott," began Kalpesh, choosing a different approach as he now took the lead from Abberline. "You've broken countless laws, performed dangerous rituals, you've plotted acts of terrorism against the crown! But however illicit your practises, you established a clear set of rules during the society's foundation."

"You think we are barbarians?" remarked Blavatsky with amusement.

"Not quite," returned Kalpesh. "But the man we are after almost certainly is."

The witch's eyes narrowed with curiosity.

Abberline took several steps backwards, giving way to Kalpesh as the young detective placed himself front and centre before the bloated prisoner.

"The Theosophical Society drew the line at killing of innocents; animal and human sacrifice is condemned, punished not only by expulsion from the order, but by leaking of the identity and address of any member guilty of violating said rules to Malleus."

Blavatsky remain silent, her attention fixed squarely on the man before her.

"Despite what else I believe about your morals, I think the very idea of ritualistic murder repulses you, and I am willing to bet you will turn this man over to us."

"I have no idea who you are talking about," returned Blavatsky, shrugging her shoulders beneath the weight of her chains and collar.

Kalpesh reached deep inside the pocket of his jacket, his fingers first finding the tarot card he had been handed the night prior, before finally settling on a folded envelope. Pulling it from his pocket, the detective drew the stack of photographs from inside. One by one he dropped them, letting each settle face up on the floor around his feet at the edge of the Faraday cage where Blavatsky could see them. The theosophist's bulbous eyes enlarged as she beheld the macabre images of mutilated women captured from both the murder scenes and the morgue.

"Recognise the handy work?" questioned Abberline, moving alongside his partner with his hands squarely on his hips.

Blavatsky ignored the question, her gaze transfixed on the grotesque images littered across the concrete.

"I know this shocks you just as much as it does us," insisted Kalpesh, pausing to see if he could illicit some response from Blavatsky. "You want magic to be decriminalised; you wish for the persecution of those who practise the mystic arts to end—but that will never happen, not whilst men like this use magic to do unspeakable things! People are right to fear the arcane when it leads to this! Surely you want this man brought to justice just as much as we do?"

Still Blavatsky refused to speak, her eyes not wavering from the photographs.

"We've heard from a mutual friend of ours that you know something about him!" insisted Abberline forcefully. "Tell us what we want to know!"

Blavatsky let out a chuckle. "You will never catch him."

"That's what *you* think," returned Abberline through gritted teeth.

Kalpesh stooped and retrieved one of the photographs from Annie Chapman's murder scene that had captured within frame the Fifth Pentacle of the Sun. "You see that?" he asked pressing the photograph as close to the cage as he could without contacting the bars. "You know what he is trying to do? You know what he is trying to summon!?"

Blavatsky met eyes with Kalpesh, smiling weakly as she nodded.

"Then help us!" pleaded the Indian. "It doesn't matter what you think of me, or of Malleus! None of it will matter if this man succeeds in opening the gates to the Abyss."

Her eyes flitted between the two inspectors, cogs visibly turning inside her mind as she weighed up her options; the decision clearly pained her, but it became apparent after time that despite her bitter resentment for the men in front of her, she was faced with few options but to aid their investigation.

"Please," reiterated Kalpesh, "you know what is at stake."

Blavatsky exhaled deeply. "A month ago, I conversed with the Mahatmas through ritual. They warned me that the Beast had returned to London."

"The Beast?" inquired Abberline.

"A powerful adept who had been gaining renown in the occult for several years. I have met him only once, little more than two years ago," she began. "Even then I could sense the darkness inside him."

"Who is he?" pressed Kalpesh.

"He referred to himself as Lord Boleskine,'"

replied Blavatsky.

"Lord Boleskine?" repeated Abberline, neither of the detectives having heard the name before.

Blavatsky nodded.

"Is he a member of the Theosophical Society?" questioned Kalpesh.

"No," the witch shook her head. "I turned him away from my order. He sought teachings of Enochian magic, in acquiring siddhis—arts not taught by the Theosophical Society: secret knowledge which the Mahatmas choose not to reveal."

"What societies *do* teach Enochian magic?" questioned Abberline.

"In depth...?" she replied, "none. Few are fluent enough in the language to know where to begin with the system."

"You are something of a linguist yourself, aren't you?" questioned Abberline.

Blavatsky cackled, uttering a sentence that seemed to jump between over half a dozen languages before effortlessly switching back into her heavily accented English. "Mortal tongues," she said, "languages that are alive and well. Trivial things compared to the tongue of angels."

"Then where do you propose our man learnt that!" pressed the chief inspector impatiently, gesturing to the photograph being presented by his partner.

Blavatsky's eyes fell sombrely to the images

littered across the concrete. "The Mahatmas have spoken to me of a coven, one I have heard of from whisperings deep in the underground world of this city. They speak of an order more secretive than any that existed before it: a society closed to all but the most powerful of sorcerers."

"Does it have a name?" questioned Abberline.

Blavatsky nodded solemnly. "The Order of the Golden Dawn."

"The Golden Dawn?" repeated Abberline, the name suspiciously familiar to him.

"The Golden Dawn is a myth," dismissed Kalpesh.

"Then you know of them?" questioned Blavatsky.

Kalpesh nodded sceptically. "A secret hermetic order allegedly comprised of influential and high-profile members of society; one that supposedly selects its own initiates from promising sorcerers that have risen quickly within the ranks of other occultist circles? A society said to be so clandestine, that its very existence is a mystery to all but the most high-profile members of the occult? Seems a little farfetched, doesn't it?"

Blavatsky responded with a wry grin.

"Malleus has been hearing about references to the Golden Dawn for years, but we've dismissed them as nothing more than rumours. The Golden Dawn doesn't exist, it is merely a myth created to intentionally obfuscate Malleus' investigations into other more prominent occult societies, the Theosophical Society chief amongst them! Every reference to them, each supposed clue, leads to nothing but a wild goose chase. It was a clever ploy from whoever first came up with the idea, to divert Malleus time and resources from real threats."

Blavatsky's grin widened.

"You can't seriously expect me to believe they exist?"

"The Golden Dawn is real," she assured him coldly. "If the Beast belongs to any occult society, it will be them. But you will never find them," she added insistently.

"He found you, didn't he?" replied Abberline smugly.

"But I was merely hiding in plain sight," returned Blavatsky. "The Golden Dawn lies completely in shadow."

"And I suspect you have no idea about how to begin finding them?" questioned Abberline,

"You do not find the Golden Dawn; they find you," insisted Blavatsky. "If they want you to join their ranks, they reach out to you. That is only way they can be found."

"Goddamn it!" snapped Abberline, snatching the photograph out of Kalpesh's hand and presenting it emphatically once more in front of the theosophist. "Two women have been butchered in two weeks! He'll kill again soon enough and be one step closer to summoning Choronzon! If you want us to fail in stopping him, then keep talking in riddles and dodging our questions! Otherwise, give us something to go on!"

"I give you something already," spat Blavatsky resentfully. "I give you his name!"

"That's not much to go on in a city of five million people!" returned the frustrated chief inspector. "And Lord Boleskine sounds like a fake name if ever I did hear one!"

Blavatsky bit her tongue, and after a moment spoke calmly. "He was young," she explained. "His age," she added looking momentarily at Kalpesh, "maybe younger."

"Anything else?" pressed Abberline impatiently.

She nodded. "I believe he is rich. He mentioned manor he purchased—in Scotland, where he intended to carry out experiment... a ritual; one not been completed before."

"What kind of ritual?" asked Kalpesh.

"One that takes months to perform," alluded the witch.

"What is the purpose?"

"To summon a guardian angel," replied Blavatsky.

"The Abramelin Ritual?" questioned Kalpesh in disbelief.

"You have heard of it?" returned Blavatsky with surprise, alluding to the limits of her own understanding of the rite.

"The Abra-what?" interjected Abberline.

"Abramelin," repeated Kalpesh. "An

Egyptian mage; his grimoire, The Book of Abramelin describes an extensive ritual..." he explained. "Perhaps the longest and most complex of any sacrament ever recorded. It has numerous prerequisites before it can even be attempted—a period of celibacy, abstinence, living off only bread and water—prayers must be carried out before sunrise and at sunset throughout... it is estimated to take the better part of eighteen months! There is even a warning at the start of the Book of Abramelin, stating that the ritual should never be attempted!"

"Why?" queried Abberline warily. "Because it is too difficult?"

"Because it is too dangerous," returned Kalpesh anxiously.

"But if it is to summon your guardian angel...?"

"It isn't intended to summon one's guardian angel," asserted Kalpesh, staring at Blavatsky.

The witch awaited his next words, confirming Kalpesh's suspicions that she in fact knew very little of the ritual in question.

"The series of operations does involve making contact with a spirit, one that is allegedly the summoner's guardian angel, though I suspect in reality the evoked entity is more likely a demon making claims to be such. But the true purpose of the ritual is far more sinister."

"Out with it, Khatri," urged Abberline. "What is it?"

Kalpesh looked to see Blavatsky awaiting the answer as eagerly as his partner. "It is to gain dominion over certain demons—powerful demons, binding them to the caster's will; doing so is said to imbue the performer of the ritual with immense power."

"Der' mo," breathed Blavatsky, swearing quietly in her native tongue. "How you know all this?"

"He reads," answered Abberline, "...a lot!"

"You said you met him two years ago," continued Kalpesh. "Do you know if he ever completed the Abramelin?"

"Summoning the Dweller in the Abyss— tearing down the four towers..." began Blavatsky. "This is something even most powerful adept would struggle with."

"Then I think we can assume he was successful," put in Abberline.

"I should have suspected something along these lines," cursed Kalpesh.

"There must be something else you can give us?" pushed Abberline forcefully.

The witch shook her head stubbornly.

"Then maybe it is time I let Detective Khatri here go to work on you?"

"I have told you what I know!" snapped the Russian angrily. "You want more, I must speak to the Mahatmas!"

"That's not going to happen," insisted Kalpesh.

"Then as long as I am caged here like animal, I cannot help you anymore," she growled emphatically, tossing her head back and forth, jangling her chains. "Let me out and I will look beyond the veil—find out what it is you want. I can help you!" she insisted.

"Nice try," smiled Abberline, "but I don't trust you as far as I can throw you... and looking at the size of you—well, I can't imagine that's very far at all now, is it?"

Blavatsky scowled vehemently Abberline's way.

"I've seen what you can do," put in Kalpesh. "That cage is what is severing your connexion from the Aether. If we let you out, you could kill us both with just a few spoken words."

Blavatsky's cheeks curled upwards into a twisted smile. "This cage is not air-tight like you believe."

"Is that so?" questioned Abberline. "Then I'm sure you can exchange a few words with your *'Ancient Masters'* from in there and tell us more about our man!"

Blavatsky's smirk faded. "The Mahatmas still whisper to me; but they are too quiet for me to make out words."

"Or maybe you are just lying," returned Abberline.

"Or maybe I am not," replied the witch sinisterly.

"I think we are done here," asserted

Abberline, glancing at his partner. The two shared a look of agreement and Abberline made a gesture with his hand to the door for the guard watching on the other side of the one-way glass to see. "Thank you for the help, Madame Blavatsky," smirked Abberline, making his way towards the cell door. "We'll look into the information you've given us. We'll be in touch when you are feeling more cooperative. In the meantime, don't go anywhere," he added mockingly over his shoulder as the electronic bell clattered outside the cell and the steel door began to draw open.

Kalpesh followed Abberline out of the cell when the Russian witch called after him. "I turned the Beast away from the Theosophical Society, not because we could not teach him what he wanted to know, but because I was afraid of him," warned Blavatsky.

Kalpesh paused beyond the threshold, looking back to hear Blavatsky's final words.

"There is a darkness inside him unlike anything I have seen before; if he intends to open the Abyss, there is nothing you can do to stop him."

The cell door slammed shut and the bell fell silent.

XX

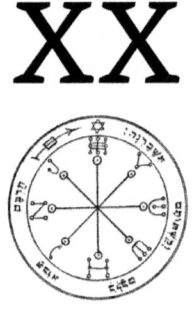

Anvil Archives, Tower of London, City of London
11:53 p.m. September 28th, 1888

Kalpesh rubbed his eyes as the words on the page once more fell out of focus. Abberline let out a soft grunt as he started to snore again, his head craned backwards over the top of his chair. The Indian detective focussed once more on the page in front of him, scanning through the endless stacks of records that had been sent over to Anvil from the Public Record Office on Chancery Lane. He sifted through countless names and addresses, all seemingly meaningless as he attempted to scour the endless lists of information in the hope of finding some breakthrough. For weeks they had been searching; no one by the name Lord Boleskine seemed to exist, or at least no one who might have borne any connexion to the occult; all they had discovered relating to the name were a few terribly written, smutty poems that had been published overseas, authored by one Lord Boleskine, of whom there appeared to be no other record.

The more they continued their research, the more Kalpesh feared Abberline had been correct in assuming that the name was a fake; either that, or Blavatsky had been playing games with them from the start. Kalpesh continued searching through the pages of legal records, trying to push the thought from his mind, yet as the clock atop Anvil tolled midnight, the idea that they had been hoodwinked crept back into his mind.

Of course Blavatsky had been lying! It made complete sense; the Golden Dawn was the dead giveaway and Kalpesh cursed himself for believing her when it had all been so outlandish. She either knew nothing of the Whitechapel killer or was defending his identity by feeding them false information. She had been too compliant, too quick to tell them what they wanted to hear, yet everything she had given them was too vague to follow up with any meaningful investigation! Her ploy had worked; they'd wasted over two weeks chasing false leads! The only comfort was that the killer had not struck again in the time they had squandered.

Kalpesh slammed the book shut in frustration, the sound startling Abberline awake. Realising he had drifted off, but clearly thinking it had been only a few seconds ago, the chief inspector quickly leant back over the page and resumed scanning the records splayed open in front of him, glancing up a few seconds later to see if his partner had noticed that he'd nodded off. Upon doing so, he saw the annoyance in Kalpesh's stare.

"Sorry," apologised the senior detective.

"It's not you," replied Kalpesh in exhaustion.

"Then what is it?"

"Everything she said was a lie, wasn't it?"

"Blavatsky?"

Kalpesh nodded.

"You've started to think that too, huh?"

Kalpesh peered off into space, his jaw tightening in frustration.

Abberline sighed audibly. "Maybe," he conceded. "Maybe she pulled the wool over our eyes; she had every reason to... But I've been in this line of work a long time, and I like to think that by now I can tell when someone is bullshitting me!"

"You reckon she was telling the truth? You reckon there really is an Order of the Golden Dawn and a man called Lord Boleskine who performed the Abramelin?"

"Maybe I've lost my gut instincts since transferring to Hammer," shrugged the chief inspector.

Kalpesh rubbed his eyes, rising to his feet to pace about the reading desks in the centre of the vast library of forbidden texts.

"We'll go question her again in the morning," insisted Abberline. "Turn the screws a bit tighter this time..."

Kalpesh nodded, pausing in front of the microfilm reader tucked in the corner.

"In the meantime, you should go home Khatri, get some rest... you've been here much longer than I have!"

"I'm fine," insisted Kalpesh flatly, taking a seat in front of the machine and peering once more through the lenses.

"I don't think you are, son," insisted his partner warmly. "You look stretched pretty thin. Just go get some kip. Meet me back here when you've had a shave and changed your shirt in the morning."

Kalpesh ignored him and began clicking through the reels of film, studying the miniaturised photographic records of suspected occultists and their known associates.

"Lad," insisted Abberline, "you've looked through that bloody thing a dozen times already this week—a file named Lord Boleskine isn't going to suddenly appear in there if you look again!"

"Maybe I've missed something," insisted Kalpesh.

"It's past midnight," reiterated Abberline.

"Just go home."

"*You* are still here," returned Kalpesh.

"I didn't get here until gone noon."

Kalpesh ignored him once more.

"Suit yourself," huffed Abberline, returning to the open page in front of him.

Kalpesh continued to flick through the film, until suddenly, he found himself on the dossier for one Samuel Liddell 'MacGregor' Mathers. He had read the file over several times, never lending it any special attention; the man was merely in the records because, being a rather eccentric individual, he had aroused suspicions with the paranoid member of the public that had reported him. He was merely on file as a formality; no serious investigation had ever been carried out into him, and the information gathered in the dossier was scant, many of the boxes on the form left blank. He had no record of employment and was seemingly something of a recluse, choosing to spend an inordinate amount of time in the British Library. What *was* noted about the intellectual, and what specifically caught Kalpesh's eye, was the extensive list of languages he was suspected to know; Kalpesh skimmed down the list, bemused that neither he, nor whoever had compiled the file originally, had noted that amongst the long listing were both Hebrew and Coptic.

Hebrew, though often implemented in various forms of Kabbalistic magic, was not terribly unusual, given the large Jewish population residing in the East End; Coptic however should have sent alarm bells ringing. The late form of Ancient Egyptian screamed of esoteric criminal intent: a dead language associated with various forms of magic utilised in everything from the Book of Thoth to the Book of Abramelin itself. Kalpesh suspected that the only explanation that could account for why Samuel Mathers had not been investigated further, was that whoever compiled the file was lacking in geographical knowledge, and merely assumed Coptic was perhaps some innocuous foreign tongue spoken in some far-flung reaches of the Empire, and thus had not bothered to follow up his report with any form of research. Kalpesh shook his head in disbelief, peering back down through the lenses once more at the magnified image of the microfilm. Enochian was not listed, but had such been the case, Kalpesh might have arrived at the conclusion that corruption rather than ineptitude had been the cause of this file being overlooked.

Coptic, though dead, was still an earthly language, one used by a real culture at an earlier point in history, whilst Enochian was never a tongue spoken by any culture at any point in time, known to humans only through John Dee and Edward Kelley's scrying. However, the thought swiftly occurred to Kalpesh that, were anyone to know Enochian, this Samuel Mathers was perhaps better qualified than anyone.

Kalpesh's attention was drawn away from

the microfilm by Abberline clearing his throat. "Khatri, I think I might just have found something!"

Kalpesh smiled, "so do I," returned the detective, "but you go first."

Abberline picked the record book up from the desk and presented it to Kalpesh. "Look there," he said prodding the page forcefully.

Kalpesh skimmed the looping handwriting of the clerk who had recorded the sale of a property on the shores of Loch Ness. Kalpesh's mouth rapidly broadened into a smile as he sighted the name of the property. "Boleskine House!"

"It gets better," insisted Abberline. "Look at the date of the sale."

"A little more than two years ago…" gasped Kalpesh as he read it over.

"It lines up with what Blavatsky said," smiled Abberline.

"It does," agreed Kalpesh. "And look at the square footage of the property and the recorded lands—if that doesn't constitute as a manor, I don't know what does!"

"I'm going to go make a call to our Edinburgh office—see if they can send a man over to go check the place out in the morning," declared Abberline.

"A *team* of men, I think," insisted Kalpesh. "If our man did attempt the Abramelin ritual at this property, then we have no idea what could be waiting for them in that house!"

"Point taken," agreed Abberline. "Did you see the name?" he added, gesturing to the page.

"No," returned Kalpesh, looking back down to skim the records.

"Sold by the Fraser family," explained Abberline, "to one Aleister Crowley."

"Aleister Crowley," repeated Kalpesh. "That could be our man."

"It might just be," agreed Abberline excitedly. "What was it you found?" he asked gesturing over to the microfilm reader in the corner.

"Oh, err... nothing. Well, not nothing," replied Kalpesh, "but this is much more important!" insisted the inspector, tapping the page emphatically.

"Come on," beckoned Abberline, "let's see if the lads up in Scotland are burning the midnight oil like us!"

XXI

Anvil Offices, Tower of London, City of London
8:47 a.m. September 29th, 1888

Kalpesh bolted awake in his chair as his head slipped from the hand propping it up. Looking around the Anvil office, he rubbed his eyes and stifled a yawn. Sorting a few papers scattered across his desk, he looked up to see Abberline stood beside him, an enamel mug of steaming coffee extended in offering to the Indian. Kalpesh smiled weakly and accepted the mug, blowing off the steam and taking a tentative sip.

"I take it you didn't get much in the way of sleep then?" asked Abberline, leaning against

Kalpesh's desk.

"I managed a few hours," replied the inspector, immediately taking a second sip of coffee before reclining in his chair. "Though, it certainly doesn't feel that way!"

"The call's just come in from Edinburgh," announced Abberline, taking a sip of his own.

"And!?" pressed Kalpesh leaning forwards.

Abberline nodded, smiling as he did so. "It's him."

"What did they find?"

"All sorts," replied Abberline more seriously. "The windows blacked out, the walls covered floor to ceiling with pentacles and every other kind of magical markings!"

"Sounds like somewhere the Abramelin has been attempted," returned Kalpesh.

"They took pictures," added Abberline. "They're posting them our way once they've been developed; we should get them in a couple of days."

"I'd like to see them."

"There's more," continued Abberline. "It sounds as if the Edinburgh boys were spooked. They reckon Boleskine House is haunted; some of them said they felt as if something was watching them the whole time they were there; doors were slamming by themselves, windows were rattling, and there wasn't even a breath of wind in the air!"

"I don't doubt it," replied Kalpesh gravely. "If this Aleister Crowley completed the ritual, who knows exactly what he unleashed!? Send word up to them to get an exorcist in there as soon as possible if they haven't sent for one already!"

"I think they've gone a step further," chuckled the aging inspector.

"What do you mean?"

"I might be paraphrasing, but I believe they said they planned to *douse the bloody floors in holy oil and burn the godforsaken hellhole down to ash!*"

"That bad?"

"It had them rattled," nodded Abberline sombrely.

"I'm not surprised," Kalpesh took another sip of his coffee. "What's next then?"

"We put together a file on this Aleister Crowley—find out who he is, any associates he has in London."

"It was too much to ask for the boys up north to have apprehended him?"

Abberline shook his head. "They spoke to the neighbours; they reckon he hasn't been back there in months."

"So, he genuinely did buy the property just for the sake of performing the Abramelin?"

"Looks that way," agreed the chief inspector. "Our man seems pretty single-minded."

"To complete the Abramelin you'd have to be."

"I'd say he rightfully earnt himself the nickname *The Beast*,"

Kalpesh nodded in agreement. "I just hope we can find him before he next strikes."

Abberline smiled weakly before standing abruptly to attention. Kalpesh swivelled in his chair to see Melville approach from behind. He rose to greet the recently appointed assistant chief constable.

"Sir," mumbled Abberline, nodding to his superior.

"Gentlemen," Melville greeted them gravely. "Both of you come with me," he added, straight to the point. "My office." Melville pivoted on the spot and took off, marching swiftly back the way he had come.

Kalpesh and Abberline shared a perplexed exchange before both men were forced to hurry after Melville.

"Sir, what is this about?" inquired Abberline as the two detectives caught up with the determinedly striding assistant chief constable.

"The Whitechapel killings," returned the man coldly as they exited the detectives' offices into the atrium of Anvil's foyer, "are the two of you closing in on the man responsible?"

"We believe we've identified him," confirmed Abberline. "We're just putting together a file."

"You need to move faster!" grumbled Melville as he took to the stairs, climbing multiple steps with each stride.

"As we've put in the reports, sir," explained Kalpesh, "we're facing off against an incredibly dangerous individual; he's earnt a reputation throughout the occult—"

"I've read your reports!" snapped Melville, cutting off Kalpesh midsentence as they reached the top of the flight of steps and made for Monro's old office. "Is it true?" he asked nervously. "Is he trying to summon…?"

"Choronzon," finished Abberline as they paused outside the door. The grizzled detective nodded. "We believe so, sir."

"Bollocks," swore Melville. He spun and stepped into his office. "Get in here. And shut the door!" he added sharply.

Tentatively, Abberline and Kalpesh stepped inside, closing the door behind them.

"Take a seat," uttered Melville flippantly.

"Sir? What is this about?" questioned Abberline again as he and his partner lowered themselves into the pair of chairs arranged in front of the desk.

Melville remained standing, striding over to the corner and pouring himself a drink from the decanter atop the spirits cabinet. He took a swig, planting the near-empty crystal glass down atop his desk before snatching up a sheet of paper.

"This here just arrived from the Central News Agency," he growled, shoving it at Kalpesh.

Kalpesh apprehensively took the page from his friend and began examining the letter penned in red.

"They had it for two days before they had the decency to send it our way—apparently they felt it was a hoax." Melville scowled as he grabbed his glass back from the table. "They must have had a change of heart though, since they've sold the story to the Daily Star, who are planning to print it in tonight's paper! They sent it to us ahead of time as a *show of good faith!*"

"It's dated from four days ago," noted Abberline.

"It's written in blood, for God's sake man!" snapped Melville.

"Are you sure, sir?" questioned Kalpesh, studying the clotted ink the letter had been penned with.

Melville nodded agitatedly. "We've already tested it. It's blood—a good chance its human too!"

"Dear god," breathed Abberline as he and Kalpesh began to read it the forward-slanting, neatly composed handwriting.

Dear Boss,

I keep on hearing Hammer has caught me but they won't fix me just yet. I have laughed when they look so clever and talk about being on the right track. Them buckling that fat old Russian gave me real fits. The Beast will not be caged so easily! I am down on whores and I shant quit ripping just yet. There is work to be done if the door to Hell is to be broken down and I'm not yet even halfway through. Grand work the last job *was. I gave the lady no time to squeal. How can they catch me now. I love my work and want to start again. You will soon hear of the fun I will have with the next one. By the time the Hammer strikes I shall have <u>disappeared</u>. Then we shall see what trouble the witch hunters have searching for an invisible man!*

I saved some of the proper <u>red</u> stuff in a bottle over the last job to write this letter. <u>Ha ha.</u> The next job I do I shall carve out the ladys eyes to show Hammer how <u>blind</u> they are, just for jolly. Keep this letter back till I do a bit more work, then give it out straight. My knife's so nice and sharp I want to get to work right away if I get a chance.

Good luck.

Yours truly
Jack the Ripper
Don't mind me giving away the trade name!

PS The <u>Devil</u> behind the gate is angry! Lets see what shall happen when the <u>Beast</u> lets him out on a leash! <u>Ha ha.</u>

A long uncomfortable silence elapsed after the two men finished reading the blood letter.

"Any chance it *is* a hoax?" asked Melville hopefully.

"No," refused Kalpesh, placing it back atop the desk. "He knows too much for it to be a fake."

"So what? The sick bastard is just taunting us?"

"Yes," returned Abberline, "but he's not *just* taunting us."

"Whatever do you mean?" questioned the assistant chief commissioner.

"He's trying to throw us off his scent."

"How so?"

"I'm far from the best critic of the written word, but I can point out all manner of punctuation errors in this thing," began Abberline.

"That's hardly noteworthy," returned Melville. "A tenth of the people in this city are straight up illiterate!"

"But when was the last time you saw a person who didn't understand grammar or bleeding punctuation with handwriting like this?"

Melville took another look at the letter, noting the elegance to the flowing script. "You make a good point, Chief Inspector," he apologised.

"You think he is feigning ignorance?" questioned Kalpesh. "Hoping that we'll mis-profile him?"

"I think that is exactly what he is doing," nodded Abberline. "He won't know that we've found out his name! He reckons we haven't closed in on him yet. He wants us to keep looking for some perverted anarchist in Whitechapel, not some toff that buys manor houses in Scotland as part of some master plan!"

"You are right," agreed Kalpesh. "He's trying to muddy the water whilst having a dig at us. But he must hate Hammer even more than most occultists to try and goad us like this—writing a letter in blood hardly constitutes as a joke!"

"This will be all over London by six o'clock tonight!" emphasised Melville. "We're going to come under a lot of fire. If we aren't careful, we'll be a laughingstock!"

"With respect, sir, we can't exactly be held accountable for this nut job sending letters to the press," put in Abberline.

"You two should have caught this man by now!" growled Melville, raising his voice. "You are two of the best bloody detectives in not just Hammer, but the whole Met, and it's taken you a whole month to come up with your first suspect— and all you have is a name!?"

Abberline sank back in his chair, accepting the scalding from his superior in silence.

"I want you two to get out there and catch this *Jack the Ripper!* Find him, bring him in, and chuck him in the darkest, deepest cell we've got!"

"Yes sir," the two detectives murmured.

"And for heaven's sake, be quick about it! The last thing we need is this cascading out of control with the papers! Whitechapel is in chaos enough as it is! We don't need any more fuel for the fire!"

An uncomfortable silence elapsed as both

Kalpesh and Abberline lowered their gaze.

"Do I make myself clear?"

"Yes sir," they repeated.

Melville huffed loudly. "Get out of here, both of you. You are dismissed!"

Keeping their heads low, they both rose from their chairs and made for the door.

"And take this bloody thing with you!" he added, snatching the letter back up from the desk and palming it off to Abberline.

The two detectives stepped out of the office, closing the door behind them.

"I appreciate his frustration," muttered Abberline as they descended the stairs together, "but it's not as if we've bloody sat around with our thumbs stuck up our arses!"

"He's just feeling the pressure," sympathised Kalpesh, feeling the need to apologise for his friend's attitude towards them. "He's only new to the job."

"That doesn't give him the right to act like a royal twat!" growled Abberline. "I felt like reminding him that it was only a fortnight ago that you brought in Blavatsky!"

"He knows that," insisted Kalpesh. "I think that's probably why he expects more from us."

As they reached the ground floor, Kalpesh turned to head back towards the office, but Abberline continued straight as if heading for the exit.

"Fred?" questioned the Indian, diverting

from his path to follow. "Where are you going?"

"Where are *you* going?" returned Abberline. "I need you out with me!"

"We're gathering information on Crowley, aren't we?"

"That's clerical paper pushing!" returned Abberline. "I've already got men over on Leman Street doing the grunt work for us. They'll have all the basics slapped into a file come lunchtime."

"Isn't it something we should see to personally?"

"Do you really think any of the stuff they'll dig up on him will actually help us find him?" questioned Abberline sceptically. "The man's a bloody ghost! If he is part of the Golden Dawn, he knows how not to be found. We're not going to turn up some current address by digging through public records—the man's in hiding!"

"I take your point," conceded Kalpesh. "But where are we going?"

"Whitechapel," returned Abberline. "I've got a few contacts that might just know something about our *Jack the Ripper!*"

"Okay," nodded Kalpesh as they neared the entrance to the cloakroom.

"Grab our jackets and hats, Inspector. We've got work to do!"

XXII

Dutfield's Yard, Berner Street, Whitechapel
1:41 a.m. September 30th, 1888

Kalpesh crouched over the corpse of a third victim. Her throat was cut down to the spine, blood pooled around the body as she lay slumped in the shadows near the corner of the entrance to Dutfield's Yard on Berner Street. Kalpesh clicked on his torch, casting the beam of light over the victim to study her in greater detail.

Outside the yard, a crowd was gathering as patrons from the socialist club next door spilled out into the gaslit road, mingling with the awoken residents of Berner Street to try and see what was going on. Just inside the entranceway, Abberline was interviewing Lois Diemschutz, the Russian jewellery merchant who had not long earlier discovered the body.

"Let me run through this again with you," insisted Abberline, skimming the scribblings in his notebook. "You were on your way back from the market at Crystal Palace?"

The Russian nodded.

"You pulled into the yard here, and your pony startled?"

"That's right," Diemschutz agreed. "Just here," he pointed to where he was stood.

"You tried to encourage your pony into the yard, but it wouldn't shift. It was then you realised there was something lying on the ground out in front—but you couldn't make out what?"

He nodded.

"You prodded it with your whip but had no response, and so, you climbed down off your cart and lit a match to try and make out what it was."

"Correct, sir."

"You say the match blew out almost immediately, but in that time, you made out the body of the deceased?"

"Yes."

"But instead of raising the alarm, you first went back into the club?"

"I did not know she was dead," explained the Russian.

"Even still, you left a woman you perceived to be unconscious alone in the street!?"

"Look..." the Russian shifted on the spot anxiously. "I thought it was my wife," he whispered. "You know... drunk—again!"

"I see," nodded Abberline taking notes.

"I went to go find someone to help me drag her inside..."

"Only to find your wife was already inside?"

"That's right," nodded the man, smiling nervously.

"So, you told the men inside the club that there was a woman lying out in the street and you did not know if she was drunk or dead."

"Yes," Diemschutz confirmed.

"And so, you and several of the patrons from the club—I presume those men gathered in the street over there trying to gawk at this poor woman's corpse, came back out with a lantern, where you discovered, to your horror, that her throat had been cut?"

Diemschutz nodded silently again, offering an anxious smile to Abberline.

"Okay," sighed the aging inspector heavily, rubbing his whiskered chin. "You are a resident of number forty here, you say? You are a steward of the working club? And your wife helps you manage it?"

"That's right."

Abberline continued to question the Russian, but their conversation faded into the background hubbub of the street as Kalpesh stopped paying attention. He arose, looking down at the victim, intrigued by the lack of mutilations that had been present on the other two cadavers. Were this indeed the work of the Ripper, the Indian would have expected another level of escalation; yet the only wound, aside a few faint bruises, appeared to be the singular deep cut to the throat. They'd have to wait for the surgeon and the photographer to arrive for confirmation, but as it stood, it seemed to be the full extent of the attack. But what surprise Kalpesh more, was the absence of a pentacle. There was no form of magical inscription of any kind in sight. Stepping further into the dark yard, he paced its circumference, shining the light of his torch over every region of the square concealed in shadow. Still he found nothing.

Returning to the body, he knelt closer to the murdered woman again. She had yet to be identified, but she matched the other victims superficially enough that Kalpesh was confident she was a prostitute. It was of course possible that this was merely a normal murder, nothing supernatural about it; they were in Whitechapel after all. But somehow, that didn't seem likely.

The Indian gently peeled back the woman's collar to further unveil the gash across her throat; though it was difficult to tell for certain, the laceration looked incredibly deep; that at least, matched the Ripper's modus operandi.

"Thoughts?" asked Abberline, stooping over his partner to get his own look at the cadaver.

"It's him," confirmed Kalpesh.

"You sure?" questioned Abberline in surprise. "What about the pentacle? The disfigurements?"

"I don't think he had time," hypothesised Kalpesh. "I reckon he was interrupted—possibly by that man you just interviewed."

"You think he fled the scene when he heard the cart coming?"

"No," refused Kalpesh. "I think he was still here, hidden in the shadows."

"And he made his getaway when Diemschutz went inside?"

Kalpesh nodded. "I reckon had he *not* gone inside, we might have been standing over *two* bodies right now."

"Poor sod doesn't know just how lucky he was," mused Abberline. "Well, there is *some* good news out of this," continued the chief inspector. "The next step in his ritual has not yet been performed."

"I'm not sure that is good news," replied Kalpesh gravely.

"What do you mean?"

"He was interrupted—he wasn't stopped. I reckon he'll kill again in quick time," warned Kalpesh, looking up at his partner. "We might have days... or maybe just hours!"

Heavy footfalls came echoing across the

cobbles from Berner Street. Both Kalpesh and Abberline rose to their feet, stepping out of the entrance to Dutfield's Yard to see who was charging their way. The crowd parted as a police constable came sprinting at full tilt from the north end of the road, skidding to a halt as he sighted Abberline and Kalpesh.

"Sir..." he gasped, "Inspector Abberline!"

"What the devil is it Mizen?" demanded Abberline.

"Sir," he breathed heavily, his eyes glimpsing down the entrance to the yard at the body cloaked in shadows.

"Shit!" breathed Kalpesh, already knowing what the constable was about to say.

"There's been another one!"

"What!?" questioned Abberline in disbelief.

"It's him, sir—she's been ripped!"

"Where damn it!?" growled the chief inspector.

"Mitre Square," he sputtered, "near Aldgate, sir!"

"How long ago?" demanded Kalpesh.

"I..." he shrugged.

"How long ago!?"

"Minutes, sir."

Before he had time to think, Kalpesh had taken off north towards Commercial Road.

"Hold up Khatri!" Abberline cried after him as the Indian took flight, but in a matter of seconds, the older of the two men had fallen well behind his partner.

Kalpesh's hard shoes rattled across the cobbles, his open coat flapping behind him as he hurtled out of Berner Street, veering left onto Commercial Road. The arc lamps hummed, flooding the main thoroughfare with cold electric light as the Indian detective now raced westward. A gust of wind channelled down the wide street, catching the brim of his hat, flipping it from his pate, sending it tumbling off to his rear. Kalpesh peered back over his shoulder without slowing, but lost sight of the garment as it vanished into the dark. He continued, charging down the five-hundred-yard stretch until he reached Gardiner's Corner, the junction with Whitechapel High Street. There, he bore left, rushing onto the final straight.

He charged passed Aldgate East, gasping deep, sharp breaths as he felt a stitch begin to tear into his side. In less than a minute he had closed the distance to Aldgate Station, cutting across the front of St Boltoph's Church. Kalpesh veered right up Duke Street, passing the primary school on his left before slowing to a trudge as he approached the dark and narrow corridor of Church Passage.

He halted, chest quivering as he caught his breath. Peering down the passageway lit by a single gas lamp at the far end, he failed to make out Mitre Square beyond the pall of darkness. Arresting his laboured breath, acutely aware of his heart throbbing beneath his chest, Kalpesh anxiously stepped into the alley.

Before he had made it halfway down the claustrophobic walkway, the light of a bullseye lantern glared from up the passage, momentarily blinding him. Raising a hand to shield his eyes, he heard a husky voice call down the way from out of Mitre Square.

"Who goes there!?"

As Kalpesh's eyes adjusted to the light, he made out two silhouettes up ahead.

"Not another step!" a second more youthful voice ordered.

"Detective Inspector Khatri," puffed Kalpesh, still not having yet fully caught his breath. "Special Branch," he added, reaching into his jacket to present his badge to the lamp light spilling down the pass.

"Thank god!" he heard one of the men sigh.

"You got here fast!?" puzzled the other in disbelief as the beam of light lowered. "Come on, she's just through here."

Kalpesh warily trudged the last few yards down the narrow alley, emerging from Church Passage beneath the corner gas lamp. The square was bordered on three sides by high warehouses; a second wall-mounted gaslight burnt on the opposite corner of the yard by the entrance from Mitre Street, yet the freestanding streetlamp centred in the square appeared to be suffering from a faulty gas line, the flame within flickering only faintly, casting barely a square yard's worth of dim light around it. As such, the men that greeted Kalpesh, like much of the square itself, were cloaked in shadow.

"I came as fast as I could," exhaled Kalpesh as he stepped nearer to the two men, seeing now that they were both uniformed constables.

"We appreciate that," nodded the first. "PC James Harvey."

"PC Watkins," greeted the older of the two men, looking the sweating detective up and down. "You ran here?"

"I only phoned through to Scotland Yard a few minutes ago!" added Harvey.

"Scotland Yard?" Kalpesh repeated, realising that he had crossed the border out of Whitechapel and thereby left H Division jurisdiction. "You two are with the City Police?"

They both nodded.

"Did you come from Anvil?" questioned Watkins, gesturing vaguely in the direction of the Thames.

Kalpesh shook his head, realising now that the Tower of London was only a half mile southward. Any minute now he could expect back up to arrive. "I was at the other site," explained the detective. "Less than a mile away."

"The other site?" the two men repeated in unison.

"You don't know..." realised Kalpesh. "This is the second time the Ripper has struck tonight!"

"God save us," PC Watkins breathed as the

two men looked to one another in dread.

"Where is the body?"

"Over there," gestured PC Harvey, indicating to a corner of the square shrouded in almost complete darkness.

Without needing to be shown, Kalpesh pushed past the two constables and shone his torch into the shadows.

"I found her about fifteen minutes ago," explained Harvey. "Less, maybe. Sent the watchman from the Kearley and Tonge warehouse for help. He's an ex-bobby."

"He ran into me not more than ten minutes ago," added Watkins. "I phoned in the murder at the police box down the road."

Kalpesh nodded, now almost ignoring the two constables entirely as he gradually unveiled the brutal crime scene with the slow ascent of his torch. Butchered on the cobbles in a still-widening pool of blood was another prostitute, this time bearing the full malefic artistry of the Ripper. Her legs were parted and her abdomen drawn open; organs torn out of her pelvis and draped across the body. Her face had been carved to pieces, and to Kalpesh's horror, as promised, the Ripper had removed the poor woman's eyes from their sockets. Raising the ray of light higher, Kalpesh revealed a third pentacle still glistening as the fresh blood congealed against the brickwork above the corpse.

The sound of horse drawn carriages echoed in the distance from down Mitre Street as Malleus began to close in on the scene from the direction of Anvil.

"Jesus!" cried PC Watkins, averting his gaze as the light unveiled the horror of the eviscerated body. "It's worse than I thought!"

"No..." breathed Watkins in disbelief. "No... she wasn't like this!"

"What do you mean?" questioned Kalpesh, turning to see the police constable swivelling his head, glancing about in frantic terror.

The man nearly leapt out of his skin, dropping his lantern as a second set of footsteps clattered from down Church Passage. Moments later, Abberline emerged beneath the lamplight, visibly out of breath.

"Khatri?" he called out, wheezing as he sighted the Indian inspector stood before the body with the two constables.

"What do you mean!?" Kalpesh repeated more commandingly, turning his attention back to the frightened constable as he watched the man slowly begin to lose his grip of the situation.

The officer's eyes bulged in terror as he raised a shuddering finger back at the corpse. "She... she..." he began.

"Out with it, man!" insisted Watkins, grabbing hold of his fellow uniformed officer to steady him.

"You don't understand!" he blurted suddenly. "She wasn't like that when I found her!"

"Wasn't like what?" wheezed Abberline as he finally reached the three of them.

"That!" Harvey shouted, pointing to the bloody mess of drawn intestines pulled from the corpse.

Kalpesh glanced back at the body, shining his light on the pentacle once again. The tumult of Malleus officers approaching the square from the south grew louder. In mere moments, their backup would be on the scene.

"He's right!" dismayed Watkins suddenly. "She wasn't like this before you got here!"

"What the devil do you mean!?" pressed Abberline.

"She wasn't opened up like that..."

"She must have been," insisted the chief inspector dismissively as he clicked on his own electric torch and started an investigative sweep of Mitre Square. "You boys are just in shock," he insisted, walking the perimeter as he waited for the ever-nearing help.

"No!" refused Harvey. "Her face was cut up — her eyes carved out... but the rest of her..." he grimaced, turning away from the gruesome sight. "She hadn't been gutted! I swear!"

Horror suddenly swept over Kalpesh as he realised the nature of the pentacle painted in the woman's blood across the brickwork.

"What's that over there?" bemused Abberline, sighting something in a corner of the square shrouded in almost complete darkness.

"Fred!" called out Kalpesh anxiously.

The faulty gaslight centred in the square flitted out, the faint glow it emitted dying away completely, darkening the square that little bit more.

"Do the rest of you see this?" called out a perplexed Abberline from across the court.

"Fred!" cried Kalpesh louder, the full weight of his realisation hitting him like a punch to the gut. The sigil painted in blood was the Sixth Pentacle of the Sun. The power it granted: invisibility. "Fred! He's still here!"

Kalpesh spun on the spot, hand instinctively reaching for his holster. On the far side of the square, Abberline was shining his torch into a darkened corner of the court, where a seeming trick of the eye was warping the beam emitted from the incandescent bulb. The rays of light seemed to bend and shimmer in a supernatural aura around an empty space tucked away in the darkness, causing a mirage-like effect that gave away the illusion for what it was. Upon hearing his partner's words, Abberline glimpsed momentarily back at Kalpesh before his hand reached for the Mauser holstered on his own belt.

Both men took aim at the mirage, behind which could only be concealed the Ripper hiding in the dark. But before either man could pull the trigger, the shroud of contorted air dissipated, and a black clad figure leapt from out of the shadows. Kalpesh and Abberline simultaneously opened fire and a hail of bullets clattered across the square.

Moving impossibly fast, their target raised a palm and a bubble of translucent energy materialised in front of him. The dome of magic rippled as it deflected the fusillade of shots fired, each bullet pinging and shrieking as it ricocheted off the arcane ward, the rounds deflecting harmlessly away in hot streaks of light.

Abberline suddenly howled in agony as a reflected slug ricocheted into his thigh. The grizzled detective toppled backwards, thumping hard into the cobbles. Kalpesh's pistol emptied, clicking uselessly in his hand as he continued to pull the trigger to no avail. The protective arcane ward suddenly evaporated, and without delay, the man behind it took flight, charging off towards Church Passage.

"Fred!?" cried Kalpesh, rushing towards his downed partner.

"I'm fine!" groaned Abberline, clutching his bleeding leg.

Kalpesh hesitated, watching the Ripper vanish down the narrow alleyway as he darted out of Mitre Square. He looked left to see the first carriage pull up outside the entrance to the court on Mitre Street; out stepped a pair of Malleus officers. He glanced back to Abberline to see his partner still glaring at him.

"I'm fine!" he repeated, sitting upright. "Get after him!"

Without needing to be told twice, Kalpesh gave chase, spurting into Church Passage, hot on the heels of the Ripper.

XXIII

Duke Street, Aldgate, City of London
2:00 a.m. September 30th, 1888

St Botolph's Church's bells clanged the hour as Kalpesh's feet hammered north up the cobbles of Duke Street. Up ahead, a dark figure scudded beneath the streetlamps, swooping right, cutting between the rows of terrace houses towards Houndsditch. Kalpesh swerved sharply around the corner, his legs moving as quickly as they could carry him as he pursued the most dangerous man in London. In seconds, he emerged onto Houndsditch, crossing the boundary between the

City of London and Whitechapel. He swivelled his head left and right, catching glimpse of the Ripper just as he slipped into the narrow alley of Gravel Lane. Following south, Kalpesh darted after his man, sighting him again directly ahead as they charged down the claustrophobic alley of slums.

"Stop!" roared Kalpesh as he slowly gained on the fleeing villain.

They flew down the steadily tightening passage, the buildings pressing inwards on either side. Reaching the end of Gravel Lane, they emerged suddenly onto a gaslit bridge above a set of railway tracks.

The Ripper glimpsed back over his shoulder as he charged out onto the overpass. Seeing his pursuer hot on his heels, he veered right, vaulting over the parapet, dropping down onto the tracks below. Kalpesh skidded to a halt in front of the low wall, peering down over the ledge to the dimly lit railway line below. The killer landed on the tracks, taking the twenty-foot-fall in his stride, barely breaking step as he darted back into a sprint. Pivoting around, he dashed beneath the bridge into the cover of shadows.

Kalpesh watched the villain vanish as he stood hesitantly peering at the drop below. It was a long way down; if he botched the landing, he'd at best break an ankle, and at worst hit the electrified rails of the track. Cursing in frustration, he abandoned any notion of leaping from the ledge, spinning on the spot to dart back across to the other side of the bridge, charging north up the road to follow the path of the underground line.

Crossing over Stoney Lane, the cut and cover rail line emerged into the open again. Up ahead, Kalpesh sighted the Ripper emerge from the tunnel, sprinting down the train tracks as he tried to make his escape. Fumbling for the ammunition pouch on his belt, Kalpesh drew a clip of cartridges whilst on the run. Jamming the charger into the receiver slot of his Mauser, he forced the cartridges downwards into the magazine and discarded the stripper, continuing to race down the narrow path of White Street parallel to the tracks.

"Stop!" shouted Kalpesh after the man again, realising he was rapidly approaching a tunnel up ahead that disappeared beneath Harrow Alley; thereafter the Metropolitan line did not resurface again until Barbican. If the killer continued on, following the Metropolitan Line below ground, Kalpesh would have no other option than to brave the jump down to the tracks or risk losing the Ripper by the time they hit Liverpool Street Station.

The Indian halted, raising his pistol, resting his forearms across the top of the parapet to steady his aim. He tracked the shadowy figure dashing across the tracks below as he approached the gaping aperture of the tunnel ahead. His finger curled, squeezing the trigger. The Mauser C96 snapped deafeningly, muzzle glaring against the night. The sound of lead striking steel whined through the streets as the bullet bounced off the line. The shot had dropped substantially, falling short of his target; he was too far out of range!

Kalpesh accelerated off the mark, giving chase once again, readying for the moment he would be forced to leap down onto the tracks to continue his pursuit. He cursed as the figure below approached the yawning tunnel entrance. Leaping up onto the wall, heart thumping in his chest, he contemplated the fall to the tracks three fathoms beneath him; he'd have to lower himself down first to lessen the distance. He crouched, readying to hang from the wall, but as he looked across the tracks, he watched the impossible unfold up ahead.

Still on the run, the Ripper began to list sideways. Despite the ground remaining perfectly flat, the killer appeared as if he were running on a camber, that with each step grew more severe, until all of a sudden, his boots stepped off the gravel lining the tracks, up onto the arched brickwork of the railway trench.

Leaping back down from the parapet, Kalpesh broke into a sprint once more, staring across the rail line in disbelief as the man he pursued scaled the near vertical surface as if he were running across a horizontal plane. In mere seconds, the Ripper had dashed up the side of the railway trench, vaulting over the parapet on the far side of the Metropolitan Line, where gravity resumed its natural orientation, planting the murderer back onto the cobbles of Artizan Street.

Still struggling to process what he had just seen, Kalpesh gave chase, cutting swiftly right along Harrow Alley over the entrance of the railway tunnel. Warehouses and terraces blurred past left and right, all the while, Kalpesh's focus remained on the man fleeing from him thirty yards ahead. Tears began to well in his eyes. His legs burned and a stitch cut into his flank, but he pushed on, ignoring the pain as best his body could allow, forcing himself to gain on the man ahead.

Reaching the end of the alley, the Ripper veered left up the curving passage of Sandy's Row. Kalpesh trailed shortly behind, catching glimpse of the man each time he darted beneath a wall mounted gaslight. A sharp turn to the right took them down Frying Pan Alley, and before Kalpesh knew any better, he had followed the Ripper into the twisting labyrinth of narrow back passages that formed the Halifax Estate.

The Ripper turned this way and that, swerving left and right as he tried to lose his tail through the warren of decaying houses. Kalpesh frequently lost sight of his quarry, following only by the rattling of hard-soled shoes echoing through the passages ahead. Several people ducked out of the way into doorways, narrowly managing to get clear of the two men hurtling at speed through the shadows of the back streets.

Kalpesh staggered suddenly to a halt. He had come to an opening: Cox's Square, right in the heart of the rookery. To his dismay, he had lost sight of the Ripper altogether. He glanced frantically about at the three possible alleys down which his prey might have fled. He listened for footsteps, hoping the sound of hard shoes against the cobblestones might betray the fleeing killer. He caught ear of what he was listening for, but for a moment he was unable to locate the source. Quickly, he snapped his head back, just in time to see a shadow vanish across the rooftops above.

"Damn it!" Kalpesh growled in frustration, desperately searching for a route upwards. With no easy path in sight, he faced his only option. He leapt up off the cobblestones, grasping hold of a downspout. He heaved himself upwards, wedging his foot in a gap left by a missing brick in the wall. Reaching overhead, his fingers curled around a splintering windowsill. Hoisting himself higher still, he planted a shoe on the metalwork that fixed a shop sign to the face of the building. Scrambling up the next floor by way of the spout and another crumbling windowsill, he hooked his fingers over the guttering and dragged his weight up onto the cracked tiles of the pitched roof.

Standing erect atop the house, Kalpesh scanned the rooves, sighting a distant shadow against the hazy amber glow of the London city skyline. Kalpesh took off, clambering up the slanted rooftop before darting along the ridged apex of the terrace row. Stumbling to a halt at the end of the run, his feet dislodged several shingles that were sent tumbling to the dark street below. Scanning the way ahead, he picked out a path and turned to dash along the next line of buildings, crossing an alleyway below via the roof of a covered passage, traversing to the next straight of rooftops across the way.

Kalpesh quickly caught up with the man he was chasing, rapidly closing to within a dozen yards. But reaching the end of the row, the Ripper charged for the precipice, leaping across a narrow alley, planting his feet on the rooftiles of the next terrace over to continue his flight. Kalpesh felt his heart rise in his throat as the gap raced up to meet him. He kicked off from the ledge, throwing his weight high into the air. His stomach somersaulted as the street below sailed under him.

He touched down hard on the other side. A tile cracked, slipping away underfoot. Kalpesh lost his balance, slamming hard onto his shoulder. All of a sudden, he was sliding down the pitch of the roof, the precipice rushing up to meet him. He scrambled with his fingers at the tiles to no avail, but as he reached the eaves, his heels struck the guttering, halting his descent before he plummeted from the ledge. Yanking himself upwards, he fought his way back to the apex of the row and resumed his pursuit.

The Ripper had pulled away in the time Kalpesh had lost, but the Indian was determined to catch up to his quarry once again. He vaulted over another narrow alley, this time nailing the landing, before, purposefully dropping onto his side, he slid down the pitch ahead of him, clearing the ledge and touching down on a lower stretch of rooftops. Turning along a perpendicular run of houses, the Indian dug into his last reserves, summoning all his strength to narrow the gap. He leapt clean across another alleyway, powering up over the ridge of the next stretch of buildings, sighting the Ripper across the way.

The chasm between them was further than anything he had jumped before now, but the route around was too far; the diversion would risk him losing the Ripper for good. Steeling his resolve, Kalpesh charged towards the brink with all his might. Hurling himself into the air, he tucked in his legs and flailed his arms as he sailed high above the cobbles of the street below. He felt himself began to drop as he cleared the apex of his parabola. His heart stopped midbeat as he realised in horror that he was going to fall short.

The eaves rushing up towards him, Kalpesh braced in dread, readying his body for impact. His chest slammed hard against the tiles, his knees smacking numbingly against the brickwork underneath. Clawing with his hands, he groped desperately at the smooth roof slates, trying in vain to clasp hold of anything within reach as he started to slip from the ledge. His fingertips snagged around a wonky tile, but to his dismay, it pulled loose in his grip. Suddenly, he was plummeting from the precipice.

Chin smacking the lip of the eaves as he tumbled towards the darkened alleyway below, Kalpesh at last felt his fingers hook around a gutter. Shoulder and arm snapping painfully taught, he came to a dead stop, dangling in mid-air from the ledge three floors above street level.

Daring to look down, his stomach turned over. The iron fixings holding the guttering in place groaned. Glancing back overhead, he could see the metalwork beginning to buckle. Using the last of his strength, Kalpesh heaved himself upwards, swinging a leg out and hooking his heel in the channel of the gutter. Scrambling on the slates, he fought his way back up onto the roof, climbing shakily to his feet.

He glanced ahead, searching for the Ripper. There, up in front, the murderer was approaching the end of the terrace. Taking after him one final time, Kalpesh raced across the rooftops of Dorset Street, determined to head the Ripper off once and for all.

Drawing his pistol, he took aim on the run. Sights swaying violently about as he sprinted at full tilt along the rooftop ridge, Kalpesh did his best to time his shot. He fired. A bullet whizzed through the air, narrowly missing his target ahead, cracking into a chimney. He squeezed the trigger again. This time, roof slates exploded beneath the Ripper's feet, shards flying in every direction.

Reaching the end of the terrace, the killer skidded to a stop inches short of the precipice.

Below, the broad expanse of Commercial Street stretched out across the way, the white spire of Spitalfields Christ Church rising on the far side. It was a dead end: a chasm fifty feet across, and a drop forty feet down. The Ripper was trapped. Menacingly, he turned to face Kalpesh.

Still advancing towards the Whitechapel killer, Kalpesh slowed from his sprint into a steady forward march as he continued to discharge shot after shot from his Mauser. The Ripper once again raised his palm, summoning another translucent shield, just as he'd done in Mitre Square. The cannonade of gunshots deflected off the arcane bulwark one by one, howling as they streaked away in glowing arcs before vanishing into the dark.

The Ripper began to move towards Kalpesh, palm still upraised, shield protecting him. Mirroring his foe, the Indian detective continued to march towards the killer, gun trained on his target, the Mauser cracking deafeningly with each bullet discharged. The gap between them closed to nothing as Kalpesh readied to fire off the last round in his magazine. He squeezed the trigger just as the Ripper's fingers closed around the muzzle of his gun. The bulwark of energy collapsed, imploding around the bullet, sealing the gunshot inside the barrel of the pistol.

The Mauser backfired. Kalpesh yelped as the barrel ruptured and an expulsion of hot gas seared across his hand. Suddenly wrenching on the gun, the Ripper twisted the ruined pistol in the Indian's grip, locking out the detective's elbow with a violent jerk.

Kalpesh winced, releasing the gun out of his grip, somehow managing to slip his finger free from the trigger guard before it broke. The Ripper suddenly pivoted, driving a shoulder square into Kalpesh's chest, knocking the already unbalanced detective clean off his feet.

Thrown to the slates, Kalpesh rolled away down the slope of the roof, narrowly avoiding a boot driving for his face. Leaping back to his feet, the Indian detective reached around his back for the kukri sheathed on his belt.

The Ripper discarded Kalpesh's ruptured pistol, tossing the Mauser into the darkness of Dorset Street below, before reaching inside his coat to draw his own blade. An incarnadine stained athame, still wet with his latest victim's blood, glinted in the pale light of the moon. Darting back up the pitch of the roof, Kalpesh lunged for his foe with a cleaving swing. The Ripper nimbly ducked aside in a display of absurd speed and agility, snapping his body back upright to riposte with a slash of his own.

Already wrongfooted, Kalpesh staggered away, barely managing to parry the counterattack slicing for his throat. Their weapon edges bound, the Ripper's athame hissing down the inward curve of Kalpesh's kukri until it bit into the notch.

Reeling back, the Indian disengaged, leaping

away to narrowly avoid a lancing redoublement from the Ripper. Swinging wildly to counter, Kalpesh felt his blade sail through nothing but clean air. Overcommitted to the strike, his leading foot lost purchase on the slanted rooftiles. Boot slipping, he stumbled passed the Ripper as he fought to stay on his feet. Capitalising on Kalpesh's mistake, the Ripper slashed effortlessly at the Indian detective, slicing through the fabric of his coat, blade biting at the flesh beneath as he cut a burning gash across his back.

Letting out a sharp scream, the detective swung back around in another wild retaliatory attack, but once again, his kukri cleft wide, missing the Ripper by more than a foot. This time, the punishment was a slice across the back of the hand.

Kalpesh gasped, involuntarily letting go of his kukri. The curving blade clattered to the tiles, and before Kalpesh could see where it had landed, a boot was planted firmly in the centre of his chest.

The world span violently as he somersaulted backwards, tumbling and flailing out of control down the pitch of the roof. He felt the eaves smack underneath him as he dropped over the precipice. By some miracle, the fingers of his uninjured hand hooked around guttering for a second time that night.

His shoulder strained as he dangled helplessly from the ledge. Averting his gaze from the fall below, Kalpesh peered upwards to see the hilt of his kukri poking out from the guttering above him. Grimacing in pain, he tried to reach for his weapon, but in that moment, a set of sinister eyes appeared above him. The toe of a boot tapped the kukri and Kalpesh watched in horror as it tumbled from the precipice, vanishing into the darkness below.

The Ripper knelt over Kalpesh, finally revealing his face in the amber haze of the streetlights. A set of sunken eyes glared down at the Indian, his irises black with malice; he was younger than Kalpesh, likely in his mid to late twenties, but what he lacked in age he made up for in intimidating presence. A wicked smile graced his thin lips as he flourished the bloody athame in his hand, and with a grotesque sense of amusement, he pressed the edge of the blade against Kalpesh's fingers.

"So," he whispered, leaning in closer so that his face was as near as he could get to Kalpesh. "You are Kalpesh Khatri, the famous witch hunter?"

Kalpesh let out a cry as the killer began to apply pressure to his blade, drawing blood.

"I'm disappointed," he mocked, licking his lips. "I had hoped our paths would cross, but I expected more from you!"

"Why are you doing this!?" gasped Kalpesh as he dangled helplessly, fumbling with his other bloody hand to try and get a second grip of the rooftop.

"Would it disappoint you terribly if I told you that it was all to satisfy my own sadistic curiosity? To sate my own despicable and wicked fetishes?"

"I know that's not true!" insisted Kalpesh. "I know what you are planning—what you want to unleash on this world!"

"If you are so certain, then tell me," remarked the man amusedly. "What exactly is it I am planning?"

"Choronzon," croaked Kalpesh as the edge of the blade cut harder into his skin. "You want to summon Choronzon!"

"Clever you," remarked the Ripper mockingly. "Tell me, why do you think I plan on calling forth the Dweller of the Abyss?"

"You want to destroy the world!" wheezed Kalpesh, his eyes momentarily flitting to the fall below. If he let go now, he'd break his legs, but he'd more than likely survive.

"I don't want to destroy it!" returned the man. "I merely want to tear it down—start anew!"

"Once you release Choronzon..." puffed Kalpesh, struggling to keep his grip, "there is no way to imprison him again!"

"You think I intend to set him free?" questioned the Ripper. "Let him wreak havoc across the world? No. I am not some anarchist without a plan!"

"You want to try and control him!?" sputtered Kalpesh in confusion.

The man issued a broad and crooked smile.

"You won't be able to!" insisted Kalpesh. "You underestimate his power!"

"And you underestimate mine!" insisted the killer smugly. "I am the Beast! Six, six, six! I am Jack the Ripper!"

"I know who *you* are," returned Kalpesh, offering his own wry smile, before whispering. "Aleister Crowley!"

Crowley rose to his feet, taking a step back. "My, my…" he mused in amazement. "You *have* been busy! Perhaps you *are* worthy of the reputation you've earnt!"

"You thought you covered your tracks…" huffed Kalpesh, his arm burning in agony as blood trickled down his hand and dripped onto his cheek. "You left loose ends! Maybe you aren't as smart as you think!"

"It no longer matters if you know who I really am," he returned. "It is too late for you to stop me."

"Maybe," conceded Kalpesh.

"It seems a shame to kill you, really," remarked Crowley, twiddling the point of his athame between his fingers.

"Why bother?" asked Kalpesh. "You said it yourself: I'm too late to stop you."

The Ripper chuckled. "Nice try," he remarked. "Although, I would very much like you to see the end result of my work."

"Malleus will stop you," returned Kalpesh.

"With or without me!"

"They have failed to so far," replied Crowley smugly. "This is the closest they've gotten—and look where you and I have ended up!"

"But we know who you are now!"

"But you don't know how to find me!"

"We'll see about that."

Crowley smiled again. "This is your lucky day, Detective. I have decided I am going to spare you after all. When this is all over, I'll find you again. We'll see who emerges the victor in the end."

Crowley stepped back from the ledge, vanishing into the shadows.

Kalpesh grimaced, clasping hold of the guttering with his other wounded hand. His arms screamed in agony as he heaved himself upwards, swinging a leg over the ledge. He dragged the dead weight of his body back up onto the roof. Gasping for air, he fought his way to his feet and searched around the rooftops. Crowley was gone. The Ripper had once again vanished into the night.

XXIV

Anvil, Tower of London, City of London
10:31 a.m. October 1st, 1888

Kalpesh sat nursing his bandaged hand, glancing at the postcard lying atop his desk out of the corner of his eye. He leant forwards and felt a twinge from the long line of stitches across his back as he retrieved the postcard and reread the flowing script inked in blood.

I was not codding dear old Boss when I said the witch hunters would be looking for *an invisible man. You'll hear about Saucy Jacky's work tomorrow, double event this time! Number one squealed a bit, couldn't finish her straight off. Ha, not the time to get eyes for Hammer. The second got ripped too quick to scream! I'm glad to hear the famous Hindoo detective is an admirer of my work. The <u>Devil</u> is in the detail after all!*

Thanks for keeping back the last letter till I got to work again. There's still one more left to gut before the real fun can start and I've got something special planned for my new friend in Hammer!

Jack the Ripper

The tapping of a walking stick across the floor tiles echoed through the Malleus offices. Kalpesh swivelled in his chair to see a haggard looking Abberline limping towards him.

"Fred!?" cried Kalpesh in confusion. "What on earth are you doing here?"

"What do you mean *what am I doing here*?" he questioned. "We've got a bloody bedlamite to catch!"

"But..." stammered Kalpesh, glancing down at the hardy detective's trouser leg visibly bulging from the bandages underneath. "You were shot!"

"The bullet barely grazed me!" insisted the grizzled inspector. "After all, it was only a ricochet."

"You were in surgery for over an hour!" returned Kalpesh. "Does Emma know you are here?"

"Yes," grumbled Abberline.

"Is she happy about it?"

Abberline shook his head, issuing Kalpesh a wry smile.

"You should go home," insisted Kalpesh. "Rest up!"

"I'm not going to help you catch this psychopath from bed," returned the man stubbornly.

"Well, at least take a seat!" insisted Kalpesh, leaping out of his office chair and offering it to his partner.

"Alright," agreed Abberline, easing himself into the chair. He grunted as he stretched out his leg and leant his walking stick against the desk. "You alright son?" he asked, looking up at Kalpesh. "I hear our man tried to throw you off a rooftop?"

"He had a change of heart," returned Kalpesh coldly.

"He what!?"

"He let me live," explained Kalpesh. "I think he wants to watch us fail in trying to stop him."

"Does he now?" growled Abberline.

Kalpesh silently gestured to the blood-smeared postcard on the desk.

"What's this?" questioned the chief inspector, picking it up to study it.

"The follow up to the letter he sent the press," explained Kalpesh as he waited for his partner to read it over.

"This bastard loves the spectacle, doesn't he!?" snarled Abberline in frustration. "What was he like in person?"

"About what you would expect," returned Kalpesh dismissively.

"That file on him arrive from Leman Street yet?"

Kalpesh nodded.

"You read it over?"

He nodded again.

"Well spill it then—what are we dealing with?"

"Aleister Crowley, originally Edward Alexander Crowley—born into wealth, the son of evangelical Christians," began Kalpesh. "His father was an engineer who earnt his fortune through the family brewing business. The man died when Crowley was eleven, after which he was sent to a religious boarding school. Needless to say, he rejected the Christian teachings, rebelling throughout his adolescence. It would seem before she died, his relationship with his mother was strained at best—it appears it was her that originally gave him the nickname, 'The Beast.' He supposedly revelled in it."

"Still does by my reckoning," put in Abberline. "What else?"

"He moved about from various schools—no

formal record of expulsion, but it would appear he was *asked to leave* a number of colleges."

"Unsurprising," remarked Abberline.

"It would seem he developed something of a fixation with prostitutes during this time," explained Kalpesh. "It appears from his medical records that at some point he contracted both gonorrhoea and syphilis."

"Well, that explains why he has been targeting whores," muttered Abberline.

"He studied philosophy and English literature at Cambridge where he became president of the chess club and developed an interest in mountaineering—something he supposedly has quite a talent for."

"What else?"

"It's hard to pinpoint, but I imagine it was during his time at Cambridge that he developed an interest in the arcane. Since he left Cambridge, our records of him become spotty. We don't have a solid timeline of his whereabouts, and the last time he showed up on any official documentation was when he purchased Boleskine House a little more than two years ago."

"Anything else?"

Kalpesh shrugged. "Though we can't determine anything for certain, we believe he has travelled around somewhat," he explained. "His passport suggests he's widely explored Europe. He's been to Russia and spent time in both India and Egypt; supposedly he was at one stage considering a career as a diplomat and thus endeavoured to learn a number of languages."

"Which he is putting to good use now," remarked Abberline cynically.

"He is suspected of having several homosexual partners," added Kalpesh, "but it seems he struggles to maintain relationships with members of either sex. People tend to find him... disagreeable—narcissistic, perhaps."

Abberline nodded. "No leads then?"

"Sadly, no," agreed Kalpesh.

Abberline huffed loudly, skimming the postcard once more. "It's difficult enough to find a man like this—someone who has learnt to keep a low profile. But when that same man can vanish from sight—teleport from one place to another unseen... how the devil are we supposed to track him down!?"

"We'll get him," assured Kalpesh, though he noted the lack of optimism in his own voice.

Abberline reached for his walking stick and grimaced as he rose out of his chair.

"Where are you going?"

"The streets," he murmured. "Whitechapel."

"Do you want me to come?" asked Kalpesh.

Abberline sighed wearily. "No," he said. "I'm probably wasting my time. I just can't sit around here whilst that monster is out there."

Kalpesh nodded.

"I'll phone in if I find anything," Abberline

added. "In the meantime, if you've got anything you want to look into, any hunches—any gut feelings, I suggest now is the time to give them a look over."

"Alright," agreed Kalpesh defeatedly.

"Don't worry, Khatri," insisted Abberline as he began to limp away, "we'll see this bastard swing soon enough!"

"I hope so," muttered Kalpesh to himself as he retook his seat and watched his partner make for the exit. He sighed heavily, tapping the postcard on the desk before discarding it atop a pile of paperwork. He hesitated, looking at the file on Aleister Crowley before pulling it aside. There, beneath the Ripper casefile, was another that had three days ago been sent to the bottom of the pile. He peeled back the folder, looking over the information he had retrieved from the archives having first looked over it in the microfilm reader. Perhaps it was time he looked into Samuel Mathers.

XXV

Russell Square, Bloomsbury
12:41 p.m. October 1st, 1888

Kalpesh turned the page of The Times as he leant against the wrought iron railings surrounding Russell Square, skimming through the broadsheet. Yet another article on the Ripper murder stretched across the page.

Two more murders must now be added to the blacklist of similar crimes of which the East-end of London has been very lately the scene. The circumstances of both of them bear a close resemblance to those of the former atrocities. The victim in both has been a woman. In neither can robbery have been the motive, nor can the deed be set down as the outcome of an ordinary street brawl. Both have unquestioningly been murders deliberately planned and carried out by the hand of someone who has been no novice to the work. It was early yesterday morning that the bodies of the two women were discovered, at places within a quarter of an hour's walk of one another, and at intervals of somewhat less than an hour. The first body was found lying in a yard in Berner-street, a low thoroughfare running out of the Commercial-road.

The discovery was made about 1 o'clock in the early morning by a carter, who was entering the yard to put up his cart. The body was that of a woman with a deep gash on her throat, running almost from ear to ear. She was quite dead, but the corpse was still warm, and in the opinion of the medical experts who were promptly summoned to the place, the deed of blood must have been done not many minutes before. The probability seems to be that the murder was interrupted by the arrival of the carter, and that he made his escape unobserved, under the shelter of the darkness, which was almost total at the spot. The efforts of Malleus to trace the murderer have been without result yet. They set to work without delay. Their first attention was directed to the inmates of a Socialist Club, close to the place at which the body had been found, but there was nothing to give ground for a reasonable suspicion about any of them; nor was there any one in the neighbourhood of the locality on whom the guilt could be presumed to rest.

The body has been identified as that of ELIZABETH STRIDE, a widow according to one account, according to another a woman living apart from her husband, and by all accounts belonging to the "unfortunate" class. Her movements have been traced to a certain point. She left her house in Dean-street, Spitalfields between 6 and 7 o'clock on Saturday evening, saying that she was not going to meet any one in particular. From that hour there is nothing certainly known about her up to the time at which her body was found, lifeless indeed, but not otherwise mutilated than by the gash in the throat, which had severed the jugular vein and must have caused instantaneous death.

Not so the corpse of the second victim. In this case the purpose of the murderer had been fulfilled and a mutilation inflicted of the same nature as that upon the body of ANNIE CHAPMAN. It was in the south-

western corner of Mitre-square, in Aldgate
that the second body was found. It was
again the body of a woman, and again had
death resulted from a deep wound across the
throat. But in this instance the face had also
been slashed as to render it hard for the
remains to be identified, and the abdomen
had been ripped up and a portion of the
intestines had been dragged out and left
lying about the neck...

Kalpesh flipped the page, not wanting to read another word. They still had yet to identify the poor woman who had fatefully ended up the Ripper's second victim of the night; her face so brutally carved to pieces that she had thus far proved unrecognisable to anyone they had brought into the morgue. The papers had sensationalised the grotesque nature of Crowley's murders, but Malleus and the Met had done well to hold several key details back from the public. For one, the surgeon who arrived on the scene swiftly after Kalpesh had given chase to Crowley noted that, in addition to the woman's eyes, the Ripper had also removed her left kidney and uterus. None of the organs had been found at the crime scene, and Kalpesh suspected that, like in the case of Annie Chapman, they had been consumed in the ritual that both granted the Ripper with the siddhi of invisibility, and compromised another

Watchtower holding shut the gates to the Abyss.

Though Malleus' involvement reliably informed the public that the murders were in some way esoteric, neither the pentacles from the Key of Solomon painted in the victims' blood, nor the ritualistic aspect of the killings were public knowledge. And just as well. Whitechapel was already on the brink of revolt; were residents of the East End to find out that the Ripper's ultimate plan was to tear down the pillars of creation and open a gate to the Abyss, the heavy police presence in the borough would not be enough to prevent the chaos that would undoubtedly ensue.

But the panic would not stop at Whitechapel, nor London, nor even Britain itself. If the true weight of the situation became widespread knowledge, the world itself could cave into hysteria. Fortunately, few even within Malleus truly understood what was at stake; demonology wasn't exactly widely understood, and even amongst those within the organisation that had heard of Choronzon, few truly comprehended what the supreme being represented. Though the air of tension was apparent throughout Anvil, the Indian detective suspected that few, if any beyond himself and Abberline, actually grasped that the world at present was teetering on the brink of the apocalypse.

The inspector pushed the thoughts from his mind and continued to skim the paper, waiting patiently as he kept one eye on the path above him, watching as pedestrians continued to stroll by. A few more minutes passed, before, as predicted, a slim, pale-skinned, moustached man in his mid-thirties strode briskly past Kalpesh. Samuel Liddell Mathers ignored the Indian reading the newspaper altogether as he crossed diagonally through traffic and made his way south down Montague Street towards the entrance of the British Museum, inside of which laid the British Library. Like clockwork, the suspected occultist had made the journey he was reported to almost every day of the week.

Kalpesh wondered exactly what it was the man was studying inside the Pantheon-esque building that sat in the heart of the Museum's courtyard. There was little in the way of esoteric material accessible to the public; the vast majority of arcane texts and grimoires were forbidden from public access. Anything that had once been housed inside the library had been relocated to the Anvil archives forty years earlier.

It was more than possible that the man merely had an insatiable appetite for reading; Kalpesh after all was a sufferer of the same addiction. The idea occurred to him in that moment that he himself should apply for access to the reading room; his promotion to inspector certainly gave him the necessary credentials. It was curious however, that Mathers had managed to gain permission when access was normally restricted to registered researchers. The man had supposedly served sometime as an assistant librarian at the Horniman Museum; perhaps that served as a sufficient qualification to gain entry to one of the largest collections of texts in the world.

Kalpesh watched the man vanish into the crowds some way away. Folding his newspaper, he turned around and strode into Russell Square. He cut diagonally across the gardens, following the path until he exited on the far corner of the square. There he opened the door to the Hackney carriage in which he had arrived half an hour earlier.

"Thank you for waiting," he greeted the driver. "Great Percy Street, if you will."

"Right away, sir," the driver remarked, and as Kalpesh stepped inside the carriage and shut the door, he whipped the reins and the horses began to move off.

Kalpesh peered out the window as the Hackney carriage jostled across the cobbles, making its way northeast across Bloomsbury. Passing Regents Square and St Peter's Church, the driver finally steered diagonally across King's Cross Street as they drew near to the address. Driving a semi-circle around the Percy Circus roundabout, the cabman steadily eased up, pulling over onto the side of the road as they arrived at their destination. Kalpesh stepped out onto the street of the well-to-do neighbourhood and paid the driver.

"Do you want me to wait again?" he asked,

pulling an apple from out of his pocket and taking a bite.

"No need," returned the Indian inspector. "I don't know how long I'll be."

The cabman nodded. "Enjoy your afternoon, sir," he smiled, crunching a second mouthful from the fruit, before with a flick of the wrist, he signalled his horses to move off.

Doublechecking the address he had scrawled on a scrap of paper, the detective slowly strolled up the hill, glancing casually about the street numbers until he arrived at the terrace house believed to be the current residence of Samuel Mathers. Coolly looking up and down the row, the detective took note of the other pedestrians walking up and down the street. Only a dozen yards away, a woman pushing a pram was slowly approaching. Kalpesh leant against the railing outside the property, unfolding the newspaper he had tucked under his arm, once more pretending to read the tiny print as he waited for the coast to clear. He smiled at the middleclass mother as she passed him by, she offered him the same courtesy, though Kalpesh suspected insincerely. Once she had reached the end of Great Percy Street, disappearing as she made her way around the circus, vanishing behind the trees, the detective glanced about the road once more, this time satisfied that he was suitably alone.

Swiftly climbing the steps to the front door, he knelt before the lock, rapidly drawing the case of lockpicks from out of his coat. Inserting a pick and torsion wrench into the keyhole and twisting the cam to the point of tension, the detective made swift progress at clicking each lever upwards into place until the final gate opened and the tension released. Rotating the wrench around, Kalpesh felt the bolt retract inside the lock. He tried the knob, verifying his success as the door eased gently open.

Kalpesh rose to his feet, and checking that he had not been observed, slipped through the door, shutting himself discretely inside. He was stood in a porchway tiled in black and white diamonds. A hat stand and coatrack were pressed up against the wall, whilst a stained-glass window arched above the doorway to the ground floor corridor ahead. Brushing his shoes on the mat to ensure mud tracked in from the street did not give away his intrusion, the detective stepped over a set of discarded slippers lying by the door and made his way through into the corridor ahead. Crimson wallpaper rose upwards from walnut half-panelling that stretched across the hallway and ascended the stairwell to the first floor above.

Tentatively, Kalpesh inched further inside, listening for any sound to suggest there might be anyone in the building. Finally satisfied he was alone, the detective made his way down the hall, opening the door to the front room and peering inside. A massive Persian rug occupied much of the floor, whilst several wingback chairs were arranged around a darkly varnished coffee table in the centre of the room. Stepping through the door, Kalpesh was immediately drawn to the three large bookcases lining the back wall; the fitted shelves were crafted from the same wood as the panelling and the cases stood full height, stretching from floor to ceiling. Every inch of the shelves was occupied, the assortment of books meticulously ordered, seemingly alphabetised and arranged by genre.

Running a finger over the row of spines, Kalpesh skimmed the titles and authors as he worked his way from one end of the room to the other. The man's reading tastes appeared as eclectic as his own. Numerous literary classics had earnt their place upon the shelves, whilst more modern works of fiction carved out their own deserved region. There were travel journals, scientific theses, medical and botanical textbooks, atlases and encyclopaedias, all arranged in a precise and well-thought-out manner. The inspector could not help but feel envious as he reached the end of the small library; he smiled in admiration before realising that he had found nothing of what he had been really looking for. Not a single book upon the shelves so much as resembled a tome or grimoire; every work of fiction and non-fiction alike was entirely legal and unrestricted, and would not so much as place Mathers on a watch list.

Kalpesh stepped away, looking around the

rest of the room, noting that there was nothing else of interest. He made his way back out, pushing towards the rear of the property. He inspected the kitchen and pantry, finding nothing of note, and even spent some time looking about the dining room to no avail. Finishing his circuit of the ground floor, he made his way upstairs. A bathroom fitted with a modern flush toilet lay behind the first door at the top of the stairs, whilst a pair of bedrooms made up the rest of the floor.

Inside the master bedroom, a fourposter bed was erected against the rear wall, whilst an armoire and dresser stood either side of the fireplace. Sifting briskly through the chest of drawers and peeking inside the wardrobe, the inspector found nothing but clothing. The second bedroom appeared unoccupied, the bed neatly made but covered with a quilted throw that seemed long undisturbed. The wardrobe in the guest room appeared to hold overspill from the master bedroom, consisting of older, less pristine garments. Yet as Kalpesh pulled the hangers across the rail, something struck him as unusual.

He pulled out what appeared to be a plain white wraparound skirt of some kind; thus far he had found only male garments. He studied it curiously for a moment, but ready to merely dismiss it and hang the garb back inside the wardrobe, it then suddenly occurred to him that the item in question was unlike any skirt he expected a woman to wear; it was short, falling just above the knee, and was too wide around the waist to rule out as children's attire. Kalpesh puzzled over the item for a long moment, finally deciding he was unlikely to come to any firm conclusion as to its presence in Mathers' wardrobe. As such, he hung it back away.

Preparing to shut the wardrobe and begin his search of the top floor, he noticed a second peculiarity hidden beneath a top hat resting on the upper shelf. Several folds of gold and black striped fabric were poking out from under the brim. Lifting the hat, Kalpesh slid the item out and inspected the strange garment.

As he let it dangle in front of him, the detective quickly realised what he was holding; it was an Egyptian headdress, not unlike what Pharaohs were depicted wearing on most of the sarcophagi on display in the British Museum: a nemes. Suddenly the white dress made sense; it was a shendyt, another garment likewise worn in ancient Egypt.

But knowing what both items of clothing were did not leave Kalpesh any less puzzled. The reason for their being there was no less clear; perhaps Mathers had at some point attended a costume party, something that Kalpesh understood happened from time to time amongst the upper classes; alternatively, perhaps the costume had an esoteric significance in some occultic ritual, though that was mere speculation. Regardless, he replaced the nemes beneath the top hat and finally left the wardrobe alone, turning his attention to the top floor.

Another bedroom sat atop the stairs, this one scarcely furnished, whilst the final room in the building was a small study complete with a writing desk positioned in front of the window. The detective moved to open the desk, only to find it locked, but a quick inspection with his fingers beneath revealed a tiny key hung from a hook concealed out of sight. Unsurprisingly, the key fitted the desk lock, and after a short moment fiddling, the detective slid it open. Sifting through an array of papers in anticipation, Kalpesh eventually let out a sigh of defeat. In his hands he merely held a few letters and financial documents, none of which were remotely incriminating.

Kalpesh closed the desk, locking it shut and returning the key to the hook where he had found it. He glanced about, hoping to see something that might prove the whole venture had not been a waste of time, but after a long moment, the detective hung his head in disappointment and made his way back downstairs.

Performing a final sweep of each of the rooms as he made his way back through the house, he once more failed to spot anything awry. Out of options, he returned towards the front door and readied to leave. Just before he stepped through into the porch, he hesitated. Something was bothering him about the property, and the more he pondered it, the more he felt it should have been obvious. Kalpesh opened the front door, stepping out into the street; sure enough, like every other house on the row, Mathers' property was in possession of a lower ground floor. Yet at no point in his search had Kalpesh come upon the staircase that should have led down to it. He had left no door unopened; it was not something he had simply missed.

Kalpesh made his way down the steps to the pavement, quickly realising why it was that there was no stairwell leading down to the partially submerged bottom floor: it had been annexed into a separate flat. Affixed to the iron railings next to a steep set of concrete steps was the flat's own house number.

Kalpesh considered accepting defeat, locking the door to Mathers' property and turning away. But Abberline was always insisting he follow his gut, and something about Mathers just didn't add up. He glanced up and down the quiet boulevard, satisfied that he was still alone, before descending the flight of steps to the underground flat. The curtains were drawn inside, obscuring any view into the small apartment. The detective rapped his knuckles on the door and waited a long moment. No reply came. He tried once more, just in case, but there was still no indication that anybody was inside.

Pulling out his lockpicks for a second time, Kalpesh got to work on the door. He inserted his torsion wrench and pick, only to quickly realise the door was not actually locked. Slightly embarrassed that he had not first thought to try the handle, he rotated the knob and pushed inwards. It failed to budge. Suspecting it was merely stuck, the inspector applied greater force, but there was still no give whatsoever. He drove a shoulder against the wood, but still the door resisted him solidly.

Stepping back, the detective rubbed his chin in confusion. He considered for a moment that he had been wrong, and that the door was in fact still locked, yet that notion quickly left him as he examined the paintwork across the doorframe and on the door itself. In various regions, the dried paint bridged across the gap; it had been painted over whilst shut, sealing the door to the frame. Judging by the cracks and weathering to the wood and paintwork, Kalpesh suspected that it had been done some time ago: months, or maybe even years. The door was sealed from the inside. The apartment was a facade.

Kalpesh knelt again in front of the door, this time using his thumbs to lever open the letter box. The flap lifted and he peered inside, yet his view through the slit was completely masked by a black veil. Something was draped over the inside of the letterbox, preventing anyone from attempting to peek in. Kalpesh smiled. If this didn't arouse suspicion, what else would?

He ascended the steps back to street level and hastily re-entered Mathers' house, tripping up on the doormat as he did so. Letting the door swing shut behind him, he rushed over to the rear end of the staircase that led up to the floor above and began tapping against the wallpaper and panelling. Sure enough, the pitch of his knuckles knocking against the wall changed as he moved along the panelling; there was a cavity behind. He'd discovered a false partition.

The detective began running his fingers and palms over the wall, examining it for any sign of a conceal doorway. It took a few moments of searching, but he quickly found a seam in the wallpaper that was not stuck down, beneath which a thin crack could be made out with his fingertips. Tracing the straight ridge down to the panelling, he noted a thin shadow gap visible where two sections fitted together, something otherwise absent in the finish of the rest of the panelling. Kalpesh smiled to himself, knowing then that he'd found the way down. Now all he had to do was find a way to open it.

Applying pressure with both hands to the centre of the concealed door, he gave a gentle shove and felt a latch spring open. The wall swung away on a set of hinges, unveiling a wooden stairwell that descended into darkness. Fumbling inside the doorway, Kalpesh discovered a light switch fixed to the bare brickwork. He flicked it, waiting for a long moment before a hanging bulb fizzled to life at the bottom of the steps. Uncertain what he was about to find, he stepped down into the secret room.

XXVI

Great Percy Street, Pentonville, Islington
1:15 p.m. October 1st, 1888

When Kalpesh reached the bottom of the staircase, he stopped dead in his tracks. More bookcases lined the wall to his left, the shelves laden with as many volumes as those in the sitting room above. However, unlike the library of literature upstairs, each and every tome was a forbidden esoteric text. Just glancing over the illicit collection, Kalpesh sighted both The Lesser and The Greater Key of Solomon, the Book of Thoth, The Book of Abramelin, The Grimoire of

Armadel, John Dee's diary, and countless other forbidden manuscripts. Mere possession alone of any single one of the grimoires lining the shelves warranted the death sentence.

Beyond the bookcases, Kalpesh sighted various glass cabinets set about the room; inside the nearest were a set of wands, each uniquely crafted with different cultural symbolism. One resembled Caduceus' staff, tipped with a set of wings and entwined by a pair of golden serpents. The implement beside it was adorned with the Star of David, whilst the next culminated with the Ankh symbol, the Egyptian 'key of life.'

The next cabinet over held various decorative athames, whilst in the final case, Kalpesh observed several mannequins adorned in vestments of various colours. Across the chest of each set of robes was emblazoned the same emblem. Kalpesh had never seen the insignia before; nonetheless, the Indian inspector's prior research assured him that he was staring at the Rose Cross of the Golden Dawn: a complex emblem comprising dozens of different symbols which represented everything from the four elements to the zodiac, including all manner of other religious and esoteric iconography. This was something many in Malleus had been hunting for for years: proof that the Hermetic Order of the Golden Dawn existed!

The secrets of the underground room did not end there; every square inch of the walls, and a good portion of floorspace, were plastered with sheets of paper, each covered in scribblings. Pinned in sequence across one wall were three scores of cotton pages; on each were inscribed a set of elaborate notes encrypted in a set of bizarre characters. It was this series of folios upon which all the other notations seemed to be the focus.

At first, Kalpesh thought that the symbols were perhaps some strange esoteric language which he had yet to encounter in all of his arcane research, yet as he examined the pages encircling the cotton paper folios, he realised the notes referencing the strange symbols were translations. He understood then that the symbols did not belong to any language, but were rather an encryption, one that he had indeed encountered before: the Trithemius Cipher, a cryptograph invented by the fifteenth century German Benedictine abbot, Johannes Trithemius.

The cypher looked illegible to the untrained eye, and perhaps it had appeared as such for Mathers when he had first begun decoding the manuscript plastered across the wall, but once understood, it was simple enough to decrypt. Two things were required: the key that denoted the symbols to their corresponding characters in the English language, and secondly, the tabula recta, a twenty-six by twenty-six-character table whereby in each subsequent row, the alphabet shifts one character to the left. When coding a message, with each letter written in the communication, the coder drops a row, thereby creating a cycling code that, without understanding, looks utterly incomprehensible. Sure enough, central to the entire decrypted scribblings affixed to the wall, were both the tabula recta and Trimethius' key.

Kalpesh moved across the wall, skimming the hundreds of pages scrawled in Mathers' hand. Concealed within the manuscript were countless rituals, and what appeared to be parts of a syllabus in esoteric education, but as Kalpesh glanced across the workings, he noted something circled in red: an address, one in Germany, that supposedly belonged to a woman by the name of Anna Sprengel.

Kalpesh stepped back from the wall of translations and continued to look about the room. He came to a second writing desk, this one left ajar, and ran his eyes over the mess of letters scattered across the desktop. Immediately, he picked out the same name and address he had seen seconds earlier on the wall; Mathers had been corresponding with Anna Sprengel and an additional man residing in London by the name of William Wynn Wescott, who from the tone of the letters, appeared to be a personal friend of Mathers. Kalpesh picked up several of the letters from the desk, rapidly sifting through them, extracting the key information and compiling it in his mind.

Their intentions were clear from the start. The letters dated the earliest discussed the founding of the Hermetic Order of the Golden Dawn, or at least, the first lodge in Britain. As the correspondence progressed closer to the current date, there were discussions of establishing a new sanctuary in the heart of London, the Isis-Urania Temple, set to be the headquarters of the clandestine order. Kalpesh continued to skim through the pages and pages of letters, hoping by some miracle to spot somewhere an address or clue as to where the secret headquarters might lie for the most covert occultist society the world had ever seen. Yet despite the clear belief amongst the three corresponding individuals that their line of communication was secure, they were smart enough never to make direct mention of the location. Instead, they spoke of a disused masonic hall, one which had served as the secret lodge for the Societas Rosicruciana in Anglia before its dissolution.

The Societas Rosicruciana in Anglia existed before Kalpesh's time in Malleus, but as far as the detective could remember, the society collapsed when several high-ranking members of the occultic brotherhood were apprehended across London over the course of a single night nearly ten years ago. It had been the culmination of years of investigation, with a Malleus agent managing to even infiltrate the lowest ranks of the order. What stuck out to Kalpesh as he remembered reading about the operation, was that despite the identities of numerous high-profile members of the society being revealed, the main headquarters of the underground society was never disclosed.

Suddenly a great realisation struck Kalpesh: a coincidence presented itself to him that seemed too great to be merely happenstance. One of the more prominent individuals apprehended during the night of arrests that collapsed the Societas Rosicruciana in Anglia was none other than architect Sydney Smirke, the man behind the circular Reading Room of the British Museum. There had to be a connexion with Mathers' excessive visitation to the Reading Room beyond his thirst for knowledge; the coincidence was too great to be ignored. It was all circumstantial; Kalpesh was merely connecting the dots; but as Abberline had once told him, that was what most good detective work was.

What if, concealed in his plans for the Pantheon-esque structure erected inside the museum's courtyard, was a hidden entrance to some underground vault, or tunnel, or hall of some kind? What if the location of the Order of the Golden Dawn's headquarters, one of the best kept secrets in the entire occult, was hidden beneath one of London's most iconic landmarks? One visited by thousands of people each day! It seemed ludicrous; but it also seemed somehow possible, and perhaps even likely.

Kalpesh checked his watch. It had just gone half one. He had seen enough. He wasn't going to find any better lead than the theory he had just concocted. Mathers regularly left the house unattended for extended periods during which Kalpesh would be able to slip back inside unnoticed in the future to gather further insights. He had evidence to prove Mathers' links to the Golden Dawn; Malleus protocol dictated that he should immediately report his findings at Anvil, but he knew he couldn't just yet. He had to delve further and see what else he could uncover before things moved ahead. Mathers wasn't going anywhere, but Crowley on the other hand, was plotting the next and final stage of his ritual to tear down the gates to the Abyss.

If Kalpesh reported his findings now, Malleus would raid the premises and arrest Mathers. The rest of the Golden Dawn would surely find out soon enough and go to ground, and Kalpesh's efforts towards determining Crowley's whereabouts could be completely undone. He had to wait; that was what Abberline would do.

Kalpesh turned back up the stairs, flicking the switch at the top, sending the room below back into darkness. Grabbing the edge of the secret door, he pulled it closed, swinging it forcefully inwards the last few inches. The latch clicked shut and Kalpesh checked it momentarily to ensure it was as Mathers had left it. He stepped around the corner into the main hallway and started towards the front door. But before he could make it so far, he sighted something that made the blood in his veins chill.

By the door, the doormat was crumpled; in his eagerness to uncover the hidden underground study, Kalpesh had tripped on it when he re-entered the house. Only now did he realised that, in doing so, he'd uncovered something concealed beneath it. Painted onto the encaustic tiles, just inside the threshold of the door, was a red pentacle. The arcane seal was still mostly covered by the mat, but its presence and location were enough for Kalpesh to deduce its purpose. It would serve as an alarm, a magical tripwire of sorts, no doubt triggered the moment anyone unauthorised set foot inside the property. Seconds after Kalpesh had broken in, Mathers would more than likely have been alerted.

Footfalls rattled up the front steps and the murmuring of voices sounded behind the door. Kalpesh froze on the spot, paralysed by the fear he was about to be discovered. A key inserted into the door, turning to discover that it was already unlocked. Immediately the handle began to revolve. The door swung open.

Kalpesh must have come to his senses, because, as daylight spilled in through the porch, he found himself cowering behind the corner, out of sight from the door.

"See!" remarked one of two men, more than likely Mathers himself.

"You sure you didn't leave it unlocked?" questioned the other.

"I'm pretty sure," returned Mathers, though there was an air of doubt in his mind.

"What do you reckon then?" questioned the other man. "Burglars?"

"In the middle of the day?" doubted Mathers as they made their way inside.

"If they knew you were out…" insisted the second individual as Kalpesh heard them step into the sitting room as they began to look around for any sign of intruders. "They might have been watching this place for some time."

Kalpesh peeked around the corner. The front door was wide open, but he knew he'd be spotted

SHADOW OF THE GOLDEN DAWN

for certain if he made a run for it. Alerting Mathers to the fact that he had been searching his property would scupper his hopes of finding the Golden Dawn's hideout. He couldn't risk being spotted, regardless of any suspicions Mathers already had. Barely daring to so much as breathe, he tiptoed further towards the back of the property, slipping inside the kitchen.

"All the furniture is still here," remarked Mathers as they emerged back into the corridor. "Do you still think it might have been a burglar?"

"Do you have anything valuable in any other room?"

"Upstairs—no."

"What about *downstairs*?"

"Shut the door," Mathers commanded.

Seconds later, the sound of the front door clicking shut sounded, followed swiftly by the deadbolt locking into the frame. Kalpesh skulked as silently as he could towards the backdoor, but as he approached, he saw movement through the windows. Several men in dark suits had entered the back garden through the gate and were ascending the rear steps towards the door.

Kalpesh screamed internally, realising his route of escape was blocked, and that if he didn't move fast, he'd be discovered. He poked his head back out of the kitchen. The door to the secret basement room was open, the light switched on, but the hallway ahead was empty. He slipped back out into the corridor just as a key slotted into the

339

backdoor in the kitchen. He heard movement from down in the secret study as he slunk past. Moving briskly for the front door, he crept through the porch, ensuring to skirt clean around the pentacle still partially concealed beneath the rumpled doormat. He reached for the lock.

"Not another move," a voice spoke coldly from behind him.

Kalpesh's heart skipped a beat as he froze on the spot.

"Turn around—slowly," the man commanded.

Kalpesh gradually revolved to see a greying bearded man in his forties stood halfway up the stairs facing him. In his hand, aimed in Kalpesh's direction, was a wooden wand.

"Who are you!?" the stranger demanded, taking several steps down the stairwell to draw nearer Kalpesh.

"No one," insisted the detective.

"I doubt that!"

Kalpesh heard movement emerging from the back end of the property. It was enough to momentarily divert the occultist's attention. Kalpesh's hand shot for his holster, drawing his pistol in the blink of an eye.

"I'm leaving now!" he insisted quietly, backing towards the front door, fumbling blindly for the lock.

"No—you aren't," came the voice of Mathers.

Kalpesh swivelled his gun down the

corridor ahead, taking aim at the adept. Like his friend on the steps, Mathers held a wand aimed directly at the Indian in the doorway.

"Get back!" threatened Kalpesh, cycling targets between the two men as Mathers continued to advance down the hallway towards him.

Out of the kitchen, three more men emerged, each holding a wand of their own.

"I'll shoot!" warned the detective as his fingers found the lock behind him and twisted it open.

"Not another move!" threatened Mathers.

"Or what?" questioned Kalpesh, feigning ignorance as to the danger the wands aimed his way posed. "I'm the one with a gun here!"

The group of men chuckled amongst themselves.

"You think we don't know who you are?" questioned one of them. "Why you are here?"

"How did you know to come here?" questioned Mathers.

"Stay back!" growled Kalpesh again, "or I swear to God, I'll shoot you!" He moved to open the door, but Mathers suddenly raised his voice.

"Don't!" the adept cried with absolute authority.

Kalpesh halted.

"You know perfectly well how inadequate a defence that peashooter is against us," continued the sorcerer coldly. "If you make another move, we will rip you limb from limb! Now step away from the door!"

Reluctantly, Kalpesh took a step back into the porch.

"Good," smiled Mathers. "Now, tell us, Inspector Khatri, how did you find out what I was?"

Kalpesh dropped the act and smiled. "We've been onto you for months," he offered smugly.

"Is that so?" returned Mathers sceptically. "You've sure taken your time in arresting me."

"Just waiting for the right opportunity," smirked Kalpesh wryly. "We wanted as many of you together as we could get when we made the arrest."

Mather's smile faded slightly as Kalpesh continued to speak.

"And here you are," the Indian chuckled. "Assistant Chief Constable Macnaghten was sure that if we triggered your detection seal that you'd come running. We hoped you'd bring friends with you, and sure enough, you did. All we had to do then was buy a little time for our men to get into position—surround the property." Kalpesh noted the nervous exchange of looks between the three men behind Mathers. "They said you liked to talk —Figured I could get you rambling long enough to buy us the time we needed to surround this place!"

The man on the stairs now averted his eyes from Kalpesh, looking momentarily to Mathers to see if the adept believed him.

"Should I head out and tell the boss that you've agreed to come quietly?" Kalpesh made a move for the door.

"Stop!" ordered Mathers.

Kalpesh did as he was told, sensing the warning in Mathers' voice. If he moved again without permission, that would be it.

"I know you are lying."

Kalpesh chuckled, trying his upmost to maintain the act. "Alright," he shrugged. "I guess they'll have to do it the hard way."

"Even if it were all true," smiled Mathers, "we'd now have you as a hostage."

Kalpesh maintained a straight face.

"No one is coming to save you. Now drop your gun."

"Okay," breathed Kalpesh, slowly lowering his Mauser as he realised he was out of options.

"Good," remarked Mathers, he and his fellow occultists relaxing slightly. "Now—"

Capitalising on his foes' lowered guard, Kalpesh seized the moment. His gun snapped back up. Squeezing the trigger rapidly, he fired wildly down the corridor, reaching for the door handle as he did so. His first shot plugged into the shoulder of one of the men stood behind Mathers, yet the second and third bullet drilled into the walls beside them, sending out a shower of plaster. Mathers reacted fast, summoning from the tip of his wand a protective ward. A glimmering shield, not unlike the one the Ripper had projected from his hand, erupted in front of Mathers, protecting him and the men behind as the next three bullets deflected away into the floor and ceiling.

Kalpesh pulled open the door, but the handle slipped suddenly from his sweaty palm as the door slammed magically shut. He felt his gun fling from his other hand, and before he could so much as react, the tiles beneath him exploded into a shower of shrapnel as gravity inverted beneath his feet. The last thing Kalpesh remembered was hurtling upwards into the ceiling of the porch, before everything turned black.

XXVII

Unknown Location
Unknown Time

Kalpesh felt his mind slipping in and out of consciousness. His head throbbed and span in the cold, damp darkness that had swallowed him. His joints burned as his limbs drew taught, his chest straining with each breath he took. Hessian fabric scratched his face, his head bundled beneath a sack hood. He was nauseous and dizzy, his mind only able to remain cognisant for a few blurred moments at a time. He could taste blood. Beads of icy sweat trickled down his naked body as he felt the wooden frame of a rack pressing into his back. Then, darkness.

Sometime later, muffled voices echoed in the black. The words vibrated in and out of focus.

"I say we kill him," muttered a man icily some distance away.

"Don't you realise who he is!?" demanded another.

"A Malleus assassin!" returned the first person sharply.

"The man who arrested both Olcott and Blavatsky!" snapped a woman.

"Blavatsky and Olcott were terrorists!" denounced a fourth voice.

"He's right," insisted a fifth, Kalpesh rapidly losing track of who was speaking in his brief moment of wakening. "They plotted to blow up Westminster Abbey and everyone in it."

"They were fighting four a cause—*our* cause!"

"We cannot condone acts of violence!"

"I agree—the Theosophical Society were no allies of ours—they deserved what they got!"

"For daring to look beyond the veil?"

"For treason! They'd receive equal punishment if their crimes had no magical association."

"Silence!" commanded an authoritative voice. "This man may be our enemy—but he is also the son of Arthur Octavian Hume!"

"We don't know that!"

"Don't we?" questioned a woman, unconvinced by the counterargument. "You saw the mark on his hand!"

"He's an Indian—it's the symbol for Om—it could very easily be a coincidence."

"You can't believe that!?"

"Hume searched this country for the better part of a decade for a child bearing that mark and found nothing," returned another person. "He is the son of Rani of Jhansi, secreted away to England before her death at the battle of Gwalior."

"Are you sure?"

A long pause followed.

"Almost certain."

"Then what should we do with him?"

"I don't know," sighed a man. "His position in Malleus complicates matters."

"No, it doesn't!" insisted someone sharply. "Hume was a friend to many of us and instrumental in founding the Golden Dawn—but he has been dead for years. This man—he may be his son by blood, but Hume never even held his child!"

"He's right," insisted a woman. "Hume didn't raise him. He's not his son—not really."

"You can try and convince yourself of that, but you know it isn't true!" another female voice argued. "If a son of yours went missing for three decades, he'd still be your child!"

"He's a bloody Hammer detective!" snapped someone angrily. "He's a sworn enemy of the entire occult."

"He cannot be blamed for what he is when no one was there to guide him during his life," argued another. "We turned our back on him when we abandoned our search. We are as much to blame for the circumstances that led him to join Malleus."

"What's done is done," insisted a male voice. "We cannot change the past, no matter our regrets. He is too dangerous to be kept alive."

"He's right. We can't let him go; he'll lead Malleus straight back to us."

"We've already cleared out Mathers' house."

"I can go into hiding," Mathers' own voice added reluctantly.

"He won't ever find us. He doesn't know the location of the Isis-Urania Temple! He has nothing to go on!"

"Doesn't he? He found Mathers' house and his hidden study!"

"A fluke, I'm sure," insisted Mathers.

"We have no idea how much he knows," insisted someone else. "This is the man who found the Blavatsky Lodge. He tracked down Olcott. He has proven that he is incredibly resourceful. If any Malleus officer can find us, it is him!"

"She makes a good point."

"He's too dangerous."

"If you are so keen to kill him, then he is right over there—go and cut his throat now if you are as eager to murder the man as you so seem."

"I don't *want* to do it, but we *have* to!"

"We don't have to do anything," insisted another. "He's not going anywhere for the moment."

"And just as well," muttered someone under their breath.

"Why don't we talk to him?"

"And say what?" someone asked mockingly. "Ask him nicely not to arrest us?"

"Talking to him will not achieve anything."

"We don't know what his motivations are. He could be sympathetic to our cause…"

"A Malleus detective sympathetic to the occult? Don't be delusional!"

"Malleus needs to exist in some capacity," insisted someone. "Look at Whitechapel, for God's sake! There will always be people like Crowley out there who need stopping."

"Then why don't you just hand yourself over to them?" patronised another voice.

"Don't be stupid!" snapped a woman. "You know he's right. Hammer needs reforming, not abolishing."

"This isn't the matter of debate—we are here to decide what to do with the prisoner."

"I say we cut out his tongue and dump him in Regent's Canal!"

"Of course *you'd* say that!"

"Silence!" boomed a voice above all others. "The decision rests with me."

"And what *is* that decision?"

"I need time to consider our options."

"Then decide quick. Malleus will soon be out looking for him."

Unable to remain awake, Kalpesh felt his groggy mind slip back into insentience.

An indeterminate length of stillness elapsed as Kalpesh continued to fade and wax, his mind occasionally conjuring murky hallucinations as he slept. Benumbing muscular spasms twanged sporadically throughout his body. Dryness crusted across his lips and tongue. Wheezing sputters rose and fell through his aching lungs. His head swam in a cocktail of concussion and the sweet chemical waft of chloroform, his brain seemingly permanently adrift in the dusk between waking and reverie.

Whispering voices roused him gradually, this time muttering closer than before.

"Are you sure about this?" questioned Samuel Mathers. "I feel killing him could be less cruel. They'll torture him…"

"You may be right," a deep voice agreed solemnly. "But Woodman believes this is the best course of action we can take."

"We don't even know if it'll work…" hesitated Mathers. "Most of this… it has never been attempted before; we don't know the extent to which flesh can conduct the Aether."

"We know enough," insisted the other man. "It will work," he asserted confidently. "The mark he already bears is proof enough of that."

"Okay," breathed Mathers.

The hessian hood was drawn back off Kalpesh's head. He gasped, coughing violently as his eyes watered open, letting in the hazy glow of a dozen surrounding candles. The place they were keeping him was dark, incredibly so. The air was dank and cold. He was below ground, but beyond that, the was no hint to his location. As his vision blurred into focus, he strained his neck to look around. His body was fettered, his arms and legs spread-eagle and chained to a rack. On the floor surrounding him, a wide intricate pentacle inside the ring of candles was chalked onto the flagstones.

Swallowing hard, he felt his swollen tongue rasp across the parched roof of his mouth. He canted back his head, letting it hang painfully. Sweat dripped from his hair, trickling into his eyes, the salt stinging as he blinked through a stream of tears. His vision finally refocussed and he saw two men partially revealed in the candlelight before him. One was Samuel Mathers, whilst the second was the bearded occultist who had also been present at Mathers' house. He suspected he was looking at William Wynn Wescott.

"What do want with me?" wheezed Kalpesh. "Why haven't you killed me yet?"

"Because," began Wescott solemnly, "we believe you can be saved."

"From what?" he breathed laboriously.

"From yourself," returned Wescott.

"Why not just kill me?"

"Because I knew your father," he explained. "And I owe him this at least."

"I don't believe you," snarled Kalpesh.

"I wouldn't expect you to," shrugged Wescott. "You see me as the embodiment of everything you stand against."

"Why are you doing this?" hissed the Indian. "Why keep me chained up here?"

"Because, we have chosen to believe that you are merely a victim of fate."

"What!?"

"You fight in a war that has been waged for centuries. You fight believing you exist on one of two sides; but it is not that simple. There are those that oppose the forces you hope to defeat with whom you should be aligned, but instead, Malleus has become radicalised towards an extremist view of the world, electing to enforce genocidal policies for the sake of protecting the many from the few."

"What do you want?" sputtered Kalpesh, struggling to remain conscious.

"To show you the truth—the way things are," answered Wescott. "To give you the ability to see this world in a clearer light. To offer you a second chance."

"What do you mean?" stammered the Indian. "What are you going to do to me?"

"There will be pain," apologised Wescott. "We will take measures to minimise it on our end, but... I fear what *they* will do to you." Wescott issued a grave expression Kalpesh's way. "I hope the fact that you are one of them will stay their hand—but I fear it may instead worsen their wrath."

"What are you going to do?" pressed Kalpesh fearfully, as now, his eyes flitted outside the pentacle, where across the floor, all manner of sharp and terrible instruments were laid out.

"There are several members of this order who have cautioned that this course of action is needlessly cruel; many agree that killing you now would be the more merciful option. But, alas, time is running short, and I genuinely believe this could be our best hope at stemming the tides of chaos."

"Please..." panicked Kalpesh. "Please don't do this!"

"I am sorry," grimaced Wescott, retreating into the darkness.

"If you survive," spoke Mathers, "if you see things clearly—seek us out again."

"What?" whispered Kalpesh in terrified conclusion.

Barely visible from within the shadows, Wescott nodded to someone stood behind Kalpesh. "Begin," he uttered coldly.

A hand grabbed hold of Kalpesh's hair, wrenching his head jarringly back. A leather bit was shoved between his teeth. Kalpesh screamed, struggling as a strap was tightened across his forehead, securing his pate in place. He felt a needled stab through the skin of his neck. A cocktail of drugs injected painfully into his blood, and in less than a second, his mind melted into darkness and oblivion.

XXVIII

Unknown Location
Unknown Time

The bustle of traffic and chattering of pedestrians steadily grew as Kalpesh painfully regained consciousness. He was bundled onto a leather upholstered bench, his knees tucked into his chest, his head slumped in a pool of his own drool. His eyes fluttered hazily open. Cold October light loomed through the drapes drawn over the window. Kalpesh swivelled his eyes about him; he was in the back of a carriage. He began to sit up and groaned in pain; every inch of his skin from his neck to his ankles was raw. He felt scabs crack and burnt flesh weep as he strained to lift himself from the seat. A woollen blanket slipped from across his shoulders as he rose. When Kalpesh looked down at his torso, he cried out in horror.

His arms and chest were branded and tattooed extensively, each inch of his skin inked and singed with arcane markings. He craned his head painfully, catching glimpse of the continuing disfigurements that stretched down his back and across his abdomen. He cast off the blanket; he was wearing a set of tattered trousers, but he could see through rips in the knees that even his thighs and calves were mutilated with esoteric symbols, all the way down to the soles of his feet. Pentacles and sigils stretched from the palms of his hands, twisting around his wrists in a series of anatomical ley lines, nadi, crisscrossing up to his torso. Runes punctuated his limbs, interweaving with Icelandic staves. Hebrew characters surrounded the Kabbalistic tree of life across his back and hermetic icons were surrounded in Enochian lettering over his chest. Throughout the tattoo canvas that seemed to darken every region of his body beneath his face, his skin was puckered into raised and weeping burns that could only have been the work of branding irons. The burns were shaped into pentagrams and arcane sigils, each differing slightly, each slotting perfectly into the macabre artwork that defiled his body.

Panic consumed Kalpesh as he rubbed his

forearms in disbelief, hoping the sweat congealing across his flesh might somehow wash away the ink; he pleaded, begging for the disfigurements to be a hallucination from the drugs lingering in his system. But it quickly became apparent the markings were both real and very much permanent.

Gasping for air, the detective tried to grapple with some semblance of composure, fighting his body back from the brink of a panic attack. His heart throbbed. His head spun. His chest quivered with hyperventilating spasms of breath. He swallowed, closing his eyes, balling his fists, punching the ceiling of the carriage. Tears streamed from his eyes and his teeth gritted together, as slowly and deliberately, he wrestled his body into submission, retaking autonomy.

Picking up the blanket from the floor of the carriage, he wrapped it tightly around his torso. Opening the door, he stumbled out into the street. He felt grass beneath his feet. He glanced back to see the carriage in which he had awoken was abandoned on the side of the square without horse or driver. He staggered forwards, swivelling his head to gather his bearings. He saw statues. Carriages rattled across cobbles. The hubbub of the city murmured through his muffled ears. A bell slowly began to toll deafeningly loud as it started to strike the hour; it was distinctive, recognisable above the tumult of London: the gargantuan cracked bell atop St Stephen's Tower. Kalpesh almost collapsed in horror as he looked up at the clocktower. Like a klaxon to signal the end of days, Big Ben continued to peal. Before him, the Palace of Westminster rose sharply from the bank of the Thames. He was stood on the edge of Parliament Square.

Kalpesh glanced around in a daze. People were stopping to gawk at him as he stumbled barefoot and dishevelled out into the street. Rain began to drip from the sullen skies above. He pulled the blanket tighter across his chest, but gusts of wind continued to buffet the cloth, threatening to unveil the skin of arcane markings that clung to his body. He stumbled, sighting up ahead a pair of City Police constables chatting to a pedestrian a hundred feet away. He hesitated, realising that at this moment, for the first time since he was a child on the streets of Whitechapel, the police were not his friends. He looked on in horror as the woman they were speaking to raised a finger, pointing towards Kalpesh and then the carriage from which he had emerged. The bobbies' eyes narrowed in on him as they clocked the Indian up ahead, before in unison, they began to stride his way to investigate.

Kalpesh panicked, stepping out into the road, weaving through the traffic as he began crossing over towards Westminster Hall. The police followed, signalling several carriages to halt as they pursued the strange man. Kalpesh staggered hastily on, narrowly avoiding being run over by a cart. Stepping out of the road, he started to jog along the pavement. He stopped, sighting another patrol of armed police marching his way; as of yet they were unaware of him. The Indian peered back over his shoulder, watching as the first two officers stepped out of the traffic and begun searching for him again on the far side of the road. In seconds they sighted him and blew their whistles, ordering him to stop.

With little other means of escape, Kalpesh dropped back down off the curb, wading once more into traffic. He slipped narrowly behind an oncoming cart, yet as he dodged further into the road, a pair of black mares drawing a hackney carriage at speed charged towards him. Kalpesh cowered in panic, flinching as he readied to be crushed beneath a set of hooves. He shielded his face with his hands and felt a surge of energy well within his forearms. The tattoos across his skin burned hot, and suddenly, the air surrounding his palms ruptured into a shockwave.

A whirlwind ripped outwards in every direction. Kalpesh heard screams and cries accompanied by the whinnying of horses. Wood crunched and splintered. Metal creaked and groaned. Slowly, Kalpesh opened his eyes. Traffic had halted across the square. Before him, the carriage set to run him down mere seconds earlier was toppled onto its side, the horses snorting and whining in panic as they were pinned atop of one another in a sprawl of broken legs. Various other vehicles had been battered aside and flipped in the immediate vicinity. Pedestrians wailed in terror, taking flight in every direction away from Kalpesh stood centred amidst the chaos.

"Put your hands up!" roared an armed policeman, daring to encroach on the Indian knelt in the road. He had raised his bayonetted rifle, aiming nervously down the sights, his partner beside him doing the same. Kalpesh glimpsed over at the pair of patrol officers that had first sighted him. One stood warily at a distance, whilst the second was making a run for the nearby police box.

"Don't move!" roared one of the Westminster guardsmen.

"Please!" whimpered Kalpesh, raising his hands in surrender, causing the blanket concealing his body to fall away. "Don't shoot!"

"Shit!" one of the officers cried out. "What is that...? His skin...!?"

"Please," cried Kalpesh. "I'm a Malleus officer!" he insisted, praying against all hope that they would believe him.

"Don't speak!" roared one of the officers, fearing that Kalpesh would at any moment begin uttering a curse or enchantment of some sort.

"Please!" insisted the detective. "I am Inspector Kalpesh Khatri of Special Branch—"

"I said don't speak!" shouted the officer again as he and his partner continued to edge nervously closer towards him, bayonets and muzzles aimed directly at his chest.

Kalpesh began to shake with terror. There was a good chance they would open fire any second. "Please!" he uttered feeling a peculiar sensation trickling through the inked lines across his arms. "Please—let me explain!"

"Not another word!" roared the policeman angrily.

"Lie down on the ground! Hands behind your head!"

Kalpesh looked down at his palms in horror. Preternatural darkness began to smoke and issue from the air around them, spilling downwards and pooling onto the ground in an obscuring veil.

"Stop it! Now!" demanded one of the policemen.

"Please!" begged Kalpesh. "I can't control it… I don't know how!"

To his relief, the inky black air started to dissipate, but one form of involuntary magic was supplanted by another. A line of flames started to trace upwards from the cobbles between himself and the encroaching officers, the fire writhing higher and hotter with each second that passed.

"Stop!" roared the policemen.

"I can't!" wailed Kalpesh.

A flicker of energy traced across the Indian detective's chest. Everything fell momentarily silent. The chaos and panic of Westminster staggered to an immediate halt. All was still and eerily quiet as the seconds splintered and drew out. Time slowed like the spinning reel of a film projector whirring down until the moving pictures stagnated to individual frames. Kalpesh looked up and watched as the policeman slowly squeezed the trigger of his Lee-Enfield rifle. The cocking piece gradually drove into the end of the gun and Kalpesh watched as a cloud of white smoke issued from the muzzle. In the fractured increments of time that followed, the bullet streaked from the barrel of the gun, rapidly taking flight towards the defenceless detective.

Kalpesh flinched, his hand moving to protect himself before the gun had even fired, yet as the bullet rushed towards him, it collided with a distorted barrier of air. The compressed shield of magical energy rippled as the bullet struck it head on, the slug disintegrating into a shower of sparks and shrapnel that tumbled away in slow motion. A second muzzle flashed, ejecting another spooling cough of gunpowder smoke, the other armed officer sending a bullet of his own Kalpesh's way. The second shot cut speedily through the air, impacting the arcane ward projected outwards from the Indian's raised palm, this time striking the curving edge of the shimmering barrier. The bullet split in two, the lead fragments shrieking as they were deflected into the cobblestones of the road.

Time re-hastened, the flitting images of the world's motion projector accelerating back to full speed. The tumultuous clamour of Parliament

Square roared to life again. Kalpesh looked down at himself, amazed to see no bullet wounds. Warily, he glanced back up at the two policemen that had fired at him. The officers hesitated, peering at each other to share looks of dismay as they realised their rifles had not so much as left a scratch.

"Please!" Kalpesh repeated in desperation. "Don't shoot—I surrender!"

The two men drew back the bolts of their rifles, discharging the spent casings and priming their chambers with the second round from their magazines. They took aim anxiously, unsure as to whether to fire again. They began to back away, stepping up onto the curb as they kept their sights trained on Kalpesh.

"Don't move!" one of them ordered, though now the authority in his voice had been supplanted by fear. Back on the pavement, at a distance they deemed to be safe, the two armed officers knelt, both keeping their rifles trained unwaveringly on Kalpesh as they did so.

The inspector glanced nervously about. He heard horseshoes clattering across the road, the squealing of axels, the groan of wheels. A police carriage skidded to a halt somewhere behind him and out issued a half dozen men. Peering around with his hands still raised, he watched in horror as a perimeter was rapidly established a hundred yards around him in every direction. Each turn of his head revealed more police arriving at the scene, as rapidly, the situation continued to escalate.

Dozens of rifles were now trained on him from every direction; any sudden movement would trigger a fusillade of bullets.

Kalpesh shivered as rain started pelting down unrelentingly from the heavens. Winds swept around the square and a black shadow steadily loomed over the House of Commons. Kalpesh glimpsed overhead in awe as a Zeppelin airship bore down out of the clouds, blotting out the faint light of the stormy skyline as the aircraft came to float a hundred fathoms over Westminster. Its array of guns were aimed groundward at him.

Malleus carriages began to arrive in force, and as Kalpesh gazed through the streaking rain at the perimeter of men, he recognised numerous faces in the wall of armed officers.

"Inspector Khatri?" crackled the voice of Commissioner James Monro blaring electronically over a loudspeaker.

"Sir!?" shouted the Indian, rainwater spitting from his lips as he looked around for the source of the voice.

A blinding floodlamp suddenly surged to light from the airship above, cutting down through the deluge to isolate the Malleus inspector knelt in the road.

"Inspector!" boomed Monro again. "You don't need to do this!"

"Do what!?" roared Kalpesh in dismay.

"Move away from the Palace!"

"I'm not doing anything!" screamed Kalpesh. "Commissioner... I've been set up!"

A terrifying silence elapsed throughout Parliament square as rain continued to batter Kalpesh's shuddering body.

"Kalpesh!?" the voice of Melville buzzed now over the loudspeaker.

"Melville!?" cried the Indian in relief. "Melville... you have to help me!" he stuttered as his body quivered. "It's the Golden Dawn..." he tried to explain. "Please... I've been set up!"

"Kalpesh," Melville's voice echoed from somewhere in the crowd. "You don't need to go through with this. You have to surrender yourself!"

"I'm not doing anything!" he stammered. "I've already surrendered!"

"Move away from the Palace!" the voice of Monro ordered. "Or we'll be forced to open fire!"

"Okay! Okay!" Kalpesh pleaded. "Don't shoot!" Slowly he began to rise to his feet, trembling as his frozen muscles fought the commands he gave them. He staggered forwards, blinded by the light and the rain. His bare foot slipped on the slick cobbles and he suddenly toppled over. A gunshot echoed from beyond the square and a cobblestone exploded into a shower of grit inches from Kalpesh's head.

"Hold fire!" cried Melville over the speaker.

Everything fell silent save for the lashing of rain.

"Kalpesh…" continued his friend. "You have to give yourself up… before it's too late!"

"I surrender!" he screamed.

"It's over son," boomed Monro. "We've found your journal!"

"What?" stammered Kalpesh in confusion as he pulled himself up off the ground, raising his hands high above his head.

"We know everything," Monro's voice crackled. "But you've failed! It's over now. Just give yourself up before more innocent people are hurt!"

"I've been set up!" screamed Kalpesh again. "I haven't done anything!"

Another stretch of unnerving silence elapsed.

"Kalpesh…" came the more sympathetic voice of Melville. "If that is true, just surrender now!"

Kalpesh spread his arms in a furious gesture. He could not think how else to demonstrate his submission any more than he was already doing so.

"Come in quietly," continued Melville. "If you cooperate, we'll give you a fair trial!"

"I surrender!" he roared over the howling winds.

Silence continued as hundreds of policemen watched him shivering beneath the spotlight of the airship. Kalpesh waited anxiously; at any moment he expected Monro to give the order for his men to open fire.

"Melville... please!" he begged, tears running from his eyes lost instantly in the rain.

"Kalpesh..." Melville spoke out.

His heart thumped as he awaited the next words.

"We're sending men over to restrain you—don't try anything!"

He nodded.

"Lie down, slowly, and spread your arms out on the ground!"

Shivering violently, Kalpesh did as he was instructed, slowly lowering himself to his knees before lying prone in the puddling road and spreading his arms wide.

"We're sending officers over to you now!" explained Melville over the speaker. "If you try anything, we'll open fire!"

Kalpesh laid perfectly still, his body on the verge of convulsing from the cold. He made out shadows cutting through the floodlights around him as a unit of heavily armed Malleus officers pressed in on him from all sides. Suddenly his arms were yanked painfully behind his back and a set of heavy iron manacles were clamped tightly around his wrists. They hoisted him violently up off the ground and a gag was forced inside his mouth. The blinding glare of the spotlight beaming down on him was abruptly blacked out as a hood bagged around his head. He felt a set of shackles snap about his ankles, before finally, a billy club struck him powerfully across the back of his skull, rendering Kalpesh immediately unconscious.

XXIX

Anvil, Tower of London, City of London
8:21 p.m. October 4th, 1888

The deafening drone of continuous lightning arced out from two massive Tesla coils; the bolts of electricity licked violently across the bars of the Faraday cage containing Kalpesh. Knowing that the forks of plasma could not penetrate inside did not quell the awesome terror the lightning projectors imbued in him. His heart throbbed, adrenaline pulsing cold in his blood as his eyes glared wide at the jittering tongues of electrical energy snaking back and forth across the metal rungs mere feet away.

Hours passed as Kalpesh knelt on the hard floor, taught chains tethering him by the collar and wrists. His body ached against the restraints, his skin still burning from the tattoos and brands recently stained and singed into his flesh. Finally, at some unknown hour, the high-pitched hum of the Tesla Coils whirred down, the lightning died to sparks, and the screech of the door's alarm bell clattered out in the corridor beyond. Seconds later, the heavy steel door to the dungeon cell revolved away, and into the room entered Melville Macnaghten.

"Melville...!" stammered Kalpesh. "Thank heavens you are here!"

"I'm sorry it has taken this long," the man uttered solemnly.

"You have to get me out of here," rambled the Indian. "I was captured—by the Golden Dawn... they... these tattoos... the marks... they did this to me!"

Melville smiled weakly, lowering his head as the cell door drew heavily shut behind him. He stepped closer to the cage, averting eye contact with Kalpesh.

"I've been set up!" insisted Kalpesh desperately.

"I wish I could believe that, old friend," Melville uttered coldly, his gaze finally rising to meet Kalpesh's.

"What do you mean?" babbled Kalpesh in

confusion.

"Please," insisted Melville, "drop the act!"

"I... I..." quivered the Indian. "Melville... you have to believe me! This isn't me! Why would I do this?"

"You tell me?" questioned the assistant chief constable.

"What!?"

"We found your journal, Kalpesh!" snapped the man fiercely. He rapidly drew from his jacket Kalpesh's black leather notebook, slapping the journal hard against the bars of the cage.

"What about it!?" demanded the Indian.

"What do you mean, *what about it?*" snarled Melville, flicking rapidly through the book. "Pages upon pages of ritual notes—pentacles, runes, staves—it's all in here!"

"No!" refused Kalpesh. "No... those are case notes!"

"In this much detail!?" demanded Melville. "You could perform hundreds of spells from the things you have written in here!"

"Melville..." stuttered Kalpesh in disbelief. "I use that book for work—You know that!"

"Do I?" questioned the man. "You are supposed to *catch* magic users, not *become* one yourself!"

"That's how I caught Olcott!" insisted Kalpesh. "I found him because I understood the rituals he was using!"

"You aren't supposed to *understand* magic!"

snapped Melville. "It's a crime!"

Kalpesh shook his head. "I've never... I've never even tried to cast a spell!"

Melville chuckled in disbelief. "We have hundreds of witnesses from Parliament Square who claim otherwise!"

"No, no! That wasn't me... I had no control —"

"We've been to your apartment," interrupted Melville. "Do you know what we found there?"

Kalpesh stared silently back at the man he had once believed was his closest friend.

"Dozens of books on the Aether...the classical elements... magical theory..."

"What?" questioned Kalpesh in confusion. "There's nothing wrong with them—you can buy them in general bookstores! They aren't outlawed."

"You can own chemicals, Kalpesh!" retorted Melville. "Sulphur—nitrates— charcoal—none of them are outlawed, but when we find someone with all three of them, we start to suspect they are making explosives!"

"Melville... this is ridiculous... please! You know me! You know I would never do anything!"

"Just confess!" cried out Melville in anger. "We know it's you. We know it has been you since the start!"

"What!?"

"These killings, Kalpesh! The Whitechapel murders!"

"You think I had something to do with them!?"

"All of the pentacles found at the murder sites are in this bloody journal! The Enochian symbols—you have all the translations written down!"

"So I could identify them if ever I came upon them in a case!" Kalpesh argued. "Which I did!"

"All the murders have happened within a mile of your address," remarked Melville icily.

"Melville... this is insane!"

"No!" he boomed. "That I didn't suspect you sooner... *that* is what is insane! You've been running Abberline around in circles, drip feeding us snippets from your grand plan, all the while you plotted your next murder! Well, it's over! We've caught you now!"

"You can't believe that... not after what I've done for Malleus!"

"You've played the part brilliantly!" smiled the man venomously. "Who better not to suspect than the great witch hunter, Kalpesh Khatri? What better a cover for a fanatical occultist than a Malleus detective?"

"Where are you getting this from!?" demanded Kalpesh in disbelief.

"Just tell me this: were you involved in the occult when I first met you?"

"Melville... please..."

"Don't lie to me!"

"I'm not!" insisted Kalpesh.

"You've been feeding us misinformation since the start, haven't you? Covering your tracks, all the while handing us over sacrificial occultists that what—? Stepped out of line? Disagreed with you? Weren't committed enough to the dark arts to aid you in this... this... evil ritual you've been plotting for years?"

"Please listen to me Melville!" begged the Indian.

"I'm all ears!"

"I was kidnapped!" reiterated Kalpesh. "By Samuel Mathers! If you look in the archives, we have a file on him. He wasn't flagged for investigation—"

"I know perfectly well who Mathers is!" snapped Melville. "We know you've been colluding with him. We know you met with him and several other occultists at his house!"

"No..." refused Kalpesh. "No, I went there to investigate him!"

"Kalpesh—"

"No, you have to listen!" he insisted. "Go there... there is a hidden room... the flat under his house—"

"We found it!" interrupted the assistant chief constable. "We found the room. We found out you had been there without telling anyone— not even your partner. We went soon after you were arrested. It had been cleared out."

"Because they released me... they knew I'd tell you about it!"

"Who Kalpesh? Who released you?"

"The Golden Dawn!"

Melville pinched the bridge of his nose in frustration. "I hardly think you are in a position to start mocking me!"

"No, please!" continued Kalpesh. "I swear... Mathers... he is a member, and William Wynn Wescott! They found out I was there... they ambushed me—"

"The Golden Dawn doesn't exist!" cut in Melville sharply. "Don't insult my intelligence by trying to convince me otherwise!"

"No, Melville," pleaded Kalpesh. "I thought so too... but they *are* real I swear! I think I know where their hideout is—"

"Enough, Kalpesh," uttered Melville definitively. "I had hoped you would cooperate. I didn't want it to come to this..."

"Melville please!" cried Kalpesh. "I'm telling you the truth!"

Melville glanced sombrely at the reflective wall of glass and issued a nod.

Fire erupted through Kalpesh's nerves, contorting every muscle throughout his body into a spasming knot. The current flowing through the chains cut out and Kalpesh was left a whimpering mess.

"Confess!" uttered Melville.

The chains buzzed again, hundreds of volts conducting through his restraints, earthing across his body into the concrete floor. His chest convulsed, his head throbbing, his fingers and toes curling as he lost all control over his muscles. Writhing agony flared blindingly across his body. The second jolt lasted longer than the first, and when the current switched off, drool sputtered from his lips as he struggled to catch his breath.

"Confess, Khatri!" the voice of Commissioner Monro crackled over the loudspeaker revealing that he was the one in control of the torture switch behind the glass.

"I can't!" slurred Kalpesh. "I've been framed!"

Hot pain raced up his arms and across his torso. He bit down hard on his tongue and felt blood gargle in his mouth. His eyes bulged from the strain. He began to fear they might pop from their sockets. His body juddered and convulsed. The pain endured as the third bout of electrocution stretched on even longer than the last. Finally, the current switched off and Kalpesh slumped against the draw of the chains, no longer able to support his own weight.

"Confess!" repeated Melville.

"Melville..." he coughed, unable to muster another word in his defence.

Melville nodded once more. A surge of electricity conducted into the chains again and Kalpesh felt the fiery pain return with a vengeance. He blacked out, coming around a few seconds after the charge had shut off, his eyes focussing blurrily on Melville's silhouette outside the limits of the cage.

"Just confess," Melville's voice echoed. "Make it easy on yourself."

This time unable to conjure a single word, he shook his head weakly in refusal.

Lightning erupted across his bones, and blackness engulfed him.

XXX

Anvil, Tower of London, City of London
7:21 p.m. November 1st, 1888

Kalpesh drifted in and out of waking. For nearly a full month he had been tortured unrelentingly as Malleus had attempted to extract a confession from him. He had been electrocuted, waterboarded, whipped, beaten, and burnt. Sometimes it had been Melville interrogating him. On one occasion Monro himself had even entered the cell to question the Indian. But more often than not, it was the pair of guards assigned to watch his cell; they rarely even bothered to ask anything at all, inflicting pain on their prisoner for the sheer enjoyment of it.

Throughout the month, Kalpesh had begged for an end; he had prayed for death. He had whimpered, cried, and cowered. He had soiled himself. He had bled. He had screamed until his voice had left him. But throughout it all, he had never given in. He had not produced a false confession, no matter how hard they had pushed him. He had not implicated Abberline no matter how many times they had questioned his partner's involvement. Nor had he ever given them any false information, nor anything for that matter that did not constitute as the truth. Despite this, he felt defeated all the same. No one had once listened to anything he had said; they chose either to ignore or disbelieve everything they had been told about the Golden Dawn, about Samuel Mathers and William Wynn Wescott, about the London Museum's Reading Room, and most frustrating of all, about Aleister Crowley.

The Ripper had not struck since Kalpesh had been arrested; that constituted as evidence enough of his guilt. Time was running out; soon Crowley would commit another ritual killing, tearing down the fourth and final pillar of creation, rending the veil, and opening the gates to the Abyss. Were such to happen, Kalpesh would possibly be absolved, perhaps not of all the crimes to which he had been attributed, but the Whitechapel murders at least. But somehow, he doubted even the continuation of the murders and the resulting apocalypse would have been enough to convince Melville and Monro; they were determined to prove Kalpesh's guilt whether they actually believed in it or not. He was a scapegoat, one orchestrated to ease public unrest under the growing criticism aimed at Malleus at their failings to apprehend the Ripper.

Regardless, any chance for Kalpesh's absolution required the arrival of the rapture, something he would gladly give his life to prevent; even if his memory had to be tainted and besmirched to paint him as a traitor in the process. His only hope now was that Abberline had been unconvinced of Kalpesh's involvement, and as such, continued his search for Crowley.

The next best thing he could hope for was that his end would come soon and that as little pain as possible would be inflicted upon him before such a time. Of the first part, Kalpesh was certain; he was more than likely only a few short days from execution. Of the second part, he had little hope; he knew if anything the torture would only ramp up in the time from now until he reached the gallows.

He dozed for a time, suspended awkwardly by his restraints that prevented him from lying down. After a while, he awoke to the powering down of the Tesla coils. An alarm sounded before the door wheeled open and Melville walked in.

"Kalpesh," he greeted the prisoner

indifferently. Realising he would receive no acknowledgement in response, the assistant chief constable continued. "Your trial was held earlier today."

"And I wasn't allowed to attend?" uttered Kalpesh sarcastically.

"You were deemed too dangerous to be removed from the dungeons," responded the man matter-of-factly.

"Was there anyone there to argue my defence?"

"You know that's not how things are done," returned Melville with a mocking grin.

"I suppose it was too much to hope for a fair trial," hissed Kalpesh bitterly. "Given how corrupt the rest of Malleus is, I can hardly say I'm surprised."

"The only source of corruption in Malleus kneels before me."

"You know that's not true!"

"You were found guilty on all counts," announced Melville. "You've been sentenced to death at noon tomorrow."

"How?" questioned Kalpesh. "How could you betray me like this? I thought you were my friend!"

"And I thought you were mine," returned the man solemnly. "But *you* betrayed *me*. You betrayed Malleus. You betrayed your country!"

"I gave you everything!" despaired Kalpesh. "I gave my country everything! I gave Malleus everything! Even when I disagreed with the way things were done... the way we treated people here...! Even when I could see it was wrong! I followed orders without question—and look where it has gotten me!"

"Treason has gotten you here," insisted Melville sharply.

"You know I didn't do anything you claim I did," chuckled Kalpesh. "But you aren't interested in the truth!"

"Malleus wasn't founded to uncover truth," uttered Melville sinisterly. "It was founded to uncover guilt. It was founded to extract the confessions needed to try those who have been seduced by the dark arts!"

"I should never have saved you all that time ago," growled Kalpesh. "I should have let those men beat you to death!"

A faint grin tugged at the edges of Melville's twisted mouth. "Given the nature of your crimes, and the extent of your treachery, the judge deemed the customary form of execution insufficient." The man's lips contorted now into a broad sinister smile. "Instead of being hanged tomorrow, you are to be burnt at the stake until dead."

Kalpesh glared back at Melville in disbelief. "You bastard!" he hissed. "Did you push for this?"

"This will be the last time you see me," uttered Melville coldly.

"Did you push for this!?" snarled Kalpesh loudly.

"I felt I should be the one to deliver the verdict to you."

"Melville, did you push for this?" repeated Kalpesh, tears forming now in his eyes.

"Farewell, old friend." Melville turned, making for the cell door as it slowly drew open.

"Melville!" Kalpesh roared after him. "Come back here you bastard!"

Melville exited the room and Kalpesh lost sight of him as he turned down the corridor, vanishing into the dark passages of Anvil's dungeons.

"Melville!" he cried again. "Get back here you son of a bitch!"

In the darkened aperture of the cell door, two figures suddenly loomed.

"I'd save your voice boy," cackled one of the guards. "You've got plenty of screaming left to do before the night is over!"

"Watch the door," instructed the second man.

As commanded, a prison guard armed with an Enfield rifle took up position in the opened aperture of the cell door.

"You are headed for the pyre tomorrow!" mocked the first torturer again as the two men stepped into the cell. "So we've got a full night of fun planned for you, wog!"

"You can fuck off!" snarled Kalpesh as the two guards sent to torture him made for the door to the Faraday cage and began fiddling with a key in the lock.

"Good!" mocked one of them. "I like it when he's feisty!"

"It's not as fun when they don't put up a fight," agreed the other.

The gate creaked as the hinges swung open, and as the two men stepped inside, Kalpesh suddenly became aware of a faint tingling that seemed to vibrate through the air. They pushed the cage gate shut, but the unoiled hinges failed to swing it all the way closed. The unusual sensation faded slightly as the aperture of the gateway diminished, but as the door came to rest a foot ajar, Kalpesh remained faintly aware of it. It took him a moment to comprehend what the odd sensation was, but as the two interrogators began to lay out a row of torture implements on the floor of the cell, he realised he was sensing the Aether.

"Where should we start first?" asked one of the men, looking at the array of pincers, pliers, knives, drills, saws, and spikes arranged neatly across a band of fabric on the floor before them.

"I say we cut his balls off!" replied the other.

"No," his partner chuckled. "We have to work up to that! Start small—We've got all night remember!"

"I still say we cut his balls off!" smiled the second of the torturers, ensuring he was making eye contact with Kalpesh as he said it.

"But there's nowhere to go from there," refused the other man.

"I can think of a few things," smirked the second guard.

"He still needs to be alive for his noon appointment tomorrow—Only just, but alive all the same."

"Alright," agreed the other. "What do you propose?"

"Hmmm," the first man beamed, looking at the array of tools he had at his disposal before selecting a set of pliers. "What about his teeth?"

"Okay," chuckled his partner.

"Hold his head."

Kalpesh grimaced as his head was yanked sharply back by the hair. He clenched his lips and jaw tightly shut, but a set of fingers dug hard into his cheeks and a hand pinched shut his nose.

"Open wide!" cackled the guard with the pliers.

Kalpesh thrashed his head about as he tried to resist, but against his efforts, the two men managed to prise open his mouth. He felt the cold pliers knock his incisors and scrape across his tongue as the man drove them into his mouth. Suddenly, the hard metal crunched one of his molars. He screamed as force was applied, the pliers wrenching at the tooth. He felt cracking as the enamel chipped away in the struggle, before, with throbbing agony, the root itself began to rip free. A swift yank finished off the pull, and from out of Kalpesh's mouth was torn one of his rear teeth. Kalpesh moaned as his mouth filled with blood, his whole head aching from the pain as the second torturer let his head sag loose on his neck.

"There!" chuckled the first man, showing Kalpesh the molar still gripped in his pliers as blood and spit oozed from the Indian's mouth. "Only thirty-one left to go!" Kalpesh watched as his tooth clattered to the floor.

"Let's try a fingernail next," suggested the other torturer gleefully as he reached down and picked up a set of his own pliers.

"Okay," smiled his partner, moving around Kalpesh to wrestle for one of the hands shackled behind the Indian's back.

Kalpesh grunted and his chains jangled as he fought against the man trying to uncurl one of his fingers from his balled left fist.

"Pass me the keys," the torturer instructed his partner. "And hold him still!"

One of the men grappled hold of Kalpesh's thrashing torso, subduing the Indian as the other struggled to insert a key into the lock for the manacle cuff.

"No!" huffed Kalpesh, refusing to give up. He threw back his head, cracking the top of his pate into the face of the man holding him still.

"Shit!" cried the guard, reeling back in pain and releasing Kalpesh.

The Indian prisoner glanced up to see the guard clutching his nose. Blood spilled out from between his fingers just as the key turned in the lock and the iron cuff around Kalpesh's left wrist clicked open.

"The fucker broke my bloody nose!"

"Calm down!" the other man laughed. "He got you good, but it is nothing compared to what we're going to do to him."

"Forget the fucking fingernail!" spat the injured guard as he threw down the pincers and picked up what looked like a pair of sheers. "I want the whole fucking finger!" he snarled, uncupping his face to reveal his crooked and blood smeared nose.

"Fair is fair," agreed the other man, snapping open the manacle and wrestling Kalpesh's arm from behind his back.

The moment the iron cuff slipped from his wrist, Kalpesh felt the vibrations in the veil intensify. The air felt alive, shuddering with untapped energy which the Tesla coils, the Faraday cage, and even the iron manacles had suppressed until now. As the levels of magical dampening were being peeled back, he was becoming steadily aware of the supernatural energies that had always permeated existence, but were now stimulating senses in Kalpesh which had previously been blind.

Kalpesh struggled as his arm was cranked out from behind his back. Fighting with all his might, he tried to keep his fist clenched tightly into a ball, yet steadily, one of his fingers was uncurled as the man wielding the shears stepped menacingly closer. The torturer smiled evilly, snapping the cutters open and closed as he taunted Kalpesh, slowly moving them nearer to his extended left index finger.

The shears opened wide around his digit. Kalpesh shut his eyes. He felt a sharp twang cut across his hand. He opened his eyes to see to his amazement that his finger had not been severed. The torturer looked down at his own hand in confusion, realising he was no longer clutching the shears.

"What are you playing at?" questioned the other man.

"But I..." stammered the guard with the bloody nose.

"Do you want to do this or not?" grunted the first as he fought with Kalpesh to keep the Indian restrained.

"They just flew out of my hand, I swear!"

"Just go fucking pick them up!" he groaned. "This bastard is fighting to get free!"

The man with the broken nose moved to retrieve the cutters now lying on the floor across the cell. Kalpesh twisted his wrist, trying to break away from his capture. Across his stomach he felt a twinge of energy trace across one of the tattoos, and suddenly his arm found the strength to tear out of the torturer's grip.

"Shit!" cursed the prison guard as he tried to regain hold of the Indian's now free arm, but before he was able to, Kalpesh snatched hold of the torturer's wrist. Fire surged immediately down his arcane tattoos, focussing into the Om symbol on his palm. The guard suddenly cried out in pain as his flesh started to sizzle and sear. The smell of burning skin flooded the cage and the torturer's agonised screams erupted throughout the cell.

"What the—!?" cried the guard with the broken nose as he spun back to face Kalpesh in alarm.

Kalpesh released his grip and watched as the torturer toppled backwards, clutching his charred forearm in despair, screaming as the cooked flesh looked ready to slop off the bone.

"Fuck!" cried the other guard, tripping as he fumbled for the gate, falling over himself in his panicked attempt to flee. Scrambling back to his feet, he tried to yank the cage door open, but Kalpesh grappled at the empty air in front of him, feeling his mind clasp hold of the gate. He rent back with his hand and suddenly the heavy grating flung open on its hinges so forcefully that it pinned the man against the bars of the cage.

The second torturer emitted his own harrowing screams as Kalpesh tightened his telekinetic hold, driving the gate into the restrained guard's body with crushing force. Limbs snapped and popped loudly before the man's gargled cries were drowned into silence in a final crunch of ribs.

"Shoot him!" shouted the guard lying on the floor to the rifleman in the doorway as he clasped his immolated forearm.

More tattoos buzzed with energy, and time seemed to slow just as it had done back in Parliament Square. Smoke issued from the Lee Enfield's muzzle, followed presently by a pellet of lead that glided swiftly through the air, sailing into the cage through the open gate. It collided with a ward of energy projecting from the Indian's outstretched palm. The bullet pinged off the arcane shield, ricocheting sideways where it plugged into the neck of the scorched guard. The deflected bullet silenced him with a spurt of jugular blood before time whirred rapidly back up to normal speed.

Kalpesh looked up to the rifleman stood in the doorway. He was gawking at the two torturers that had been butchered with ease by a prisoner with one hand chained behind his back. With little hesitation, the armed guard took off into a stumbling flight down the dark passageway. Kalpesh looked at his palm, studying the tattoos stretching up his wrist. Somewhere on his body he suspected there must be a rune or pentacle for opening locks.

He clenched his hand into a fist, focussing on the collar around his neck. A patch of skin on the small of his back flared with energy, and sure enough, the lock clicked open and the collar released its cold grip of his neck, thudding to the concrete floor. Seconds later, his remaining manacle and the shackles bound around his ankles sprung apart. He was free!

He stood up, rubbing the sore skin of his wrists and neck, looking to both the open cage and cell door that had been left ajar. He stepped forwards, tentatively emerging out of the Faraday cage, when suddenly, alarm bells and the building-wide claxon started to howl outside the cell. If he wanted to be the first prisoner ever to escape Anvil alive, he'd have to move fast.

XXXI

Anvil, Tower of London, City of London
8:52 p.m. November 1st, 1888

Electric alarm bells rattled throughout the dungeons as Kalpesh darted out of the cell. Veering left down the passage, his bare feet slapped hard against the cold concrete. He heard the stomping of boots from up ahead as guards mobilised down the corridor; they were heading in the direction of his cell. He skidded to a stop, catching glimpse of shadows blurring across the walls. Two guards charged around the corner. Spotting Kalpesh inexplicably out of his cell, they confoundedly came to an abrupt halt. Their moment's hesitation was all the opening the Indian needed.

Both guards raised their guns in panic, stocks snapping into their shoulders, fingers squeezing hard at their triggers. The two muzzles clapped, the corridor filled with smoke, and from out of the flash of gunpowder, a pair of bullets tore into the air. The lead slugs twanged off Kalpesh's arcane shield, each bouncing harmlessly away. Then, before either guardsman could take a second shot, he made his move.

Kalpesh darted towards them, closing the gap in less than a second. The Anvil guards thrust at the charging prisoner with their bayonets. The two gleaming blades sliced towards the Indian, yet before they could connect with his flesh, he felt a chain of runes link up along the vertebrae of his spine. A dizzying compression of space drove towards him, and in the blink of an eye, Kalpesh had teleported a dozen feet ahead, materialising behind the two guards.

Twisting his body rapidly around, Kalpesh drove a heel into the back of one of the soldiers' knees, catching the barrel of the other man's rifle as it spun to slash at him. The first man crumpled, crying out as his leg gave way. The second drew back the bolt of his rifle, ejecting the spent cartridge and loading the next into the barrel.

Still clutching the rifle in his hand, Kalpesh jerked it violently aside, redirecting the guardsman's aim as the gun went off. The bullet cracked loudly into the tunnel wall and the gun barrel turned blisteringly hot in his palm. Gritting his teeth against the pain, refusing to release his grip, he drove a shoulder into the rifleman, pinning him against the wall of the passage.

In the scuffle, Kalpesh's hand shot for the guard's sidearm revolver. Gun still in the holster, he squeezed the trigger twice. The revolver's first click merely turned over an empty chamber, but with the second, hammer struck firing pin and the revolver went off. The rifleman's knee exploded as the bullet tore down through his thigh, and as Kalpesh released him, he slid down the wall in a fit of agonised screams.

Pirouetting away, revolver now in hand, Kalpesh turned back to the first soldier. Still reeling from the kick he'd taken to the back of the leg, he gawked in horror at the pool of blood rapidly widening around his downed partner. He swung his rifle and took aim at Kalpesh, but in that moment, a rune twinged across the Indian's collar bone.

With a flick of his fingers, Kalpesh telekinetically pulled back the bolt of the Enfield. The firing mechanism snapped back and the bullet loaded in the chamber suddenly ejected from the barrel before it could be fired. The soldier clicked the trigger a split second later to no avail. A shot of desperation struck the soldier's face as his gun seemingly misfired.

Panicking as Kalpesh then began to move towards

him, he lunged with his bayonet at the escapee.

A slowing of seconds enabled by the tattoos across his chest gave Kalpesh ample time to dodge the blade lancing for his gut. Moving swiftly past his foe's defences as time reverted to normal pace, the Indian swung the gun in his hand, cracking the butt hard into the rifleman's temple. Eyes rolling back, the guard flopped unconsciously to the floor at the Indian's feet.

Kalpesh cocked back the hammer of the revolver, taking aim at the whimpering guardsman he'd shot through the leg. The soldier had been reaching for his rifle, but finding himself now gazing down the barrel of a gun, his hands rapidly retracted, slowly rising in surrender. Kalpesh clicked the hammer forwards, lowering his pistol, satisfied the injured man no longer posed a threat. Giving him one final look, he took off once more through the dungeons.

The men who had tortured Kalpesh had deserved what they got; had they the authority, they would happily have tortured him until his heart had given in completely. But most of the people in Anvil were just doing their jobs. Kalpesh refused to needlessly kill any prison guards in his escape attempt, even if it would ultimately cost him his chance at freedom. He glanced down at the pistol clutched in his hand; he could use it to threaten, and maybe to wound, but killing was off the table.

Weaving through the underground

labyrinth, he once more caught sound of stampeding boots cutting through the din of alarm bells. The marching soldiers were drawing rapidly towards him; this time there were more than two. Swivelling his head in search of options, Kalpesh sighted an open, empty cell. Slipping inside the steel door and drawing it to, he flopped onto the bunk, pulling a tattered blanket across himself and tucking in his head as he disguised himself as a sleeping prisoner. The footsteps thundered nearer as Kalpesh lay in wait. Heart pounding in his chest, he remained perfectly still, waiting for the rhythmic trudging of boots over concrete to crescendo as the men charged past. Finally, the footfalls faded, the contingent of men utterly failing to notice him as they stormed off in the direction from which Kalpesh had come.

Throwing off the blanket, he slipped out of the cell, checking the coast was clear before rounding a turn as he made for the way out. He avoided another unit of men sent to recapture him by detouring down a side corridor of cells, emerging several moments later behind the unit of none-the-wiser riflemen, back en route to the exit. He peaked around the final bend, glancing down the passage ahead to the spiral staircase and adjacent elevator that led out of the dungeons. Two guards were stood blocking the way, rifles trained straight down the corridor towards where Kalpesh was hiding, waiting in anticipation for any escaped prisoner to come charging around the turn. Stifling a gasp, the Indian rent his head back into cover and pressed his back against the wall. Finally satisfied the guards hadn't seen him, he braved another glance. This was the only way in and out. Kalpesh had to find a way past them before reinforcements arrived.

The Indian looked down at his hands and smiled. Twirling his fingers, he began to summon a preternatural black smoke. The cloud of opaque inky gas expanded, spooling onto the floor, creeping along the concrete until a deluge of the thick vapour gushed around the corner.

"What the fuck is that!?" demanded one of the guards up ahead as he first caught sight of the rapidly swelling cloud of shadow.

Within seconds, the two men found themselves confronted with a corridor flooded in impenetrable darkness that blotted out the hanging Edison bulbs, totally obscuring the corridor beyond.

"It's him!" cried the second man. "Quick, shoot!"

Bullets whistled through the blackness, occasionally pinging off the dome of protective energy cast from Kalpesh's outstretched hand as he rounded the corner and progressed up the corridor toward the soldiers blocking his way. A brand at the base of his neck hummed with energy and his eyes lit up, his magically augmented vision penetrating the shroud of blackness, demarcating the outlines of the passageway and the hot glow of the guardsmen's bodies up ahead.

"Shit! Where is he!?" despaired one of the men as they continued to fire blindly into the smoke clawing up the corridor towards them.

"It's getting closer!" cried the other, as they repeatedly slid back the bolts of their rifles, sending bullet after bullet screaming uselessly into the darkness.

Kalpesh drew to within striking distance, the red and amber blur of his foes visible a dozen feet ahead as he remained hidden behind the veil of preternatural shadow. As the advancing pall threatened to envelope the men, they began to panic; yet before they could turn and flee up the stairs, Kalpesh teleported for a second time, snapping back into existence between the two guards.

Pouncing on the first of the men, Kalpesh grabbed the guard's head in two hands, driving his pate into the wall with full force. The rifleman went instantly limp as his head smacked the stone, thumping to the floor as Kalpesh swivelled around to face his partner.

Having spotted the escapee appear out of thin air, the second guardsman was fumbling desperately at a clip, failing to slot it into the rifle's magazine in his fluster.

Kalpesh swung his arm violently and a magical whirlwind of force lashed outwards from his body. The shockwave of energy barrelled straight into the rifleman, launching him clean off his feet and into the opposite wall. Like his partner before him, he was rendered instantly unconscious as the back of his head struck stone, slumping into a heap on the floor.

Kalpesh spurted away, darting into the helical stairwell as he bounded up the steps. But after ascending a full turn of the spiral staircase, he halted abruptly; an oncoming resonance signalled more men descending the steps towards him. Retreating back down into the dungeons, Kalpesh looked to the elevator. The lift suddenly hummed loudly as the motors kicked in and it began to ascend the shaft. Knowing he had mere seconds before the guards on the stairs flooded out into the passageway, Kalpesh tore apart the elevator shutters and stepped inside the shaft as the lift rose overhead. He leapt, curling his fingers around a steel beam on the underside of the elevator, hanging beneath it as it continued to ascend. Half a dozen guards spilled out of the stairwell just as Kalpesh rose out of sight, not a single one of them spotting him as he made his escape from the dungeons.

Dangling from the elevator undercarriage, Kalpesh drew in his legs, hooking his feet around a second beam, tucking his body flat up against the bottom of the lift before it could rise past the ground floor. He glimpsed out through the grating across the lobby of Anvil's grand atrium. He watched the front doors draw close as detectives, uniformed officers, and tower guards alike darted about the foyer to lock down and secure the building.

The elevator continued to climb, ascending past the first floor towards the upper levels of the building. The lift ground jerkily to a halt, and as Kalpesh kept his body rigidly fixed to the elevator undercarriage, he heard the shutters draw apart and someone step inside. A pair of familiar voices began to speak above him.

"What do you bloody well mean *he's escaped*!?" demanded Commissioner Monro.

"Apparently he's running about free down in the dungeons!" explained Melville.

"How the devil did he get out of his cell!?"

The elevator shutters closed.

"I'm not sure. I'm told he managed to kill the two men interrogating him—lord only knows how he broke out of the restraints!"

Kalpesh relowered his legs as the coast drew clear on the floor below. Swinging across towards the gates, he planted his feet on the lip of the opening. The elevator above buzzed as it suddenly lurched into descent.

"I thought you said he had no control over his powers!?" snapped Monro.

"Clearly I was wrong!"

"Well, just make sure he doesn't make it out of the dungeons alive!"

Kalpesh rapidly prised open the shutters, slipping through the gap before the elevator could crush him. Glancing back over his shoulder, he watched Monro and Melville descend into view, the elevator continuing past on its way down.

"Son of a bitch!" growled Monro in disbelief as he sighted Kalpesh.

Kalpesh issued them both a wry grin, accompanying it with a mocking salute.

"He's made it to the third floor!" shouted Melville at the top of his lungs, hoping someone in the building would hear him.

The commissioner slammed the emergency stop and the elevator ground to a halt halfway between floors. Monro picked up the receiver of the lift telephone and began dialling through to the security office. Melville drew a sidearm from his belt and aimed it through a gap in the grating. The Luger coughed rapidly in short succession, a cannonade of shots flying through the lattice shutters towards Kalpesh.

Another barrier projected from the Indian's palm, effortlessly deflecting the lead slugs. Melville's magazine snapped empty and the assistant chief constable slammed the pistol against the grating in frustration.

Kalpesh gave his old friend the 'V' sign, smiling in satisfaction as he took off down the corridor. He rounded a turn, bare feet thudding across the floorboards as he passed the doors to a dozen offices, when the building-wide Tannoy system crackled to life.

The voice of Commissioner James Monro buzzed over the loudspeaker, cutting through the wailing sirens. "Attention all guards! The prisoner has been sighted on the third floor! All men converge on his location. Repeat: Inspector Khatri has escaped the dungeons and is possibly making his way towards the roof. The escapee is armed and dangerous. Engage with caution! Shoot to kill!"

Kalpesh's soles squeaked across the polished floorboards as he rounded a corner sharply. Monro's voice continued to repeat the warning, alerting everybody in the building that he was close to making an escape. By now, most of the guardsmen stationed in Anvil would be down in the dungeons, having believed that was where Kalpesh was until a few seconds ago. As such, the best route of escape was indeed the roof, even if everyone in the building now knew that was where he was heading.

The ground floor exits would by now be completely locked down, and it wouldn't take long for the majority of soldiers to emerge from out of the dungeons; though they'd head straight for the upper floors to try and head him off, they'd no doubt sweep the lower levels as they made their ascent. The roof wasn't just Kalpesh's best option, it was seemingly his only one. But with every soldier in Anvil believing that was where he was going, his chances of making his escape from the rooftop seemed slim to none. His only hope was to somehow convince the rest of Malleus that he had other plans.

An office door opened ahead and a clerk and his secretary stepped out into the hallway. They immediately caught sight of the Indian hurtling towards them. The typist emitted a high-pitched shriek and the clerk tossed a stack of paper he was carrying skyward as he leapt away in terror. Kalpesh rushed past them, tearing through the cloud of fluttering pages, charging towards the rear stairwell that served as the building's fire escape.

"There he is!" roared a voice from behind.

Gunshots popped deafeningly from down the corridor and the floorboards and wall panels surrounding Kalpesh began to explode in a maelstrom of splinters. The Indian ducked inside an office and another clerk cried out in alarm. Stooping low beneath the windows to deprive the guards of a line of sight, Kalpesh shielded his eyes as they shot out the glass overhead.

"Stay down!" commanded the Indian as he skirted behind the desk, taking cover beside the clerk.

Bullets continued to streak overhead as Kalpesh hunkered down, shattering further windowpanes and showering the floor of the office with broken glass. Taking stock of his surroundings, he searched quickly for an escape route. The internal office had only one door, but it was bordered on three sides with corridor, partitioned off by the rapidly disintegrating series of windows.

Behind the desk, Kalpesh glimpsed a vacant hallway obstructed only by a checkerboard of still intact windowpanes. Needing a larger opening through which to make his escape, the Indian flailed his forearm, lighting up a series of tattoos as he unleashed another whirlwind of air. The remaining panes exploded, tearing with them a hole in the framework.

He had a way out, but Kalpesh was now surrounded by a sea of shattered glass. He glimpsed down at his bare feet and growled in frustration. Bullets still tearing through the office, he peered around, searching for some kind of solution, when, to his amazement, he spotted a set of muddy walking boots tucked under the cover of the desk next to him.

He turned to the clerk cowering beside him. "I'm taking these," he announced calmly.

The man whimpered, managing a despairing nod.

Kalpesh blindly fired several covering shots from his revolver over the top of the desk to deter the advance of the men pressing towards him, before, as quickly as he could manage, he stuffed his feet inside the boots. They were a size too big, but they weren't at risk of dropping off his feet on the run.

Taking advantage of a lull in the oncoming gunfire, the Indian leapt out of cover and vaulted through the gap in the window into the corridor beyond. Broken glass crunched under his newly acquired boots as Kalpesh took off again, the drumfire of rifles resuming at his back as he made for the fire escape on the far side of the building.

Skidding around a corner, he burst through a door, finding himself inside the stairwell. He peered up the narrow concrete atrium, sighting the exit to the roof two floors above. Peering down, he spotted a group of five guards charging hastily up towards him. As of yet, they seemed unaware that Kalpesh was inside the stairwell with them. The Indian waited patiently, praying he'd managed to give the men that had just been chasing him across the third floor the slip; if he hadn't, he'd know soon enough when they came barging through the door at his rear.

Tentatively watching the soldiers ascending towards him, he hung back to ensure he wasn't spotted. He waited, listening to the crescendo of footfalls echoing throughout the concrete stairwell. Counting down, Kalpesh moved closer to the railing, watching as they cleared the second floor and began ascending the final set of flights towards him.

Delaying until the very last moment, Kalpesh suddenly vaulted the banister, grappling the lower rail, swinging his body down onto the landing below. Touching down hard on the second floor, he dropped behind the unit of soldiers, the five men still unaware of his presence. But now, the time had come for Kalpesh to reveal himself.

He drew his gun from out of his waistband

and fired upwards at the men on the landing across from him. The bullet shattered against the far wall and the soldiers hit the deck in reaction. Taking cover against the steps, they searched rapidly around for the source of the gunshot, immediately returning fire the instant they spotted the Indian.

Breaking the line of sight, Kalpesh darted down the stairs to the floor below as a bullet howled narrowly past his ear. Descending the remainder of the flight in a single bound, he swerved around the middle landing, hurriedly making for the first floor.

"After him!" roared one of the men above as boots began to stomp in pursuit of the Indian.

Kalpesh skidded to a stop on the first-floor landing, backing himself hard in against the corner. He outstretched his palms in front of him, praying to any divine entity that might be listening that one of the hundred odd arcane symbols permanently marking his skin transcribed the siddhi he needed. He pressed shut his eyes, knowing that if this plan failed, he'd be caught for certain. Boots thundered down the concrete stairs, rapidly rushing towards him.

"Don't let him get away!"

Kalpesh's heart skipped a beat as a cooling sensation dispersed over the skin on his stomach, flowing towards his extremities, washing steadily out through his fingertips. As his eyes slowly peeled open, he watched the distorted images of five guards charge heedlessly past without paying him any notice. They continued to race towards the levels below, ignoring Kalpesh entirely as he remained wedged tight in against the corner of the stairwell.

At the rear of the unit, the final man began shouting into a shoulder-mounted Airwave receiver. "We've just lost visual of the target. He's heading back towards the ground floor. Repeat: he's heading back towards the ground floor!"

Kalpesh smiled as the men disappeared down the steps out of sight. Breathing a sigh of relief, he dispelled the veil of invisibility that had shrouded him. With the stairwell above now completely vacant, Kalpesh darted back up the steps, rapidly climbing towards the roof. As he ascended, he heard the echo of the building's Tannoy system. Monro was broadcasting throughout Anvil once more, relaying the information he had just received. Now, as far as everyone knew, Kalpesh was trying to make an escape through the front door.

Summiting the stairwell, the Indian drove a flying heel into the final door in his path, bursting suddenly out on to the rooftop. For a moment, he thought he had emerged out into broad daylight. Shielding his eyes against the blinding glare, Kalpesh quickly realised that the source of the intense light bathing the rooftop of Anvil was not the sun. Instead, a dozen floodlights beamed down from the Salt Tower up ahead and the surrounding curtainwall. Kalpesh was stood out in the open, lit up from all sides, completely exposed. His blood froze in his veins. The soldiers manning the spotlights had been waiting for him to burst through the door. He'd run straight into the trap that had been set for him.

The crosshairs of a Maxim machine gun swung over Kalpesh. Time unravelled to a crawl. Up atop the Salt Tower, a muzzle flared in staccato as an ammunition-belt fed cartridge after cartridge into the water-cooled automatic machine gun. Streaking tracer rounds ignited through the air and spent casings rained out of the front of the rapid-fire weapon.

The flagstones under Kalpesh's feet shattered and disintegrated as a rain of bullets screamed down from the parapets above, annihilating the rooftop in a hailstorm of shrapnel.

Palm rising desperately in defence, Kalpesh managed to somehow summon another arcane bulwark around him before any of the bullets landed on target.

The unrelenting fusillade drilled into the shield. Streaks of hot led zinged off the bubble of magical energy, but the unceasing barrage soon began to prove too much for Kalpesh's ward to sustain. Thin fracture lines started to weave across the shimmering wall of energy, growing steadily into larger and larger fissures as the cannonade continued unabated. Soon, each round that smashed into the shield gouged out a chunk from the bulwark. Bullets began to slip through, shattering as they once more struck the flagstones surrounding him. Then, reaching the point of catastrophic failure, the ward detonated, launching Kalpesh clean off his feet.

Slamming hard onto his back, Kalpesh skidded and rolled in a dizzying tumble, finally coming to an abrupt halt as he slammed into the parapets. The Maxim ceased drumming as the floodlights on the surrounding towers and walls swept across the rooftop in search of the Indian.

Kalpesh groaned dazedly as he fought to regain his wits, but in mere seconds, they'd found him again. The Maxim whirred back to life, sending a line of bullets cleaving across the roof towards him. Leaping back to his feet, he once more raised his hand in a last second defence, summoning another shield, but as the barrage drilled into the bulwark, the force of the impact sent the Indian reeling.

The small of his back smacked into the parapets as he struggled to keep his footing. Then, to his horror, Kalpesh felt his boots loose purchase on the slick flagstones. Before he knew it, he felt his centre of gravity lurch over the wall and he was tumbling backwards, plummeting headfirst from the roof of Anvil down towards the outer bailey below.

Flailing his arms and legs in desperation, Kalpesh watched the ledge sail out of reach. The ground was spinning as it hurtled towards him, but in a sudden sickening rush of vertigo, it seemed to then veer away. Stomach churning in a somersault, Kalpesh thumped shoulder-first into stone, his body reeling as he landed hard on his side.

Somehow uninjured, he heaved himself back to his feet, but despite his best efforts, he couldn't reorientate himself. His head continued to spin dizzyingly, until all of a sudden, he realised gravity itself had rotated. The ground beneath his feet wasn't the ground at all. He was stood rooted to the exterior wall of Anvil, suspended above the outer bailey, perpendicular to the ground.

Alarms continued to knell throughout the Tower. Several fathoms below, men were scouring the inner bailey, searching for any sign of the escaped prisoner. Across the way, the outer curtain wall rose from the Tower grounds, standing as the last barrier between Kalpesh and escape. Freedom was close at hand, he could practically taste it, but he still needed to figure out a way across.

The gap wasn't massive, perhaps forty feet across, but in his current orientation, it was forty feet overhead. Spotlights began sweeping across the bailey below as they hunted for Kalpesh; for the moment, he was hidden, but he figured he wouldn't be safe for long. He was within line of sight of the Develin Tower, where no doubt a second Maxim gunner would be searching for him.

Eyeing the distance one last time, Kalpesh

readied to attempt the crossing. He took a final deep breath, but in that moment, the glare of a searchlight swept over him. The Develin Maxim gun began to chatter and a volley of gunfire drilled into the wall. Kalpesh kicked off from the crumbling stonework, throwing himself into the air, out across the bailey. Men below cried out in alert as they caught sight of him soaring overhead, but in the blink of an eye, Kalpesh vanished.

Space and distance contracted in a vertigo-inducing lunge. Rematerializing in mid-air, Kalpesh began to fall. The ground reorientated in a stomach-churning flip of gravity, before, as the oncoming curtain wall rushed up towards the Indian, it swung through like a pendulum. Outstretching both arms and legs, Kalpesh touched down halfway up the wall. Overcoming a momentary spell of motion sickness, he rose to his feet, once more perpendicular to the ground, and stumbled forwards into a sprint, charging up the vertical face of the outer curtain.

The glare of a searchlight skimmed across the stone behind him, bullets peppering the wall at his heels as several Maxims drummed throughout the Tower. Reaching the ramparts, Kalpesh vaulted up onto the walkway. Gravity reverted. Bullets riddled the air. Floodlights blazed in searing beams crisscrossing the night. Out of time, nowhere left to run, Kalpesh dove clean over the battlements, vanishing into the murky waters of the moat below.

XXXII

West India Docks, Blackwall
10:31 p.m. November 1st, 1888

Kalpesh sputtered and retched. Noisome, greasy Thames water vomited from his mouth. His fingers squelched through silt and mud as he heaved himself exhaustedly up the bank. He shivered in the cold night air. Water dripped from his sodden hair and stubbled chin, gleaming in the smoggy moonlight as it beaded across the intricate network of tattoos and brands that emblazoned his torso.

Heavy traffic continued to chug up and

down the vast waterway, barges negotiating in and out of the London Docklands where millions of tonnes of cargo were loaded and unloaded daily in the world's busiest port. In the distance, a dozen Zeppelin airships hung suspended above the hazy London skyline. Their searchlights carved sweeping rays over the river upstream around the Tower of London; no doubt they were searching for the first man to ever escape Anvil.

Removing his pair of stolen boots, Kalpesh emptied them of water. Donning them again, he wrenched himself up to his feet. Wading through the saturated mud, he fought his way up the bank beneath the shelter of Limehouse Pier towards the wharf. Heaving his feet out of the ankle-deep sludge, he clambered wearily up the steps to the pier. Stumbling along the quayside, he made his way past Pier Wharf, heading northward in the direction of Limekiln Dockyards.

Keeping to the shadows, Kalpesh peered out at the dry docks ahead; they were mostly empty at this hour, but a few watchmen patrolled the perimeter of the wharf, keeping guard against anyone who might attempt to make off with any unattended cargo, or try to stow aboard the ship in dry dock.

Waiting for the nearest patrolman to turn his back, Kalpesh slipped out from between the warehouses, sprinting across the wharf and leaping from the quayside. The void lurched beneath him as he catapulted through the air and planted his hands and feet against the hull of the docked barge. Gravity swivelled with the tug of several runes tattooed up his calves, pressing him against the metal hull. Scampering up the perceived slope of the ship's bulwark, Kalpesh vaulted over the side, letting the downward pull of the Earth tilt once more upright to anchor his feet firmly on deck.

He stooped into cover behind the gunwales as the watchmen turned to investigate the source of the noise. Skirting out of sight through the shadows, he reached the portside of the dry-docked ship. Stepping up onto the far side gunnels, Kalpesh darted out across a section of scaffolding erected against the hull. His ankles tingled with magical energy as distortions in the Aether overrode his innate sense of balance, poising him unwaveringly upon a beam with catlike grace. Scampering across the rail, Kalpesh dropped down from the scaffold across the wharf and slunk out of sight between a stack of crates.

Using a short-lived veil of invisibility, he crept beneath the arc lights humming around the circumference of a second, smaller, dry dock, before arriving at the quayside of Limekiln Dock itself. Waiting for an opening, the Indian fugitive ducked out of cover, crossing the brightly lit wharf and making for the nearest ship.

Crates were being unloaded from the barge ahead via a crane, whilst workers used several ramps to transfer smaller goods from a pair of lighters moored up alongside the ship. Whilst no one was about, Kalpesh spurted across the quayside and leapt up onto a bollard. His supernatural grace took effect once more as he scurried out onto the mooring line, sprinting along the tightrope as if it were solid ground underfoot. He dropped silently onto the deck, skulking around the dimly lit stern, deftly avoiding the unsuspecting dock workers as they continued to go about their business mere feet away. Reaching the opposite side of the barge, Kalpesh planted a boot atop the bulwark, throwing himself out across the water. The air shuddered and compressed just before he was set to splash into the water. In an instant, he was transported forwards an extra dozen yards, decompressing back into full form on deck a lighter gliding through the dock.

Kalpesh dropped rapidly behind a row of barrels as the lighterman cocked his head back to inspect the origin of the sudden rocking caused by the Indian's landing. Peeking out from behind cover, he watched the oarsman shrug to himself, reverting his attention back to propelling the small barge across the water. Kalpesh felt the supernatural markings slowly recharge along his spine, and as the Aether resettled around him, he readied to teleport once more.

Presently, the lighter manoeuvred close to the north side of the dock. Kalpesh powered his legs into a short runup and cleared the edge of the barge, vanishing in mid-air and reappearing perched horizontally on the quayside just above the waterline. Pulling himself up onto the quay, he darted swiftly into the warehouse across the way, skirting the inner periphery of the building to avoid detection. Slipping through an open window, the Indian planted feet on Narrow Street. The road was empty, but as Kalpesh turned to begin his way eastward, he heard the incoming clopping of hooves across cobbles, accompanied by the rattling of carriage wheels.

He shifted his feet rapidly, ducking inside the shadows of Thomas Rents alleyway. Kneeling in the dim surroundings, he projected another veil of distorted light to conceal himself from the passing carriage. As it drew past, Kalpesh realised it was nothing less than a police wagon. Two constables rode atop the carriage, both sweeping their lamp beams left and right as they search the street.

The light of one of the bullseye lanterns momentarily fell on Kalpesh, but the veil of invisibility casting out of the Indian's palm did its work, bending the light, concealing him in a trick of the eye. The wagon jostled by leaving him undetected.

The passing of the police carriage had not been a mere coincidence; Malleus were widening their search for him. With each increment of time that passed, they knew Kalpesh could be farther and farther afield. Soon enough the entire city would no doubt be searching for him. The smartest course of action would be to flee London altogether, but Kalpesh had no intention of leaving the capital. He had unfinished business.

The fact that he was now a fugitive, on the run from the very organisation he had only weeks earlier loyally served, made no difference to the fact that the world was on the brink of collapse. Aleister Crowley, Jack the Ripper, was still at large, and only one gate to the Abyss remained unbreeched. No matter what corner of the globe Kalpesh fled to, if Crowley succeeded in summoning forth Choronzon, all would be lost.

He had to continue his investigation, but he knew he wouldn't be able to stop Crowley in his current state; he was half-naked and unarmed; the revolver he had secured back in Anvil was now lying somewhere at the bottom of the Thames. He was sleep-deprived and starved, his body on the verge of collapse from lassitude. He needed to gather himself. He needed to lie low. But most of all, he needed to find help.

Finally satisfied the coast was once again clear, Kalpesh emerged from the alleyway and began the long walk back towards Whitechapel.

XXXIII

Brady Street, Whitechapel
11:59 p.m. November 1st, 1888

Kalpesh perched on the corner of the rooftop of the animal charcoal works. He peered down across Brady Street to the corner of Thomas Passage. The front of his apartment building was clear, but tucked in the shadows down the alleyway, and both a hundred feet up and down Brady Street itself, were parked three indistinct black carriages. They appeared abandoned, no drivers seated up front, but to Kalpesh, it was obvious that each was packed with Malleus agents poised to strike the moment he dared make an appearance.

Coming back to his apartment was an incredibly stupid decision. There had been no question as to whether or not Malleus would be keeping watch in case he decided to return. The moment Kalpesh was confirmed to have escaped Anvil, orders would have been sent for men to keep watch at his home. It was the first and most obvious place anyone fleeing the law and lacking common sense would run to. As such, Kalpesh was hoping that coming here was so outlandishly reckless and idiotic, that it might in fact catch Malleus by surprise; there was a good chance that the units of heavily armed men concealed inside each of the carriages were paying little attention to the rundown apartment on the top floor of the end terrace house. No ex-Malleus detective in their right mind would ever be stupid enough to attempt a trip home. Kalpesh was counting on this; if his suspicions were at all correct, he might just be able to sneak inside and retrieve the things he wanted unseen.

The windows were dark, suggesting no one was inside. The lights would have to remain off when he entered, else the men watching from the carriages would be immediately alerted; fortunately, Kalpesh no longer required light to see.

The bell of St Phillip's Church by the Royal London Hospital tolled midnight. The rooftop of the charcoal works was suddenly vacant. Across the street, Kalpesh slid quietly down the rooftiles, slowing himself as he reached the dormer to his bedroom. Poking his head around to the window, the Indian blinked forcefully, triggering the arcane markings across the nape of his neck. His vision adjusted to the dim light in a muted colour palette, allowing Kalpesh to see in detail the interior of his apartment as if it were brightly lit, yet only in shades of grey. Gesturing with his finger, he reached telekinetically through the window and flicked open the latch. Pressing a palm against the pane, Kalpesh slowly creaked it open and clambered inside.

Looking about his bedroom, he could immediately tell his flat had been raided. The bed was overturned, the pillows slashed, the dresser broken into, and the wardrobe agape, with every item of clothing he owned discarded into a series of crumpled piles on the floor. Kalpesh quietly crept towards the open door on the far side of the room, peering through the darkness down the corridor. The kitchen was vacant, yet a muffled snoring was coming from within the sitting room.

Glimpsing inside, Kalpesh agonised at the sight of his once disordered library now in utter ruins. A large number of the books had been confiscated, whilst the works of fiction that had been of no interest to Malleus were strewn about, the pages crimpled, the covers buckled, the spines split, each having been flicked through and carelessly tossed aside as those that raided the apartment had scoured the place for any piece of incriminating evidence they could find. Slouched in Kalpesh's chair in the corner was a Malleus armed officer; his head hung forwards, his chin in his chest and his arms crossed as he dozed in the corner. His rifle was leant against the wall, whilst his belt holstering his Mauser C96 with a sheathed Malleus kukri attached, was hung over the back of the chair.

Kalpesh quietly approached the man, standing over him as he slept, fighting back the urge to throttle him as recompense for the state of his home. Instead, he cautiously lifted the belt from the rear of the wooden seat and left the man to sleep blissfully unaware of his presence. Quietly exiting the dingy lounge, Kalpesh shut the door and stepped back inside his ruined bedroom. Hanging the belt over the leg of his upturned bed, the Indian detective doffed his ragged trousers and sodden boots and started rifling through the heaps of crumpled clothing strewn about the place. In the minutes that followed, he dressed in a set of loose-fitting trousers and hardwearing boots, donning a stiff-collared shirt and waistcoat over his torso. Buckling the belt around his waist, he adjusted the positioning of the pistol and kukri and checked the contents of the ammo pouch to find several stripper clips of 9mm rounds for the adjacently holstered Mauser. Finally, Kalpesh donned a hooded duffle coat, fastening the toggles to the top and raising the hood.

Readying to leave the apartment, Kalpesh kicked aside the blanket screwed into a ball in the centre of the floor and smiled as he realised the floorboards had been undisturbed. Kneeling down, he drew his newly acquired kukri and slid the edge of the blade into a gap between the boarding, carefully lifting the singular loose plank that had previously been concealed beneath the bed.

Sliding the board aside, Kalpesh revealed the contents of the exposed cavity: a small leather satchel. Opening the bag, he was relieved to find everything in its rightful place. Inside was five pounds sterling in a combination of pound notes and coins of varying denominations, a few cherished photographs depicting Kalpesh's time in India, a single picture of him in Malleus uniform, a spare pocket watch, and finally, a fountain pen and black leather journal akin to his Malleus notebook. Flicking through the mostly blank pad, he finally arrived at the front pages where a few leaves were neatly scribed with notes and images copied across from the twinned journal now held in Anvil's evidence lockup.

Clipping the chain of the watch to his waistcoat buttonhole, Kalpesh pocketed it, before stuffing the remaining items back inside the small satchel, fastening it to his belt beneath his coat. Finally, stepping past the overturned bed, he vaulted over the windowsill, climbing back out of the dormer onto the rooftops.

Malleus would soon learn of the visit to his apartment when the slumbering officer inside awoke to find his weapons missing and the window ajar; but by that time, Kalpesh would be long gone.

XXXIV

Commercial Road, Whitechapel
12:31 a.m. November 2nd, 1888

Abberline stepped out through the rear kitchen door, emerging into his fenced backyard. He sat on the doorstep, scraping out the inside of his pipe before stuffing it with tobacco. He struck a match, sucking as the dried leaf took the flame, before stamping it out on the ground. He inhaled a long-extended drag. Lowering the pipe from his lips he slowly puffed a cloud of smoke from his nostrils into the chilly November air.

Picking up a crystal glass brimming with

gin from the doorstep behind him, Abberline slowly rose back to his feet and shuffled across the untended weed-ridden grass forming his small patch of lawn. He breathed in another lungful of tobacco smoke and took a long swig from his glass.

Several fathoms overhead, the drone of propellers steadily crescendoed as an airship scudded across the night sky, its beaming searchlights scouring the streets below. As the Zeppelin drifted northwards, the whirring faded, supplanted shortly thereafter by the stampede of hooves thundering down Commercial Road. Abberline sighed to himself, gulping another mouthful of spirit before he sucked heavily again on his pipe.

A citywide search was underway for his ex-partner; somehow the Indian had managed something no one had ever successfully achieved before. Breaking out of Anvil's jail was no small feat; it was the most secure and heavily guarded detention centre in the entire world. Several had managed to make it out of their cells in the decades since Anvil's construction, yet none had ever escaped the dungeons and lived; that was, until now.

The news had been delivered to Abberline almost two hours ago. Just after half ten, there had been a knock on the door; on the doorstep had stood a constable from Leman Street Police Station, there to deliver the news telephoned in from Anvil: Kalpesh Khatri was at large, and was now number one on Malleus' most wanted list.

Abberline thanked the young constable for delivering the message. Stepping back inside, he had poured himself a drink before he'd even begun to process what he had just been told.

He was under surveillance; of that he was certain. The fact that he had yet to receive a visit from anyone at Hammer was proof of that. In the morning, no doubt he would be called into Macnaghten's office; Monro would also be there. They would once again break the news to him of what had happened the night before, most likely withholding key details to see if the aging detective already knew more than he should about his ex-partner's escape, all the while, they would be studying him for any hint of his collusion. During that same time, he suspected his house would be searched, turned over floor to ceiling for any sign of Kalpesh or any shred of evidence that might suggest the aging inspector had aided or abetted him. Monro and Macnaghten would ask for his cooperation in locating Kalpesh; he would be tasked with finding him and bringing him in; failure to do so could even result in his own imprisonment. If Malleus decided he had played a part in any of what had transpired, they would find evidence against him, even if it wasn't there.

In the meantime, Abberline was being watched. Hammer were surveying his house from out of sight, watching the front door, waiting to see if he went anywhere to meet anyone, or if anyone attempted to pay him a visit during the night. Right now, he was Hammer's number one suspect; the fact that Kalpesh had been his partner was enough to draw all manner of suspicion upon him.

Abberline sighed, exhaling a breath of pipe smoke. He still hadn't gotten his head around what had become of Kalpesh; one moment he was Hammer's star detective, seemingly incorruptible, as straight as they came; the next, he had committed himself entirely to the very same illegal practises he seemed determined to stamp out. The Indian had always known a lot about the dark arts, perhaps a suspicious amount, or perhaps merely enough to make him adept at his job, but aside from this, nothing seemed to line up with the man's fall from grace. Abberline had always prided himself on his gut instincts, and his instincts had always told him, right from their very first meeting, that Kalpesh had been a good man. He had been naïve of course, and in desperate need of mentorship, but never in the two months they had worked together had Abberline suspected the Indian would be capable of this level of subterfuge. How could the man's allegiance to the occult have gone unsuspected and undetected for so long?

Whatever the case, it mattered little now. What was done was done. Now all that was left was for Abberline to try and find Kalpesh and bring him in. If the lad was smart, he'd be on a ship right now bound across the Channel. Part of Abberline hoped that he truly had escaped, never to be found, regardless of what it would mean for himself. But the other part of the inspector was more cynical; Kalpesh had betrayed Hammer, he had betrayed his country, but above all, he had betrayed Abberline. The chief inspector would look for his ex-partner in earnest, and had the Indian been stupid enough to remain in London, he would find him and bring him in dead or alive.

Abberline tapped out the embers from his pipe on the edge of his fence, taking another swig from his glass, polishing off the remainder of the drink. His head buzzed hazily from the effects of the gin; the garden was on the verge of spinning. He hadn't planned on sleeping tonight; he doubted he'd ever manage to drift off given the maelstrom of thoughts chaotically whirling through his mind. But all of a sudden, he felt overcome with exhaustion, ready to collapse into undisturbed slumber until the grogginess of dawn. Turning to make his way inside, he shuffled his feet back across the yard, pocketing his pipe. But before he could reach the doorstep, he found himself frozen to the spot.

"Fred," breathed Kalpesh, drawing back a dark hood to reveal his haggard face.

Abberline struggled to summon words. He stepped back clumsily, eyeing the man stood in front of him with disbelief.

"Fred, I need your help," Kalpesh smiled

weakly.

"You shouldn't be here!" slurred Abberline. "They're watching me."

"I know," nodded the Indian. "I slipped past them. They won't know I am here."

Abberline glowered at Kalpesh, suddenly overcome with rage at his friend's betrayal. His drunken fingers fumbled around the pistol holstered at his waist, and before he could think, he had drawn his gun and was aiming it directly at Kalpesh.

The Indian stood his ground, not so much as flinching as Abberline curled his finger around the trigger.

"I should kill you!" Abberline hissed. "You bloody traitor!"

"Whatever they have told you is a lie!" insisted the Indian firmly,

"I trusted you...! I believed in you!" stammered Abberline bitterly. "I invited you into my house! My wife... Emma... she cooked you dinner!"

"I didn't betray anyone," reiterated Kalpesh coolly. "I was set up."

"Of course you'd say that!" shrugged Abberline dismissively. "You'll say anything! Well, I'm done swallowing your bloody lies, Khatri!"

"I've never lied to you," insisted Kalpesh. "Not once."

"It's over. I'm taking you in. You can either come quietly, or you can kill me...like you did those whores!"

"You know that's bullshit!" snapped Kalpesh. "You know perfectly well who butchered those women!"

"What, your pal Crowley?" chuckled Abberline cynically. "Convenient that he managed to get away from you! Even more convenient that he let you live!"

"Use your brain, Fred!" growled Kalpesh. "Use your gut… like you kept telling me to do. You know I had nothing to do with any of the murders."

"Is that right!?" hissed Abberline thrusting the pistol Kalpesh's way in a threatening gesture.

Suddenly the Indian lunged for him so blindingly fast that Abberline barely had time to blink. The inspector looked down at his empty hand to see the gun missing from it. Kalpesh was now holding the weapon as he looked down the sights at Abberline several feet away.

"If I really did what Malleus claimed I had, why would I be speaking to you now? I could have snuck up behind you and killed you before you even realised I was here!" Kalpesh repeatedly drew back the slide to Abberline's Mauser, ejecting the unspent cartridges rapidly in succession from the pistol until both the magazine and chamber were empty. "After what they did to me—I don't even need a weapon to kill you. It would be so easy—just a wave of my hand…"

"Then why don't you?" growled Abberline.

"Because that isn't me! And you know that!"

"Then how the bloody hell do you explain...?" Abberline gestured in a fluster at Kalpesh. "How the bloody hell do you explain what you can do!? How do you expect me to believe that you have been set up when everyone says you can do things few adepts can manage after a lifetime of studying!"

"I can't explain completely," returned Kalpesh, slowly unfastening the toggles of his coat before setting to work on the buttons of his waistcoat and shirt. "But I imagine it has something to do with these!" he uttered, finally revealing a good portion of the tattoos and brands across his chest.

"Christ...!" stuttered Abberline.

"Do you really think I'd do this to myself?"

Abberline stepped closer, examining the markings in disbelief. "What... what are they?"

"Siddhis... somehow marked into my skin," he hypothesised. "Abilities, each of them; every mark corresponding to a different power, somehow linking my body and mind to the Aether."

"Who did this to you!?"

"The Golden Dawn."

"The Golden Dawn...?" repeated Abberline. "But I thought you reckoned—"

"That they were a myth," nodded Kalpesh. "I thought so, until I found them—by chance of all things!"

"But... why? Why would they do this to you?"

"I don't understand entirely myself," returned Kalpesh. "As punishment perhaps? They wanted me to be condemned by Malleus, of that I am sure—but I suspect they also wanted me to escape."

"But..." stammered Abberline in confusion. "That makes no sense!"

"I think..." continued Kalpesh. "They seem to believe I am the son of a founding member of their order—a man named Arthur Octavian Hume."

Abberline narrowed his eyes suspiciously. "Are you?"

"It..." Kalpesh sighed. "It seems likely," he admitted in defeat.

"I still don't understand," insisted Abberline. "Why would they do this to you?"

"I believe they want me to help them—to stop Crowley."

"But isn't Crowley one of them!?"

"No," returned Kalpesh. "No... I don't think he is. I think he might have been—once. But I believe they want to stop him just as much as we do."

"You think they are on the same side as Malleus?" returned Abberline sceptically.

"Not necessarily," Kalpesh shook his head. "But to paraphrase the Arthashastra—"

"The enemy of my enemy is my friend," put

in Abberline.

"Yes," smiled Kalpesh in surprise.

Abberline shrugged, acknowledging the perplexed expression Kalpesh was giving him. "I do read—*occasionally.*"

"I think..." continued Kalpesh. "I think you are more right about magic than I first realised," confessed the Indian. "There are those who use it for criminal intent, but..."

"You reckon it could also be a force for good?"

Kalpesh nodded, almost ashamedly.

"Well," sighed Abberline heavily, "I reckon you better hope to god that's true now." He gestured to Kalpesh's chest as the Indian refastened his buttons.

"I'm not done yet," insisted Kalpesh. "I think there is still a chance to catch Crowley—before it is too late."

Abberline shook his head. "No. You can't do anything. You need to get out of here! Every officer in London is out looking for you! Find a ship and sail as far from this godforsaken city as you can. I'll find that bastard Crowley, don't you worry."

"No," refused Kalpesh. "You need me—now more than ever. I'm not going anywhere."

Abberline grumbled. "I had a feeling you'd say something like that, Khatri. But I can't let you!"

"With all due respect, sir," Kalpesh smiled, "there is nothing you can bloody well do to stop me!"

Abberline bit his lip in frustration. "Alright," he finally agreed. "But you need to get out of here. If anyone finds out you were round my house, they'll chuck me straight in that cell you just broke out of— and they'll throw away the key!"

Kalpesh nodded. "Okay," he agreed. "I'll be in touch."

The Indian turned away, readying to teleport back up to the rooftops, yet as the tattooed runes down his back began to hum with energy, Abberline spoke once more.

"Khatri."

"Fred?" the Indian turned back to face his partner.

"If you need somewhere to lie low—our mutual friend will probably take you in."

Kalpesh glanced back quizzically at the chief inspector.

"Let me know how it goes if she suggests you play cards again!"

Kalpesh smiled, nodding a silent farewell, and before Abberline could so much as blink, he had vanished from the yard. Abberline emitted another low sigh. He trudged wearily towards the back door, ready now for bed. He prayed to god that no one had been listening in on their conversation.

XXXV

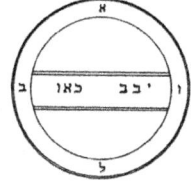

St Mary Matfelon's Church, Whitechapel Road, Whitechapel
7:56 p.m. November 5th, 1888

Fireworks popped, fizzed, and whistled in the skies above Whitechapel. A black vortex of smoke specked with glowing embers pillared upwards from the immense bonfire below. Kalpesh clung to the spire of St Mary's church, watching the annual festivities that marked the anniversary of the Gunpowder Treason Plot unfold on the church green. In 1605, a plot to blow up the House of Lords and assassinate King James

I and the rest of the English aristocracy during the state opening of parliament was thwarted; the plot was an attempt made by numerous occultist conspirators to spark a revolution and throw the country into upheaval. With plans to kidnap James I's daughter Elizabeth and instate her as a puppet queen, the ultimate aim for the movement was to repeal the Witchcraft Act of 1542 and legalise sorcery.

The plot inevitably failed when an anonymous letter was sent to the king, forewarning him of the attempt on his life. Guido Fawkes, one of the occultist plotters, was discovered at midnight on November fourth in the undercroft beneath the House of Lords guarding thirty-six barrels of gunpowder. The esoteric terrorist was found in the last moments of a ritual that would have magically concealed the stockpile of explosives and begun the countdown of an arcane fuse, detonating the barrels the following morning during the state opening of Parliament, reducing the old Westminster Palace to ash, and immolating the country's ruling class and head of state within.

The foiled plot had the opposite effect to what the conspirators desired; public opinion hardened against witchcraft and sorcerers, and Malleus were given greater powers and authority to stamp out occult societies across Britain. On November the fifth every year since, the entire country celebrated the failed Gunpowder Plot and the survival of King James I, parading through the streets during the day and letting off fireworks and gathering around vast bonfires throughout the night.

Atop each bonfire was burnt an effigy, traditionally of Guido Fawkes; but tonight, atop the bonfire on the church green of St Mary Matfelon's, and countless other bonfires across the country, burned an effigy of the Whitechapel Murderer.

From his perch on the church spire, Kalpesh watched a jeering mob celebrate as the straw and hessian rendition of an Indian Malleus detective caught alight in the conflagration. As the depiction of himself crackled and disintegrated in the searing heat, Kalpesh shuddered, knowing that his actual self had barely escaped the very same fate on Tower Green two days earlier.

Soon after Kalpesh's very public arrest on Parliament Square, Malleus had released a statement, claiming that the identity of Jack the Ripper had been uncovered, and that the perpetrator of some of the most heinous crimes the city had ever seen was none other than the Indian detective in Malleus that had helped thwart the Jubilee Plot the previous year.

Needless to say, the papers had run rampant with audacious claims and headlines, painting Kalpesh as a mastermind Malleus conspirator serving as a triple agent for the Theosophical Society, playing both sides against each other, thwarting the Jubilee Plot one moment whilst planning his own terrorist agenda the next. Once again, public opinion had hardened against the occult, but perhaps more worryingly, there had been a recent racist backlash against the East End's Bangladeshi community.

Kalpesh despaired at how little of the truth the public actually knew. Crowley was still anonymous, his links to the murders covered up in Malleus's attempt to frame Kalpesh. And now that he had escaped Anvil, the city-wide manhunt for him meant all of the police's resources and attention were focussed elsewhere; the real Jack the Ripper was now free to complete his dark ritual unopposed.

Though Kalpesh's escape from the Tower of London hadn't yet officially been made public, rumours were circulating fast. The night of his escape, Malleus had scoured London top to bottom in search of him. People inevitably took notice, and come morning, most of the Newspapers were printing rumours of a prisonbreak from Anvil's dungeons. Nobody outside of Malleus knew for certain who had escaped, but many had arrived at the correct conclusion.

The city was still on high alert. Officers from local divisions and Malleus alike were out patrolling the streets nonstop, searching for any sign of Kalpesh's whereabouts. As of yet, he had not been detected, but Indians were constantly being stopped in the streets by both the police and the public if they even so much as faintly resembled Kalpesh. As such, Kalpesh was limited in his movements, able only to emerge from his single room rented from Vittoria Cremers in Dorset Street under the cover of dark. The streets were almost entirely off limits to him; instead, he was forced to navigate Whitechapel via the rooftops in his search for Crowley; but tonight was different.

Easing his gravitational grip of the slanting church spire, Kalpesh allowed his weight to gently slide down the slates. The bell began to clang the hour as Kalpesh clambered nimbly down from the tower to the pitched roof of the church. Descending further, past the eaves, he stealthily dropped into the shadows of the churchyard. Emerging out into the street, Kalpesh joined the throngs marching up and down Whitechapel road, blending in with the dozens of costumed caricatures of the traitors Guido Fawkes and Kalpesh Khatri. Any other time, the Indian fugitive would have been unable to walk down the high street so openly, but tonight, there were so many people dressed up as himself that he had become simply a face in the crowd. A patrol of constables strolled by, scanning the gathering; neither of the bobbies even noticed the Indian as he walked past within a few feet of them.

Kalpesh rounded the corner onto Union Street, making his way around the bonfire, merging through the crowd gathered around it.

The head of his effigy dropped off the charred torso atop the blaze; the crowd jeered loudly as the straw-stuffed sack vanished into the fire below.

"Fred," Kalpesh greeted the man beside him in a low voice from beneath the shadow of his hood.

"Inspector," Abberline returned equally quiet, without so much as glancing at the shady individual that had sidled up beside him.

"Any news?"

"None to speak of," replied the chief inspector, not averting his eyes from the conflagration before him.

"You are still being watched," whispered Kalpesh, nodding subtly at the undercover Malleus officers stood in the crowd several feet away.

"No shit," breathed Abberline sarcastically.

"You think they suspect you?"

Abberline shrugged. "Probably not. They raided my house and didn't find anything—Emma was furious!"

"I'm sorry," apologised Kalpesh.

Abberline grinned faintly. "They were just... things—things can be replaced."

"If it is any consolation, they turned over my apartment too."

Abberline afforded himself a look at Kalpesh, ensuring the Indian fugitive caught the glower he shot him. "Why would that be a consolation?"

"I..." began Kalpesh. "I guess it wouldn't be."

"You definitely got the shit end of the stick," Abberline conceded, "but being guilty by association is—"

"You don't have to help me," put in Kalpesh. "You've done enough already."

"No," returned Abberline. "No, son, I owe you far more than what I've done. We all do... everyone here," he mumbled, glancing around at the assembled crowd. "Even if they'd like to watch you burn."

"Tonight, they get their wish," sighed Kalpesh as the depiction of him continued to reduce to ash.

"You and I both know who should be on top of that bloody fire!"

Kalpesh nodded.

"We need to find him—before it is too late!"

"I don't know what to do," muttered Kalpesh. "All I can think is to scour Whitechapel by night... try and catch him in the act."

"What about..." Abberline hesitated. "What about the Golden Dawn?"

Kalpesh paused for a long moment before turning to look briefly at his partner. "What about them?"

"Didn't you say you knew where they were? Their temple?"

Kalpesh gazed down at his hands, his eyes tracing along the lines of tattoo ink visible just beneath the cuffs of his duffle coat. "I'm not sure I can go back... not after last time."

"I understand," nodded Abberline. "But you said you thought they wanted you to escape Anvil. You said you thought they wanted your help?"

"I know," agreed Kalpesh. "But I'm not sure I can risk it—if I'm wrong, surely they'll just kill me this time."

Abberline frowned. "All you can do is go with what your gut says."

Kalpesh nodded.

"Whatever you decide..." continued Abberline, the crimson inferno glinting in his eyes, "just be careful, son."

"I'll try," agreed Kalpesh.

A shrieking firework shot high above the church spire overhead, erupting in a glittering explosion of crackles. When Abberline glanced back down beside him, Kalpesh had vanished.

XXXVI

Great Russell Street, Bloomsbury
9:51 p.m. November 8th, 1888

Kalpesh crouched atop the roof of Montague Mansion, staring across the street at the lit-up facade of the British Museum. Night-watchmen patrolled the circumference of the building; no doubt there was a similar presence walking the corridors within, though Kalpesh figured he'd have little trouble slipping past them. Infiltration had become something of a specialty for the ex-detective given his newfound abilities. But getting caught by museum security was of minor consequence for him; his true fear, were he to find an entrance to the Isis-Urania Temple concealed somewhere within the Reading Room, was being caught by the Golden Dawn.

They had let him live the last time they had caught him somewhere he shouldn't have been; though handing him over to Malleus in the manner they did was arguably less of a mercy than if they'd simply killed him outright. Had Kalpesh never escaped, he would have been executed by Hammer on the Golden Dawn's behalf, yet only after the month of torture and interrogation he had been subject to.

Desperation had driven Kalpesh to return; Abberline's suggestion had given him the final push, but the truth was, Kalpesh had been contemplating William Wynn Wescott's final words over and over again since his escape: *if you survive, if you see things clearly—seek us out again.* Kalpesh saw things clearer than ever; without the Golden Dawn's help, he'd never find Crowley in time.

They wanted him to return. In Kalpesh they saw a powerful ally, or perhaps more likely, a tool they could use to their own ends. Irrespective, Kalpesh believed the Golden Dawn wanted Crowley stopped, and even if they didn't, they alone, it seemed, might know of his whereabouts. Kalpesh's conviction had undoubtedly been shaken by the month of torture he had endured; in the past, he would have marched inside the hideout of the Golden Dawn guns blazing had he believed it might grant him the information he needed to stop the Ripper. But now, Kalpesh's stomach was turning over at the thought of once more being at the mercy of those who wanted him dead.

It had taken him several days to build up the courage to come here, driven only in the end by the realisation that Crowley would imminently strike again. The word was finally out: Jack the Ripper, the famous witch hunter turned sorcerer Kalpesh Khatri, was at large once again. With his escape from Anvil now public knowledge, Crowley no doubt knew he had the perfect cover to carry out the final stages of his dark ritual; with all of Malleus out hunting for Kalpesh, he was free to act.

Sliding down the vertical face of Montague Mansion, Kalpesh dropped to the ground. Emerging out onto the street, he projected a distorted field of light ahead of him, cautiously creeping behind the cover of the magical illusion across the lamplit road. Dispelling the veil of invisibility, he ducked behind one of the limestone pillars of the front gates and scampered effortlessly up the face until he was perched atop the rectangular column.

Waiting for the nearest security guard to reach the most distant point of his patrol route, Kalpesh then dropped down inside the gates and sprinted across the grounds. Footfalls magically muffled as he darted across the paving, he vaulted a low wall ahead, racing over the lawn, before, in a few brief seconds, he had closed the distance to the Museum front. Bounding upwards, the Indian felt the runes running along his vertebrae surge with latent energy, and in a head-spinning contraction of three-dimensional space, he was launched into the air. His body rematerialised stood horizontally on one of the neoclassical columns three quarters of the way to the roof. Boots clomped below and Kalpesh glanced down at the passing watchman oblivious of the intruder clinging to the pillar overhead.

Creeping on hands and feet, Kalpesh scampered up the face of the portico, soon reaching the pediment above. Pulling himself up over the ledge, Kalpesh stood atop the copper roof cladding and stared out across the courtyard, over the top of the Iron Library, to the domed Reading Room beyond.

Sprinting across the rooftop, Kalpesh wove around the various skylights, rapidly making his way around to the western side of the court. Skidding to a stop, he stepped up to the precipice, glancing across the expanse of iron bookstacks erected throughout the court to the round building in its centre. From where he stood, the chasm measured nearly seventy-five feet to the far side; significantly further than he had managed to teleport to date.

Kalpesh had not yet tested how far he could travel in a single jump, but he suspected the expanse before him would push the limits. The Indian sorcerer glimpsed down into the court itself; several watchmen were patrolling the circumference of the Iron Library, guarding the way in. If he were to try and touch down on the perforated iron panels that roofed the bookstacks surrounding the Reading Room, his landing would no doubt ring out across the court, irrespective of any magical sound suppression he employed; the patrolling watchmen would be immediately alerted to his presence.

He stepped back from the ledge, deciding instead to brave the leap across the full distance to the Reading Room itself. He backed up, retreating all the way to the far side of the roof. Planting his foot against the low wall behind him, he stooped into a crouch. His heart pounded. He exhaled deeply, visualising the jump ahead in his mind. Closing his eyes, he took a final quiet moment to ready himself.

Kalpesh's hamstrings snapped taught as he exploded off the mark. Legs pumping powerfully across the museum roof, the lip sped rapidly towards him. He planted a final foot inches from the ledge, bounding upwards with all his might. He was sailing through the air, legs and arms flailing as he continued to run. He felt a twinge of magic trace across his thighs, and for a few strides, the air beneath his boots turned rigid, granting him an extra couple steps that carried him beyond the precipice, out across the Grand Court.

But the solid air quickly gave out, and after only a few footfalls, Kalpesh's feet failed to find purchase. He began to fall, descending over the peak of his parabola, plummeting faster and faster towards the ground below. The runes up his spine surged to life. The distance to the other side rapidly shrunk. Gravity betrayed its normal orientation like on the deck of a capsizing ship, and as Kalpesh's body manifested back into material space, it fell the final dozen feet across the chasm. His boots struck the round concrete outer wall of the Reading Room and the shock of the force shot through the Indian's ankles and knees. He rolled off his feet to lessen the impact, recovering into a crouch, stifling the gasp of pain his mouth involuntarily emitted.

He looked overhead, back across the expanse he had just cleared, glancing next down to the guards below; they were still ignorant to his presence. Finally, Kalpesh turned his attention skyward, climbing the face of the wall to reach the expansive dome that capped the Reading Room. Clambering over the ledge, he sprinted across the arc of the roof, gravity slowly realigning such that it remained perpendicular to the outer face of the curve throughout Kalpesh's traversal to the oculus at its pinnacle. Dropping from his feet, he slid the remaining distance heels-first over the copper roofing towards the narrow window ahead. His boots impacted the glass, yet instead of smashing through the pane, a glyph above one of the sorcerer's elbows quivered; the glass rippled, parting like the surface of water as Kalpesh glided silently through.

Dropping swiftly on the inside of the oculus, Kalpesh felt his stomach invert as the tug of gravity flipped him wrong-side-up. His coccyx burnt as he slammed uncomfortably hard on his backside into the inwardly domed ceiling of the Reading Room. Rolling over in pain, he rubbed the small of his back and steadily rose to kneel upside down, glancing overhead at the maze of bookcases arranged on the floor below.

The Indian let out an audible gasp as he beheld the immense library beneath him; it was grander and greater in every way than he could previously have imagined. Miles upon miles of bookshelves stretched around the circumference of the immense building, whilst fanning out from the centre of the room were dozens of tables capable of seating over three hundred readers at any one time.

As Kalpesh examined the room from his unique top-down perspective, he was struck by something obvious that he suspected from floor-level might have been altogether inconspicuous: centred in the Reading Room sat the circular catalogue desk for the library's superintendent, around which curved a series of reading desks that cut outwards in two tangents towards the entrance of the round library. The result was that the desks took up the appearance of a keyhole shape when observed from a bird's-eye view. The imagery could not be merely coincidental: a keyhole suggested that something could be opened, the only question was, what fit the lock?

Rising to his feet, Kalpesh descended the interior of the dome, allowing his weight to slowly shift from inverted to horizontal, before finally rotating back to its normal orientation as he reached a bookcase ladder. Sliding briskly down the rails, Kalpesh dropped off the bottom rung and cautiously made his way across the carpet towards the heart of the room. He strolled around the circular arrangement of reading tables, towards the catalogue desk sat directly beneath the immense oculus overhead.

A glimmer from the crescent moon spilled down from the visible circle of sky, dimly illuminating the centre of the reading room. Kalpesh gently took a seat in the superintendent's chair, pausing for a moment to gaze across the catalogues sprawled out in front of him. He rapidly skimmed over the pages, glancing then to the various labelled drawers within his reach, searching for anything that seemed out of place; perhaps there might be a symbol scribbled on a page, a rune carved beneath the desk, or maybe some concealed switch or mechanism hidden out of plain sight. But there was nothing. The catalogue desk appeared to be just that, nothing esoteric about it whatsoever.

Kalpesh rose from the chair, wandering

aimlessly about the vast circular building. It seemed cliché, but perhaps somewhere there was a false book that when pulled might activate a hidden mechanism of sorts. He scoured the bookcases, his eyes jumping from spine to spine, hoping by chance he might somehow catch glimpse of a title that spoke to him, but there were thousands upon thousands of books shelved inside the Reading Room alone. Hoping to merely stumble upon something meant to remain hidden was surely a near impossibility; regardless, Kalpesh continued his hunt, his eyes running rapidly over the lower shelves of the bookcases.

Completing the full circumference of the room in what likely exceeded an hour, Kalpesh found himself seated once more in the superintendent's chair, his neck reclined over the headrest as he gazed up through the vast circular skylight in the dome overhead.

Kalpesh's gut now told him that he had been wrong. The British Museum all of a sudden seemed like an absurd place for the Golden Dawn's secret temple to exist; and even if he had been right, what chance would he have of finding it? He hadn't the faintest idea of where to search, and though access for the public was restricted, the Reading Room was busy enough that it seemed an impractical place to conceal an entrance to a secret hideout for the most clandestine occult society in existence. Any hidden door or mechanism that opened to a secret temple in a place such as this risked discovery, especially given the layout; there was barely anywhere within the entire room that was not visible to anyone stood elsewhere inside; only by stooping or crouching behind the assortment of desks and shelves could one hope to vanish from view, and even then, total concealment seemed impossible given the raised walkways skirting the upper shelving.

Kalpesh sighed in annoyance, ready almost to give up, when a thought occurred to him. Why should a secret society comprised of the most powerful adepts throughout the occult even need a door? The powers that they had imbued Kalpesh with gave him the ability to teleport over short distances, vanish from sight, and even pass through solid materials; surely then, some ingenious arcane means might be employed to conceal an entrance inside the Reading Room; one that could not be happened upon by accident, for only those with the means to do so could ever stand a hope of finding it.

Furthermore, perhaps the secret gateway would only ever open if the person attempting to pass through was unobserved. This then led to another realisation: such enchantments were more than likely detectable. There were several technological instruments that in theory would be able to home in on any subtle distortions to the Aether caused by their presence. An electromagnetic field meter would probably do the job, but without sneaking back into Anvil, Kalpesh suspected finding such a piece of equipment would be nigh on impossible. However, prior to the modern age, witch hunters had often used the occults own techniques against them when tasked with magical detection.

Dowsing rods were first employed by Malleus in the early period after its conception, despite the fact that dowsing was in and of itself a form of divination that the 1542 Witchcraft Act outlawed. Sorcerers in the past would often use the practice as a means of locating ground water or precious minerals, but dousing was just as effective at locating sources of magic. Historically, Y-shaped rods, most often fresh cuts of willow or hazel, were used, however, in the period leading up to the industrial revolution, before the advent of modern technological techniques, Malleus developed a system utilising two L-shaped metal rods.

The principle was simple enough: the douser either held the Y-shaped stick or pair of L-shaped rods out in front of themselves, and slowly walked around an area suspected to contain whatever the douser was searching for. In the event that something was detected, a Y-shaped stick would begin to twitch, whilst the L-shaped rods would either cross over one another or point apart. No doubt Kalpesh could employ this technique to locate a hidden entrance inside the Reading Room were one to exist, but once more, there were no fresh cuts of hazel or willow nearby, nor did Kalpesh have access to a pair of Malleus dousing rods.

However, in that moment, Kalpesh began to wonder if he would need any. The siddhis he been granted by the arcane sigils inked across his body were largely abilities linked to spells and rituals that already existed. What made the tattoos remarkable was the fact that Kalpesh was effectively able to cast said spells without the requirement of any ritual components. He didn't need to recite any incantations, he had no requirement to hold or wave around a wand, nor did he need to spend time scribing out intricate sigils where he intended to cast a spell. The abilities he'd been granted he could perform at will, using only his body and the connexion the tattoos granted him to the Aether. Given that magical detection by arcane means was well established, Kalpesh suspected that one of the many siddhis imbued into his flesh might just grant him the ability to dowse without the need for rods.

In the time that had passed since his escape from Malleus, Kalpesh had discovered a number of abilities bequeathed to him by his tattoos, but to date, many of the markings that graffitied his flesh were unaccounted for. It stood to reason that he was still in possession of several undiscovered abilities. If the Golden Dawn wanted Kalpesh to find them, logic dictated that they would have given him the necessary tools to do so; finding and unlocking the secret door to their temple perhaps being chief amongst them.

Kalpesh rose out of the seat, flexing his fingers and rolling his shoulders. He focussed his eyes about the room, raising both palms, hoping to sense something in the Aether. At first nothing happened, but as he allowed his mind to meditate, his senses began to awaken to the distortions in the veil. There was something beneath him: a vast emptiness underfoot that stretched away in every direction. A tingling sensation quivered through his fingertips as Kalpesh became suddenly aware of a faint energy radiating from the far side of the desk.

The Indian sorcerer slowly edged around the circumference of the keyhole arrangement of tables, approaching closer to the source of the magic. Like drawing near to the warmth of a fire, Kalpesh felt the arcane sensation well across the rest of his skin as he drew close. Suddenly, he could see something. It had materialised presently in the air before him: a fissure in space through which his eyes struggled to focus. He moved nearer to investigate, when without warning, a symbol on his abdomen fired to life. The portal's aperture gaped rapidly open, instantly swallowing Kalpesh whole.

A judder of momentum swept through the sorcerer's body, and suddenly he found himself stood silently in the dark. He was no longer inside the Reading Room; he was beneath it. He blinked his eyes, activating his mystic night vision. There was no doubt about it: he had found the secret hideout of the Golden Dawn.

XXXVII

The Isis-Urania Temple, Bloomsbury
11:06 p.m. November 8th, 1888

Kalpesh glanced around in the darkness as his eyes magically amplified the faint traces of ambient light. He was stood inside an immense underground gothic chapel, constructed in typical cruciform architecture; yet the temple was not shaped like a Christian cross, but instead, laid out as per the Golden Dawn's rosy cross, with triangular recesses cutting diagonally outwards from the crossing between the transepts to represent rays of divine light.

Kalpesh was stood in the centre of the crossing, beneath an immense domed ceiling that no doubt aligned perfectly with the round Reading Room above. Across the inside of the dome, the limestone ceiling was sculpted into a massive rose of twenty-two petals, each ornately carved and painted with the rainbow of colours Kalpesh had seen depicted in the lamen stitched into the robes at Samuel Mathers' home. Each petal was embossed with a mystic symbol complementarily coloured to the petal in which it was sculpted, whilst at the heart of the flower sat a second smaller depiction of the rosy cross. The decorative ceiling continued across the transepts, east around the semi-domed ceiling of the apse, before stretching westward towards the nave.

In the absence of stained-glass windows, various tapestries depicting historically significant sorcerers hung from the walls, portraying everyone from John Dee to Nicholas Flamel, to Morgan le Fay, and Merlin himself. Beneath the rows of wall hangings, bookcases lined with tomes, grimoires, and scrolls stretched against the walls of the chapel, representing perhaps the greatest collection of esoteric texts found anywhere in the world. A ritual altar sat in the expected position to the east end of the subterranean cathedral, as did a marble baptismal font, yet between the rows of pillars throughout the nave, where one would expect the church pews to be arranged, a long table stretched with heavy oak chairs positioned down its length.

Kalpesh crept forwards to investigate, but with the first plant of his boot across the flagstones, the temple awoke to his presence. Four sconces fixed to the main supporting pillars of the crossing flared to light, setting off a chain reaction as torches began illuminating in pairs, steadily lighting the transepts, the apse, and finally the full length of the nave. When the final row of sconces caught aflame, Kalpesh realised that he was not alone.

"Please, sit down," commanded William Wynn Wescott from the far end of the table.

"You took your time," muttered Samuel Mathers sat opposite him.

"It matters not the timing of our friend's arrival," put in the third man, who was sat at the head of the table. "What is important is that he has come, and not a moment too late."

Kalpesh hesitated, his feet remaining rooted to the spot as he gazed down the length of the nave to the three founders of the Golden Dawn, whom he could only assume had been seated in the dark awaiting his arrival.

"Come now, Inspector," insisted the elderly man at the head of the table, "we promise to be more hospitable then when last you were here."

"I've been here before?" questioned Kalpesh, glancing around the immense underground sanctuary.

Wescott nodded. "It is to here that you were

brought after we subdued you at Mathers' home."

"My *old* home," remarked Mathers snidely. "I believe it is safe to say I am now homeless, thanks to our friend here. Unable to show my face in public without fearing arrest!"

"You want to complain about being a fugitive to *me* of all people!?" snapped Kalpesh angrily as he began to stride down the nave towards the trio of men. "You broke the law! You are lucky to be on the run. Meanwhile, *I* was set up!"

Kalpesh watched as Mathers' hand slid nervously inside his robes, no doubt seeking the assurance of a wand in his grip.

"We all have done things we must answer for, inspector," insisted the elderly man seated between Mathers and Wescott. "You shot and wounded a philosophus in our ranks, and ousted both Samuel and William's identities, forcing them underground. As recompense, we branded you, marking you as a traitor to Malleus—but we did not kill you, as easily as it could have been done."

"And why is that?" questioned Kalpesh as he continued to slowly approach the three men.

"The answer to that is complicated."

"We've got all the time in the world," returned Kalpesh, halting before them.

"Alas, if only that were true."

"If only," agreed Kalpesh with a grumble.

"I have you at a disadvantage," the man

continued. "I am Dr William Woodman, Imperator of the Golden Dawn. I believe you are already familiar with Samuel and William?"

Kalpesh nodded.

"I understand you desire answers," conceded Woodman. "Eventually there is much that can be explained to you in great detail, but we fear time is currently of the essence, therefore I trust you will understand if I give the abridged answer to some of your questions?"

"Very well," agreed the Indian reluctantly. "Let's start with: Why am I here?"

"You came here on your own accord, did you not?"

"Fine," returned Kalpesh sharply. "Why did Wescott tell me to seek you out?"

"Because, as much as we hate to admit it," answered Mathers, "we need your help."

"You want me to stop Crowley for you?"

"Not for us," corrected Woodman, "for everyone."

"You no doubt understand exactly what is at stake in all of this?" questioned Wescott.

Kalpesh emitted a laboured sigh. "*Everything* is at stake."

"Indeed," confirmed Woodman.

"But *why* do you need me? Why do *this* to me?" Kalpesh gestured to the dark lines inked across his skin.

Woodman chuckled. "We need you, because we have failed for the better part of a year in locating Aleister," he explained. "You, it would seem, hold a talent for seeking out those who wish not to be found."

"As to why we chose to gift you the powers you now possess," continued Wescott, "there are a whole host of reasons."

"Such as?" pressed Kalpesh.

"Firstly, because given your bloodlines, we were confident the process would be successful," explained Matters.

"We chose to grant you the siddhis you now wield in the hope that they would allow you to confront Aleister," elaborated Woodman.

"I don't understand," returned Kalpesh. "If you three are amongst the most powerful adepts in the entire occult, could you not oppose Crowley yourselves?"

"Perhaps, if we could find him," agreed Wescott. "But as an expelled member of the Golden Dawn, he knows us three far too well to ever let himself be discovered by us. Need we remind you, inspector, our field of expertise is in the study of the mystic arts, not hunting those who choose to practise."

"If you think that I know how to find Crowley, I hate to disappoint," explained Kalpesh frustratedly. "That's why I am here now. That is why I was in your house," he pointed at Mathers. "I haven't the faintest idea of how to locate him! I came here hoping you might offer me some insight!"

"Then it is *us* who must disappoint *you*, Inspector, for Aleister Crowley has foiled every attempt we have made to locate him since the very first days he was expelled from the Golden Dawn. He has taken every precaution to prevent anyone from scrying his whereabouts."

"Why was he expelled?" questioned Kalpesh.

"For a long time, we held suspicions of his motives; eventually it became clear that his interests in the dark arts were far more than academic. At the time he was driven out, we did not yet know the full extent of his plans; had we, I assure you he would swiftly have arrived on the doorstep of Anvil. The Golden Dawn was founded on the principles of the pursuit of enlightenment. Since our inception, we have worked hard to purge the likes of Crowley, those who seek to perform malfeasance and bring untold horrors into this world, from the occult. Our order was established in juxtaposition to Malleus: our methods are not opposed but parallel to one another's, our goals are the same. Both Malleus and the Golden Dawn seek to prevent the perils of magic, but where Malleus' approach is to abolish all practises of the mystic arts, the Golden Dawn seeks to use the arcane in eradicating the few schools of magic designed to do harm. We believe fundamentally that magic is neither inherently a force for good nor evil; it is the intent of the sorcerer and the means they use that determine such.

"Aleister Crowley was admitted to the Golden Dawn in error; I myself, along with many other high-ranking members, were blinded by the raw potential we could see, unwittingly choosing to ignore the darkness that resided in him. He is charismatic and highly intelligent, easily manipulating those around him, seducing nearly everyone he encounters into his twisted web of deceit. We believed him a kindred spirit: a young sage hunting for meaningful existence in a complex and arcane universe. But Aleister Crowley's goal has always been the pursuit of power. He sought out the Golden Dawn for the secrets we safeguard. He rose swiftly through our hierarchy, befriending many whilst positioning himself as a rival to others, yet throughout his time in the Order, his ultimate goal was always to progress to a rank where our most protected secrets and knowledge would be available to him.

"Aleister was successful in deceiving us long enough to learn much of what he sought. Over time, it became clear that his fascination with the Abyss, with siddhis, and Enochian rituals —it stretched far beyond academic intrigue. We cast him out, fearing what he might attempt were he allowed to remain within the order. Alas, he had uncovered more than we had suspected, somehow learning secrets that should have been well above his station, unearthing dark rituals that should never be attempted. Upon his expulsion, he took many members of the order with him—those he had seduced with the promise of power. He established his own occult society, 'A∴A∴,' often referred to as Angel and Abyss—amongst other names."

"You mean Crowley isn't working alone?" questioned Kalpesh in horror.

Wescott shook his head. "By now he may even have scores of followers."

"Perfect," uttered Kalpesh sarcastically.

"The men and women of A∴A∴ are little more than puppets," insisted Woodman. "They consist mostly of members of the occult too weak-willed to resist the allure of Aleister; he is the true threat. Once he has been stopped, the remainder of A∴A∴ will crumble. What poses the true danger is what Aleister hopes to summon forth into this world."

"Choronzon," put in Kalpesh.

"Correct," confirmed Woodman.

"I don't yet understand *why* Crowley would want to summon Choronzon," returned the Indian. "Why would he want to bring about the apocalypse?"

"Aleister does not wish to simply unleash Choronzon," explained Woodman, "he seeks to subdue him—enthral him under his own will."

"He wants to control him?"

"Yes," nodded Wescott gravely.

"Do you think he can succeed?" asked Kalpesh.

"If anyone were capable of doing so,"

uttered Mathers, "it would be Crowley."

"Then what do we do?" questioned Kalpesh. "How am I of all people supposed to face him?"

"As we have already explained to you, you are not simply *anyone*," insisted Woodman.

"I know you think that," returned Kalpesh, "but I assure you that you're wrong."

Woodman and Wescott exchanged a smile with one another.

"Inspector," beamed Woodman, "that you are stood here now before us is evidence to the contrary. Were you, as you claim to be, a *nobody*, the ritual to endow you with the powers you now possess could never have worked. You are a result of the brief romance that existed between the Indian sorceress queen, Rani of Jhansi, and a powerful occultist by the name of Arthur Octavian Hume. Arthur was a close personal friend of mine; it is from him that we first acquired the cipher manuscripts that were fundamental in the founding of the Golden Dawn. He dedicated his life to the safeguarding of magical lore, ensuring that the arcane secrets gathered by a multitude of occult societies throughout the centuries did not vanish from history at the hands of Malleus. He believed that one day attitudes to the mystic arts would change, and that when that time came, the Golden Dawn would emerge from the shadows, assimilating with Malleus, beginning a new age of enlightenment where only those who sought to wrongfully manipulate the Aether to their own ends would ever need fear persecution.

"Arthur was a mentor to us all. And he was your father. We know this because of the mark you bear on your palm; it is not a simple caste marking, but a symbol of power. It was not only intended to identify you upon your arrival in England; it acts as a direct connexion to the Aether. No doubt it has served to protect you throughout your life, perhaps without you even realising so.

"Alas, following your mother's death in the aftermath of the siege of Gwalior, you were lost upon your arrival in London through some cruel act of fate. Arthur spent the remainder of his life searching for you, never giving up on the hope that one day he might find his son. He may no longer be with us, but now you are here in his stead. The siddhis we have gifted you are not yours alone; whilst Crowley has performed dark deeds, paying the necessary costs in attaining such powers with blood, the Golden Dawn worked together, channelling the energies of the cosmos to imbue you with similar powers through the Order's combined will.

"To say that we did not pay a price to grant you these abilities would be a lie; but know that the cost was gladly given, unlike the lives taken by Aleister in his own pursuit of power. Know that the reason we paid such a price, was because of who you are, and the debt that we owed to your father. Thus I must ask, out of respect for that which was sacrificed to make you what you are, that you do not deny *who* you are. Be true to yourself. You may never have known Arthur, but I can assure you, even in your absence, he loved you dearly."

Kalpesh nodded sombrely, unsure how to respond. "I'll help you," he assured. "I'll find Crowley. I'll find a way to stop him."

"Our guidance is with you," insisted Woodman, "but we have gazed beyond the veil at the uncertain future before us. Our part in the events to come is nearing its end; from hence forth, I fear it is up to you alone to stand against the rapture. We have done all that is within our power to aid you."

"I understand," nodded Kalpesh.

"Godspeed," said Wescott.

"Good luck," added Mathers.

"Go forth now," instructed Woodman. "Time is short. Already the final stages of Aleister's plans have been set into motion."

Kalpesh gazed back over his shoulder. Before the temple's altar, a portal was beginning to take shape.

"Wait..." stammered Kalpesh, turning back to the three men. "I still have more questions!"

"They will have to wait," apologised Woodman.

The most distant torches across the pillars of the narthex were suddenly extinguished, followed rapidly by the next inward set of sconces. Kalpesh felt the portal at the distant end of the temple begin to tug at his body.

"No wait...!" insisted Kalpesh, feeling darkness begin to press upon him as more lights went out, the chain reaction now beginning in reverse.

"I am sorry," returned Woodman as he and the other two men were plunged suddenly into shadow. "You are on your own now."

The length of the Isis-Urania Temple compressed suddenly behind Kalpesh, whilst the darkness ahead of him stretched endlessly into the distance. He felt his stomach turn over, his head spinning with dizzying intensity as the vast underground cathedral collapsed inwards around him, and against his will, he was sucked through the portal. With the dying of the final lights, Kalpesh was swallowed by darkness.

XXXVIII

Millers Court, Dorset Street
11:45 a.m. November 9th, 1888

Kalpesh sat bolt upright in bed. The hammering that had awoken him continued to sound. He leapt out from beneath the tattered blanket, only to realise, it was not *his* door that was being broken down. He shuddered as he stood shirtless in the frigid air, his heartrate slowing to its normal cadence. Taking a solitary step across the tiny room, he drew back the grimy rags hung across the pane-less window and peered down into Millers Court. The splintering of wood cracked below as a door staved inwards, but from inside his room, Kalpesh was unable to see what was happening down in the courtyard. He stepped back, rapidly dressing, finally strapping on his belt and holster. Checking the door to his cell-like bedsit remained securely barred shut, the sorcerer pushed open the window and vaulted out onto the roof slates.

Sliding down across the tiles, Kalpesh came to rest perching over the eaves, peering down into the narrow courtyard below. A single uniformed constable loitered in the gloomy court, standing guard outside one of the ground floor flats; behind him, the door to number thirteen hung ajar, the frame fractured where the lock had ripped through the wood. Kalpesh focussed his magically enhanced hearing, discerning amidst the uneasy mutterings from inside the flat the voice of Abberline.

Sergeant Edward Badham anxiously gripped his billy club as he stood watching the arched entranceway to Millers Court. In Dorset Street beyond, a crowd was starting to gather, curious about the police presence on the worst street in London. It had been more than a month since the Double Event, and a sense of normality had begun to return to the East End during the time that the Ripper had been locked up in Anvil; but now, in the wake of Kalpesh Khatri's escape, Whitechapel was once again on edge. For the last week, people had been wondering how long it would be before the Ripper struck again; soon, it would be obvious that time had come. When word got out, there was a good chance the masses would begin to riot. Badham could only hope that back up would arrive from Leman street before then. As it stood, he was the only uniformed officer on the scene; if things turned sour, he would be ripped to shreds by the angry mob.

A blur of shadow streaked downwards in the corner of his eye. Badham span on the spot to see a hooded figure drop straight out of the sullen skies above, boots planting firmly on the cobbles of Millers Court. The police sergeant nearly leapt out of his skin. Blind panic took hold. He stumbled backwards, nearly toppling clean off his feet. He fumbled for his truncheon, but the club flung magically from his grip with a flick of the Ripper's fingers.

"Inspector!" Badham managed. "Inspector... its him!" he babbled, backing into the corner of the court as the most wanted man in the country cocked his head as he watched the policeman cower in front of him. "He's here!"

Abberline loomed from out of the broken doorway. "Heavens Khatri, you got here quick!"

"Is it him?" asked Kalpesh, pulling back his hood.

Abberline nodded through a grimace. The chief inspector turned to observe the whimpering uniformed officer. Badham glanced back at the inspector in terrified confusion.

"Good grief, Badham," growled Abberline, "pull yourself together!"

"But… Sir…!?" he stammered, pointing nervously Kalpesh's way. "It's him!"

Abberline shook his head disgruntledly. "Contrary to official reports, Inspector Khatri is not the man we are after."

Badham glanced timidly back at Kalpesh.

"You'd do well to forget that you saw him here," the chief inspector grumbled menacingly.

Badham continued to cower with his back pushed as far into the corner as he could manage.

"Do I make myself clear!?" demanded Abberline furiously.

The sergeant nodded uneasily.

"Good," he smiled wryly, before gesturing for Kalpesh to come inside.

The Indian followed his ex-partner, leaving Sergeant Badham to continue trembling alone outside.

Kalpesh stepped across the threshold into a scene evocative of hell itself. Sprawled out across a set of blood-soaked bedsheets was a butchered corpse so horrifically desecrated that she was barely recognisable as human. The murdered woman had been carved open from groin to chest, her abdominal cavity emptied of its entire contents. Her face had been peeled away, her chin, lips, cheeks, eyelids, eyebrows, and forehead all skinned, with her nose cut clean off. The victim's breasts had been entirely removed, her legs spread apart, the flesh flayed down to the exposed bone. Every part of the corpse had been attacked; each piece cut away with violent strokes of the knife until barely anything remained of her humanity.

The neck bore the Ripper's trademark laceration that no doubt cut deep to the bone; the rapid exsanguination would have rendered the poor prostitute dead in a matter of seconds, after which, Crowley would have begun his monstrous mutilations. Beneath the woman's head, Kalpesh made out what appeared to be her kidneys and uterus; her intestines were drawn out across her right side, whilst her spleen was resting on the crimson sheets to her left. What appeared to be her liver and one of her severed breasts were arranged about her feet, whilst the table stood beside the bed was heaped with flaps of skin and flesh removed from various regions of the body.

"Horrifying, isn't it?" came the voice of Inspector Edmund Reid stood in the corner of the tiny room.

Kalpesh nodded, his stomach turning at the grotesque scene of the macabre ritual killing.

"I don't think 'horrifying,' quite covers it, Reid," huffed Abberline.

"We stand witness to the depths of the Ripper's depravity," returned Reid, "a scene where he was allowed to perform his dark deeds undisturbed in private."

"This is…" struggled Kalpesh as he beheld

the sickening room in disbelief, "...it's a whole new level!"

"So, what now?" questioned Abberline. "That's it, isn't it? His ritual is finished. Is the Abyss now open? Has he managed to summon Choronzon?"

Kalpesh hesitated. He listened to the growing uproar from the crowd amassing around the entrance to Miller's court. "No," he declared finally. "I suspect that if Choronzon had been unleashed we would have known about it long before this body had been discovered."

"So, what then?" questioned Abberline. "The ritual failed?"

"Maybe," shrugged Kalpesh. "But the Golden Dawn seemed convinced that Crowley would succeed."

"The Golden Dawn?" repeated Abberline. "You met with them?"

Kalpesh nodded solemnly. "Last night."

"They give you any idea how to find him?"

"No," responded the Indian flatly.

"Shit," hissed Abberline under his breath. "What then? What now?"

"There must be another stage to the ritual," surmised Kalpesh. "Some final step..."

"Another killing?" queried Abberline. "I thought you said there were only four watchtowers... four seals...?"

"Representing the four classical elements," confirmed the Indian. "Only..."

"Only what!?"

"Only there aren't four elements… there is a fifth!"

"A fifth?" repeated Reid from the corner of the room.

"The Aether," put in Abberline.

"That's right!" returned Kalpesh, somewhat surprised.

"The Aether is an element?" asked Reid.

"Yes," he affirmed. "Though it differs in nature from the other four. It is not always considered an element in and of itself because it is not bound by the laws of physics in the same way as the other classical elements; instead, it serves as a medium that ties the other four together —Hindus refer to it as the Akasha, Aristotle described it as the *first* element, Sir Isaac Newton used it to explain gravity. It is poorly understood, but we know it to be the vital medium that conducts and convects magic."

"Alright," nodded Abberline. "You reckon there is a fifth stage to the ritual— but why, if there are only four watchtowers, would there be five stages?"

"Perhaps the four watchtowers serve as the locks," proposed the Indian. "Each has been unlocked, but the door has not yet been opened."

"Special Inspectors?" interrupted Reid, who had up until this point been for the most part stood meekly in the corner of the room.

"Reid?" questioned Abberline.

"Perhaps the answer is simpler," he suggested.

"Go on?" questioned the Malleus detective, eager to hear what his replacement at H division had to offer.

"At each of the murder scenes thus far, in addition to a mutilated body, our killer has left in his wake what you men of Malleus refer to as a pentacle, marked in the victim's blood. Yet, despite the disturbing extent to which this body has been dissected, there appears to be no such esoteric symbol."

"By god!" breathed Abberline, his eyes now flitting around the room. "He's right! We were so focussed on what he did to this poor woman that we didn't even see there was nothing painted on the walls!"

"Perhaps then the answer as to why the gates to hell have not been breached is merely that, this ritual, much like with the murder of Elizabeth Stride on the night of the Double Event, was interrupted before our killer could complete his grisly rite?" suggested Reid.

"Perhaps indeed," agreed Abberline, befuddled as to how he had missed such an obvious omission from the crime scene.

"No," refused Kalpesh.

"What do you mean, 'no'?" questioned Abberline. "You reckon he did the ritual somewhere else after he gutted the woman here?"

"No," repeated Kalpesh, sensing the residual

energy in the Aether. "A ritual definitely took place here," he insisted as he paced over towards the hearth. The Indian crouched over the fireplace; he moved his hand near to the ashes, feeling the warmth still radiating upwards. Careful not to burn himself, he pulled something out of the cinders. Examining the curved tube of iron, Kalpesh held it up against the kettle hung above the grating to confirm he was holding the missing spout.

"The fire burnt hot," deduced Reid as he observed Kalpesh. "Hot enough to melt the soldering."

"A ritual fire," confirmed Kalpesh. "Her clothes were used as fuel," he determined, noticing a few charred shreds of fabric that had settled on the floor in front of the hearth. "And no doubt a number of her organs were consumed in the flames," added the Indian as he rose to his feet, moving closer to the eviscerated body.

"Her name is Mary Jane Kelly," declared Reid as Kalpesh stooped to peer inside her hollowed-out thorax. "Once more a victim of circumstance, akin to most residing here on Dorset Street."

"Was the woman from Mitre Square ever identified?" questioned Kalpesh.

"Catherine Eddowes," replied Abberline. "Identified by the pawn tickets she had in her pockets of all things," he added.

"She's missing her heart," concluded Kalpesh, having spent several seconds gazing at the few remaining organs inside the woman's chest.

"I can't see it anywhere," grimaced Inspector Reid as he searched around the room at the haphazardly positioned viscera.

"Well, we know where it went then, don't we!" concluded Abberline as he now too stooped by the fire to examine the embers. The detective stood after a moment, turning once more to Kalpesh. "Alright, Khatri," he began, "let's say you are right —let's say he did perform his ritual here; why aren't we looking at another seal from the Key of Solomon?"

"Who own's this bedsit?" questioned the Indian, looking now to Reid.

"Miss Kelly was renting it," explained the Inspector. "The landlord who owns this flat also owns the row of properties attached to the front of it, twenty-six through number thirty Dorset Street. It appears he acquired all of them sometime last year, but no one seems to know much about him."

"Does he have a name?" questioned Abberline.

Reid nodded. "John McCarthy."

Abberline's face suddenly turned pale as he gazed back at the man from H Division.

"What is it?" questioned Kalpesh in confusion.

"I might be mistaken…" started the chief inspector. "When you were locked up in Anvil, I did some research. I figured if our man had one alias, *Boleskine*, he might have others."

"And does he?" questioned Kalpesh.

Abberline nodded. "I spent weeks digging them up; I reckon he might have hundreds of bloody names!"

"Was John McCarthy one of them?" questioned Inspector Reid.

"Not quite," returned Abberline. "But the initials... J. Mc. C.—I found them a good few dozen times. He's published poems and books abroad under those initials—I'm sure its him!"

"If not then it is an incredible coincidence," conceded Reid.

"Then if Crowley owns this apartment...?" Realisation suddenly hit Kalpesh.

"He could come and go here as he pleased," inferred Abberline.

Kalpesh hesitated, looking around at the room at the wallpaper; aside from the recent bloodstains, it was in good condition, new even. He closed his eyes, feeling a rune tingle on his chest. His eyes opened once again. "Shit!"

"What is it?" Abberline questioned, unnerved somewhat by his ex-partner's pupils now glowing with magical energy.

Kalpesh blinked, his vision returning to normal. Slowly, he edged around to the far side of the bed, carefully stepping over the pools of congealed blood, to the splatter marks up the wall. A shred of wallpaper curled up from the surface.

Kalpesh tugged at the scrap, slowly peeling away a larger and larger section from the wall until suddenly he had removed the entire blood-soaked strip, revealing beneath the fourth and final pentacle from Crowley's dark ritual.

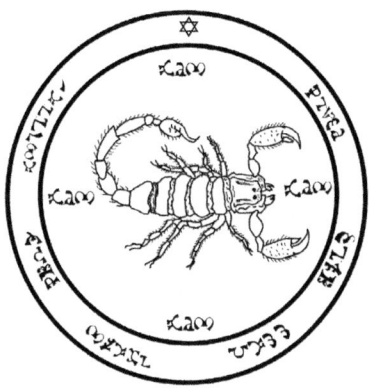

"Oh," mumbled Abberline, otherwise lost for words,

"The fifth pentacle of Mars," announced Kalpesh. "Causes all demons to obey the wishes of the conjurer." The Indian stepped back to observe the pentacle comprised of two outer rings encircling the depiction of a scorpion surrounded with numerous Enochian symbols.

"Christ," breathed Abberline in dread.

"It gets worse," assured Kalpesh, stepping closer again to tear away more of the wallpaper. The more the sorcerer peeled back from the surface, the more sigils and runes he uncovered. In a matter of moments, he had exposed a good portion of the wall, revealing an expansive network of interlocking symbols and arcane graffiti surrounding the central pentacle positioned above Mary Jane Kelly's body.

"What are they?" questioned Reid as he stepped out of the corner, peering back at the wall behind him, correctly assuming that beneath the remaining wallpaper, every inch of the bedsit was covered with the same esoteric etchings.

"Mostly invocations for siddhis," replied Kalpesh, recognising numerous sigils that matched his tattoos. "But a number of these... the pentagrams—they are demon summoning circles."

"Demons that Crowley now controls?" questioned Abberline.

"Demons free to enter the material plane now that the gates have been unlocked," explained Kalpesh.

"Inspector Reid, sir?" called the voice of Sergeant Badham from the court outside.

"What is it, Badham?" questioned Reid, stepping out through the door into the yard.

A bloodcurdling scream blurted from outside. Kalpesh and Abberline locked eyes with one another, their hands swiftly moving for the pistols holstered at their waists. Kalpesh was first out of the door. The angry din of the mob crescendoed suddenly to a deafening volume.

Kalpesh watched Badham crumple to the ground as a knife was rent from his gut. Stood over the sergeant's body was a short man in his late forties, darkly dressed, wearing a bowler hat; in his hand he clutched a narrow blade dripping with Badham's blood, in his other, he gripped the cane inside which the same weapon had moments before been sheathed. Screams roared as the crowds outside of Miller's Court bore witness to the police officer's brutal murder and the mob rapidly dispersed in terror.

"Lusk!?" questioned Reid in disbelief as he stood gazing in horror at Badham's body lying in a rapidly swelling pool of blood.

"Aleister Crowley sends his regards, inspectors!" the man chortled before suddenly lurching forwards with incredible speed.

A swing from the man's cane connected powerfully with Reid, launching him clean off his feet. The inspector flew tumbling sideways through the air, colliding with a window before crashing to the cobbles in a shower of glass. Lusk lunged next for Abberline but was met with a fusillade of bullets as two Mauser C96 pistols fired in rapid succession. The bullets punched into Lusk's torso, each slug plunging through the man's chest in a puff of vaporised blood, yet the assailant continued to spurt Abberline's way, altogether immune to the cannonade riddling his body.

A split second before the man sank the point of his knife into Abberline's neck, Kalpesh collided with the attacker. Together, he and the man in the bowler hat smashed through the already cracked glass of number thirteen Millers court, slamming hard onto the floorboards beside the bundle of blood-soaked bedding. Lusk began to thrash violently, and before the Indian could pin him down, he threw Kalpesh off himself with a sudden jerk of his shoulders.

Flipped onto his back and suddenly pinned to the floorboards, now Kalpesh was underneath, struggling beneath the flailing thug on top of him. The edge of the knife slashed the fabric of his duffle coat as he blocked a stab for his ribs with an elbow. Kalpesh pressed the muzzle of his Mauser into the man's gut and pulled the trigger a half dozen times. The gun clapped hard in his grip and more bullets ripped through Lusk's stomach. Kalpesh felt hot blood spill across his midriff, yet the bullet wounds didn't even seem to so much as slow the crazed aggressor.

The Mauser clicked uselessly, magazine now spent. He snatched hold of the stranger's forearm, straining against the seemingly impossible strength of his assailant as Lusk attempted to force the point of his blade down into Kalpesh's heart. A second drumfire of shots went off as Abberline appeared in the doorway. More bullets plugged into his foe's back. The attacker's strength momentarily faltered, giving Kalpesh a brief opening. The Indian lurched up with his elbow, driving it hard into the man's temple.

The knife stabbed downwards, missing by an inch, sinking through a wooden floorboard. Kalpesh felt a line of runes singe across his right arm. A whirlwind of force tore outwards and the man atop of him was launched skyward. The crazed assailant crunched into the ceiling, crumpling the plaster and laths. Kalpesh flipped back to his feet as the man dropped, his bloodied body slapping hard against the floor.

"What the hell!?" demanded Abberline as the man fell limp.

"I..." gasped Kalpesh, struggling for breath. "I don't know!" he wheezed, watching now in disbelief as the man started to twitch.

Lusk's head snapped backwards, his body contorting as broken limbs twisted and popped sickeningly back into shape. His eyes locked on Kalpesh and Abberline, irises burning like hot coals as black smoke billowed from the corners of his eyes. The monstrous fiend cackled, his sinister laugh echoing with dark malevolence. His mangled form leapt up from the ground, before, in a frenzy of gnashing teeth and flailing limbs, the nightmarish aberration charged for Kalpesh.

The Indian sorcerer raised a hand in defence, summoning an arcane shield just before the demon drove into him, yet the fiend had rushed him with such force that the bulwark of magical energy only served to buffer the blow. Kalpesh found himself rolling head over heels across the cold cobbles outside. Ignoring the throbbing ache in his side, he dug his boots into the paving, grinding to a halt. He looked up to see the demon launch across the yard, soaring fifteen feet into the air in a single bound.

Kalpesh dodged away as the fiend slammed down next to him. Knife clutched in a deformed talon, the demon slashed for his neck. Kukri hissing out of his scabbard, Kalpesh managed to raise his blade just in time to parry the next thrust from his foe. Time slowed as the tattoos across his chest awakened, the temporal distortion serving as a foil for the fiend's blinding haste.

The playing field levelled, Kalpesh managed to duck beneath the next swing with ease. Slashing overhead as he slid under the attack, he felt the curve of his Ghurkha blade carve deep into Lusk's armpit. The beast emitted a terrifying wail. Kalpesh stepped rapidly clear, watching as the fiend's knife clattered to the floor, arm hanging limp at its side.

The demon's flaming gaze locked once more on Kalpesh. It flailed the walking stick in its other hand, swinging wildly for the Indian, yet another subtle distortion to the passage of time saw the sorcerer dodge cleanly away. Darting back into close quarters, he grappled the fiend from behind.

Struggling against the demonically possessed man thrashing violently in his embrace, Kalpesh drew the edge of his kukri across the fiend's throat. The blade cut deep through flesh and Kalpesh felt the edge score vertebrae as he nearly decapitated the demon altogether. What blood remained inside the otherwise eviscerated corpse spilled out across the cobbles, yet the animated cadaver continued to writhe powerfully as it fought to free itself from Kalpesh's grapple. A wayward limb batted the kukri from Kalpesh's grasp and the blade rattled across the courtyard as it was knocked clear.

Kalpesh battled to restrain the demon, yet it thrashed and wrestled against his waning strength. Fingers groped at the Indian's neck, the creature's sharp fingernail's digging in as it attempted to gouge at his face. Kalpesh locked an arm around the demon's throat, clasping its forehead with his second hand. A tattoo illuminated on Kalpesh's palm, the Om symbol given to him by his mother; suddenly, a searing heat began to expel from the mark.

The demon howled in agony as the tattoo on Kalpesh's palm branded its forehead. Hot white light scalded the monster's flesh, penetrating into the host body, immolating the dark spirit inhabiting the vessel in radiant energy. The white fire seared outwards through the fiend's red glowing eyes, and with a sudden flash of brilliant light, the demon was exorcised and the body slumped dead in Kalpesh's grasp.

The Indian released his grip and the man flopped into an exsanguinated heap in the middle of Miller's Court.

"Sweet Mary!" cried Abberline in disbelief.

A groan came from a few feet away as Reid heaved himself agonisingly up from the ground. The inspector limped warily over to inspect the corpse, checking it was well and truly dead this time. "George Lusk," he wheezed.

"As in, head of the Whitechapel Vigilance Committee?" questioned Abberline as he too moved closer.

"The very same," confirmed Reid. "Do you think he was in league with Crowley?" questioned the inspector, trying to fathom what had just happened.

"It's possible," nodded Abberline. "Rumour has it, he received a letter from the Ripper not a month back: it was addressed *'From Hell,'* and supposedly it came enclosed with a piece of Catherine Eddowes' kidney!"

"Lord have mercy," breathed Edmund Reid.

"I think it is possible he might be just another victim left in Crowley's wake," suggested Kalpesh as his eyes flicked momentarily into penetrative vision. "Although..." he continued, drawing back the mans ripped and bloody collar to reveal a pendant hung around his neck.

"He was a freemason," declared Abberline, instantly recognising the square and compass masonic amulet.

A police whistle sounded in the distance, followed swiftly by a second blast far nearer than the first. Kalpesh magically attuned his hearing, catching ear of rapidly approaching boots down

Dorset Street.

"Get out of here," insisted Abberline, looking first to the body of Lusk, then the corpse of Sergeant Bradham. "If they catch you here then there will be no hope of ever clearing your name!"

"And you'll be locked up with me!" added Kalpesh.

"Godspeed," uttered Reid.

"Find me again," insisted Abberline.

"I will," nodded Kalpesh, outreaching a hand. Across the court, his kukri skipped over the cobbles before leaping up from the ground and back into his grip. The Indian sheathed the blade Before issuing a final farewell. He turned away and fled up the vertical wall ahead, vanishing swiftly across the rooftops as a dozen constables and Malleus officers spilled into Miller's Court below.

XXXIX

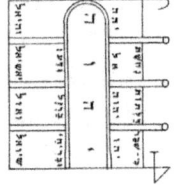

Christ Church, Spitalfields
04:00 a.m. November 11th, 1888

The bell of Christ Church Spitalfields tolled for a fourth time, heralding the end of the devil's hour. The din of jeering echoed throughout the East End. Smoke plumed from buildings aflame, whilst bonfires blazing in the centre of the streets cast the city in an ominous amber glow. The occasional scream cut through the roar of rioters, punctuated often by the shattering of glass, as shop fronts were smashed in and looted. Chaos had descended across the city in the single day since the events in Millers Court. Both the Met and Malleus had withdrawn from much of the East End altogether, their efforts directed to restoring order in the City of London and Westminster. The men of H Division had erected various barricades down Leman Street, managing to secure a small area of Whitechapel against the violent mobs parading through the borough, where those fleeing the chaos could find refuge. Yet the rest of Whitechapel and the other surrounding regions were no man's land, where anyone caught out in the open was set upon by those driven to frenzied violence by the breach in the gates to the Abyss.

Before complete control had been lost, there had been reports across London of crazed bedlamites attacking police and civilians alike; Kalpesh had caught the tail end of a conversation between two constables, one of whom claimed he had witnessed a woman withstand over a score of bullets before a final shot to the head was enough to bring her down. Word had not yet broken that these rabid lunatics terrorising the streets were in fact cases of demonic possession, yet suspicions were growing even in light of the otherwise widespread violence across the rest of the population.

Crowley's rituals had succeeded entirely; the capital was on the brink of collapse, and Kalpesh suspected the time of the final stage of his master plan was close at hand. The chaos raging across London was no doubt a necessary part of the ritual to invite Choronzon through the interdimensional gate. It could be merely a matter of hours before Crowley would summon forth the Dweller of the Abyss, triggering the apocalypse in full. Kalpesh knew that time was rapidly running out, and if Crowley was to be stopped, he had to find him fast.

The Indian sorcerer clung to the church spire, surveying the pandemonium in the streets below. Above, a Zeppelin airship was scudding through the smoke and ash towards Commercial Street. A broad searchlight swept down from the aircraft as it glided past the spire, the harsh beam centring on a hoard of rioters smashing an overturned tramcar with crowbars and cricket bats. The airship loudspeakers crackled and a distorted voice blared across the thoroughfare.

"Attention citizens! Disperse! Vacate the streets and return to your homes or we will be forced to open fire! Repeat: disperse or we will open fire!"

"Fuck you!" Kalpesh heard from the street below.

A firebomb flew upwards, the arc of its trajectory falling well short of the Zeppelin as it plummeted back towards the road, the bottle shattering against the cobbles into a wide pool of conflagration. Seconds later, the sound of a revolver fired, the shot pinging against the hull of the airship. The resulting response came rapidly. Smoke grenades streamed downwards from the

Zeppelin, swiftly followed by the deafening drumfire of the ship's guns. Cobblestones cracked and exploded beneath the cannonade as several rioters were immediately mown down in the hail of bullets. The shooting rapidly halted, the message received clearly; the mob scattered into the refuge of various side streets and back alleys. Smoke continued to billow upwards from the grenades as the Zeppelin's propellers whirred louder, accelerating the airship away to the south in search of another group of anarchists to supress.

With a semblance of order momentarily restored in the immediate vicinity, Kalpesh made his move. He slid down the spire, leaping from the tower out across Commercial Street. Runes flashed up his back and the distance across the thoroughfare shrunk immediately before him. He landed on a roof above Dorset Street; the crime-ridden alley below was for once uncharacteristically vacant. He traversed across the row of dosshouses, making his way back in the direction of Miller's Court.

A thought had occurred to him some time after he had fled the scene of Mary Jane Kelly's murder: on the night of the Double Event, Kalpesh had chased the Ripper from Mitre Square north-eastward, their confrontation happening on the very rooftop upon which he now stood. At the time, Kalpesh had merely assumed that Crowley had been fleeing in a random direction in his attempts to lose the pursuing Malleus detective, and that their standoff had occurred above Dorset Street for the simple reason that the maniacal occultist had run out of rooftops and been cornered; but now the alternative seem far more obvious.

Crowley did not stop to fight Kalpesh above Dorset Street because he had nowhere left to run; the man, like Kalpesh, could teleport, and as the Indian had just deftly demonstrated, the crossing from Dorset Street to Christ Church was entirely possible for someone with their capabilities. No; Crowley had stopped to fight Kalpesh where he did because the Indian had chased his foe all the way to the very destination to which he had been fleeing. The Ripper had hoped he'd lose his tail long before he ever reached Dorset Street.

Dorset Street was the location of Crowley's hideout. The fact that Kalpesh had earlier learnt that the man owned not one, but an entire row of houses in the slums, seemed only to confirm this theory. It should have been obvious from the start: the most demented killer in Whitechapel's long history would surely seek refuge from the law in the one place where the law daren't set foot; it was exactly what Kalpesh himself had done.

That was what had made the revelation all the more infuriating; for the last week, since his escape from Anvil, Kalpesh had been living less than a dozen yards away. Crowley had murdered Mary Jane Kelly and torn down the final pillar of creation whilst the Indian slept peacefully in a flat in the same square! All this time, Kalpesh had been closer than ever to the man he had been searching for, and yet he had been totally oblivious to his presence. But that all changed now; he was certain Crowley's base of operations resided in one of the properties he owned on the worst street in London, and the Indian sorcerer would find it, even if it took all night.

He came to a stop not far from Miller's Court; from where he stood, he could see the dormer of his own bedsit. He took a few deep breaths, clearing his mind. He pressed his eyes tightly shut, feeling a familiar sigil beneath his shoulder blade tingle with magical power. As his eyelids slowly lifted, his eyes began to penetrate the surfaces around him. He directed his vision across the rooves of number twenty-seven through thirty; the shingles faded into transparency, the blurred images of what lay beneath drawing faintly into focus. At first the shapes of furniture and people crammed into the various attic rooms took form only in wispy outlines, yet as the Indian sorcerer narrowed his gaze, greater and greater detail condensed in the hazy images flickering through his vision. His arcanely attuned hearing likewise pricked up, combining with his piercing sight to concentrate on the interior of the buildings.

The first sound and picture that became clear enough for Kalpesh to make out was a sobbing child curled in her mother's lap. The woman cradled the toddler, clutching a weeping baby in the other arm. The entire attic space was rammed with beds, each occupied by families taking refuge from the madness of the streets outside. Kalpesh found himself unable to endure the images for long, and quickly strode over the roof to the next property in the row.

Once more, the Indian focussed his boring vision on the slates under his feet. As the room below focussed into view, he made out several subdivisions to the attic space, inside of which were more occupied beds, though unlike the house before, there were no families in sight. Kalpesh did not need to look long to realise he was peering inside a brothel, and though most of the working women and their clients were finished for the night, there were a number of prostitutes still plying their trade, some more vigorously than others. Once more eager to avert his gaze, though this time for completely different reasons, Kalpesh hurried across to the next rooftop, hoping to discover a scene less vulgar than the last.

Hesitating over the next property, Kalpesh took a short moment to cleanse his mind of the graphic scenes he had just been privy to, before once again turning his attention on the rooftiles underfoot. This time, the Indian sorcerer found himself peering into a veil of darkness; a fog effervesced before his gaze, its smoky shadow impenetrable even to Kalpesh's tunnelling sight. He swept his vision away, focusing across the rooves towards his own tiny apartment, finding that he was able to peer through the slates to see his bed and trunk inside. Yet as he returned his attention back towards the building in question, he was once more unable to peer through an obstructive screen.

Kalpesh smiled, realising now he was staring at a manifestation of some kind of anti-scrying enchantment. He could not see inside for the simple reason that someone had put up an arcane barrier to prevent anyone from doing so. People were often nosy, regularly taking interest in the affairs of their neighbours, and when there was the off chance that your neighbours had the ability to see through walls, every precaution had to be taken to prevent your illicit activities from being discovered. There were other sorcerers residing in the vicinity of Dorset Street; both himself and Vittoria Cremers resided merely a few doors down, and no doubt there were other nearby individuals seeking refuge from the law that had the capacity to scry inside this apartment. Not only that, but the Golden Dawn themselves were actively searching for Crowley's whereabouts. The magical shroud would be enough to prevent anyone from discerning the Ripper's location. There was little doubt in Kalpesh's mind that he had at long last found Crowley's hideout. Now, all he had left to hope was that he might catch the deranged occultist inside.

Kalpesh scrambled down the slope of the

roof, snagging hold of the flashing around a dormer. Craning his head around to the window, the detective peered through the murky glass into a darkened room. The window was too grimy to see much of what laid beyond, but the ex-detective could tell well enough that nobody was inside. Disappointed, but no less determined, Kalpesh flicked open the latch inside with telekinesis and pulled himself into the room. Clicking his fingers, the sorcerer magically lit a candle stump melted into the bedside table, illuminating the room with the faint flame.

Kalpesh had been right: this was Crowley's hideout; or at least, it *had* been. In the centre of the floorboards, the charred runes of a burnt-out teleportation circle was laid bare for the Indian to see. A few blood stains splattered the floor, leading from the door of the room to the corner, where a heap of clothes soaked in blood and excrement lay discarded on the floor. A few empty jars and vials were knocked over atop a table, but it appeared as if everything of further use to the Ripper had been taken. Yet across the wall, pinned into the crumbling plaster, were several sheets of esoteric scribblings.

The detective cracked the candle from the waxy puddle on the nightstand and edged closer to the wall of arcane notations. As the amber light flickered over the pages, Kalpesh made out the plans for the Ripper's work. He spotted a crude sketch of the Third Pentacle of Mars as it had appeared above the body of Polly Nichols. Aside it was the Fifth Pentacle of the Sun that had been painted in Annie Chapman's blood. Next came the Sixth Pentacle of the Sun that had granted Crowley the power of invisibility in Mitre Square on the night of the Double Event. And finally, there was the scorpion seal of the Fifth Pentacle of Mars, still as of yet unremoved from the wall of Mary Jane Kelly's apartment on the ground floor below. Yet there was another seal, a fifth pentacle inked onto a sheet of paper far larger than the other four.

Kalpesh set the candle down on the desk, leaning closer to inspect another seal from the Lesser Key of Solomon: a cross patteé encircled within two rings, once more incorporating various Enochian symbols inside.

Each arm of the cross was representative of one of the classical elements, with the crossing marked as the convergence of the four, symbolic of the Aether. A translation of a versicle from Psalms was written beneath it, scribed in the same flowing script Kalpesh had seen in both the *'Dear Boss'* letter and the *'Saucy Jack'* postcard.

Thou hast broken my bonds in sunder. I will offer unto thee the sacrifice of thanksgiving, and will call upon the name of the Supreme Being

Kalpesh did not need to consult his journal; he had now spent so long studying the seals from the Lesser Key of Solomon that he recognised each and every one of the forty-four pentacles contained within the grimoire and knew all of their effects. He was looking at the Seventh Pentacle of the Sun, the final piece of the puzzle, the last part of the ritual. It should have been obvious to Kalpesh ahead of time that this would be the final seal; he visualised the description from the grimoire inside Anvil's library, reading it again in his mind's eye.

If any be by chance imprisoned or detained in fetters of iron, at the presence of this Pentacle, which should be engraved in Gold on the day and hour of the Sun, he will be immediately delivered and set at liberty.

This was the final key to Choronzon's prison. The gates to the Abyss had already been opened, yet Choronzon's chains had not yet been broken. Once this final part of the Ripper's ritual had been enacted, the dweller of the Abyss would be summoned into this world where Crowley would attempt to bind him to his own will.

Kalpesh went through the remembered instructions once more in his head. The rite needed to be performed on the day and the hour of the Sun. It was a reference to the planetary hours of Hellenistic astrology. The day of the sun was of course Sunday. Kalpesh's heart froze. He dug his hand swiftly into his waistcoat pocket, pulling out his watch to check the time, though he knew already it was too late. It was coming up to a quarter past four in the morning, Sunday. Kalpesh panicked. He was too late! The day of the sun had already come, and the first hour of each day was ruled by the planet of the day. The hour of the sun on a Sunday was always the first hour of the day!

"Shit!" cursed Kalpesh under his breath, pocketing the watch in frustration. He had failed. It had all been for naught. The end of the world had no doubt already come; Crowley had summoned Choronzon. Had he been sharper, quicker to think, he might have realised the location of Crowley's hideout sooner. He might have discovered the

Ripper's plans in time to stop him, but it had taken him the better part of a day to realise, and even then, he had waited for the rioting to lull before he had come to investigate.

The Indian thrashed his arm in fury and a blast of wind ripped out from his hand, flipping the bed in the corner onto its side, toppling the nightstand beside it, and cracking the plaster of the far wall. He gritted his teeth, wracking his brain for any solution. Surely there was something that could be done. Perhaps there was a way to exorcize Choronzon and send him back to the Abyss. But there was no solution. It was too late.

Or was it? A glimmer of hope suddenly flickered through Kalpesh's despair. He had been mistaken! True, the first hour of Sunday was the hour of the sun, but unlike normal timekeeping, the planetary hours of the day did not begin with midnight, but rather sunrise. There was still time!

Kalpesh brought his breathing back under control. He paced back and forth as he tried to think clearly. It was November, little more than a month away from the winter solstice; the nights were long, the sun setting in the afternoon, shortly after four. But what time did it rise? Seven; sunrise was just after seven! He had less than three hours!

His heart slowed as he regained his composure. Kalpesh continued to pace. He knew what time the final stage of the ritual was going to take place, but he had yet to ascertain where it would happen. It had to be somewhere significant. Every aspect of the Ripper's crimes had been enacted like a grotesque pantomime. With the exception of Mary Jane Kelly, all of the murders had been committed out in the open under the very noses of the police and Malleus. Any old location would simply not do for Crowley's grand finale; it would have to take place somewhere of importance! But where?

Kalpesh returned to the pages of pentacles tacked to the wall, studying once more the final puzzle piece: The Seventh Pentacle of the Sun. He stared at the image, hoping against all hope that some hidden tidbit of information might reveal itself from within the esoteric pen strokes. Yet despite his familiarity with the Lesser Key of Solomon, the magic was still for the most part beyond his comprehension. He understood the purpose of the pentacle, but as to *how* it operated, Kalpesh was in the dark. He could translate the Enochian alphabet with the aid of a cipher, but he could not perform the magic himself.

The Indian continued to stare blankly at the page, until finally, something unusual did stand out to him. It might have been a simple mistake, but in light of Crowley's meticulous attention to detail, demonstrated both in the other pentacles on the wall before him and those he'd painted above the bodies of his victims, Kalpesh became immediately suspicious. The pentacle seemed accurate in every respect, except that the Enochian markings denoting east and west on the left and right arms of the cross appeared to be flipped.

Kalpesh reached inside his breast pocket, fishing out his journal, and flicked mechanically through the pages. He studied the Hebrew version of the pentacle and then referenced the Enochian cipher scribbled on one of the back pages; sure enough, the east and western arms of the cross were switched, but furthermore, there was something that Kalpesh had not previously noticed: each and every one of the Enochian characters appeared to be a mirror image of those transcribed into his journal.

Kalpesh pocketed his notebook and ripped the sheet of paper from the wall. As he held it in his hands, the light from the candle flickering on the table diffused through the paper, revealing printed lines on the reverse of the page. Kalpesh rapidly turned the sheet overleaf and realised he was holding in his hands a map of London. Now, as the light from the candle continued to glow from behind the page, the Seventh Pentacle of the Sun was visible through the paper, superimposed over the map, both the Enochian characters and the east and west arms of the cross visible in their correct perspective.

Kalpesh exhaled in disbelief. Upon the map were four X's marked in red ink, each residing inside one of the four arms of the cross. Kalpesh flitted his eyes between them, picking out their locations, sifting through his knowledge of Greater London until he realised what stood at each of the four positions. They were coal power stations, each newly built to supply the most advanced city in the world with electricity. In the northern arm of the cross aligned the Edison Tesla Electric Company's Holborn Viaduct Power Station. In the eastern arm laid the Pioneer Bankside Power Station at Meredith Wharf. To the south, the enormous, recently commissioned Battersea Power Station fitted just within the boundaries, and to the west was the Kensington Electric Lighting Station.

Kalpesh puzzled over the crosses for only a brief moment before everything became clear to him; the electricity generation plants were themselves a part of the ritual, providing the immense quantity of power that would be necessary to break the fetters binding Choronzon inside the Abyss; the power attained from a singular ritual sacrifice was unlikely to be enough to provide the necessary energy for such an extreme magical feat. But the vast quantity of energy generated by the four stations would be more than capable of fuelling the final act of Crowley's master plan! But where would the actual ritual take place!?

Kalpesh slowly traced his eyes over the map to the seal's crossing. At the heart of the pentacle, where the four elemental arms converged in the centre of the page, sat the Palace of Westminster. The Houses of Parliament: that was where the finale to Crowley's epic performance was due to take place! That was where Kalpesh needed to go! That was where the world would end in less than three hours' time!

XL

Liverpool Street, City of London
4:39 a.m. November 11th, 1888

The dial tone continued to buzz as Kalpesh held the phone receiver to his ear.

"Come on, come on!" he muttered impatiently as he peered out through the door of the police box to the rioters torching a carriage up the street. The phone continued to ring for several more moments without an answer before Kalpesh slammed the receiver down on the hook in frustration. "Damn it!" he cursed furiously, stepping back out onto the street.

Sighted immediately by the gang of arsonists, Kalpesh darted across the road as they began hurling slurs his way. The rioters gave chase to the Indian, yet as Kalpesh reached the face of Bishopsgate Station, gravity swung horizontally underfoot and he spurted cleanly up the face of the building, disappearing over the rooftops to his pursuers' confusion.

He gazed over the London skyline to the southwest. All across the horizon, smoke was rising from buildings alight. The entire city's fleet of airships patrolled the skies. Kalpesh glanced back down at the police box below; it was the third he had found, and the first among them that had not been destroyed by rioting vandals. But no one at the other end of the line was picking up the phone. Kalpesh was hardly surprised. The city was in turmoil. Every policeman and Malleus officer in London would be out on the streets tonight. The Met and Malleus were stretched well beyond their limits; one could hardly expect someone to be manning the phones. Even still, Kalpesh needed some way to contact Abberline. He couldn't stop the ritual alone. He needed help. But Abberline could be anywhere in the city right now, and Kalpesh had no time at all to search for him.

Wherever he was, Abberline would likely have some line of communication; no doubt he and the other Malleus officers out on the streets would have been issued with Airwaves. If Kalpesh had one of the Hertzian devices of his own, he might have been able to get hold of his ex-partner, but he'd didn't have the time to go searching for one. There simply wasn't the time.

Kalpesh's mind traced back to the moment he had first laid eyes on the Mark II version of the Hertzian wave communicator. A remark Abberline himself had made stood out to him. The chief inspector had likened the technology to telepathy. Telepathy had long been the bane of Malleus, as it allowed for members of the occult to speak to one another over great distances without risk of interception of their communications. There were many spells that allowed for telepathic communication, but they all more or less followed the same basic principles. Telepathy was largely attributed to the occult's ability to remain underground and undetected by Special Branch; it allowed for a relatively coordinated network of societies and lodges to exist. There were limitations to the spells. Range was one of the limiting factors, another was the requirement for communicating individuals to perform the spell synchronously with one another. Kalpesh had once heard the process likened to trying to make a telephone call where neither phone was able to ring to alert the person on the other end of the line that someone was attempting to reach them.

There was a good chance that amongst all the abilities the Golden Dawn had endowed Kalpesh with, telepathy was one of them. But given that Abberline was not only unaware that

Kalpesh wanted to reach him, but was, more importantly, unable to perform the necessary spell himself, the chances of Kalpesh being able to contact the chief inspector telepathically seemed equally slim. A thought did occur to Kalpesh, however; one that seemed outlandish, yet altogether possible.

Kalpesh was well versed enough on the science behind the Airwave to know that Hertzian waves were a form of electromagnetism. Likewise, it was reasonably well understood that the Aether affected electromagnetism in a variety of ways. Tesla theorised that both were merely different manifestations of the same phenomenon; could it therefore be possible for Kalpesh to communicate with Abberline's Airwave via telepathy?

Covent Garden, City of London
4:45 a.m. November 11th, 1888

Abberline took cover behind a pillar as several shots from a Colt revolver chinked off the stone. The chief inspector stepped back out from the protection of the column, drawing back the bolt of his Lee Enfield rifle, loading the next cartridge into the chamber. He peered down the sights. The shambling demon locked eyes onto him and charged his way at full tilt, discarding the empty gun in its hand as it flailed its talons and snapped its maw. Abberline exhaled and squeezed the trigger. The firing pin struck the modified cartridge, exploding the gunpowder inside the chamber, propelling an iron slug rapidly down the barrel. The muzzle flashed and smoke plumed as the shot hurtled from the gun, driving through the skull of the charging demon. The creature's legs gave out and it toppled to the floor, sliding to a halt in a fit of spasms. A normal lead slug would have done little but slow the fiend, yet an iron bullet was effective enough to stop a demon in its tracks. It continued to writhe about for several more moments before finally its thrashing limbs fell limp.

Abberline wiped the sweat from his brow, reloading his rifle as he glanced warily about in the eerie silence. He rubbed his whiskered chin anxiously, gazing at the fire raging from the Royal Opera House. He sighed in dismay; so much of the city was in ruin. It would take years to rebuild what had been lost. Abberline heard footsteps approaching. He spun on the spot, raising his rifle as a figure emerged from out of the smoky shadows of the market.

"Don't shoot!" warned the familiar voice of Sergeant Cumming. "It's me!" he insisted, lowering his own Greener Police shotgun.

"Jesus, Cumming!" snarled Abberline in relief. "I nearly blew your bloody head off!"

"Sorry," apologised the Malleus sergeant. "I didn't intend to sneak up on you." The man was clutching his arm, his sleeve soaked with blood.

"You alright?" questioned Abberline, nodding at the wound.

"Yes," he grumbled. "One of those bloody things took a bite out of my arm!"

"You sure you're okay?"

"Yeah, yeah," insisted the sergeant. "I blew the fiend's head clean off!" he gestured to his lowered shotgun. "The iron shot seems to do the trick alright. Good job you gave us all forewarning."

"Pays to be prepared," agreed Abberline. "You should have seen the trouble Reid and I had in Whitechapel without any iron shots. Had to cut Lusk's head near clean off to take him down!"

"Is that the last of them?" questioned Cumming as he looked at the lifeless body face down in front of Abberline.

"I reckon so, for now," confirmed the chief inspector. "Best call everyone back in—regroup," he smiled weakly as he reached for the receiver of his Airwave, yet before he could click down the transmit button on the mouthpiece, the speaker started to crackle. At first merely white noise fizzled from the communicator, yet as Abberline and Cumming looked at one another in confusion, a voice slowly whined and popped into frequency.

"Fred... Fred... are you there.... Can you hear me!?"

"Is that...!?" questioned Cumming in disbelief as he recognised the voice.

"It better be!" nodded Abberline before

he depressed the button and spoke into the mouthpiece.

"Khatri... is that you?" he questioned tentatively, praying none of his superiors were on the same frequency.

"Fred!" sighed the wanted man through the static. "Thank heavens!"

"What is it, lad?" questioned Abberline.

"Fred... I've found his hideout! I know where he is going to be!"

"Crowley!?" questioned Abberline in shock. "You know where he is!?"

"Not right now," returned Kalpesh. "But the final stage of the—" the transmission cut out for a brief second. "—today, Fred! At dawn today! We—"

An ear-piercing whine shrieked over the speaker.

"You're breaking up!" insisted Abberline impatiently. "Retune your Airwave."

"I'm not using an Airwave!" replied Kalpesh, the interfering noise intensifying before the channel cleaned up. "We only have a few hours!" insisted the Indian. "It's happening at Westminster—Parliament! I'm heading there now!"

"Westminster?" repeated Cumming.

"We read you, son!" returned Abberline. "We'll get everyone in Hammer over there to stop that bastard!"

"No!" interrupted Kalpesh. "No, it's not just Westminster!"

"What do you mean?" pressed Abberline as Kalpesh's volume faded.

"He's drawing energy from powers stations!" explained the Indian. "For the ritual. You need to get men to each of them!"

"Power stations?" parroted the chief inspector. "What power stations?"

"Coal plants!" explained Kalpesh. "There are four: Holborn Viaduct, Battersea, Kensington, and Bankside!"

Abberline repeated the locations back to Kalpesh and Cumming nodded to confirm he had heard the same.

"That's right!" returned Kalpesh.

"That's a pretty wide spread!" replied Abberline anxiously. "I'm not sure we can get men to all of them!"

There was a long pause before finally Kalpesh responded. "I'm en route from Liverpool Street. I'll head to Bankside on my way to Westminster—but I need you to take care of the others."

"Alright," conceded Abberline. "I'll see what I can do."

"Thank you!" replied Kalpesh. "I have to go. There's not enough time!"

"Kalpesh wait!" insisted the chief inspector, determined to get a last word in before the Indian cut off communications.

"What is it?"

"Good luck, son."

"You too."

Silence fell.

Abberline looked up at Cumming. The man appeared as if he had seen a ghost. "Well don't just stand there!" barked the chief inspector. "Did you hear the lad or not?"

"Sir?"

"Call the boys in. I'll contact Anvil—we've got work to do!"

XLI

St Paul's Cathedral, City of London
5:12 a.m. November 11th, 1888

Kalpesh sprinted across the lead roofing of St Paul's Cathedral as he charged southward in the direction of the river. Cutting around the domed crossing, the Indian hurtled along the apex of the nave, veering left to slide down the pitch. Leaping back to his feet, he scampered along the edge of the roof until he hit the narthex and darted south, skirting the periphery of the clock tower, skipping over a void onto a smaller pitched roof. Planting a foot firmly on the parapets, he threw himself skyward, feeling the ground lurch beneath him. He slingshotted magically over the street, his feet landing hard atop the next building. Knees buckling in the impact, he rolled over, flipping swiftly back into a sprint as he continued to race onwards.

Hurtling over the next expanse of rooftops, he lunged across Carter Lane, landing firmly across the way. On he rushed, cutting a line diagonally over the next stretch of rooves. Swerving left, he hurried south, reaching the precipice of Knightrider Street. Throwing himself from the ledge without hesitation, Kalpesh streaked across the chasm, touching boots down next atop the roof of the General Post Office Savings Bank.

The Thames was fully in sight now, and across the river, Kalpesh could make out the enormous brick chimney rising from the centre of Bankside Power Station. Diving from the brink ahead, his body sailed through the air across Queen Victoria Street, and in a rapid truncation of distance, he was teleported onto another stretch of rooftops. Cutting a line dead south, he jumped once more, this time crossing Upper Thames Street in a single arcane bound, finding himself finally atop the row of warehouses lining the northern bank of the river.

The power station was dead ahead, but in order to reach it he'd have to cross the river. Normally the Thames waterway was the busiest in all the world; under most circumstances, the river was so congested that even someone with no magical teleportation abilities could feasibly cross from one bank to the other by leaping from lighter to lighter without ever touching the water. But with the city in chaos, traffic along the river had ceased altogether and the murky expanse of water ahead was almost completely devoid of ships.

Kalpesh begrudgingly turned west, across the wharfs and warehouses, heading for the next nearest option over the river. On he ran, rapidly approaching St Paul's Station up ahead. Bounding in a series of leaps over various docks, Kalpesh threw himself across the final chasm, teleporting atop St Paul's Station. Darting south, he reached the end of the roof. He dropped from the ledge, slapping a palm and kicking a boot against the wall. Gravity tilted back on itself and the Indian slid rapidly down the face of the railway station, the soles of his boots braking his descent as they grated against the brickwork. Landing hard on the tracks below, Kalpesh felt his ankles and knees burn for a few seconds following the impact.

Limping the first few steps, he broke into a sprint once more, heading south across Blackfriars Railway Bridge, his feet pounding across the wooden sleepers underfoot as he charged out over the water. His lungs burned, his heart throbbed, his mouth gasped rapidly at the air as his legs carried him on. The three-hundred-yard stretch came to an end as Kalpesh reached Blackfriars

Goods Station on the far side of the Thames. He charged into the station, leaping up onto the platform. Racing towards the stairs, he took the steps five at a time. In a matter of seconds, he had reached the embankment, the power station just up ahead. The immense three-hundred-and-twenty-five-foot-high chimney loomed overhead as he charged towards it, issuing a steady torrent of black smoke that blotted out the moon.

Rushing up towards the wall, Kalpesh collided with the bricks, revolving the tug of gravity as he planted his boots against the western face of the power plant. He sped up the eighty-five-foot height, vaulting swiftly up onto the roof. Finally, he slowed to catch his breath at the top.

Edging over towards the skylights up ahead, Kalpesh peered down into the turbine hall. His heart sank in dread. The rows of generators below were being guarded. Kalpesh flitted his eyelids, his arcane vision making out dozens of shambling figures highlighted below patrolling between the dynamos. He sighed laboriously; as far as he could tell, each and every one of the generators had been graffitied in an array of Icelandic staves, all designed to draw power, syphoning it elsewhere to a specified geographical location.

Furthermore, it appeared the arcane markings were not simply painted onto the generators, but instead, engraved into their casings. Given that the staves couldn't be dispelled without gouging lines through each of the sigils, the only way to disrupt the flow of power to Crowley's ritual would be to kill the switches and cut off the turbine from the generators. He hadn't known what to expect before he'd arrived, but he had hoped it would be easier and quicker than this.

If he was quiet, there was a chance he could sneak past the demons to begin with. They might not notice anything was wrong until he started cutting off the turbines. Whatever he was going to do, he needed to act fast. Kalpesh leant against the glass of the skylight, triggering a glyph above his elbow. The glass parted like the surface of a pond and Kalpesh slipped through. Clutching hold of the nearest steel rafter, he swung himself back upwards to the inside of the ceiling, shifting his weight so that he was crouched upside down.

From the bird's-eye view he continued to survey the scene below. The men and woman shuffling sinisterly about the walkways below were all adorned in black robes. They were occultists by appearance, no doubt the lackeys of Crowley, neophytes of A∴A∴, perhaps voluntarily surrendering their bodies to demonic possession, or perhaps just as likely possessed against their will. Whichever was the case, it mattered little now. They had aligned themselves with the wickedest man alive, and as such, had condemned their souls to the Abyss.

Kalpesh continued to observe, hoping he might see some semblance of routine to their patrols along the walkways, but it was seemingly random. If he were to sneak around, he would have to use every spell in his arsenal and rely heavily on luck. He readied himself to drop from the ceiling, tracing his eyes one last time over the numerous possessed neophytes below, when suddenly, his heart skipped a beat.

Down below, one of the demonic occultists was gazing up at him; even worse, she was aiming a wand his way. Time slowed with the familiar burn of the marks across Kalpesh's chest, giving the Indian the extra few split seconds he needed to react. He flung himself from the rafters, just as the steel he had been clinging to buckled under a blast of energy.

Kalpesh was free falling, the air rushing rapidly past his ears as he tried desperately to orientate himself in the air. He pivoted, conducting the Aether down the run of his spine. He vanished, reappearing on top of the demon that had taken a shot at him, and with a swift unsheathing of his Kukri, he sunk the blade clean into her throat. Kalpesh rent the knife free and blood spouted from her carotid artery. The demon reeled back, her eyes burning hot like the very coals fuelling the power station, and emitted a gargling screech that alerted every other fiend inside Bankside to the intruder.

Kalpesh slammed his palm across the woman's bloody face, rapidly exorcising her with a blast of radiant energy. White flames licked suddenly from her eye sockets, replaced immediately by cavities of darkness as the lifeless vessel of her body thumped onto the steel walkway.

Kalpesh spun to the sound of footsteps. He raised a hand in defence, conjuring his shield as another blast of kinetic energy ejected from a wand. The fist of magic smashed into Kalpesh's ward, driving him backwards. The small of his back impacted the walkway railings and he felt his weight topple helplessly over the banister. Flailing a hand, he snagged hold of the walkway with his fingers. His body swung beneath the steel mesh platform, and as he released his grip, Kalpesh felt the runes across his thighs invert the direction of his fall. He arced back up towards the underside of the walkway, but instead of planting his boots against the metal grating, he felt his mass sink through the mesh in much the way he had ghosted through the glass skylight. Now he was falling up, behind the possessed occultist that had taken a shot at him seconds earlier.

He managed to grab a handful of the man's black robes, dragging them over his head as once more the pull of the Earth reoriented itself. Kalpesh changed direction again, landing on his feet back where he had been stood a moment ago, and with a swift yank at the fabric clutched in his fingers, he managed to pull the demon off its feet and slam it down into the steel mesh platform. Kalpesh's kukri dismembered a hand clutching a wand, and as the creature squealed from the blow, he performed a second blinding exorcism.

A bullet twanged as it ricocheted off the steel casing of the turbine adjacent to Kalpesh, the shot narrowly missing his head. The next bullet pinged off an arcane shield, but before the revolver could let off a third shot, Kalpesh had rapidly drawn his Mauser and returned fire. An iron slug lanced through the gut of the demon charging his way, knocking the fiend square off his feet. The monster hissed as steam bubbled out of the bleeding wound in its abdomen, the iron burning away at its insides. Kalpesh stepped over the aberration, squeezing his trigger a second time to send a finishing shot through its skull.

Twirling away from the lunge of a cane sword, Kalpesh skipped back several steps, right into the embrace of a behemoth of a man further strengthen by the vigour of a demon possessing the body. The bald-headed heavy tightened his bear hug around Kalpesh and the Indian felt his lungs ready to rupture as every wisp of air in his chest suddenly expelled through his mouth. He groaned, certain his ribs were about to give out.

The female demon carrying the unsheathed cane sword took a running jab for his abdomen. The run of tattoos up Kalpesh's spine rapidly fired and the Indian teleported swiftly from death's embrace. The giant that had been crushing him a moment before was suddenly run through by the sword, whilst the demon clutching the blade was simultaneously impaled by a kukri as Kalpesh reappeared behind her.

Using both his own and the woman's momentum, Kalpesh drove the two fiends into a turbine. The impaled demon at the rear struck the spinning flywheel with the nape of his neck and his pate was swiftly cracked clean open. Kalpesh pressed the muzzle of his pistol into the back of the woman and fired. The iron slug tore through her heart, exiting her body and penetrating through to the animated corpse behind. The two lifeless bodies slumped to the walkway.

Kalpesh turned, narrowly reacting in the suspension of time that his tattoos afforded, ducking just beneath the swing of a crowbar. The metal clanged loudly against the steel turbine. Locking his arm around the elbow of the demon assailing him, Kalpesh delivered a swift thrust from his shoulder, dislocating the joint. The crowbar fell loosely from the creature's broken grip, clattering to the steel walkway at their feet.

The demon snarled and Kalpesh suddenly felt teeth clamp through the fabric of his coat, trapping the flesh beneath tightly in the fiend's powerful maw. The Indian cried out as a set of fingernails gouged his skin. He tried to struggle, yet the creature only tightened its grip, locking its thighs around Kalpesh's waist as it tried to maul his neck.

Gravity revolved and suddenly they were plummeting sideways as a pair. The demon cushioned the blow of the railing as the two men flipped over the side, and as the flow of their weight reassumed its natural course, they dropped towards the ground below. Once more, the fiend softened the impact as they collided with a dynamo on the ground floor. This time, the Indian felt several bones break in the body of the demon beneath him. He tumbled off the top of the beast, slamming hard onto the concrete floor.

Wheezing, winded from the collision, Kalpesh tried with all his strength to heave himself back to his feet. Yet to his dismay, the demon was not yet dead. A talon snatched hold of his ankle as the Indian tried to stand, and suddenly the creature was dragging itself on top of him.

Kalpesh struggled, kicking wildly with his free foot, planting a heel firmly into the demon's forehead. The blow freed his ankle, allowing the Indian to roll over onto his back. He took aim with his Mauser from the floor as the fiend lunged back towards him, and with a sudden clap of the muzzle, a bullet plugged through the demon's eye, finally slaying it.

Kalpesh once more tried to get back to his feet, but before he could do so, a hand clasped firmly around the scruff of his collar. He choked as he was dragged across the floor and hoisted suddenly upwards. A set of feminine hands clamped like vices around his throat, pressing shut his airways as the fiend began to throttle him. Kalpesh thrashed his legs as he dangled by the neck. Darkness was pressing rapidly in from the corners of his vision as he tried desperately to prise away the fingers locked around his airways. He lashed out with a hand, clawing at the smouldering eyes of the demoness strangling him, but the creature barely seemed to notice the fingers numbly groping at her face as she grinned sinisterly, watching the life slowly fade from her victim.

In a last-ditch effort to free himself before blacking out, Kalpesh strained and planted his palm against the demon's cheek. A smite of radiant fire singed from his skin, scalding the fiend's face; as her flesh bubbled, she loosened her grip fractionally. Kalpesh locked his palm on her wrist, emitting the same white fire from his hand, burning the creature beneath his grip. She recoiled, releasing the Indian sorcerer entirely.

Kalpesh collapsed, his legs failing under him. He gasped, sputtering against his bruised throat as he forced air through his constricted trachea, straining to inflate his lungs. He looked across the floor, spotting his Mauser lying several feet away. He outreached his fingers and the gun slid across the concrete into his grip. He felt a boot plant firmly on his chest, pinning him down. The pistol went off in his hand, a slug tearing through the shin of the woman as he pressed the muzzle against her leg. The bone shattered and the fiend wailed in agony, collapsing beside Kalpesh.

Suddenly Kalpesh was on top of her, branding her brow with his palm until the glowing embers of her eyes burnt out with a flicker of white. The sorcerer staggered to his feet as he heard boots clomping down steps from the platform above. Kalpesh retreated into the shadows as four more fiends approached. Raising his palm, he projected a shimmering veil of distorted light to obscure himself from their view. The demons rapidly sighted the corpse that he had just exorcised and rushed closer to search for the perpetrator. Meanwhile, Kalpesh slunk away behind the cloak of magic, his footsteps muffled by the tattoos on his legs.

The Indian watched from the shadows, waiting for a moment to strike. Soon enough, the quartet of demons searching for him fanned out, each taking a different route between the whirring generators. Creeping behind the nearest of the fiends, Kalpesh suddenly dispelled the veil of concealment hiding him in the dark and struck with incredible pace. He clasped his hand over the woman's mouth to stifle her cries, cutting her throat in a swift slash before exorcising her in the seconds that followed.

The next demon reared his head, certain he had heard some suppressed cry through the drone of the power plant, yet he was unable to locate the source of the sound and resumed searching the way ahead. Sneaking deftly up behind the man, Kalpesh struck from around the corner, lunging with his knife to slice open the man's gut, simultaneously slapping his hand against the fiend's face to deal a final exorcising blow. This time his prey's screams rung out over the roar of machines, alerting the two remaining fiends to his location. Yet before the nearest creature could even react, Kalpesh teleported across the turbine hall, closing the distance on the abyssal spirit in the blink of an eye, banishing the demon from its bodily vessel with a palm of white-hot fire.

A gunshot echoed through the powerplant and a streak of hot lead sliced a line across Kalpesh's ribs. The glancing shot crunched into the brickwork behind, spitting a shower of dust outwards. Ducking away, Kalpesh threw himself behind the nearest turbine just as the gun went off again. Skirting rapidly around the rear of the generator, he darted suddenly out of cover, hand projecting an arcane shield as he charged the final demon. The Indian let out a terrifying battle cry as a fusillade of bullets shattered against his protective bulwark, and in a few short powerful steps, he had closed in on the possessed occultist.

Dispelling his shield, Kalpesh stooped beneath the lunge of a heavy spanner and swung his Kukri with full force. The edge of his Ghurkha knife clove deeply into the creature's face, dealing a blow that would instantly kill any normal man, but as the Indian rent the blade from the fissure he had carved between the demon's eyes, the beast swung the spanner again. Kalpesh blocked the blow with his forearm, the shaft of the wrench sending a dull throb up the length of his arm. The

Indian struck again, cleaving with all his might. The edge of his blade hacked at flesh and bone repeatedly, cracking through the occultist's frontal plate until the kukri was cutting deep into brain matter.

Finally, the fiend relented in its advance, the strings of the spiritual puppeteer severed from the corpse. As the last demon fell dead, Kalpesh dropped to his knees, his chest straining to keep up with his drumming pulse. He felt dizzy and weak, unable to stand, unable to continue. He had pushed himself to the very limit and only just escaped with his life. All he wanted was a moment's rest. But there wasn't time. He still had to uncouple each generator from the turbines, and then after, make his way over to Westminster, where the Ripper would no doubt be awaiting him.

XLII

Bankside Power Station, Southwark
6:21 a.m. November 11th, 1888

Kalpesh threw another switch and listened as the dynamo inside the generator whirred down.

'Fred?' he thought, focussing his mind once more to try and narrow down on the Hertzian frequency that his partner's Airwave was tuned to. 'Fred, can you hear me?'

"Khatri?" fizzed a voice faintly inside Kalpesh's mind, accompanied by the popping of gunfire. "I'm a little busy right now!"

'Fred, you need to let everyone know to

expect heavy resistance at the power plants. There were nearly a dozen demons here at Bankside!'

There was a long pause before Abberline's voice sounded once more faintly inside the Indian's mind. "No shit!" remarked the aging inspector sardonically as a scream was also picked up by the Airwave. "It's a fucking bloodbath here in Holborn!"

'Are you okay!?'

"Shit!" cursed Abberline as the firefight faded. "They got Cumming!"

'Fred!?'

"Man down," sighed Abberline, the sound of the exchange having died completely.

'Damn,' lamented Kalpesh defeatedly.

"This place is clear," returned Abberline.

'You'll need to shut down the generators. If it's like here, the glyphs will be too difficult to dispel in time!'

"Copy that," returned the chief inspector. "We've got men en route to Kensington and Battersea but... hell, I'm not sure they'll make it there in time!"

Kalpesh hung his head low as he heaved down another switch to uncouple a generator from the turbines. 'I understand.'

"I'm sorry lad."

Kalpesh remained silent as he moved on to the next switch. 'I'm just about finished up hear. We'll have to hope what we've done is enough to slow the ritual.'

"I don't know," returned Abberline warily. "If these generators have been going all night... if they've been syphoning power as long as I think they have..."

'Then Crowley might already have enough energy to power the ritual in full.'

"Exactly!" agreed Abberline.

Kalpesh pulled the final switch, and as the last generator cycled down, the room was filled only with the hum of steam turbines. 'I'm done here,' he explained. 'I'm on my way to Westminster Palace.'

"I'm not far behind," insisted Abberline. "I'll meet you there."

'Fred?' began Kalpesh, realising this could potentially be the last time they might ever speak.

"What is it, lad?"

'Thank you,' he issued. 'For everything.'

"No. Thank *you*," returned the chief inspector insistently.

Kalpesh smiled.

"Ten Bells tonight? Meet you there at eight?"

'Sounds good,' returned the Indian, suspecting he'd be unable to make it.

"First round is on me," insisted Abberline.

'I'll hold you to that,' chuckled Kalpesh as a tear beaded in the corner of his eye.

"Good luck, son," returned Abberline.

'I'll see you on the other side.'

Kalpesh cut off his telepathic link, kicking opened the side door and exiting the power plant back out onto the embankment. The Indian hurtled down the waterfront, back towards Blackfriars Goods Station, his feet drumming across the paving as he began the final leg of his mad sprint from Whitechapel to Westminster. He dashed up the steps, emerging rapidly onto the darkly lit platform. Dropping onto the tracks, he turned south, exiting the station as he sped along the raised railway, crossing over the tramline below. On he raced, rapidly heading southward through Christchurch Ward. The lines diverged as the tracks crossed over Dolben street. Kalpesh bore right, his feet pounding over the sleepers, breath rasping as he ran.

As the tracks ahead spanned over a perpendicular line, Kalpesh swerved towards the edge of the bridge, vaulting swiftly over the railings, dropping from the side. He fell a dozen feet, air rushing past as he plummeted. He teleported downwards, lessening the drop, yet his feet still burned as his boots drove into the ground. Shaking off the pain of the fall, limping back into a sprint, he continued westward along the South Eastern and Chatham Railway line. Kalpesh fought on, chest straining, legs screaming. Several signal bars blurred by overheard as he followed the tracks forking left.

Waterloo Station loomed out of the darkness ahead. Smoke was rising from the streets below, fires raging from numerous buildings, the tumultuous roar of rioting crowds sounding across the city. The Indian sorcerer sped ahead, racing beneath the cover of Waterloo. He leapt up off the tracks, vaulting between the carriages of several abandoned trains as he crossed between platforms. Making for the exit, he bounded down the steps, emerging out onto the streets. A mob was gathered along York Road, forcing Kalpesh to veer right up College Street, cutting across a crescent before turning south on Belvedere Road.

Wharfs and warehouses rushed past on the right, finally granting Kalpesh a view across the river of Westminster Palace. The quarter bells inside Big Ben's belfry began to toll. Three quartets chimed in succession as Kalpesh swerved right towards Westminster Bridge. Quarter to seven: mere minutes until sunrise. Racing up the slope towards the river crossing, Kalpesh glanced back over his shoulder to descry the hazy light of dusk rising in the east. Up ahead, storm clouds were brewing over the Houses of Parliament.

Kalpesh charged out onto the bridge as winds began to pick up across the Thames. Dozens of carriages were overturned in the road, forming a series of blockades. Dead horses lay broken in pools of blood, the occasional human casualty visible in the wreckage as flames burnt amidst the ruin.

A gun went off up ahead and a bullet scored the cobbles beneath Kalpesh's feet. He looked on to see an occultist taking aim at him from behind the cover of an upturned stagecoach. Kalpesh raised his shield, deflecting the next bullet aimed his way, closing the distance to the shooter in a matter of seconds. He whipped his arms sideways as he rushed up to meet the man and a rip current of air tore out from his wrist. The occultist screamed as he was catapulted skyward by the arcane torrent, his cries fading as he was flung from the bridge, splashing into the waves below.

Kalpesh dropped off his feet, sliding beneath the wreckage of a hackney cab, leaping back into a sprint on the far side. His reactions fastened and time momentarily slowed. He cocked his head to the right, just in time to see a Malleus officer take aim at him with a Greener Police gun. He lunged with his hand, clasping his fingers around the barrel, redirecting the shot as a demon-slaying-slug exploded from the muzzle. Kalpesh's ears rung as he rent the gun from the officer's grip, swinging the stock wildly around to clout the man squarely across the temple. The blow rendered the policeman unconscious and he immediately collapsed.

Kalpesh swivelled just in time to see another man from Hammer emerge from the wreckage and take aim at him, this time with an Enfield. Yet before the officer could pull the trigger, a shadow lurched from out of a veil of smoke, tackling the man from Special Branch to the ground. In a sprawl of claws and teeth, the demon savaged the officer, chomping a meaty chunk clean out of his neck.

Kalpesh drew his Mauser. The muzzle coughed repeatedly, spitting out four slugs in rapid succession. The shots plugged one by one into the demon, riddling its body, sending it reeling back off the brutalised Malleus officer. The final shot drove through the fiend's cheekbone, exploding out the back of the creature's pate in a crimson spray.

Kalpesh rushed over towards the wounded officer, locking eyes with the man as he clamped a hand over the spurting arterial spray gushing from his throat. In mere seconds, the life left his eyes.

"Damn it!" cursed Kalpesh as he turned away, readying to continue his fight across the bridge.

He gazed up in horror as black clouds swirled above the palace's clock tower. Lightning crackled across the eye of the vortex, once at first, then a second time, before moments later, continuous searing bolts of electricity began to set the sky ablaze. The howling winds intensified, now directing outwards from Westminster Palace, sweeping up dust and ash, canting the rising flames into angular tongues of fire, and pushing pieces of debris along the bridge.

Kalpesh shielded his face against the eye-watering gales, fighting his way upwind. A white halo of light suddenly descended upon him. He looked back over his shoulder into the sky, watching in disbelief as an airship juddered out of the storm towards him, its search light beaming down on him from above.

"Kalpesh Khatri!" the blaring voice of Melville Macnaghten crackled over the loudspeakers. "Surrender now! Stop this madness or we will open fire!"

Kalpesh gazed up into the glare of the spotlight. "This isn't me, you idiot!" he roared, his voice barely audible over the storm. "The man responsible is up there!" he screamed, pointing towards the Houses of Parliament.

"We gave you fair warning!" fizzled the voice of Monro, revealing he too was onboard.

"You bastards!" snarled Kalpesh, realising what was about to happen.

The Indian broke into a sprint just as the artillery guns of the Zeppelin opened fire. Deafening drumfire ripped through the storm and suddenly the bridge began to disintegrate around Kalpesh. He teleported, vanishing from the cobbles to atop a flipped Malleus carriage. He dropped down, dashing once more towards Westminster as the shelling accelerated towards him. The winds screamed past as they began to tear water up from the surface of the Thames. The cannonade of explosions drummed at Kalpesh's heels. Earth, air, wind, and fire raged around the Indian sorcerer in a deafening maelstrom as he charged heedlessly across the bridge.

Forks of lightning lit up the black heavens above, arcing outwards from the storm. Kalpesh peered back overhead at the pursuing airship and watched in disbelief as the outer hull of the Zeppelin was struck repeatedly by a series of lightning bolts. The chattering of cannons rapidly cut out. Hydrogen leaking from the ship suddenly caught alight, and in a matter of mere seconds, a fireball of titanic immensity was raging in the sky above Westminster. The skin of the airship blistered away and the massive steel skeleton began to plummet down towards the bridge.

"Shit!" screamed Kalpesh in horror as the inferno plunged towards him. The Indian teleported again, bursting back into a sprint as he reappeared. He felt the scorching heat burning across the back of his neck; the entire face of the Houses of Parliament lit up beneath the ball of fire. The raging firestorm continued to drop. The steel skeleton collided with Westminster Bridge, buckling in the heat, detonating in a secondary explosion. The shockwave knocked Kalpesh clean off his feet and he collided sideways into a hackney carriage.

The Indian's back spasmed in pain as he peeled himself up off the cobbles. He gazed back at the rising conflagration as the melting steel frame of the Zeppelin bent and groaned. The aft of the airship tore away, plunging into the grey water of the Thames, sending up immense plumes of steam that were swept off in a torrent of wind. Kalpesh gazed around, amazed at his survival. Had the winds raging from the storm overhead not been so fierce, the airship would have come down directly on top of him and he would have been consumed within the same hellish inferno that had killed both Melville and Monro.

Regathering himself, he caught sight of the amber glow of dawn faintly visible through the pillars of black smoke rising from the bridge. He turned back towards Westminster Palace, glancing up at Big Ben. He had minutes left, but as he gazed upon the clockface, the time was the least of his concerns.

XLIII

Palace of Westminster, Westminster
6:58 a.m. November 11th, 1888

Kalpesh stared up at the clockface of Big Ben; across the dial was painted the Sigillum Dei, the Seal of God.

The highly intricate sigil, labelled with the names of God and his angels, was something straight out of myth and legend. Deep in the Malleus archives existed a thirteenth century grimoire: *The Sworn Book of Honorius.* Purported to be the translation of a much older ancient Greco-Roman tome, the book was one of the earliest existing Solomonic grimoires. Within its pages was depicted a close approximation of the detailed pentacle Kalpesh was looking at now. The power it allegedly granted was to possess the abilities of God himself: control over all celestial spirits.

It was well known among scholars however, that the depiction of the Sigillum Dei in The Sworn Book of Honorius was inert. Some speculated that the pentacle was merely a fabrication, and that no sigil could ever truly grant the powers the Seal of God claimed to. Others suggested that the Sigillum Dei was real, but that the pentacle had been erroneously transcribed at some point in history, some minor detail missed out or copied out incorrectly, with the original version having been lost to time. Whichever the case, the Seal of God as depicted inside The Sworn Book of Honorius was altogether powerless.

But Kalpesh knew instinctually as he gazed up at the clockface of Big Ben, that this revised Enochian version of the Sigil was undoubtedly the real artifact. This was how Crowley intended to control Choronzon; the sigil granted power to control angels, and though twisted and warped by an eternity of imprisonment, the Dweller of the Abyss had once been an angel himself!

The immense hands of the clock were likewise marked, with two gaps in the clockface left blank. The hour hand was just about ready to slot into place over the seven, but the minute hand was still several ticks out from the eleven-minute-mark. Once both hands moved into their correct positions, they would complete the Sigillum Dei, triggering the ritual, freeing Choronzon from the Abyss, releasing him into the material plane. But not if Kalpesh could stop it!

He had less than thirteen minutes! Breaking back into a run, he clambered rapidly over the wrought iron fence and darted across the Speaker's Green, flipping his weight to the south as he planted his feet on the walls of St Stephen's Tower. The belfry began to chime, the quarter bells clanging as Big Ben readied to strike the hour. Kalpesh raced up the clocktower, his feet treading rapidly between the arrow slit windows in the gothic stonework.

Then, Big Ben tolled, the enormous, cracked bell signalling the hour, the thunderous peal reverberating through the stonework, sounding across London in every direction. The Indian sorcerer raced up towards the dial, yet before he could complete his two-hundred-and-fifty-foot climb to the clock, a shadowy figure materialised out of the storm in front of him.

Kalpesh skidded to a halt as he found himself stood face to face with Jack the Ripper.

"You!? I should have known you'd come," remarked Crowley as he stood horizontally above. "But it's over now. You've run out of time to stop me!"

"You overestimate yourself!" roared Kalpesh over the howling winds. "All this time I've been just a few steps behind you—but now, I've finally caught up. This is the end alright—the end for you!"

Crowley's lips twisted into a sadistic grin. "You think the gifts the Golden Dawn have given you make you a match for me?" he chuckled. "The magic of the Golden Dawn is mere child's play. They were always too afraid to experiment—they never dared pushed the boundaries of what is possible. I have transcended their teachings. I have forged my own path. I have torn down the veil between worlds and gazed into the very depths of the Abyss! I am the most powerful sorcerer the world has ever seen! And soon, I will be more powerful than God himself!"

Big Ben tolled a final time.

"You are a madman!" cried Kalpesh in fury. "You will doom the world in your own crazed pursuit for power! You cannot control Choronzon —no one can!"

"You fail to understand," returned Crowley. "I don't just intend to control Choronzon—I *am* the beast!"

"You want to become him!" realised Kalpesh. "You're planning on letting him possess you!? You're going to summon him into your own body?"

"You are sharp," smirked Crowley. "You'd make a powerful sorcerer—all you need is someone to teach you!"

"I not going to join you, you sick bastard!" cut in Kalpesh before Crowley could even make the offer.

Crowley cackled. "Suit yourself. You stand no hope of stopping me! No one can!"

"You should have killed me when you had

the chance!" warned Kalpesh. "I will stop you!"

"Just try it!"

Kalpesh's hand shot for his holster. He drew his Mauser in the blink of an eye and opened fire. Bullets streaked through the air, smashing into a shield of force summoned from Crowley's palm. Kalpesh advanced up the face of the clock tower as he continued to squeeze the trigger. Bullets wailed as they ricocheted off the bulwark of magic until Kalpesh's magazine ran empty and the gun clicked uselessly in his grip. Crowley dispelled his shield and flicked his fingers sideways. The gun ripped out of Kalpesh's grip, tumbling down towards the green below.

Crowley vanished, closing the distance between them as he teleported. He reappeared, athame drawn, slashing it down towards Kalpesh, but the Indian already had his kukri in hand. Their blades clashed. Kalpesh parried, forcing Crowley's knife away, immediately creating an opening in which to strike, yet before he could deal a riposte, the Ripper balled his other hand into a fist and a shockwave of energy ripped outwards. The blast of magic staggered Kalpesh backwards and shattered the surrounding windows. Glass jangled as it rained down all around.

Shielding his face against the shower of glass, Kalpesh managed to regain his footing on the side of the building, but as he lowered his hand from his face, he caught sight of Crowley summoning a ball of fire in his palm. The Ripper hurled the bolt of flame Kalpesh's way. Unable to dodge aside, the Indian sorcerer released his gravitational grip of the wall, plummeting from the side of the clock tower. The ball of fire streaked after him, smoke and ash trailing behind it as it homed in, yet the moment before contact, Kalpesh evaporated, rematerializing above Crowley.

Still falling, downward momentum conserved through the teleportation jump, he drove his boots hard into the Ripper's back, delivering a flying kick straight into the unsuspecting sorcerer. Crowley crumpled in the impact and was dislodged from the clock tower. The tattoos on Kalpesh's legs lit up and he landed back on the wall to watch as the Ripper was sent tumbling rapidly towards the ground.

As Kalpesh heard his foe's screams fade below him, he turned to run back up towards the clock dial, yet he barely made it more than a few fathoms higher before the limestone in front of him was struck by a lightning bolt arcing up from below. The stonework exploded, taking out Kalpesh's feet from under him. He slammed hard into the wall, smashing out another window with his knee as he tumbled. Rolling over, he narrowly avoided another fork of electricity aimed his way. Flipping back to his feet, he glanced down to see Crowley charging up the clock tower towards him. The black magician conjured another thunderbolt from his palm. The runes across Kalpesh's chest lit up, bending the flow of time long enough for him to teleport to safety.

Reappearing within a few feet of the Ripper, Kalpesh lunged with his kukri, once more clashing blades with his nemesis. Ghurkha blade and occultist athame clanged and chimed in a flurried exchange of blows before the brief spout lulled and the two men were left circling one another.

"You cannot stop me!" snarled Crowley as he licked his lips. "You are nobody! I am the beast! I am destined to succeed!"

"No. You are wrong. I am not nobody," breathed Kalpesh. "I've been telling myself that my whole life; but it's not true!"

Crowley's eyes narrowed. "Who are you?" he demanded.

"I am Kalpesh Khatri, son of Lakshmibai, the Rani of Jhansi, son of Arthur Octavian Hume, founder of the Golden Dawn!"

Crowley's grin faded as if he had somehow been cheated of a fate he had long been promised. "No," he shook his head in disbelief. "No, that can't be true!"

"It is," returned Kalpesh, for the first time truly believing it himself.

"No!" roared Crowley. "No, it doesn't matter who you are. You cannot stop me! I am more powerful than the Golden Dawn. I am more powerful than *you* will ever be!"

"You aren't more powerful than the Golden Dawn," ridiculed Kalpesh. "You are merely a shadow of it!"

"Shut up!" Crowley screamed. "Shut up!"

The Ripper lunged for Kalpesh in a berserking rage. Time slowed and the Indian sorcerer dodged nimbly away. They clashed blades again and Kalpesh dealt Crowley a swift knee to the gut. The Ripper grunted, stumbling back as he hunched over from the blow. The dark sorcerer flailed an arm, conjuring a whip of fire out of the air. The flaming tendril lashed for Kalpesh, colliding with the Indian's shield. The fiery serpent darted away as Crowley rent back his hand and slashed downwards again. Yet this time, Kalpesh vanished before the blazing whip struck, causing it to carve against a patch of unoccupied limestone in a shower of sparks.

Kalpesh reappeared behind Crowley, and before the Ripper had time to turn and face him, he struck with his own arm, feeling the tattoos across his wrist twinge with power. A blast of energy tore out of his hand, surging across the face of St Stephen's tower, striking Crowley off his feet. The Ripper yelped as he was knocked off the northern face of the clock tower, vanishing as he plummeted over the corner to the south.

Kalpesh spurted forwards, leaping as he reached the edge. He raised his kukri high overhead as he dived around the eastern face of the tower. Kalpesh arced downwards, cleaving his kukri against Crowley's upraised athame. The Ripper's long ritual knife slid along the inside curve of the kukri, dropping into the notch positioned above its haft, and for a moment the two blades locked together in a bind. A contest of might broke out between the two men as they strained against one another's strength in an attempt to break the deadlock.

Crowley managed to twist his knife inside the notch and the point swivelled towards the Indian's chest. Suddenly, Kalpesh felt a heel hook around the back of his knee. His leg buckled and he tripped backwards, slamming into the wall. Crowley forced his weight on top of him, pinning Kalpesh into the stonework. The dark sorcerer gripped the pommel of his athame in two hands, pushing all of his weight into the blade. Kalpesh cried out as he began to lose the struggle, the point of the athame sinking through the fabric of his coat, digging into his skin below.

Crowley grinned menacingly through crooked teeth as he continued to force the blade down on Kalpesh. "My knife is so nice and sharp!" he chuckled, quoting the letter he had sent as Jack the Ripper. "I want to get to work right away if I get a chance!"

Kalpesh screamed louder as the blade sank deeper.

"Shush," insisted Crowley calmly. "It's over. Just let it happen."

Kalpesh strained with all his might, but Crowley was stronger than him. The knife continued to sink through his flesh; in a second it would slip between his ribs and pierce his heart.

"The end is nigh," smirked the Ripper.

Kalpesh nodded. "For you!" he spat.

Kalpesh felt all manner of tattoos suddenly blaze to life across his body. The athame suddenly sank deeper, but instead of piercing flesh, its point chinked into solid limestone, ghosting clean through Kalpesh's vaporous form. Gravity pulled the Indian away as he dropped out from beneath the Ripper, and as his body solidified back to normal, the pull of the world below spiralled in a stomach-turning parabola. Kalpesh tumbled downwards, then sideways, then up, his body agilely somersaulting with the distorted fall.

Suddenly his feet planted firmly back onto the side of St Stephen's Tower as he landed next to Crowley. Reacting in a panic, the Ripper stabbed for him. Time slowed momentarily and Kalpesh managed to grapple hold of his foe's lunging arm by the wrist. Hot fire seared out from Kalpesh's palm, branding the flesh above Crowley's elbow. The Ripper screamed as his skin smoked and bubbled. His athame slipped from his fingers, tumbling out of sight towards the ground below.

Crowley's eyes widened in horror as he realised at the last moment that he was at Kalpesh's mercy; but there was no mercy to be had for Jack the Ripper. Kalpesh sunk his kukri deep into Crowley's gut. The murderer gasped, his eyes bulging in their sockets. The Indian rent his blade downwards, its curving edge slicing through the Ripper's abdomen, disembowelling him in a singular brutal cut. Blood trickled from the corner of Crowley's mouth as his swollen eyes locked with Kalpesh's in a look of disbelief.

Kalpesh tore his blade free of the Ripper's gut. The magic holding Crowley against the wall failed, the natural orientation of the world's grasp retaking effect. Kalpesh watched the Ripper tumble downwards, his black robes billowing in the wind as he plummeted towards the ground. The body thumped into the grass below and lay there motionless in a slowly expanding pool of blood.

Overhead, the tempest rage more powerfully than ever. Crowley was dead, but the ritual was still in full effect. Barely any time remained, and as Kalpesh turned to gaze back up at the clockface, he watched the minute hand click to within a single movement of completing the Sigillum Dei.

Sheathing his kukri, Kalpesh raced up the remaining height of St Stephen's Tower. In a matter of seconds, he reached the clockface. Stepping out onto the dial, he let the glass ripple beneath his feet as he sank through. Landing on a wall behind the face, he dropped down on to the floor. He looked up at the great axel driving the arms overhead and realised the mechanism laid in the room behind.

He darted through a narrow doorway, stepping into the mechanism room. A massive machine of clicking gears ticked loudly above.

Mere seconds remained before the minute hand would revolve into place and complete the Sigil of God. Kalpesh somehow needed to stop the Great Westminster Clock, yet he gazed at the immense intricate machine in befuddlement. There had to be some lever or something of the like somewhere that would uncouple the hands from the driving pendulum; there were several handles in various places, but they could just be to wind up the weights. He wracked his brain, studying the device, all too aware that he was running out of time.

He made out the escapement, and he could see the pendulum swinging through the floor below, but despite being something of a polymath, the Indian was no clockmaker; he had no idea how to operate the great machine. But he knew somebody who just might.

'Fred!' he cried out telepathically.

"What is it?" Abberline replied over the Airwave.

'You were a clockmaker—How do I stop a clock!?'

"What...!? Why!?"

'Quickly!'

"I..." stammered the detective. "Easiest way: smash it!"

"Fuck it! Alright." Kalpesh chuckled nervously, realising Abberline was right. He darted back out the door through which he had come, into the space behind the clockface. The arc lights illuminating the dial buzzed loudly, revealing the lines of the Sigillum Dei painted onto the glass face beyond. The clock ticked. Time slowed. The tattooed runes down Kalpesh's arm fired violently. A torrent of wind surged from within the clock tower, and as the wave of energy ripped from Kalpesh's body, the glass of the clockface cracked and shattered, exploding outwards, obliterating the immense pentacle marked across the dial.

The minute hand ticked into place, but without the rest of the pentacle intact, the graffitied hand merely rotated a six-degree turn, ticking over like it did for any other minute of the day. The storm raging above the Palace of Westminster began to slowly quell, and as Kalpesh found himself gazing out from the destroyed clockface, the sun crept up over the London skyline, setting the city ablaze with the light of a new day.

XLIV

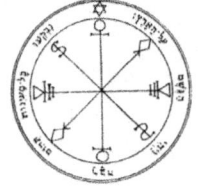

Parliament Square, Westminster
11:00 a.m. November 11th, 1888

The sun shone brilliantly down across Parliament Square as Big Ben finished striking the hour. Abberline watched as policemen from both Hammer and the Met aided the surgeons and doctors called to hand to tend to the wounded. The night of horror had ended suddenly. The demons terrorising London had all at once vanished, fleeing the bodies which they had possessed the moment the sun had risen across the city. It seemed that with the death of their master, they too had perished; or perhaps, they had merely fled back into the Abyss before the gates had sealed shut once again. Such notions were the optimistic thoughts of the men of Malleus, but Abberline himself was not quite convinced.

The veil between dimensions had been torn, and though the aging chief inspector was no expert in magical affairs, he suspected that the breached gates to hell had not been barred shut simply because the Ripper was killed. The demons had merely fled when their leader fell. Maybe they'd never return; or perhaps they were merely licking their wounds, biding their time. Whatever the case, Abberline suspected it was not entirely over; but he was always happy to be surprised.

"You there, sir," a voice called out to him, "Chief Inspector Abberline, is it?"

"Yes," confirmed Abberline, turning to see a bald bearded man approaching. "Prime Minister, sir!?" he stammered, abruptly standing to attention as he recognised Lord Robert Cecil.

"I understand you are the man to talk to about all of this?" smiled the politician.

"Sir?" questioned Abberline.

"Given the tragic death of Commissioner Monro and his assistant chief constable, I'm told by the other inspectors that you hold the greatest authority here?"

"I suppose that is true," agreed Abberline. "What exactly is it you want to know, sir?"

"I want to know what the devil happened!"

"Very well, sir. I trust you are well aware of the spate of occultist murders that have recently transpired in Whitechapel?"

"Yes," nodded the prime minister. "Jack the Ripper, as the papers have called him; better known now as Kalpesh Khatri."

"Not exactly, sir," returned Abberline.

"What do you mean, Chief Inspector?"

"Well, we have made recent discoveries that suggest Kalpesh Khatri was in fact framed by the man who was actually responsible for the killings. The same man who brought this city to its knees last night."

"And who might that be, if you don't mind me asking?"

"A powerful occultist by the name of Aleister Crowley," explained Abberline.

"And is this man still at large, Chief Inspector?"

"No, sir," smiled Abberline. "He was stopped before his plans could come to fruition. By none other than Khatri himself."

"He was stopped by the man falsely accused?" questioned Lord Cecil in confusion.

"That's correct, sir," nodded Abberline.

"But was Khatri not an occultist himself? Please, Chief Inspector, explain to me why a man guilty of witchcraft would stand in the way of this Aleister Crowley? Was it to clear his name?"

"No sir," Abberline shook his head in hesitation.

"Speak candidly with me, Chief Inspector," insisted the prime minister.

"Candidly?" mused Abberline.

"Yes," insisted Lord Cecil. "I want to hear it how you see things."

Abberline sighed, fearing he might regret what he was about to say. "Honestly sir—things are not as black and white as we've pretended them to be for the last four hundred years."

"Oh?"

"Kalpesh Khatri may be guilty of witchcraft, but none of what he has done can hardly be considered a crime. You may disagree with me sir, and after I express this view, I fear you may have me dismissed from Malleus altogether, but: whilst there are those out there who seek to use magic to bend this world to their own ends, I believe there are also those out there who use it for good."

"Is that so?" mused Cecil, raising his eyebrows.

"Kalpesh Khatri is a good man," insisted Abberline. "I know the law dictates that he should hang from the gallows on Tower Green for what he has done, but frankly sir, the law is an ass! Without that man, you and I would not be having this conversation. Westminster would be levelled, and the world as we know it might well have ended. So, see that I'm dismissed, or hell, even lock me up as a sympathiser or co-conspirator! But those are my views, and with respect Prime Minister, you asked for them."

A long silence elapsed as Lord Cecil studied the chief inspector. Abberline had spent a career as a detective learning to read people, but like the master politician Robert Cecil was, he gave nothing away.

"You surprise me, Inspector," smiled the prime minister. "Many men join Special Branch because they despise the arcane. To hear a differing opinion is—refreshing."

"Sir?" question Abberline in confusion.

"The world is changing at an ever-increasing pace, Inspector Abberline. We'd do well to change with it, or risk being trampled by the wheels of progress."

Abberline merely nodded, not sure how else to respond.

"As I understand it, a number of vacancies appear to have opened up in the ranks above you. I trust you'll see that the necessary applications arrive where they need to be?"

"Err… yes sir," nodded Abberline.

"Very good, Inspector," beamed Lord Cecil. "I trust we'll be seeing more of each other in the future. Enjoy the rest of your day." And with that, Lord Robert Cecil bid Abberline farewell, turning to march towards the Palace of Westminster.

Abberline shrugged, not sure what to make of the encounter.

"I think he took a liking to you," the voice of Kalpesh crackled over Abberline's Airwave.

Muffling the speaker with his hand,

Abberline rapidly checked he was out of earshot of anyone else. Just to be sure, he strolled away from the square before he replied into the mouthpiece. "I'm not so sure about that, lad."

'No, he definitely did,' insisted Kalpesh telepathically as he watched his partner from atop Westminster Abbey.

"Let's hope he'll take a liking to you too returned Abberline. "Or maybe just pardon you—either will do."

'We'll see,' returned Kalpesh coolly. 'For now, I'm still a wanted man.'

"For now," agreed Abberline. "And if I am not mistaken, it is my job to arrest you!"

Kalpesh smiled as he watched the chief inspector scan the surrounding rooves in search of him. 'Then I'd better start running.'

"I doubt I'd stand a chance of catching you, even if I tried."

'You could if you knew where I'd be,' returned Kalpesh.

"I don't even know where you are now!" chuckled Abberline.

'Then I guess you'll have to wait until the Ten Bells tonight!'

I hope you have enjoyed reading Shadow of the Golden Dawn.

A lot of hard work, planning, and research went into writing it, and I am proud of the end result.

Ratings and reviews are invaluable to independent authors, especially to those, who like me, are just starting out.

It would therefore mean the world if you could rate this book, and if you have time, leave a short review on Amazon.

If you are interested in discovering more of my work, please head over to my website:

https://www.drhillauthor.com/

BOOKS BY THIS AUTHOR

The Archmage Saga

When Rhys North awakens to find himself the sole survivor of a dark curse known as the Grey, his life is upturned. Driven by the need to uncover the truth behind the fate of his village, Rhys pledges himself in service to an ancient order of magical warriors, the Circle of Magi, sworn protectors of the continent of Cambria.

In his quest for answers, Rhys becomes quickly entangled in cataclysmic events that have been building for centuries. With peace throughout Cambria threatened, Rhys embarks on an arduous journey across the continent, seeking out long lost stone circles to restore the balance of magic throughout Cambria, in order to save the world from a fanatical mage of unspeakable power.

Flight Through Infinity

The Nomad is alone.

On an endless journey across the stars, hunted by a race of mysterious machines, he must fight to survive.

Armed with only his single-manned fighter, the Nomad must scavenge what little can be found in a dead and decaying universe. His equipment steadily breaking down, the Nomad is forced to rely on his ingenuity and piloting skills to keep both himself alive and his ship in the sky.
Set amidst the backdrop of an endless, desolate, infinity, the Nomad travels from star to star, planet to planet, searching for salvation.

A hard sci-fi survival adventure filled with emotional strife, deep introspection, and tense action.

Printed in Great Britain
by Amazon

60810209R00323